PRAISE FOR *A DARK MATTER*

'I was addicted from the first page; gripping, gritty and darkly funny as hell' Erin Kelly

'*A Dark Matter* is Doug Johnstone at the top of his game, spinning a thrilling tale with style and wit. Readers will want to come back again and again to these three generations of Skelfs, a mother, daughter, and granddaughter so beautifully drawn you'll feel like they're your own family. That rare book with heart and smarts to lift it above your average crime novel' Stuart Neville

'*A Dark Matter* showcases a writer at the peak of his powers, except that with every book, Doug Johnstone just gets better' Val McDermid

'Emotionally complex, richly layered and darkly funny. An addictive blend of *Case Histories* and *Six Feet Under*' Chris Brookmyre

'What's not to like about a novel that centres around three of my favourite things: dead bodies, detectives who aren't really detectives, and a funeral parlour. Throw in a troubled family plus a sprinkling of metaphysics, and this dark but touching thriller makes for a thoroughly enjoyable slice of Edinburgh noir' Mary Paulson-Ellis

'Doug Johnstone is one of Scotland's best writers. *A Dark Matter* is a novel that cements that position. Dark, engrossing, impossible to put down. In turns a crime thriller, a family saga, and a page-turner, this book has everything!' Luca Veste

'A fiendish mystery that is also deeply moving and laced with suitably dark humour. The start of a must-read series, *A Dark Matter* is set to be one of the books of the year and sees Doug Johnstone raising the bar yet again' Mark Billingham

'It's a tense ride, but what is most enjoyable is seeing the complexities of the relationships between the three generations of women unfold as they help and impede one another and deal with their grief in their own particular ways' Kerry Hudson, *Big Issue*

'I can never get enough of Doug Johnstone's thoughtful, observant, soul-lifting writing' Louise Beech

'Piercing, wonderfully real and so very readable, this is another cracking novel from Doug Johnstone ... sitting as it does in death, crime and wrong-doing, it still felt like a breath of fresh air, it really is a fabulous read and I loved it!' LoveReading

'This is confident, assured characterisation that carries the story brilliantly well and keeps the reader utterly immersed in the interwoven story strands' Live & Deadly

'*A Dark Matter* is further proof that Doug Johnstone is as versatile a writer as they come ... there's rhythm and music in his words' From Belgium with Booklove

'Doug Johnstone captures the reader's attention from the original opening, tension mounts as each chapter ends, and with a winning combination of diverse characters *A Dark Matter* is a thriller that begs to be read in one sitting. Highly recommend' The Book Review Café

'Deliciously chilling, with a wry humour running throughout. *A Dark Matter* is toxic, unsettling and just perfect. I loved it and recommend it highly. Bravo Mr Johnstone!' Random Things through My Letterbox

'Fresh, compelling, brilliantly structured, with twists that make you shout! 10/10 ... I think this might just be the perfect book' Philippa's Quick Book Reviews Podcast

'Drenched with murder, mystery and intrigue, you're going to want a buddy reader because you WILL want to talk about it' The Reading Closet

'Beautifully written it follows the three strong women through the trauma of coping. Told with humour, it is also very dark but I loved it. I look forward to the next book in this series. Well done, Mr Johnstone' Bookseller

PRAISE FOR DOUG JOHNSTONE

Shortlisted for the McIlvanney Prize for Scottish Crime Book of the Year

'It's a lovely, sad tale, beautifully told and full of understanding' *The Times*

'*Breakers* is the most powerful and moving book from Johnstone yet – a calling card that no-one can ignore' *Scotsman*

'Doug Johnstone's best book yet. An unsparing yet sympathetic depiction of Edinburgh's ignored underclass, with terrific characterisation. Tense, pacy, filmic' Ian Rankin

'Doug's books are what the phrase "no filler, all thriller" was invented for. His no-nonsense style is tight and taut but still carries emotional depth. A tough, gritty and effective ride into the dark side of Edinburgh' Douglas Skelton

'Pacy, harrowing and occasionally brutal, it's a stunning thriller about poisonous families and one decent kid's desperate attempt to do the right thing. Had me in tears at the end. Couldn't recommend more. Oh God' Paddy Magrane

'*Breakers* again shows that Doug Johnstone is a noir heavyweight and a master of gritty realism. This may be his finest novel yet' Willy Vlautin

'*Breakers* is bloody brilliant. Gut punch after gut punch after gut punch and you can't put it down. But it's the final, huge punch to the heart that blows you away. Pages you can't stop turning, characters that linger long after you've finished the book. This is premier-league crime writing' Martyn Waites

'Loved this one. Think it may be Doug Johnstone's best, in fact ... unusual perspective on Scottish crime that just knocks it out the park. Go read, folks' Russel McLean

'I thought *Fault Lines* was good, but *Breakers* is off-the-scale amazing! Stayed up almost all night to finish it. Absolutely brilliant' Louise Voss

'It's as psychologically rich as it is harrowing. I've come to expect nothing less from Doug Johnstone, one of the genre's premiere writers' Megan Abbott

'Absolutely brilliant. A brooding, intensely dark thriller with a defiant beating heart. Evocative, heartbreaking and hopeful – the power of the human spirit to shine in the most desperate place. STUNNING' Miranda Dickinson

'Redemptive, insightful and compelling. Johnstone's best work' Vaseem Khan

'I loved this poignant and pacy book. It looks at so many important issues and was full of heart' Niki Mackay

'As much as the book is brutally realistic, it is also tinged with sensitivity and compassion, with a strong message that a less than promising start in life is not necessarily proof of a moral deficiency, and that a good nature can overrule bad nurture ... a superb read' Raven Crime Reads

'There is a gritty finesse to Johnstone's writing. The dialogue between characters is snappy and he also does a great job of bringing Edinburgh to life, whether it's the poverty-stricken or more affluent areas of the city' The Tattooed Book Geek

'PURE BRILLIANCE!' The Reading Closet

'Johnstone pulls no punches ... I'm going to be thinking about this book for a long time as I try and mend the heart that Johnstone has shattered into pieces' Live & Deadly

'A darkly brilliant thriller filled with tension and humanity' Portobello Book Blog

'Fast-paced, gritty and dark but there is hope at its centre. I found this novel impossible to put down and I'm in awe of how good it is' Rather Too Fond of Books

'What can I say about this book, other than it is bloody fantastic. It had me engrossed throughout ... impossible to put down' Books Are My Cwtches

'Doug Johnstone expertly fleshed out every character, showing both the good, bad and everything in between ... Deep, dark and dangerous!' Rae Reads Book Blog

'First off, what a book!! ... The plot, obviously, is brilliant. It's tense, taught and fraught with all the emotions that a human soul can experience ... brilliant and heartbreaking' Mac Book Reviews

'A very good book, one that will draw you into the dark side of Edinburgh, which Doug Johnstone describes so, so well, making his writing very immersive' Hooked from Page One

'This was a fast-paced, gripping read that I just couldn't put down, as I found I had to know what would happen to the characters' Over the Rainbow Book Blog

'A brilliant book, it is a painfully honest, complex and urgent social commentary that should remind us all that every person has their own story to tell. Highly recommended' Hair Past a Freckle

'Johnstone has created that rare thing – a novel that's punchy and gritty yet also full of heart and capable of being deeply moving, grim and yet optimistic' Mumbling About...

'An emotionally charged, beautifully written and evocative book. Most definitely recommended' Jen Meds Book Reviews

'*Breakers* is a compelling, gritty crime novel that shattered my heart ... This character-led psychological thriller is filled with astute observations, vivid descriptions and punchy dialogue. Taut writing means that every word counts. It's tense and shocking and felt very real' Off-the-Shelf Books

'It's a captivating fast-paced thriller; urban crime that has the brusque, authentic feel of life and not of fiction' Cheryl MM Book Blog

‘A proper page-turner of a novel that you don’t want to put down. It’s fast paced, shocking at times, and Johnstone uses every literary tool in the box to develop a multi-faceted novel that generates a multitude of emotions in the reader’ Segnalibro

‘A thrilling and gritty read, taking you deep into Edinburgh’s dark side and onto a roller coaster ride’ What Do I Read Now

‘Beautifully and sensitively written and the characterisation, especially of Tyler is great’ Beverley Has Read

‘A gritty and at times an emotional read ... If you like tense books this is a must-read. I am definitely going to be adding Doug Johnstone’s other books to my reading list’ Booking Good Read

‘An incredibly dark, eye-opening novel that highlights the lengths people can go to if they are forced, or if they have no other option ... This is such an addictive, heart-wrenching, dark and poignant read’ The Writing Garnet

‘This is a marvellous mix of hard-bitten crime thriller with all its twists and turns, and some emotive characterisation with emotional, family dynamics ... This is a fast-moving and relentless thriller that keeps you on the edge of your seat’ Books Life and Everything

By the same author and available from Orenda Books:

Fault Lines
Breakers

A Dark Matter

ABOUT THE AUTHOR

Doug Johnstone is the author of ten novels, most recently *Breakers* (2018), which was shortlisted for the McIlvanney Prize for Scottish Crime Novel of the Year. Several of his books have been bestsellers and award winners, and his work has been praised by the likes of Val McDermid, Irvine Welsh and Ian Rankin. He's taught creative writing and been writer in residence at various institutions, and has been an arts journalist for twenty years. Doug is a songwriter and musician with five albums and three EPs released, and he plays drums for the Fun Lovin' Crime Writers, a band of crime authors. He's also player-manager of the Scotland Writers Football Club. He lives in Edinburgh.

Follow Doug on Twitter @doug_johnstone and visit his website: dougjohnstone.com.

A Dark Matter

Doug Johnstone

Orenda Books
16 Carson Road
West Dulwich
London SE21 8HU
www.orendabooks.co.uk

First published in the United Kingdom by Orenda Books, 2020

A catalogue record for this book is available from the British Library.

ISBN 978-1-912374-98-4
eISBN 978-1-912374-99-1

Resource: Image by acworks from silhouette-ac.com

Typeset in Garamond by typesetter.org.uk

Printed and bound by CPI Group (UK) Ltd, Croydon CR0 4YY

For sales and distribution, please contact info@orendabooks.co.uk or visit www.orendabooks.co.uk.

A Dark Matter

This one is for Chris Brookmyre, who has more faith in me than I have in myself.

1
Jenny

Her dad took much longer to burn than she expected.

Jenny watched the deep flames lick his body, curl around his chest and crotch, whisper in his ear. His thin hair crisped then turned to smoke, grey sinewy strands reaching into the mottled sky. A sprig of juniper in his hand caught alight and threw out blue sparks, and Jenny smelt the scent, reminding her of gin. The spruce and pine logs packed around Jim's body were blazing bright and hard. The fire had destroyed his suit already and his skin was tightening around the bones as moisture evaporated from his body.

But still, it seemed to take a long time.

The funeral pyre wasn't much more than a makeshift, oversized barbecue, two rows of concrete breezeblocks with a metal grill suspended between them. Underneath was a long silver tray borrowed from the embalming room, which they would use to gather his remains once the pieces were small enough to fall through the grate. Archie had been working on the pyre in the garden ever since Dorothy announced what her husband's last wishes were.

It was contrary, Jenny had to admit. Her dad spent forty-five years orchestrating the funerals of thousands of people, arranging music and flowers, orders of service, funeral cars and sermons. Making sure every detail was right for the bereaved, ensuring all rival factions got what they wanted and the deceased was sent off in style. And yet his own funeral was the opposite. A pyre in their back garden, no speeches, no sermons, no friends or flowers or ceremony, just the five of them standing next to the throbbing heat of an illegal fire.

Jenny looked away from the flames to the others standing around the fire. Her mum stood at the head of the pyre. A dancing mote of ash landed on her flowery yellow dress and she flicked at it with a bright fingernail. She brushed a strand of wavy grey hair from her forehead and lifted her face to the flames, eyes closed, like she was sunbathing.

Next to Dorothy, Hannah and Indy had their arms linked together, Hannah leaning her head on her girlfriend's shoulder. They were so striking together, Hannah's pale features and long, black hair the opposite of Indy's brown skin and blue bob. Jenny wondered what was going through her daughter's mind as her grandpa's remains went up in smoke. It still seemed crazy to Jenny that she had a grown-up daughter in a relationship.

The flames were higher now, black smoke stretching into the air. The smell of pine and spruce made Jenny think of Christmas. Dorothy had placed bunches of herbs on the corpse before they began, and now bay and sage came to Jenny's nose, mingling with the smell of burnt flesh to remind her of Sunday roast dinners.

She looked to the far end of the pyre, beyond Jim's melting feet, and exchanged a look with Archie. He was busying himself with the logistics of the process, peering underneath, checking that the grate was holding up to the weight and temperatures, using a long pair of tongs to replace a fallen log by Jim's shin. Jenny saw an iron poker and rake on the grass behind him, for sifting through the ashes once the flames had died.

Archie was short and thick, a heavy brown beard and shaved head, the way he moved suggesting something of a Tolkien character. He was the same age as Jenny but seemed older. He'd been Jim and Dorothy's right-hand man for ten years, but it felt like he'd always been here. Archie was one of Dorothy's strays, she had a habit of taking in lost souls, becoming an anchor in their lives. He had appeared one day to arrange his mother's funeral. Over the next month he was often seen at cemeteries and cremations, crashing the funerals of strangers, trying to feel connected. At one in Craigmillar Castle Park, Dorothy approached him with a proposition, and within two weeks he was driving the hearse in a suit, changing into overalls to hammer together coffins, eventually taking over the embalming under Jim's training. And Dorothy stuck by him when the details about his condition came to light. She sought a second opinion, kept an eye on his medication and therapy sessions, and trusted him around the place, which went a long way to saving his life.

The same went for Indy, another stray who pitched up three years ago to bury her Hindu parents, dentists killed in a car accident, leaving behind a rudderless daughter. But Dorothy saw something in her, and a month later she was answering phones, gathering information from clients and sorting admin. Now she was training to become a funeral director in her own right. Meanwhile she had slipped her way into Hannah's heart and persuaded her to move into the flat she'd been left by her mum and dad, ten minutes' walk away on Argyle Place.

Jenny stared at her dad as he charred and shrivelled, his essence mingling with the flames and smoke, dissipating into the universe. Part of her couldn't believe she would never hear his dumb jokes again, that terrible vampire accent he put on sometimes to talk about death. The way he would wink at her, his little girl, during services, at the most inappropriate moments, making her cover her mouth and leave the room she'd sneaked into, because death was fascinating to kids.

But that fascination waned, being brought up around funerals began to take its toll. As a teenager she distanced herself, left home as soon as she could, studied journalism, worked, fell in love with Craig, had Hannah, divorced Craig, all the time staying away from death as much as possible.

But now death was back in her life.

She looked around. Tall oaks and pines lined the far wall of the garden, blocking the neighbours' view. Over to her left was the open garage with the silver hearse parked inside, next to the workshop and embalming room. Those rooms adjoined the main house behind her, the large, three-storey Victorian sprawl that had been the Skelf family home for a hundred years. It had doubled as a funeral director's for all that time, and a private investigator's for the last decade, the businesses taking up the ground floor, the family living on the two floors above.

There was a rustle in the bushes to Jenny's right and Schrödinger padded out from the foliage. The most recent of Dorothy's strays, Schrödinger was a ginger tabby with the wiry body of a street cat and a supreme air of confidence. The name was Hannah's idea and it stuck. As he got closer, Jenny saw something in his mouth. A bird, flashes of red, white and black on the face, yellow under the wing. A goldfinch.

Schrödinger never usually came near Jenny, she was a stranger round here, but he walked past the others and placed the finch at her feet. The cat glanced at the fire enveloping Jim's body, sucking the energy from him, then wandered back into the bushes.

Jenny looked down at the goldfinch, blood smeared across the puncture wounds on its chest and throat.

Another dead body to dispose of.

She scooped it up in her hand and threw it onto the pyre, watching as its feathers burst into flames. She wiped the bird's blood on her jeans and breathed deeply.

2
Jenny

Dorothy raised her glass. 'To Jim.'

The three women clinked tumblers and sipped Highland Park. Jenny felt the burn as it went down. Any half-decent gin was her usual drink, but Dad loved whisky and this was for him. She placed her glass on the kitchen table and ran a finger over the grain of the oak, thought about the thousands of meals she'd eaten here as a kid.

Dorothy took a gulp of whisky and played with a clay dish in the middle of the table, something Hannah made at primary school with the yin and yang symbols on it. She made it for Dorothy, even back then interested in her gran's worldview, the balance and connectedness of the world. The dish had a used-up tea-light in it, and Jenny thought of her dad in the garden, smouldering away as they sat here. She took another drink.

Archie was still down there tending the fire. When he'd begun using the poker on Jim's body the three women had adjourned upstairs to the kitchen, Indy slipping off to look after reception. The same front desk dealt with both funeral and investigator businesses, different numbers to call but they came through to the same phone.

Jenny looked round the large open-plan kitchen. They were at the old table next to the functional kitchen stuff – cooker, fridge-freezer, cupboards – running along two walls. The adjacent wall was taken up by two large bay windows looking out over Bruntsfield Links. From here Jenny could see the crenellations of Edinburgh Castle ahead and the dome of Arthur's Seat to the right. In between was the tree-lined park, a stream of students and school pupils crisscrossing from Bruntsfield to Marchmont and back the other way.

The final wall of the room had large whiteboards from waist to head height. One had 'FD' in thick letters across the top, the other 'PI'. The kitchen doubled as the ops room, from which both businesses had been run for the last decade, since Jim surprised everyone by announcing he intended to expand out of the death industry into private investigations. Maybe it didn't surprise everyone, Dorothy didn't bat an eye, but Jenny struggled to get her head around it, and Jim evaded any questions from her.

The funeral whiteboard was the busier of the two at the moment. Four names were written in black marker under 'FD' – Gina O'Donnell, John Duggan, Arthur Ford and Ursula Bonetti – all in Dorothy's neat hand. Beneath the names were various details for each. Where the body was to be picked up and whether it had been done yet, so one said RIE for the hospital at Little France, another read Marie Curie for the hospice in Frogston, the third was the city mortuary. The mortuary meant the police were involved and a post mortem had been done. Jenny was surprised that she remembered all this, despite never being involved in the business and not having lived here for twenty-five years.

Under each body's pick-up information were the time, date and venue for the funeral, a spread of churches, cemeteries and crematoriums across the city. Warriston Crematorium for one, Morningside Cemetery for another. There were other shorthand acronyms for each service, how many cars were needed, who the celebrant was, what type of service. On the wall next to the whiteboard was a large map of Edinburgh covered in different coloured pins. A map of the dead of the city. Jenny imagined the pattern that would emerge if you joined all the dots together.

In comparison the PI board was pretty empty. It was less regimented too, a bit like those boards in police dramas but without the pictures of mutilated women with red lines to serial killers or terrorist suspects. Instead there was a name at the top, Jacob

Glassman, with another name, Susan Raymond, written underneath. Then some scribbles in Jim's handwriting that Jenny couldn't decipher. She stared at the writing, a thread connecting her dad to a world that was trundling on without him. Outside the window, school kids were kicking a football around, an old woman walked her sausage dog, two cyclists in Lycra zipped along the path to the Meadows, none of them aware of the man crumbling to ashes in the garden downstairs. The only dad she would ever have.

'I can't believe Grandpa's dead,' Hannah said. She held her tumbler to her chest. Not much of a drinker, something Jenny was happy about. Such a different attitude to alcohol now in Scotland. As a teenager, Jenny was sneaking half-bottles out onto the Links to drink with her mates, Dorothy and Jim oblivious. It had left her with a legacy of drink in her veins. Not a problem, she wouldn't call it that, but alcohol was background radiation in her life, a trace of it in everything.

She finished her Highland Park and poured another for her and Dorothy.

'I know,' she said.

Dorothy breathed in through her nose and out through her mouth, a considered movement from decades of yoga.

'He had a good life,' she said, a hint of her Californian accent still there after all these years.

'I'm not ready for him to go,' Jenny said.

Dorothy leaned back and her chair creaked. 'There's nothing we can do.'

Jenny shook her head and sipped her whisky.

'What was that all about, anyway?' she said, angling her glass towards the door.

'What?' Dorothy said.

'The human barbecue downstairs.'

Dorothy shrugged. 'It's what he wanted. He was sick of the formal stuff, the ceremony of it.'

Hannah frowned. 'But he always said people needed the rules and structure to give them closure.'

'Maybe he thought we didn't need that,' Dorothy said.

Jenny wanted to kick her chair back and scream out of the window, lift her tumbler and smash it against the funeral board, splatter whisky over those other deaths. She sat still.

'But it was illegal,' she said. She knew enough about the funeral business to know that burning a body in your back garden was not OK.

'No one will know,' Dorothy said. 'Or care.'

'You think?' Jenny said. She hated how she sounded, like the bratty teenager she once was, sitting at this same table, moaning that Dorothy and Jim wouldn't let her go to some all-night rave at Ingliston with two thirty-year-old men she barely knew. Here she was, a forty-five-year-old divorcee with a grown-up daughter, and she still felt like a brat. Maybe it was Dad's funeral bringing it all to the surface, or maybe it was simply being back in this house of death.

'I know this is hard on you,' Dorothy said. 'Both of you.'

Jenny felt ashamed. This was Dorothy's husband of fifty years she was saying goodbye to, they had all lost a massive part of their lives. It wasn't a competition.

'And for you, Mum,' she said, reaching her hand across the table.

Dorothy chewed the inside of her cheek and took Jenny's hand. Her skin was still soft at the age of seventy. She seemed much younger than that, and always had a look on her face, even now, suggesting she was at peace with the world.

Hannah put her hand on top of Jenny's and Dorothy's, which made it feel like they were a gang about to execute a heist. They each pulled away just as the doorbell rang downstairs.

Dorothy sighed and pushed back her chair, but Hannah put a hand out to stop her.

'Indy can handle it,' she said. 'You know that.'

Dorothy hesitated then nodded.

Hannah was so in love it made Jenny's heart swell. Jenny had only felt the overwhelming power of love like that once before, with Craig. And, well.

She heard muffled conversation downstairs, then steady footsteps and a tap on the open kitchen door.

'Dad, you came.' Hannah jumped up with a scrape of her chair and ran over to Craig standing in the doorway. He held a bunch of red lilies and had a demure expression. Hannah put her arms around him and squeezed, and he hugged her back.

'Hi, Angel,' he said.

Hannah released him and he looked towards the table and nodded. 'Jen.'

'Craig.'

He walked into the room, offering the lilies. 'These are for you, Dorothy, I'm sorry about Jim. Hannah told me and I wanted to pay my respects. He was a good man.'

He glanced at Jenny and she rolled her eyes. Damn it, he still looked good. He never seemed to thicken around the middle like most guys his age, and the flecks of grey through his hair made him look better somehow. Maybe being a dad again to little Sophia was keeping him young, or maybe it was the sex with Fiona, the blonde dynamo who was now the second Mrs McNamara. That was the most annoying thing, that he'd cheated on Jenny with someone the same age, a diminutive Reese Witherspoon type, go-getting and ambitious.

Enough. She resisted the urge to say something sarcastic. It was ten years ago and he'd always been a good dad to Hannah. None of which made it easier.

'They're beautiful,' Dorothy said, accepting the flowers and a kiss on the cheek. She fetched a vase from a cupboard. 'Stay for a drink.'

Craig looked at Jenny. 'I don't want to impose.'

Dorothy poured water into the vase and arranged the lilies. Jenny could smell the flowers, powerful and musky. Lilies always struck her as masculine.

'Stay, Dad,' Hannah said.

Craig looked at Jenny with his eyebrows raised, waiting for her to say OK.

She swept a magnanimous hand across the table. 'Sit.'

When he first told Jenny he was having an affair and leaving her, it almost killed her trying to stay civil in front of Hannah. But she was damned if she was going to let hate and bitterness eat her up, and she didn't want all that toxic shit infecting her daughter. As the years went by it became easier, much to Jenny's surprise. You could get used to anything, it seemed. But she still had to bite her tongue, stop herself becoming the vicious harpy, the wronged woman. Of course, that let him off the hook.

Dorothy put the lilies on the table then got a whisky tumbler from the cupboard and poured Craig a drink.

'So when's the funeral?' Craig said, sipping.

Hannah frowned. 'We just did it.'

'When?'

'Now, in the back garden.'

Craig look confused. 'Wait, that's the smoke over the house?'

Hannah nodded. 'Just us, no service.'

'Are you allowed to cremate folk here?'

Hannah shook her head as Dorothy sat down and refilled her glass.

Jenny's phone vibrated in her pocket and she pulled it out. Kenny from *The Standard*. He never called. Always email, a quick back and forth about her column, then copy submitted on deadline.

She stood up and walked towards the door. 'I need to take this.'

She pressed reply in the hallway. 'Kenny.'

'Hi, Jenny.' His tone of voice was not good.

'Copy's not due for a couple of days.'

She walked to her childhood bedroom, now redecorated as a minimalist guest room, pine bed, stripped floorboards, narrow shelf holding the overspill from Dorothy's book collection.

She heard a sigh down the line. 'There's no easy way to say this, we're cancelling your column.'

'What?'

'You know what it's like here, *Marie Celeste* meets the *Titanic*. The numbers don't add up.'

She wasn't surprised but she wasn't prepared either. Everyone she knew who'd started as a journalist at the same time as her had wangled an exit strategy, gone into PR like Craig, or teaching or consulting, or even politics. A career in journalism was death by a thousand cuts, and here was the final knife in her guts.

'When?'

'Immediately.'

'Kenny, I need this, it's the only regular gig I have left, you know that.'

She fingered a book on the shelf, pulled it out. *Zen and the Art of Motorcycle Maintenance*. She remembered seeing it around the house growing up, a flower blooming from a spanner on the front cover. She'd never read it.

'I'm sorry,' Kenny said.

'I can't pay the rent as it is.'

'Not that it's any consolation, but I'm getting the bullet soon as well.'

'You're right,' Jenny said. 'That's no consolation.'

She walked to the window and looked out at the back garden. Archie was tending the pyre, which had reduced to a low pile of smouldering remains. Black and white and grey, ash and bone, Archie raking round the edges, dust sifting onto the body tray below. Jenny saw charred blobs where Dad's shoes had been and wondered about his feet. Size eleven and thin, the second toe longer than the big one, something she and Hannah both inherited.

'We're slashing across the paper,' Kenny said.

'Freelancers first.'

'You know how it is.'

No contracts, easy to terminate at zero cost. Just shift the work of filling pages in-house, make the subs who are left write the columns and reviews and everything else, and if they don't like it some bright wee sod from journalism school will do it for nothing to get their name in the paper.

Out of the window Jenny saw Schrödinger stalking along the hedge line, his eye on a woodpigeon roosting in a bush. He leapt for it, but the bird fluttered to the top of the hedge and looked down at him. Schrödinger was nonplussed, life was all a game.

'Let me know if there's anything I can do,' Kenny said.

'OK.'

'I have to go. Stay in touch, yeah?'

Jenny ended the call. She was still holding that book, the flower and the spanner, one transforming into the other as if it was that easy to change your life. Maybe if she read the book she could come up with another way to live, another way to see the world.

She returned the book to the shelf and went back to the kitchen. The three of them were sitting around the table sighing like people do after someone says something funny but poignant. Jenny always seemed to miss the joke. They lifted their drinks in unison as if hearing a telepathic message that Jenny was deaf to.

Craig looked at Dorothy.

'But what about the businesses?' he said, as if continuing a conversation.

Dorothy smiled. 'I have Archie and Indy.'

'Indy's training to become a funeral director,' Hannah said, beaming with pride.

'That's great,' Craig said. He lifted his glass and pointed at the two whiteboards on the wall. 'But there's a lot to do. Jim was...' Maybe he didn't want to remind the women of their loss.

Dorothy nodded, acknowledging Craig's diplomacy, then gazed into her glass, swilled the Highland Park, watched as it clung to the sides then slipped down.

Jenny knew what was coming, she'd expected it since she got

the news about Dad. She was surprised it hadn't been mentioned earlier, but here it was, she was ready.

Dorothy took a sip, stared at her glass. 'I thought maybe Jenny could help out. Stay for a bit, keep me company.' Now she looked up. 'Just for a while.'

Jenny thought about the phone call, her overdue rent, that stupid book with the flower on it. She could smell lily pollen and whisky and she thought about never seeing her dad again.

'Sure.'

3
HANNAH

Hannah took Indy's hand as they walked through the front garden. She glanced back at the first-floor window knowing Gran would be there. She smiled and waved then turned away. It felt weird leaving her alone, but Mum was just nipping to her flat across town in Portobello to pick up a few things and coming straight back. It was good they'd be spending time together, they needed each other right now. Everyone needs someone. She leaned over and kissed Indy on the cheek.

'What's that for?'

'Can't I kiss my girlfriend's beautiful face?'

Indy mimed being sick, fingers down her throat.

'Piss off,' Hannah laughed.

They went past the gateposts at the end of the drive and Hannah smiled at the address carved into the stonework, 0 Greenhill Gardens. Number zero, just one of the things that marked this place as special. She asked Dorothy and Jenny about it when she was younger, but Gran just shook her head as if it was a cosmic joke, and Jenny shrugged like it never occurred to her that it was odd. Hannah did some research and it turned out their house was added to the street later than others, by an eccentric brewery owner in the late 1800s. In those days you could make up your own address, but instead of creating a new street name Mr Bartholomew plumped for number zero on the street already there, right next to the existing number one. Posties had been confused ever since.

Something about it appealed to Hannah's mind. Zero was hard to define mathematically and asking about it led into philosophical territory, which she loved. She was studying metaphysics as an optional course, and sometimes popped into lectures on category theory, the maths of maths, to get her brain fried. That abstract space, the way matrices, theories and equations interlinked, the way they mapped out a universe you could superimpose on the real world, she was into it.

'What are you smiling about?' Indy said.

They were round the corner and into the park. The web of paths was full of students and workies heading home after lectures and the office. Hannah loved that everyone lived cheek by jowl here, she felt part of something.

'Just happy to be alive,' she said.

'Oh my God.'

'Which one?'

A running joke, Indy a lapsed Hindu.

The truth was Hannah really was happy to be alive, despite just watching her grandpa being cremated. Maybe because of that. Dorothy once told her that some people got horny at funerals, determined to get on with the business of living in the face of death. Hannah could relate.

They crossed Whitehouse Loan onto the north part of Bruntsfield Links where the pitch and putt was. The undulations of the ground always made Hannah think of the ancient burial site under the surface. She wondered how many of the kids and parents knocking golf balls around realised there were hundreds of seventeenth-century plague victims buried below. Another layer of existence beneath reality.

They cut round the top of the Links to Marchmont then onto Melville Drive. The sun was still high this early in autumn, and the light through the chestnut trees strobed across her eyes. She looked at Indy's face as it dappled between light and shade. In fourth year at school Hannah briefly dated an epileptic boy who had to cross the road when low sunlight flickered through railings. She wondered about that loss of control, reactions in the brain making you who you are. Depression, anxiety, love, hate, anger. She thought about neurons firing, particles shifting state, quarks changing their distributions.

She caught the smell of charcoal and burgers from barbecues across the road. The Meadows were full of students exploiting the last warm days before the country shut down for winter. Frisbees, football, in the distance some girls playing quidditch. *Harry Potter* was before her time, she preferred *The Hunger Games*, stronger women for a start. But you couldn't exactly play Hunger Games in the park.

They reached the flat and bounded up to the top floor. Indy opened the door and they fell inside. Hannah worried that she was supposed to feel down because of Grandpa, but she felt full of possibility. Jim wouldn't want her to mope around, even though she missed him. And maybe Dorothy was right, maybe death makes you horny.

She grabbed Indy's waist and spun her round, kissed her, stared at those brown eyes. 'Love you, babes.'

Indy looked at her sideways. 'What's got into you?'

Hannah kissed her again, long and deep, eased her against the wall.

Indy pulled back. 'Just a minute.' She called out. 'Mel?'

They waited for a reply.

'She must still be at King's Buildings,' Hannah said. Though she knew lectures were over for the day, and it wasn't like Mel to head to the pub afterwards, like some of their classmates. Hannah had skipped lectures on special relativity and quantum field theory this afternoon, Mel saying she would let her know if she missed anything.

Hannah went to kiss Indy again and Indy responded, then a phone rang. It came from Mel's room.

'Leave it,' Indy said, her hand on Hannah's back.

Hannah frowned. Classes were over. Mel was super-reliable and organised, and never went anywhere without her phone.

Hannah unpeeled herself from Indy and went to Mel's door,

knocked twice. Waited. The phone kept ringing. She pushed the door open. Everything seemed normal, the single bed made, the desk neat with piles of notes and textbooks, Mel's photo montage on the wall, pictures of her with friends and family.

The phone was on the desk, still ringing.

'Mum' flashed on the screen.

Hannah felt Indy at the doorway behind her as she picked up the phone and answered.

'Hi, Mrs C, Hannah here.'

'I told you before, call me Yu. What have you done with my daughter?' Her voice was bubbly, strong Canton accent, but there was an edge.

'I don't know, me and Indy were out all day and just got in. I found her phone in her room.'

'I'll kill her,' Yu said, in a tone that meant she would do the opposite. 'She was supposed to meet her father and me for lunch. It's my birthday.'

'Happy Birthday.'

'Thanks, dear, but I wanted to spend it with my daughter.'

Melanie never missed appointments and she would never, ever miss her mum's birthday.

'I'm sorry,' Hannah said, trying to keep her voice light. 'When I see Mel, I'll tell her she's in trouble.'

'You have no idea where she might be?'

Hannah looked out of Mel's window. Her room faced onto Argyle Place, but you could still see a swathe of the Meadows, a sliver of Salisbury Crags in the distance. 'We had classes this afternoon. I wasn't there, it was my grandpa's funeral.'

'Oh, baby, I'm sorry.'

'It's OK. But I know Mel was going to lectures. She probably just got caught up with something at uni.'

That was no excuse at all. The classes were in the afternoon, nothing to do with lunch, but Hannah couldn't think what else to say.

'OK, dear,' Yu said. There was hesitation down the line. 'You get her to call me as soon as she gets home, understand?'

'I will,' Hannah said. 'Bye.'

She hung up and turned to Indy, raised her eyebrows.

Indy stepped into the room. 'I heard.'

She walked to where Hannah was standing, staring at the home screen of Mel's phone, a picture of her with Xander from their year, the two of them dressed up for a Valentine's Day dinner. Hannah remembered helping Mel decide what to wear that night.

'Something's wrong,' Hannah said.

4
DOROTHY

Dorothy stood in the embalming room and stared at what was left of Jim. An outdoor funeral pyre doesn't reach the temperature of a cremation oven, a couple of hundred degrees lower, so his remains were chunkier than they usually got back from crematoriums. Also, crems sift the remaining bone fragments and pulverise them in a cremulator, so the bereaved get a nice pile of grey sand for scattering.

In comparison, the bone fragments and dust in front of her were real. And it was dust, not ashes, that was a misnomer. She was thankful that the fire hadn't left any large bones for her to deal with, nothing longer than a few inches amongst the dirt. She imagined lifting an intact skull from the pile, addressing it like Hamlet. Or one of Jim's femurs, waving it around like a cavewoman.

She looked up from the table. It was too bright for this, but it was a workplace after all, Archie needed plenty of light. Apart from Jim on the table, the place was spotless, Archie always made sure of that. The six body-fridges along one wall hummed, the names and details of the dead inside written on magnetic cards stuck to the front of each fridge. Arthur Ford, five foot eleven, viewing required, embalming needed, no jewellery, removed from the Western General. It tied in with the whiteboard upstairs, and for a moment Dorothy had a flash of the business as a single giant organism.

She turned back to Jim's remains. Picked up a four-inch shard of white bone. It was as light as balsa wood but solid, all the organic content and moisture vaporised. She held it up to the light, turned it in her fingers. It had one straight edge and one gently curved, and was wider at one end than the other with a round indentation at the wide end, like it might've been a socket for a ball joint. The narrow end was sharp, and she pushed her thumb against it, felt the pain. She kept pushing until it broke the skin, watched as a droplet of her blood spread along the tip of the bone, darkening it. She sucked her thumb and put the bone in the pocket of her cardigan.

She thought of all the atoms from Jim's body now floating in the sky across Edinburgh, rising into the upper reaches of the atmosphere. She thought of other atoms from his pyre dropping onto the soil in their garden, their neighbours' gardens. She thought of the atoms in the brush Archie used to tidy up, the atoms stuck in her own hair, on her clothes, her shoes, in her nose and ears and throat. She licked her pinkie finger and dipped it in the dust on the tray, then sucked it.

He tasted of bonfires and dirt. All that was left of fifty years together. She breathed deeply and looked at the embalming table alongside, bottles of chemicals and pumps lined up on the far workstation, razors, scissors, creams and sprays, the collapsible gurney they brought the bodies in on. Collecting bodies was a two-person job, Jim and Archie for years. Now someone else would have to step in, maybe her. She'd done the funeral arranging together with Jim for years but she hadn't got as involved with the body side of the business. She was good at logistics, good with people, had worked for the company part-time on and off her whole life, while raising Jenny at the same time. Indy could step up, she was training to be a funeral director anyway, she was small but strong, tough in a way none of the Skelfs were. Dorothy saw it in her the moment they met, same with Archie. All part of their extended surrogate family. A family that had now lost its heart.

She left the room, switching the light out on her husband, the ashen taste of him still on her tongue, his sharp bone with her blood on it nestled in her pocket.

She sat at the desk in the small office and frowned, paperwork scattered in front of her. She took a sip of whisky and sucked her teeth. She'd been drinking too much all week, since she found Jim on the bathroom floor, eyes open, pyjama trousers at his ankles.

She picked up the bank statement again, adjusted her glasses, and compared it to another piece of paper. She needed more light in here, or better glasses. She thought about Jim's eyeballs, evaporated into nothing. She looked at an open book of accounts and squinted as she ran her finger down the page. Something didn't add up.

Jim always handled the business side of things, Dorothy was hopeless with numbers. Hannah got her love of maths from him. Maybe Dorothy was misunderstanding it, but there seemed to be money missing. Not a big lump sum gone wandering, but a steady amount leaving the business account for months. No, years. Into a sort code and account number she didn't recognise, with no reference name. She shuffled papers, looked again, took another hit of Highland Park. The whisky wasn't helping.

She sighed. Maybe she was overlooking something simple, something that would explain the five hundred pounds coming out of their account every month for years. She must know about this, Jim would've told her. Because if he didn't tell her, that meant it was a secret, and she couldn't cope with that. She needed to speak to someone but the person she always spoke to when something was wrong was Jim.

She searched amongst the papers on the table and found her old Nokia, thumbed through the handful of contacts and stopped at Thomas. She looked at his name for a few seconds then called, pushing her glasses onto the top of her head. She drank whisky and sat back in her chair, then pinched the bridge of her nose and listened to the ringing.

'Hello?'

'Hi, Thomas, it's Dorothy.'

'It's a little late.' He sounded sleepy. 'Are you OK?'

She glanced at the clock on the wall, 1 a.m. 'Did I wake you?'

'What's up?'

They'd been friends for five years, since he came to her yoga class. He'd attracted everyone's attention, any man at a yoga class gets attention, especially a tall black man with an accent drifting between Scotland and Sweden. When the women discovered he was a police officer it was too much. Dorothy liked him straight away, he was softer than the Scottish men she knew, despite being a cop. Two months after that first class she bumped into him on Chambers Street and they went for coffee. It felt good to be talking with a man who wasn't her husband. Nothing more than that.

Then two years ago Thomas's wife Morag died suddenly. A heart attack while riding her bike through Southside traffic, she hit the kerb and bounced into a parked van. The Skelfs did the funeral. Wasn't too much of a reconstruction job, would've been much worse if she'd fallen into an oncoming vehicle. Thomas and Morag didn't have kids and all his family were in Sweden, so Dorothy helped out and they became close. Jim knew they met for coffee and maybe he thought it was strange but he never said anything.

Thomas's grief gradually subsided, a scenario Dorothy had seen a hundred times before. She wondered about her own grief. It was so individual for each person, she knew that well from the business. After the initial shock of finding Jim she'd wallowed for days. Arranging the pyre had focused her, but it also made her kind of numb. Again, she'd seen that so often with clients. She wondered when the waves would hit, how bad they would be, how deep she would go. But she would survive, everyone did, and the pain would reduce with time. That was almost as unbearable, the knowledge that the grief, along with her memories of Jim, would fade.

'Jim's dead,' she said.

'Oh, Dorothy.'

She rubbed at her forehead. 'Heart attack.'

The words hung between them, giving them a link to each other, both their partners killed the same way.

'I'm so sorry,' Thomas said.

'It happened a week ago,' Dorothy said, swirling the whisky in her glass. 'During the night, while he was on the toilet. I found him in the morning. Where's the dignity in that?'

She hadn't told anyone the details of how she found him. She'd removed his piss-stained pyjama trousers and put them in the wash basket. Grabbed a new pair from the chest of drawers and pulled them up his legs, then dragged him into the bedroom and heaved him onto the bed. He'd been dead for hours, skin cold, a feeling she was used to in this business. She lay down and held him for half an hour, tried to clear her mind. She didn't phone a doctor for another hour, because once she did that, Jim wasn't hers anymore, his death was everyone's. She wanted to keep it to herself as long as she could.

'A week ago?' Thomas said.

There was a slight reprimand in his tone. Why hadn't she told him sooner? He could've helped.

But how could he?

'We cremated him today.'

'If you'd told me, I would've come.'

'We didn't tell anyone.'

She heard him shift his weight and wondered if he still used the same side of the bed as when Morag was alive. She hadn't spread herself out in the last week, to use Jim's side of the bed seemed an insult to him.

'If there's anything I can do,' Thomas said.

Dorothy lowered her glasses to her eyes and stared at the paperwork on the desk.

'There is a way you can help,' she said, lifting a bank statement. 'I want you to look into something for me.'

5
HANNAH

Hannah was properly worried. She stood in Mel's room feeling like an intruder. It was dark outside now, the sodium lights from the street making the room feel seedy. She ran a finger along a bookshelf, opened a drawer of the desk and found stationery, not much else.

She'd checked all Mel's social media, once earlier this evening, then again twenty minutes ago. No activity. She'd called round all their friends and no one had seen Mel today. As far as Hannah could work out, she was the last one to speak to Mel, at breakfast. There was a full day of classes, fluid dynamics labs in the morning, two lectures and a tutorial in the afternoon, and Mel wasn't at any of them. And she had specifically said she would take notes for Hannah.

Hannah had called Xander first, who said he hadn't seen her since lunchtime yesterday. He was an astrophysicist, a subject even more complex than the stuff Hannah and Mel were studying. She tried to think what she knew about him. He was in the Quantum Club with Hannah, Mel and a few others, and his parents had something to do with the military and lived abroad.

She called a few other names in Mel's phone, but no one had heard from her. That included her brother Vic who worked at the Fruitmarket Gallery in town. He was close to his sister and said he'd spoken to her yesterday, just small talk about her meeting their folks for lunch. He was shocked when he learned Mel hadn't turned up.

Hannah posted on the third-year physics undergrad message board, asked if anyone had seen her, tried to keep it low key. She checked Mel's WhatsApp and text messages, nothing that would raise an eyebrow.

She went over this morning's breakfast in her mind. She hadn't exactly been focused, thinking about Jim's cremation. Had Mel seemed a bit off, a little nervous or anxious? Maybe Hannah was superimposing her current frame of mind onto her memories.

She looked at the time on Mel's phone, almost 2 a.m.

Indy was behind her now in the room. 'What are you thinking?'

Hannah shook her head, pulled out her own phone and dialled 101. She shared a look with Indy as she waited for them to pick up.

'Hello,' she said. 'I'd like to report a missing person.'

6
Jenny

Jenny felt the edges of the single mattress under her with her hands and was confused for a moment, then she remembered and opened her eyes. She was glad the room had been redecorated since her childhood, it gave her a little distance. It would've been too much to be back here as a middle-aged woman in the same bed she lay in as a teenager, thinking of Kurt Cobain and touching herself.

But there were still one or two reminders. The creaky floor-board next to the bed had never been fixed, and the noise it made as she stood up was overpoweringly nostalgic, sending her hurtling back through the decades to when she was a child. On the wall next to the door she could see the dent in the plaster where she'd punched it several times, furious that Susan Wilson was going out with Andy Shepherd, even though Susan knew Jenny liked him. And in the bottom corner of the window her initials were still scraped into the glass, as clear as if they were tattooed on her chest.

Being back here, Christ. Mum needed her but Jenny wasn't kidding herself this was temporary. At forty-five years old Jenny had nowhere to live, no assets, no job, no marriage. She might as well be here, where better to end your days than in a funeral home?

She looked at the open suitcase on the floor, her clothes spilling out in a mess. The rest of her belongings were in a handful of boxes in the storeroom downstairs. Archie had helped her do a moon-light flit from the Portobello flat last night. Packing up all her stuff had taken a depressingly short time, and she left the crappy furni-ture as part payment for her rent arrears.

She couldn't fathom how it had come to this. Twenty years ago, when they started renting that place on Bellfield Street, she was married, pregnant and in love. She and Craig were skint, both freelance journos, her doing cultural commentary, him covering politics. There was no chance of getting on the housing ladder with no steady income, but they'd presumed things would look up. Instead the journalism industry collapsed, Craig left her, only then starting to make money in PR with the business he set up with Fiona.

Dorothy and Jim had offered to take Jenny and Hannah in. Jim especially was incensed at Craig leaving, furious at the idea of any man betraying his family. He, more than Dorothy, tried to cajole Jenny and Hannah back into the fold, long play sessions and ice creams with his granddaughter, late-night phone conversations with Jenny, pleading with her to come home. But something about that rankled her. The idea she couldn't provide for her daughter. Which was stupid pride, looking back. Plus she didn't want Hannah growing up around dead bodies, the way she had. So she redoubled her freelancing efforts, busted herself trying to pay rent, perhaps at the expense of her relationship with Hannah. Maybe it was the wrong decision, one of the millions of wrong life decisions that had brought her back to the Skelf house.

She imagined the thousands of bodies that had passed through this place, pictured them rising from graveyards across the city, hordes of zombies marching towards Greenhill Gardens to reclaim their links to the living. Maybe she was doing that too, trying to get her father back, reconnect with Mum.

She pulled on a dressing gown from her open suitcase and padded through to the kitchen. Schrödinger was perched on a battered leather chair by one of the windows, face turned to the sun glinting through the trees. He didn't acknowledge her. Jenny grabbed a mug, poured some coffee and water into Dorothy's large stovetop pot. She could only ever be bothered with instant at home so this Columbian roast would blow her head off.

She walked to the window.

'Hey, cat.'

Nothing. She stroked the nape of his neck. 'Look, we need to get along, I'm going to be here for a while.'

Schrödinger stretched away to the other side of the chair, his claws digging into the leather.

'Fuck you,' Jenny said.

'Who are you swearing at?' Dorothy came through the door looking surprisingly fresh-faced.

'Your cat,' she said. 'He hates me.'

'He responds well to being sworn at, just like humans.'

Jenny smiled and returned to the stove, started making coffee. 'Want one?'

Dorothy shook her head. 'I'm going out, meeting a friend.'

'Who?'

Dorothy stopped. She was wearing loose cotton trousers and a maroon silk blouse, open at the neck. They both suited her, she always knew how to dress well. Jenny was envious, her elegant mother gliding through life. Her calm air gave the impression that nothing fazed her. Jenny couldn't understand why she didn't seem more upset about her dad.

Dorothy put her hands on her hips. 'Thomas Olsson.'

Jenny had heard his name mentioned before but never met him, a Swedish cop friend of Dorothy's. The Skelfs had buried his wife, and Indy said he was a bit of a silver fox.

'You're off to meet a handsome widower the day after cremating your husband?'

Dorothy raised her eyebrows at Jenny's tone. 'I can do whatever I want.'

'Just like you did in eighty-seven.'

Dorothy froze. Eighty-seven was shorthand for what came to be regarded within the family as 'Dorothy's episode'. A solo trip to visit her mum in Pismo Beach, supposedly for two weeks, turned into almost two months. Jim and a hormonal Jenny were left in Scotland wondering what the hell was going on. Turned out Dorothy was hooking up with an old school flame, recently divorced, the pair of them trying to grab on to their disappearing youth one last time. In the end, Jim had to fly to California to talk Dorothy into coming back. Jenny never really understood how, but her mum and dad managed to put it behind them. Jim forgave Dorothy and she was clearly full of remorse, but Jenny never properly got over it. A germ of an idea about the possibility of betrayal and deceit sprouted in her mind, then years later, when Hannah was almost the same age as she had been, Craig went and did the same thing, only much worse. That reopened the wound, made it hard to accept her mum's comfort and support through her own separation and divorce. And now this, Jim's burnt remains downstairs on a slab, and Dorothy dressed nice and heading out to meet an eligible widower.

'Don't you dare,' Dorothy said. 'You have no right to bring that up.'

'Whatever you say.'

'Your dad was the love of my life. What happened back then was a mistake, one I've always regretted. And to bring it up now, my God.'

Jenny held out her hands. 'OK.'

'I don't need permission to live.'

'Fine.'

The coffee pot burbled on the stove as Schrödinger wandered over to Dorothy and ran his tail round her legs. She stroked him and pointed at the doorway.

'I need you to cover the front desk for a while,' she said. 'It's Indy's day off.'

Jenny felt a bubble of anxiety rise inside her as she poured the coffee. 'I don't know what to do.'

'Just answer the phone if it rings and take down details. You've seen me do it often enough.'

'Not recently.'

'You'll be fine.' Dorothy lifted her cardigan from the back of a chair and put it on. Jenny smelt the smoke on it from yesterday, imagined her dad's spirit in the wool.

'I'm sorry,' she said. 'Are you OK?'

'No,' Dorothy said, not unkindly. 'Neither of us is OK, and I don't expect we will be for a long time. But we need to carry on, don't we?'

'Do we?'

Dorothy took Jenny's hand. 'What else can we do?'

The phone rang.

Jenny was in the embalming room staring at the pile of dust that was her dad when she heard the ringing from reception. She wasn't sure how long she'd been standing there, could've been seconds or weeks.

She walked through to reception. Such a contrast to the embalming room, here were plush carpets, carved oak fixtures, bouquets of flowers in a corner waiting for the next service. Egg and dart cornicing around the ceiling, a stylish desk with a laptop and telephone. From reception she could see the whole customer side of the business on the ground floor – the small chapel to the left, the arranging room to the right, and the three viewing rooms along the back.

She sat in the chair and stared at the phone, then picked it up.

'Hello, Skelf's?' She remembered not to say funeral director or private investigator, because it could be either.

Sniffling down the line.

'It's OK, take your time.' Jenny pictured her mum saying the same thing thousands of times over the years.

'It's my William.'

Jenny heard her mum's voice in her head. *Just be there, you don't have to say anything. People want to feel connected to someone, to anything.*

More sniffing. 'I need to arrange his funeral.'

'I'm sorry to hear that.'

The woman burst out crying and Jenny felt helpless. If they'd been in the same room she could've offered a tissue or patted her hand. Or given her a bear hug like she needed herself, maybe share some tears, break out the single malt and drown their sorrows together. How fucked up was it to be sitting the day after your dad's funeral listening to the worst moment of someone else's life?

'What's your name?' Jenny said.

A while before she answered. 'Mary. William and Mary Baxter.'

As if they were still a couple, as if she hadn't just had her soul ripped out. Jenny heard Mary breathe and try to regain control.

'It's OK,' she said. It wasn't OK, it was a stupid thing to say, nothing was ever going to be OK again. 'Tell me about William.'

So Mary did. She talked about her dead husband, how they met at the dancing on Lothian Road in the 1950s, he'd been in the navy, dashing in his uniform, seen the hydrogen bomb tests over Christmas Island in the Pacific but lived a long life despite that, worked at Ferranti building cockpit instrument panels for fighter planes, raised four children, one of whom was dead already. That made her pause. Jenny couldn't bear it, she wasn't cut out for this, didn't have what Dorothy and Jim had, or Indy. She kept thinking about her own dad in a heap on a metal tray in the room through the back.

Mary was still talking, about her grandkids, William's pacemaker and plastic hip, how he loved gardening and walks in the Meadows, still held her hand on the way to the shops, always a romantic. Jenny wrote it all down, although it mostly wasn't pertinent. Mary mentioned pneumonia, pulmonary something, then she ran out of steam, couldn't bring herself to talk about the end.

'And where is William now?'

A long pause while Mary composed herself. 'He's in St Columba's. He passed in the night. They said it was peaceful, he wouldn't have felt anything.'

How did they know? Maybe he spent an hour tortured by pain, unable to breathe, panicking to stay alive, grasping at his sheets in terror at the black hole coming for him.

Jenny really wasn't cut out for this.

'OK,' she said. 'We can look after him for you, don't worry. Would you like to come in and speak to one of our funeral directors about arranging things?'

No answer.

'We're on Greenhill Gardens, do you know it?'

'Yes.'

'When would suit you?'

Jenny imagined her sitting at home, alone, nothing to do.

'This afternoon?' Mary said.

'Let's make it two o'clock.'

'Thank you, you've been very helpful.'

Jenny wondered if she was being sarcastic. 'You're welcome.'

Mary hung up and Jenny sat looking at the phone in her grip, felt the sweat on her palm. She swallowed hard and began tapping the handset against her forehead, gently at first then harder and harder, until she could really feel the pain.

7
DOROTHY

Dorothy loved Middle Meadow Walk, the stream of students coming and going, cyclists passing in a blur, even the weird buskers. A guy up the road was playing a funky shuffle on a beaten-up old drum kit, and she smiled as she pictured her own kit gleaming in the second-floor studio back at the house. The festival was over and she was relieved when the city stopped being an assault course of kids trying to push flyers into your hand, but she missed that energy too. It was quickly replaced by students excited about a new adventure in the big city. The Walk was a long, wide boulevard stretching from Marchmont to the heart of the Old Town. Students lived in the former and studied in the latter, so it felt like an artery, and Dorothy imagined she was a blood cell, heading to another part of Edinburgh's body, transporting her nutrients to where they were needed.

As she reached Söderberg she saw Thomas sitting outside. He wore a dark-green jacket, white T-shirt, jeans, black-rimmed glasses. The day was bright and clear, a slight edge in the air, the whisper of winter coming. He was reading a book, and as she reached him she saw it was by a Japanese woman.

She touched his shoulder. 'Any good?'

He turned and removed his glasses, smiled and closed the book. 'Very.' He stood up and embraced her. 'It's good to see you.'

'You too.'

'How are you?' The question was loaded.

She considered it instead of just saying she was fine. 'I'll be OK, I think.'

'I'm sure you will,' Thomas said, pulling out a chair for her.

They were at a small table outside the café. The building was large and glass-fronted, part of the modern Quartermile development nestled amongst the spires of the old hospital and university buildings. There was an open-plan Swedish bakery through the back, one of the reasons Dorothy liked it. Light, classy Nordic furniture everywhere made her long for a place of clean lines and minimalism she'd never been to.

They ordered pastries and coffee, Thomas swapping a few Swedish words with the student waiter who took their order.

'He's studying philosophy,' Thomas said when the waiter was gone.

'Good luck to him.'

Dorothy enjoyed the way their voices told a story. Her faint traces of California, his edge of Scandinavia, the two of them in middle and old age, sitting in the weak Scottish sunlight, both immigrants because of love, now alone. When you live somewhere else for a long time you don't really have a home anymore. She loved Edinburgh, loved the Scottish self-deprecating humour, but her heart yearned for the honesty and ambition of the Pacific Coast. She wondered what Thomas missed of Gothenburg.

'So,' Thomas said, reaching into his jacket pocket. 'Your mysterious bank payments.'

No nonsense, something else Thomas had in common with Jim. But she had to stop thinking like that. He unfolded a piece of paper and flattened it on the table. He put on his reading glasses and blinked.

'They go back around ten years,' he said.

'Always the same amount?'

Thomas nodded.

Jesus, that was over fifty grand.

Thomas shifted his weight. 'Does the name Rebecca Lawrence mean anything to you?'

Dorothy thought for a moment. So many people had passed through her life, so many names. 'I don't think so.'

'She's forty-five years old, lives in Craigentinny with her ten-year-old daughter Natasha.'

The same age as Jenny, that made Dorothy think. And with a daughter. 'No, it doesn't mean anything.'

Thomas ran a finger down the page as the waiter brought their order. He waited until the kid walked away.

'She works as a receptionist at a doctor's surgery. Has done for years.'

Dorothy shook her head.

'One interesting fact,' Thomas said, looking up. 'She's a widow. Kind of.'

The smell of their coffee and the sugar from the pastries made Dorothy feel momentarily dizzy. Three young women walked past talking loudly about their night out, laughing, touching each other with ease and confidence.

'What do you mean, kind of?' Dorothy said.

'Her husband went missing,' Thomas said. 'Ten years ago. She filed an official missing-person report.'

'And?'

Thomas shrugged and took a sip of espresso. 'He never showed up. Three years ago she applied to the courts to get a declarator of death. That means he's legally dead. You can do it once someone has been missing for seven years. It means she got a death certificate, would be entitled to his state pension and so on.'

Something niggled in the back of Dorothy's mind. A middle-aged couple in tweed meandered past their table, overtaken by a scrum of teenage boys in sportswear.

'So he went missing around the time these payments started?' Dorothy said.

'A couple of months before.'

'That's a coincidence.'

'It is.'

Dorothy touched her temple.

Thomas sighed and splayed his hands. 'I'm sure there's a reasonable explanation for this.'

'That's not the police officer talking. This stinks and you know it.'

'Jim would never...' He had the decency not to finish the sentence.

'What's the missing husband's name?'

Thomas looked at Dorothy. 'Simon Lawrence.'

Oh shit, she knew him.

8
HANNAH

At first she thought no one was on reception, but then her mum raised her head above the front edge of the desk as if she'd been sleeping there. Jenny blinked heavily. A strand of her red hair had come away from the loose pony at the back and was stuck to her lip. She pulled at it and coughed.

'Hey,' she said.

Hannah had only spent a few minutes on the phone to the police last night, it was a non-starter. She thought maybe they wouldn't do anything because it hadn't been twenty-four hours or whatever it was supposed to be. But the jaded cop with wheezy breath told her down the line that was just a television cliché. The truth was there was no time limit on missing persons, and the police didn't investigate unless the person was vulnerable, like an old lady with dementia wandering off, or a schoolchild. There was no law against responsible adults going missing, apparently. Hannah checked after the conversation, and annoyingly the police officer was right. He'd almost laughed when Hannah voiced her concerns, especially when he heard Melanie was a student. A twenty-year-old student hadn't come home yet, call out the search parties. Hannah insisted on getting the cop's name and a reference number for the call, but it was just bluster.

Then at seven this morning Yu Cheng phoned just as Hannah was about to call her. Real worry in Yu's voice when Hannah told her she hadn't heard from Mel. Hannah had been keeping a lid on it until then but after speaking to Mel's mum she felt a tightness in her stomach. Checked social media again, texted a bunch of people in Mel's phone, nothing.

It was staring her in the face when Indy said it. Mel was a missing person and this was a case. If the police won't investigate, someone else has to, so here she was. Only trouble was, Grandpa was dead.

Jenny righted herself.

'I need a private investigator,' Hannah said.

Jenny came from behind the desk. 'What's up?'

'Mel's missing.'

Hannah saw lines around her mum's eyes that she hadn't noticed before. She also had a red mark on her forehead and looked exhausted. Jim's death had hit them all, but Hannah sometimes forgot he was Jenny's dad. She pictured her own dad on a funeral pyre, how she would feel about that.

'She's probably just at her boyfriend's,' Jenny said.

Hannah shook her head. She was already tired of going over the details, but she would have to again and again if she was going to do something about it.

'Xander hasn't seen her, no one has.'

'Family?'

'Yu is worried sick.'

'So contact the police.'

'They're not interested.'

'What?'

'They don't know her. This isn't like her at all.' She felt something rising in her chest, breathed to keep it down. 'I need help, Mum. I need to find her because no one else will.'

Jenny studied her.

'OK,' she said eventually.

Schrödinger purred as Hannah stroked him from neck to tail. He moved away to find sunshine by the window.

They were back at the kitchen table. Hannah rubbed at a sticky whisky ring on the wood. It was a beautiful day outside, light flooding in. She looked at dust drifting in the light and thought about subatomic particles, even though she knew particles weren't really particles at all, they were waves or fields or forces, any number of different metaphors that didn't quite fit the numbers and equations we throw at the universe.

'I'm not a private investigator,' Jenny said, sipping coffee. Her mug had an Indian depiction of Buddha on it. The coffee smelt strong.

'Neither am I.'

'So we can't do this.'

Hannah raised her eyebrows. 'You always used to tell me I could do anything if I put my mind to it.'

Jenny rolled her eyes. 'Come on, that's what parents tell kids so they don't end up as junkie pole dancers.'

Hannah drank her green tea. 'Thanks.'

Jenny waved a hand at the PI whiteboard on the far wall. 'Your gran will know better, she watched Dad do it for years.'

Hannah leaned forwards. 'You're my mum, I'm asking you for help.'

Jenny shook her head.

Hannah felt her anger rising. Her mum was such a shrugger, what was it Gen X called themselves, 'slackers'? Just an excuse not to engage with the world, not to expose yourself to real feelings.

'What's wrong with you?' she said. 'I'm asking you to help me.'

Jenny sat up. 'My dad just died, or did you forget?'

Hannah stared wide-eyed. She wanted to apologise but she also wanted to shake some sense into her mum.

Eventually Jenny spoke. 'Anyway, I have no clue where to start.'

That was acquiescence of a kind. Enough for now.

'How hard can it be? We just investigate,' Hannah said. 'We talk to people, trace Mel's movements, look into things.'

'She's probably already safe and sound back at your place.'

'Indy would've called.'

'I just don't think it's a big deal.'

Hannah pulled out Mel's phone, clunked it on the table. 'She would never go anywhere without this. And it's over twenty-four hours since anyone saw her.'

'You're acting like people aren't allowed to do their own thing,' Jenny said. 'Not everyone has to be contactable every minute of the day.'

'Please spare me the rant about the old days, four television channels, no remote controls, no Internet. You made your own fun with a hoop and a stick.'

'Maybe she went away for some peace, to study, or take drugs, or have glorious sex with unsuitable men.'

'She didn't take any clothes or her phone or a toothbrush. If she was having mad sex with a biker gang she would want clean teeth.'

'She'll turn up.'

Hannah pushed her chair back. 'I hope so, but in the meantime let's look for her.'

Jenny held her hands out, ceding the floor. 'How do we do that?'

Hannah strode to the whiteboard and stared at the names there. She took the lid off a marker pen, the smell reminding her of tutorials. She wrote 'Melanie Cheng' on a blank area of board then drew lines from Mel's name and added: 'Boyfriend Xander', 'Family', 'Classmates', 'Uni Staff'.

'What would a detective do?' she said, looking at Jenny.

Her mum shrugged.

Hannah tapped the pen against her hand. 'Start with the boyfriend.'

'What about the other categories?' Jenny said.

Hannah looked at the board and shook her head. 'I can't think of anything.'

'Family stuff? Cultural problems for a young, independent Chinese-Scottish woman?'

Hannah pressed her lips together. 'That's racist. Yu and Bolan are liberal academics, very open-minded.'

'She has a brother, right?'

'He's cool.'

'You sure?'

Hannah couldn't imagine Vic doing anything to harm Mel.

'What about extra-curricular stuff?' Jenny said. 'Societies, weird kinks?'

Hannah drew another line from Mel's name and wrote 'Quantum Club'.

'Is that a Dungeons and Dragons thing?' Jenny said.

Hannah gave her mum a look. 'It's a debating club, kind of philosophy. We both go.'

'I never heard you mention it.'

'You never asked.'

'What do you talk about?'

'Anything, really. The implications of modern physics on life, the universe and everything.' Hannah knew her mum wouldn't get the *Hitchhiker's Guide* reference. 'It's run by one of the postgrad tutors, Bradley Barker.'

Hannah added his name to the board. She could see the shadow of previous scribbles by Grandpa underneath what she'd written, and thought about the molecules of whiteboard and marker ink intermingling, blending this case with every older one, both solved and unsolved.

'OK,' Jenny said. 'So one of us should speak to Xander and the other talks to this Bradley.'

'There's no one downstairs,' Dorothy said, making Hannah turn. Her gran was in the doorway holding a folded piece of paper in her fist. She looked at the whiteboard then at Hannah and Jenny. 'What are you up to?'

Hannah looked at Jenny then back at her gran.

'We're on a case,' she said.

9

DOROTHY

Archie tapped the carotid artery like a nurse and Dorothy watched as the pump did its work, pushing embalming solution into the woman's body, which forced out the blood. The buzz of the pump and the chemical smell reminded her of Jim. But everything reminded her of Jim, maybe she should sell up and move back to Pismo Beach after fifty years, never be haunted again.

'Hi, Archie,' she said from the doorway.

He looked up. 'Hello.'

She approached the body, pale and rubbery. Not like bodies on television dramas, that was something forensic shows got wrong. They were obviously actors lying there still breathing, blood oxygenating in their veins, hopes and disappointments still messing with their minds. The woman in front of her had no more disappointments, no more hope.

'Gina O'Donnell,' Archie said.

Dorothy reached out and her fingers hovered over the abrasive marks on Gina's neck. Suicide at thirty-nine, hanged herself from the light fitting in her bedroom with a belt. Dorothy could see the buckle indentation still on her skin.

Archie followed her gaze. 'Should be easy enough to cover up.'

Dorothy nodded. Archie wasn't as skilled as Jim with the bodies, but he was good enough and he was conscientious. 'It's the sister organising, isn't it?'

'Yes.'

'Has she brought in clothes yet?'

Archie checked the pump, the peach-coloured liquid disappearing. 'Yesterday. After...'

He meant after they burnt Jim.

Dorothy watched as he checked the needle in the artery, the tube running to the pump. Someone else might have let him go when they discovered the nature of his illness, but Dorothy supported him and it had paid off. After his mother's death he'd developed Cotard's Syndrome, a psychological condition where the patient has periods believing they're actually dead. It can occur with post-traumatic stress and Archie's bereavement was clearly a trigger. He began hanging around cemeteries and crematoriums, attending the funerals of strangers, because he felt he was amongst his own. One of the weird things about it is that sufferers don't contemplate suicide, because they believe they're already dead. In severe cases people starve themselves to death.

Archie's was never that serious but he suffered in silence for the first year he worked here. Dorothy noticed his increasing listlessness and subtly enquired. He was still doing his tasks but only the bare minimum, never otherwise interacting. Dorothy persuaded him to seek medical help, and after months round the houses, a switched-on psychiatrist came up with the diagnosis. There were a couple of years of trying out different anti-psychotics and mood suppressants, trial and error, until they found a balance that levelled him out. But it was always there in the background, the idea of his own death never fully left his mind.

Dorothy tried to imagine it, believing your soul had left your body and you were a walking corpse. Worse than real death, trapped in a decaying body, stuck between this world and the next.

'I want to ask you something,' she said.

'Of course.'

She looked at Gina on the table, those marks on the neck.

'What do you remember about Simon Lawrence?'

Archie stopped adjusting chemicals on the tray. 'Why do you ask?'

'He came to mind recently, that's all.'

Now Archie looked up. 'Not much. He was here for the first few months after I started. Driving mostly, some carpentry.'

'What was he like?'

'I never really knew him, to be honest. What's this about?'

Dorothy suddenly felt the room was too bright, the lights overhead like interrogation lamps. She felt warm despite the cool temperature.

'Do you remember why he left?'

Archie shook his head. 'I think Jim said he got another job somewhere in an office. I'm not sure how much he liked this work. It's not for everyone.'

Dorothy glanced at the pump, half full of embalming fluid, gently rippling like a slushie machine. She placed the tip of her finger on Gina's hand, cold like rubber, not human at all.

'No,' she said. 'It's not for everyone.'

10
HANNAH

Southpour was a typical hipster bar, exposed brickwork, light fittings with designer rust, throbbing old filament bulbs that threw out no light. The menu was sourdough bread, craft beers and a long list of boutique gins with bespoke garnishes and twenty-first-century mixers, whatever they were.

In the five years since Hannah first tasted alcohol, most of the remaining old-man pubs had vanished from the Southside. Hannah was ambivalent about it. At least young women could now drink something that tasted nice without getting felt up, although of course the hassle never stopped. On the other hand, you paid a tenner for a drink and a bag of handcrafted artisan crisps.

Xander was behind the end of the bar, chin resting on the heel of his hand, as if the blonde he was staring at was saying the most interesting thing in the world.

He spotted Hannah and his eyes changed, followed by his body language. He edged away from the woman and turned to Hannah.

'Have you seen her?' he said.

'I was about to ask you the same thing.'

'She didn't come home last night?'

Hannah shook her head. She looked at the gantry lined with spirit bottles, fairy lights draped along wooden beams. The bar was almost empty at lunchtime and she imagined grabbing Xander by his shirt and pulling him over the bar and onto the floor.

'I need you to tell me everything you know,' she said.

On hearing Hannah's tone the blonde lifted a cherry-coloured drink full of mint and moved away from the bar. Xander watched her go.

Hannah nodded at the girl's bum. 'Moving on quickly.'

'She's just a punter.'

'OK.'

'Have you spoken with Mel's folks?'

Hannah examined him. He was over six feet and gangly, more like an arrangement of soft noodles than a human skeleton covered in flesh and skin. She'd always presumed he was harmless, but Mel's disappearing act had hardened something in her, and now she looked at everything with suspicion.

Hannah nodded. 'She didn't meet them for lunch yesterday. They came down from Dundee.'

Xander looked worried. 'That's not like her.'

Hannah dug into her pocket and pulled out Mel's phone. 'And she doesn't have this.'

'Shit.'

Hannah moved her thumb over the phone screen and the picture of Mel and Xander popped up. The phone wasn't even locked, what a naïve wee soul. 'So when was the last time you saw her?'

Xander wiped at the bar with a towel even though it was clean. 'Are you a detective now?'

Hannah thought about that. 'I just want to find my friend. And we prefer investigator to detective.'

'Seriously?'

Hannah shrugged. 'You don't seem that bothered Mel is missing.'

'Of course I am. You're the only one who's allowed to care, is that it?'

Hannah hadn't had much interaction with Xander in the past. She remembered when he and Mel hooked up after a Physics Society mixer at King's Buildings House. It was lame, as all these things are, and the lights were too bright in the bar, but she watched as the two of them sat talking in a corner, eye contact and obvious body language. Mel was beautiful in a prim kind of way, severe fringe, her black hair always glossy, no make-up but impeccable nails. The way she carried herself was contained, organised. She hadn't really talked about boys before, so Hannah was surprised she and Xander hit it off so quickly. Compared to Mel, buttoned-down and precise, Xander was like a drunken giraffe, flopping around in a daze. Or maybe, as she watched him now, he was more together than that, more aware.

'You're allowed to care,' Hannah said, planting herself on a barstool. 'Can I get a drink?'

Xander shook his head as if to say he didn't understand women, which he undoubtedly didn't. 'What can I get you?'

Hannah scanned the gantry and saw a bottle she recognised. 'Highland Park, straight.'

Xander's eyebrows raised as he reached for the bottle. His T-shirt rode up and she saw the Superdry logo on his underwear.

'I didn't have you pegged as a single-malt girl.'

'You don't have me pegged at all.'

It wasn't him necessarily, but something about this situation had her hackles up. Maybe the way he was talking to the blonde when Hannah walked in, or just his unearned confidence. Or the fact that the most sensible girl Hannah knew had disappeared off the planet.

The whisky clunked on the bar and Hannah paid. She lifted it to her nose and breathed, felt the molecules of vapour burn her nostrils. She thought of Grandpa. How would he find Melanie?

'Tell me when you last had contact with her,' Hannah said, taking a sip.

'Had contact?'

'You know what I mean – saw, spoke to, WhatsApped, sexted.'

'We never sexted.'

Hannah knew that already from checking Mel's texts.

Xander scratched at an imaginary mark on the bar. 'I never saw her yesterday. She was supposed to be in afternoon classes, so I messaged her but didn't hear back. She was round at mine the night before, but she didn't stay over because she wanted to be in her own bed in the morning, get ready to meet her folks.'

That tied in with Mel's phone, but Xander knew Hannah had it, so it would be stupid to say anything different.

'How did she seem?'

'The usual.'

'What did you do?'

'We ate pasta. Mel made it.'

'She cooks at your place?'

'She likes to cook, you know that.'

'So you let her.'

'Why not?'

'Was anyone else there?'

Xander shifted his weight and shook his head. 'The guys were in the pub watching the Champions League.'

Hannah wondered if she should be taking notes on her phone or recording the conversation. Maybe get one of those notepads that TV cops use, lick the end of the pencil before taking down particulars.

'The guys?' she said.

'My flatmates.'

Mel had mentioned Xander's flatmates, and reading between the lines they didn't much like her for taking away their buddy.

'Names?' Hannah said, getting her phone out of her pocket.

'Really?'

'Don't you want to find her?'

'This has nothing to do with them.'

'How do you know?' Hannah sipped her whisky, felt the spirit of Jim give her strength. 'How do you know what's important and what isn't? Anything could be crucial, you don't know.'

Xander looked around the bar for a customer to come and save him. 'Darren and Faisal.'

She thumbed the names into her phone. 'Surnames?'

'Is this really necessary?'

She looked at him, expectant.

He sighed. 'Grant and McNish.'

'Do they get on with Mel?'

'Sure, she's great.'

'Did they see her at your place at all?'

Xander shoved his hands in his pockets. He had a Fitbit knock-off on his wrist and Hannah wondered if it was trackable. Not that she knew how to do that. He shook his head. 'They stayed out after lectures and went straight to the pub.'

'And after pasta?'

He looked sheepish. 'You know.'

'You had sex.'

His cheeks flushed. 'Christ.'

'Then what?'

'Watched a movie on my laptop.'

'What movie?'

'Does it matter?'

'It all matters.'

'*Annihilation*. Sci-fi on Netflix.'

'So what time did she leave?'

'About midnight, I walked her home.'

That tallied with what Hannah remembered, Mel coming in about quarter past. She finished her drink and placed the glass on the bar.

'Can I see your phone?'

'What for?'

Hannah shrugged. 'Just to check a few things.'

Xander picked up her glass and passed it between his hands.

'No,' he said. 'It's an invasion of privacy.'

'Only if you've got something to hide.'

She wanted to provoke him, make him say something that gave him away.

'Fuck you, Hannah,' he said, placing the glass in the washer. 'I hope you find Mel, but fuck you.'

11
Dorothy

Craigentinny didn't look like anyone's idea of Edinburgh. It wasn't the castle and spires of the tourist centre or the jumble of tenements in the Old Town. It wasn't the Georgian townhouses of the New Town or the scrappy schemes of *Trainspotting*. These were wide, bland roads full of 1930s bungalows, small gardens and garages attached, the occasional caravan in a driveway. This was suburbia close to the sea flanked by a council golf course and a recycling centre. Dorothy looked at the backside of Arthur's Seat, gentle gorse-laden slopes compared to the steep cliffs of the front, like seeing under the skirts of Edinburgh's grand old lady.

She checked the address Thomas had given her, 72 Craigentinny Avenue. Grey brick, dormer window at the front, white Ford Ka parked outside. Someone's perfect little home. Dorothy never got used to the lack of space in Scottish houses. People seemed to be happy with a tiny sliver of land, living on top of each other. Back in Pismo Beach they weren't exactly rich, but she grew up in a house as big as the Skelf place, sprawling, low-level with new additions jutting out in different directions. In comparison, Scottish houses seemed dour, repressed. Like the people in them, maybe.

She linked her fingers over her heart for a moment, breathed in through her nose and out through her mouth, tried to find her centre. She reminded herself that this woman wasn't expecting her, it would be a shock. And what the woman had to say might also shock Dorothy.

She opened the black gate, walked up the path and rang the doorbell.

Waited.

Saw movement through the dimpled glass of the door then it was opened by a girl, maybe ten years old, in school uniform, white polo shirt with a maroon cardy. The gold crest on her cardy read 'Craigentinny' across the top and 'I Byde it' underneath. In between was a hunting horn, what looked like candy canes and an artist's palette. Dorothy knew enough Scots to know 'byde' meant 'live', but that didn't make sense. 'I live it', what kind of school motto was that?

She smiled. 'Hi, what's your name?'

'Natalie.'

'Is your mum or dad in?'

She nodded and turned. 'Mum.' This was a holler up the stairs. 'She's just coming.' Natalie stayed at the door staring at the pattern on Dorothy's blue dress.

Dorothy heard footsteps then the door widened.

Rebecca Lawrence was Jenny's age, young enough to be Jim's daughter. Dorothy watched Natalie skip to the living room and tried to keep dark thoughts away. Rebecca was curvy in a way the Skelf women never were. Wide hips, full breasts, round face. If a Skelf woman put on weight she became dumpy, but Rebecca was more sexy than dumpy. Her hair was several shades between blonde and brunette and she was wearing a grey skirt suit, office material. Black tights but no shoes, which felt oddly intimate.

'Can I help?' she said. Her accent was at the smarter end of Edinburgh, polite, approachable.

'Sorry to bother you, my name is Dorothy – Skelf.'

Rebecca's face tightened at the surname. 'What do you want?'

'I want to talk about your husband, Simon.'

'Simon is dead.'

It sounded like she was still trying to convince herself.

'So is my husband, a week ago.' Dorothy touched the wall by the door and a fleck of dust came away. 'Can I come in?'

Rebecca sighed then stood back, showing Dorothy to the kitchen.

The cabinets and hob were tired, hadn't been replaced in a long time. A couple of cracks in the floor tiles by the fridge. Natalie's drawings were stuck on the fridge door with magnets, along with bits of paper about school gymnastics and cheerleading.

Rebecca leaned against the worktop with her arms folded. 'Well?'

'This is awkward.'

'Yes, it is.'

'We never met when Simon worked for us.'

'No,' Rebecca said. 'He liked to keep work separate. Didn't want to bring death home with him.'

Dorothy's home was full of death. 'I can understand that.'

'What do you want, Mrs Skelf?'

'Dorothy, please.'

Rebecca twitched her nose at that as Natalie came in and tugged on her mum's sleeve. 'Can I get a snack, please?'

Rebecca glanced down, her body instantly more open and welcoming. 'In a minute.'

Natalie wandered off again. Dorothy could hear cartoons in the other room.

'She's lovely,' Dorothy said.

'She's a handful, like all kids.'

'And you've brought her up yourself.'

'What is this about?'

Dorothy looked around. Utensils hanging up, a half-full wine rack, Jamie and Nigella cookbooks. 'Jim died last week, like I said.'

'I'm sorry to hear that.'

Dorothy waved that away. 'I've been going through some paperwork, Jim's personal stuff, the business accounts and so on.'

'Uh-huh.'

The air was suddenly cooler, Dorothy felt her skin prickle with goosebumps.

'I discovered there have been payments coming from our business into your bank account. Five hundred pounds every month. For years.'

'That's right.'

'I didn't know anything about it. Would you mind explaining why?'

Rebecca shrugged. 'It's Simon's life assurance.'

Dorothy rubbed at her elbow. 'We don't run a life assurance scheme, Rebecca.'

The use of her name seemed to get her back up, like it was too informal, too close.

'That's not what your husband said.'

'When?'

Rebecca closed the kitchen door and the sound of cartoons died. 'This was years ago, it's in the past.'

Dorothy touched her temple. 'With all due respect, it's not. The money is still coming out of our account.'

'I told you it's my life assurance, for Simon.'

'That doesn't make sense,' Dorothy said. 'Even if we did run a scheme, the money wouldn't come directly from us, it would come from the insurer.'

'That's not what Mr Skelf told me when he came to explain it.'

Dorothy looked around as if Jim's ghost might jump out of a cupboard. 'He came here?'

Rebecca nodded. 'In his suit, with a briefcase. Got me to sign some documents.'

'What documents?'

Rebecca folded her arms. 'I don't remember, legal stuff, it was a decade ago.'

'Do you have a copy of these documents?'

'Somewhere, yes.'

'Can I see them?'

'No.'

'I didn't find any documentation about this amongst our paperwork.'

Rebecca raised her eyebrows. 'That's your problem.'

Dorothy rubbed at the bridge of her nose. 'Maybe you could tell me what happened to your husband.'

'Maybe you could mind your own business.'

'I just want to understand,' Dorothy said. 'You say he's dead but that's not strictly true, is it?'

'Have you been checking up on me?'

'Please.'

Rebecca walked to the kettle as if to put it on, but only touched its metal side. 'He's dead to me.'

'He went missing.'

Rebecca leaned against the worktop, this time as if she needed support. 'I don't know why you're digging this up. He left for work one day and never came back. I phoned Skelf's in the evening and spoke to your husband, who said Simon never turned up that day. There were no clothes missing, no bags, he didn't take anything with him. He never accessed our bank account. Just gone.'

'What did the police say?'

Rebecca laughed, a bitter sound. 'There's no law against going missing, thousands do it every year. The implication was that he'd had enough of me.'

'And your daughter.'

That brought a hard stare. 'I was pregnant with her when it happened.'

'Did you try to find him?'

'How?'

'Hire a private investigator.'

'I didn't have any money.'

'Did you know Jim was a private investigator as well as a funeral director?'

Rebecca looked at her like she was mad. 'No.'

Dorothy tried to get it right in her head. It was about that time the investigation business started, so she wasn't sure whether it was up and running when Simon went missing. Shit, maybe Jim started it because of what happened to Simon, did that make sense? Jim had always told her the PI stuff came about because a bereaved customer from the funeral side wanted to find a long-lost cousin. But Dorothy was starting to doubt everything. Jim definitely lied about Simon, he told Dorothy that Simon just quit, but he told Rebecca that he never showed for work. Why would he lie? Why wouldn't he offer to look for Simon? Why did he pay Rebecca?

'Tell me about the life assurance,' Dorothy said.

'Jim came here when Simon was declared a missing person. He said Simon had taken out a scheme with the company, that the Skelfs owed me money.'

Dorothy shook her head. 'You know how weak that sounds.'

Rebecca pushed away from the worktop, arms by her side. 'You should leave.'

'I guess you didn't want to think too much about free money.'

Rebecca opened the kitchen door. 'Go.'

'Is that my snack?' Natalie said from the other room.

'In a minute,' Rebecca shouted back.

'Unless there's something you're not telling me.'

Rebecca shook her head. 'How dare you come here and call me a liar. If you don't leave right now I'm calling the police.'

What did Dorothy have except confused ten-year-old memories and a history of payments? She walked past Rebecca, feeling the anger radiate from her. She pictured bad juju seeping through her own skin and into her soul.

She stopped at the doorway to the living room, saw Natalie watching something with talking animals and ghosts.

'Nice to meet you, Natalie,' she said.

Natalie turned. 'Bye.'

Dorothy felt Rebecca's touch on her shoulder and walked to the front door. Rebecca showed her out, a firm hand on her back.

'Don't come back,' she said as the door closed.

12
Jenny

King's Buildings was a rabbit warren. Hannah had warned her, but Jenny presumed her sense of direction would win out. But the campus seemed designed to confound, full of cubbyholes, nooks and crannies, hedges and foliage hiding the pipes, concrete and chipped paint of the science buildings.

It was weird being surrounded by students, like they were an alien species. There was an energy here, though, a recklessness to their goofing around that suggested they had no idea of the shit-show life had in store. Jenny pictured herself at the end of *Invasion of the Body Snatchers*, waiting for them all to point and scream then lunge after her. She felt out of place with her slouchy, middle-aged body, her cloud of cynicism, her slack skin. And she felt short too, how were young people all so bloody tall?

She walked past a group soaking up the sun on a grassy slope. There were more women here than she'd anticipated, putting her prejudices in place. She had been surprised by Hannah's love of maths and science, her curiosity about the universe and how it worked. She'd encouraged it like any parent would, but she never understood it. Maybe STEM subjects were the way forward. When society collapses and we end up in a bleak apocalypse, the scientists and engineers who can build stuff, purify water and make fire will be in charge. She saw a notice for the Centre for Science at Extreme Conditions and wondered about that. The science of having a breakdown or getting a divorce? She spotted the entrance to the James Clerk Maxwell Building and headed towards it.

She entered and looked at the signposts, Condensed Matter to the left, Stellar Evolution to the right, Atmospheric Dynamics through the back, Complex Systems upstairs. Each phrase seemed like a code for something unknowable. Hannah would understand what they meant. Jenny had a flash of dislocation, the fact that a person she'd created all those years ago had such a different life, different mind, to her own. When Hannah was five, they used to play a simple colour-combination guessing game, and Jenny could always win if she wanted to because she knew her daughter so well she could predict what she would choose every time. No hidden thoughts, no secrets, no independent ideas. Of course that changed, it was natural, but it still left a hole in Jenny that couldn't be filled.

She followed the signs upstairs, fourth floor, room 4.16 at the end of a corridor. There was a poster for the Quantum Club taped to the door, a picture of a tardis on it. They were meeting in two days at The Old Bell up the road. Underneath was another piece of A4 with four names on it, including Bradley Barker.

She took a picture of the door with her phone, then knocked.

'Come in.'

The voice sounded surprised, as if no one ever came here. She pushed the door. Squeezed into a tiny office were four desks with laptops, piles of textbooks and papers, notices for physics conferences on the walls alongside a poster for *Dirk Gently's Holistic Detective Agency*. There were two guys and a girl here, the air thick with the smell of cheap noodles. The three of them stared at Jenny like she'd grown a second head.

'I'm looking for Bradley Barker.'

The kid nearest her nodded. 'That's me.' Soft Aussie accent and curly dark hair in a mess. He was wearing small-rimmed glasses and an *Agents of S.H.I.E.L.D.* T-shirt.

'I want to talk to you.' Jenny felt in control here, but had no idea where that came from. Maybe just the age difference, life experience.

'And you are?'

Bradley's hands hovered over his keyboard, and she could see he was playing a game on screen with coloured balloons floating through hoops. The balloons gradually fell to the ground and popped.

'I'm a private investigator. I need to talk to you about Melanie Cheng.'

'What?'

'You heard me.'

'Has something happened to Mel?'

'That's what I'm trying to find out.'

The other two in the room squirmed with embarrassment.

'Sorry,' Bradley said. 'What's your name?'

'It's Jenny, Jenny Skelf.'

'Skelf, like Hannah?'

'Is there somewhere we can talk alone?'

Bradley looked at the other two, eyebrows raised, looking for help. They both shrugged, not getting involved.

Bradley pushed his seat away from the desk and closed the laptop. He got up and towered over Jenny, another giant from the super-tall next generation. She caught a whiff of a scent on him, surprisingly expensive and non-toxic. He was trying to assert some authority as he pushed past her into the corridor.

'Come on,' he said, walking off.

She closed the door and followed him, up two flights of stairs to a doorway onto the roof. Out in the fresh air they scuffed over a concrete floor, a weather station to their left and beautiful views to the right. They were next to a golf course and fields, then the Pentlands hunkering in the distance like watchful gods.

Bradley turned at the ledge with the sun behind him, and Jenny put her hand up to shade her eyes. With him looming over her, she suddenly felt less in control.

'What's this about?' he said.

'When was the last time you saw Melanie?'

'Is she missing?'

'Give the boy a gold star.'

'Jesus, poor Mel.'

'So what can you tell me?'

He shifted from one foot to the other, lots of nervous energy. 'This is terrible but I don't know anything about it.'

'How well do you know her?' Jenny moved to the side so that she could see Bradley's face better. She heard the thwack of a golf ball out on the course, the sound of a van driving by the building.

'She's in one of my tutorial groups,' Bradley said. 'Solid state.'

Jenny didn't know if that was the class or some other weird code.

'Do you ever see her outside of class?'

'Sure, at the Quantum Club. Hannah goes there too.'

Jenny hadn't confirmed she was related to Hannah, and she wasn't about to.

'What is this club all about?'

Bradley shook his head and shrugged, his shoulders jiggling.

'Just philosophy of physics, really. Knockabout stuff. Did you know that until recently physics was still called natural philosophy at Edinburgh Uni?'

'And do you like Mel?'

He frowned. 'Yeah, she's lovely.'

'I mean "like" like.'

'I don't know...' He tailed off, rubbed his chin, pushed his glasses back up the bridge of his nose. 'I mean, she's pretty, for sure.'

'You fancy her.'

'She has a boyfriend.'

'So?'

'Shouldn't you be talking to him? I don't understand what you're doing here.'

'No one has seen or heard from Mel in thirty-six hours, including her boyfriend, flatmates and family.'

'I haven't seen her.'

Behind him, an anemometer spun lazily, the cups pushing warm air around.

'So if I check Mel's phone messages and emails, I won't find you in there.'

He stuck his bottom lip out. 'Just about tutorials and the club, I think.'

'You never sent her anything more personal?'

He swallowed and pulled at his earlobe.

Jenny folded her arms. 'I have her phone and laptop, they're not locked. You might as well save me the time.'

'Maybe I sent a couple of texts.' He looked as if he was about to vault over the ledge. 'Asking her out.'

'Even though she had a boyfriend?'

He shrugged.

Jenny had been through Mel's phone and there was nothing in there from Bradley except emails about the club. That meant Mel had deleted the texts asking her out. Maybe she deleted other things too.

'Is that it?' Jenny said.

She wondered about digital forensics, getting back deleted data, whether she knew anyone who could do that stuff. But she was the wrong generation, if anyone could do it, it would be kids like Bradley or Hannah.

'That's all, I promise.'

Jenny decided to push it. 'That's not what her phone tells me.'

'Really?'

Jenny stared. It was amazing the force of a hard stare from an angry middle-aged woman. He was wilting. He was used to being in control, the usual white, male privilege, maybe a dollop of Aussie bravado in there too.

He looked at the Pentlands in the distance, shrouded in advancing clouds.

'Maybe I sent her a picture.'

Jenny managed to stop herself from sighing. 'What kind of picture?'

He rubbed at the small of his back, arched his shoulders.

Jenny shook her head. 'A dick pic?'

He looked at the ground. Jenny heard golfers swapping banter over the hedge below.

'What the hell is it with guys and dick pics?'

His face flushed and he avoided her stare.

She leaned in. 'Would you like it if I sent you a photo of my vagina? Would that get you excited?'

He recoiled at the word vagina, like he'd never heard a woman say it before.

'Well?'

She felt like a schoolteacher reprimanding a little kid. A mum putting him on the naughty step.

'It was nothing,' he said eventually.

He backed away as Jenny advanced towards him. She could see a tractor chugging through a field in the distance, a flotilla of gulls and crows in its wake.

'Really?'

She was close to him now, caught his scent again in her nostrils.

'Show me your cock then, if it's nothing.'

His back was against the ledge and he was sweating. He had no experience of this, hadn't ever had to fend off a sexual advance, an unwanted hand, an accidental squeeze of your breast that wasn't accidental at all.

'Come on,' Jenny said under her breath. 'Get your cock out.'

He tried to puff out his chest. 'Don't be ridiculous.'

She grabbed his crotch, felt his bollocks in her grip, squeezed.

'Jesus,' he said. 'You're crazy.'

He went to pull away but she squeezed tighter and he winced.

He was so tall that she had to go on tiptoes to whisper.

'No woman on the planet is interested in seeing your scabby junk,' she said. 'Got that?'

He nodded, eyes wide.

'Now,' Jenny said, calming her voice. 'Do you know anything about Mel's disappearance?'

She put more pressure on his crotch.

He shook his head, tears in his eyes. 'I don't know anything, I swear.'

She stood deciding whether to believe him or not. Still gripping his balls, still angry. She heard a golf club hit a ball, then a man swear.

'Please,' Bradley said. 'Let me go.'

13
Hannah

She wandered round the exhibition waiting for Vic. She liked The Fruitmarket, the natural light here on the first floor, and the art was always nuts. Next to her were thousands of cigarette papers stuck to the wall in precise order, while in the far corner were some oversized foam sculptures that looked like the bones of a giant extinct species. She wanted to touch everything but the staff were watching.

'Hannah.'

Mel's brother was in a tight black T-shirt showing off his tattooed arms, Celtic and Canton swirls from the wrist to the bicep. She hugged him. He smelt zingy and felt very solid indeed. He had every right to be showing off that body. His hair was precisely side-parted and gelled, rectangular glasses that might've been for show.

'Shall we grab a drink?' he said, ushering her downstairs to the café.

They took a table far from the baristas and the noise of the espresso machine. Hannah wasn't sure what Vic did here, something to do with community engagement, but he always looked at home amongst the design books, weird art and warehouse décor. The café was busy with young arty types and the older gentry of Edinburgh, red trousers and pashminas. This was one of the spots in the city where elderly bohemians would gather as if responding to a call only they could hear.

A tall waitress with bright-green hair and matching eyes took their order and slunk behind the counter.

'Thanks for coming,' Vic said. A brief smile, replaced by a worried look.

'I was glad you called,' Hannah said. 'I wanted to talk to you.'

'I spoke to Mum and Dad,' Vic said. His hand went to his hair, a nervous move, checking his parting, sliding his fingers along the scalp.

'How are they?'

'Worried sick but pretending not to be.'

Hannah nodded as the drinks arrived. Green tea for her, a herbal infusion for him that smelt of berries and hay.

Vic smiled at the girl with a look of complicity, colleagues together, then turned to Hannah.

'So tell me what you know.' His accent had a Dundee twang that Mel's didn't. It was strange how people could grow up in the same family and sound so different from each other.

She told him the timeline since Mel went missing. The conversation with the police, the chat with Xander. She hadn't heard from Mum yet about Bradley Barker.

Vic's frown deepened and his hand went to his hair again. She watched the muscle in his arm flex.

'What do you make of this Xander kid,' he said.

He was only three years older than Mel but seemed mature enough to think of students as kids.

Hannah shrugged. 'Not sure. He was flirting with a girl when I walked in, but if every guy who flirted was guilty, well.'

Vic nodded. He'd never flirted with Hannah but he knew she was gay from the start, which made a difference. Maybe he was gay himself, though Hannah didn't think so. The way he looked at the waitress a minute ago.

Vic leaned forwards like he was part of a conspiracy. 'Did she ever mention anyone else?'

'How do you mean?'

'Another guy.'

Hannah chewed at her lip then sipped her tea, not bitter enough. 'I would've known if she was seeing someone else.'

'Are you sure?'

'Did she say something to you about another boyfriend?'

'She didn't, but I had a feeling.'

'Why?'

'We had lunch last week and she mentioned being out the night before in a hotel bar. I thought that was strange, students can't afford to drink in hotels. I asked but she was vague, said she was on a date then changed the subject.'

'That doesn't sound like Mel.'

Vic shrugged. 'How well do we know anyone? Mum and Dad don't know Mel at all, they don't like the idea of her being with any guy, let alone more than one. There's a whole bunch of stuff they don't know about.'

'What do you mean?'

Vic sighed, leaned back. 'She was pretty wild at school.'

Hannah laughed at the idea. 'Come on.'

The look on Vic's face stopped her laugh.

'She didn't want her uni friends to find out,' he said. 'She changed a lot when she came here. Straightened out.'

'What sort of stuff?'

'She just had no off switch. Lots of booze, coke and ketamine. Boys. And men, older men. She had a reputation in some of the Dundee clubs.'

'Where did that come from?'

Vic shook his head, as if everyone's motivations in life were a mystery. 'Maybe that's why she wasn't shouting about this other guy.'

'But she would tell you, wouldn't she?'

'Unless she had a reason not to.'

Hannah rattled the teaspoon in her saucer. 'Married.'

Vic opened his hands. 'Maybe it's nothing.'

Someone dropped a plate in the kitchen, the clatter of ceramic on tile, a muttered swearword. At the table next to them, a family of Mediterranean tourists were looking at pictures on the daughter's phone. Hannah could smell poached eggs and it made her hungry.

'But she got a few texts while we were eating,' Vic said. 'The first one made her smile. I teased her about it but she didn't rise to it. Then she got another one and didn't look so happy. Then one more a few minutes later that made her switch the ringer off. I asked but she refused to talk.'

'When was this?'

Vic sipped his tea, thought for a second. 'Last Tuesday lunchtime.'

Hannah pulled Mel's phone out of her pocket and went into the messages, flicked through with her thumb.

Vic narrowed his eyes. 'What are you doing?'

'Checking her phone to see who the messages were from.'

Vic shook his head. 'That's not her phone.'

Hannah held it up. 'Yes it is.'

'Well it's not the phone she was using last week.'

Hannah stared at Vic, then at the queue for the taxi rank outside the window.

'Shit,' she said. 'She has a secret phone.'

14
DOROTHY

Dorothy watched Abi pound the drums to Sleater-Kinney. The girl had raw talent but didn't have control yet. So what? Which thirteen-year-old girl has control of any aspect of her life? What Dorothy did with girls this age was show them ways of drumming that didn't involve having a dick. Janet Weiss was a good role model, powerful when she needed to be, primal even, but never showy like male drummers, never wanking all over the song.

Abi hit the middle eight and tried a fancy fill round the toms, didn't quite make it back in time. Sleater-Kinney was good for practising tom work too, got Abi away from her hi-hat obsession. The girl's ponytail was swinging as she focused, eyes closed, slight nod of the head as she powered through the final verse into the chorus. She was in the zone, Dorothy knew the feeling well, when you lose yourself to something bigger, become part of the music and the music becomes part of you. Rhythm was so elemental, taking us back to early humanity on the African plain, tapping into something unspeakable.

Dorothy looked out of the window. They were on the second floor of the house, in the studio, small windows and soundproofing but better views than downstairs in the kitchen. The jagged teeth of the castle sloped into the mess of the Old Town, the glass spread of Quartermile in front, glinting in the sun, Viewforth Church close by, puncturing the tree line of the park.

Abi overreached again, making Dorothy turn. The girl looked sheepish, realised what she'd done, which was half the battle. A boy her age would've blundered through, expecting the song to catch up with him. Abi realised that less was more, she just hadn't quite got it in practice yet, but that would come. You don't have to fill all the space in a song, nine times out of ten it's better with room to breathe. But that's a hard lesson to take on board at any age, let alone as a hormonal teenager.

Dorothy thought of herself as a hormonal teen, her second-hand Pearl drum kit set up in the den, bashing away, drumming along to The Kinks and MC5. Her parents had been open-minded about all that stuff, although they never pretended to understand her obsession. It was a crazy time for music, The Beatles and The Stones, of course, but she'd always liked the more underground stuff, and that continued over the years.

She remembered Jim's face when she said she wanted to get a drum kit set up in the top floor of the house. She'd been in Scotland for two years at that point and was missing Pismo Beach like crazy, and she needed some way to connect to her sun-soaked adolescence. Jim understood that. And once the kit was there, it wasn't much of a stretch to think about teaching. She was good enough, there was hardly anyone else doing it, and it was decent extra income. It was the early seventies by then, so loads of kids were getting into their own rock bands, and Dorothy loved helping them, keeping up to date with music trends at the same time. It was healthy, the physical exercise of it, making her as strong as the yoga kept her supple. And it was a mirror of that meditation too, losing yourself to something bigger.

And new students kept turning up, despite drum machines and rave music and all the rest. The money was useful, of course, but the sense of identity was more important, giving her something outside of the death business that was hers alone.

The song finished and Abi sat back, the tip of her tongue between her teeth. She was tall for her age, long legs in denim shorts and wearing a baggy white T-shirt that read 'Feminist as Fuck' with roses tangled in the lettering. Her face was greasy with sweat and she looked at Dorothy for approval.

'You know, don't you?' Dorothy said.

Abi nodded. She was growing confident, Dorothy loved that.

'Lost it in the middle,' Abi said. 'Too much.'

'It sounded great, though. You're really nailing the floor tom in the verses.'

Abi grinned. It was so easy to make a kid feel good.

Dorothy looked at the clock on the wall. 'OK, that's us for this week.'

Abi put the sticks down and untangled herself from behind the kit. It was a beautiful sunburst vintage Ludwig, shallow toms and snare but still packing a punch. Dorothy was a little embarrassed at how much she loved the kit. It was a material thing, after all, but the craft that went into it and the purpose it served made it something more.

'Thanks, Mrs S,' Abi said. 'And, you know, sorry about Mr S.'

Dorothy paused for a moment. 'See you next week, Abi, and remember to listen to some of Janet Weiss's other band, Quasi, she really lets herself off the leash with them.'

Abi pointed both her fingers at Dorothy like guns then left, and Dorothy stood in silence. She got behind the kit, picked up the sticks and started a country shuffle, throwing in offbeats and trills. She swung it onto the ride, opened her body, splashed around the cymbals and toms every few bars. She was trying to feel what Abi felt a few minutes ago, but all she could think about was Jim lying in ashes two floors beneath her, Rebecca Lawrence and her missing husband and ten-year-old daughter, all the money Jim paid her over the years, the secrets that money represented. Her drum fills now were too much, trying too hard, exactly what she told Abi not to do. But she did it anyway, trying to lose control, trying to lose any sense of herself and feel part of something bigger than her own stupid worries.

It didn't work.

People never thought about how hard it was to dress a corpse. The pants were relatively easy, but even then, getting one leg in then the other was a pain. The bra was a fiddle, rolling Gina's body onto her side so Dorothy could fasten it up the back. The tights were the hardest part, lifting and turning, squeezing and massaging. It was a two-person job, and while she and Archie had it sussed, it was still a hassle. Gina was to wear a red dress, but the material was sheer and Dorothy worried it might catch on one of the staples that pinned the lining to the coffin when they tried to get her in. They did the arms of the dress first with her lying down, then sat her up and pulled the dress over her head and down her back. They laid her down, then Archie lifted the small of her back as Dorothy pulled the dress over her bum, straightening out the hem at her knees, adjusting the straps at the shoulders and bust, making everything symmetrical.

Archie had already done her make-up and hair before Dorothy arrived and he'd done a good job as always, she looked close to the pictures they had propped by the embalming table. Dorothy wriggled Gina's feet into the red heels, thinking about how she would never take them off again, never feel the relief of freeing herself from the straps after a night out. She put in the small hoop earrings, feeling the cold of Gina's earlobes, brushing a stray thread from the dress away from her lips.

Archie wheeled the coffin over on the gurney and ran his hand around the inside, checking for splinters or staples, rough bits on the lining. He lowered the gurney until the opening was at the same level as the embalming table. They stood at either end of Gina's body and put their hands under her armpits and knees.

'One, two, three,' Dorothy said, and they lifted her sideways into the box on three, lowering her slowly. Dorothy sorted the dress, which had ridden up on one side, straightened Gina's feet, placed her hands together in her lap and ran a finger up her arm to her collarbone. Archie had successfully covered the marks on her neck, you could only see them if you looked very close.

'She looks peaceful,' Dorothy said. 'You did a good job.'

'Thanks.' He put away the bag her clothes came in, began wiping down the table.

Dorothy placed the lid on the coffin and wheeled the gurney from the embalming room to the main house, through the connecting corridor and past Indy on the front desk, then into the viewing room.

Indy followed her and helped get the coffin off the gurney and onto the table in the middle of the room. Simple white cloth, tall vases of lilies either side, blinds throwing subdued sunlight across it all. Two armchairs and a small dresser with a box of tissues on it, a painting of a sunset on the wall.

'Ms O'Donnell, right?' Indy said.

'Gina, yes.'

Dorothy looked at Indy. They both knew how Gina had died and shared an unspoken sadness. But it doesn't matter how you die, Dorothy thought, it matters how you live.

'Are you conducting the funeral?' Indy asked.

Dorothy nodded.

'Need any help?'

'Archie and I have this one covered.' Dorothy touched Indy on the arm. 'Don't worry, I still want you to step up.'

'I wasn't worried.'

Dorothy lifted off the coffin lid and checked Gina hadn't moved in transit. She still looked the same, pale skin against a red dress.

'She looks good,' Indy said.

'Archie knows what he's doing.'

Indy straightened the hem of Gina's dress, fluffed up some of the coffin lining around the edges. She had a good eye for detail. She'd been very precise about her own parents' funeral, something that could've been taken for coldness, but Dorothy knew otherwise. It was a way of keeping control when chaos has taken over your life.

'I remember when we first met,' Dorothy said. 'I was very impressed with you.'

Indy looked up. 'How so?'

'It was obviously a very difficult time.'

Indy angled her head in acknowledgement.

'But you had a stillness about you,' Dorothy said. 'You've always been very centred.'

'I didn't feel like that at all,' Indy said. 'I felt lost. But you found me.'

Dorothy smiled. 'You found yourself. You just needed a point in the right direction.'

Indy shook her head and looked down at Gina in the coffin. She reached out and put a finger to her neck, where Archie had covered the belt mark.

Dorothy remembered the young woman Indy was when she arrived at the Skelf house to arrange her parents' funeral. Her hair was bright red back then, and while her face was flushed and puffy from crying, there was something meticulous and centred about her, even amongst the pain. She was studying psychology at Napier Uni but said she saw no point in continuing. She wanted to know how people worked, but the car accident that took her parents on a wet road at night made it clear that everything was just random, from the cradle to the grave and beyond, if you believed in that. Indy had never believed, she told Dorothy, despite her Hindu heritage, but her parents didn't mind, and allowed her to choose her own path without friction. Once they were gone, she was even more free to choose her own path, but there seemed no point, no purpose anymore. Dorothy was worried and stayed in touch, as she often did with the younger bereaved, and when she realised Indy was serious about quitting her studies, she stepped in with a job offer.

'It was more than that and you know it,' Indy said. 'I was a wreck. You changed my life, Dorothy. I mean, obviously it still hurts, thinking about Mum and Dad, having to live on without them. But I have a purpose here now. I have Hannah. I wouldn't have had any of that if it wasn't for you.'

'You're a natural here,' Dorothy said. 'You're brilliant with the clients. They all adore you.'

'I like to help people.'

Dorothy nodded. 'That's what I mean. And you're great for Hannah, too.'

'She's great for me.'

It was said matter-of-fact, but true all the same.

Something occurred to Dorothy. 'Has Melanie turned up yet?'

Indy frowned and shook her head. 'Han was talking to her brother earlier, and Jenny was down at uni speaking to a tutor.'

'She'll turn up,' Dorothy said.

'I'm not so sure,' Indy said.

'What makes you say that?'

'Just a feeling,' Indy said. 'I know Han laughs at things like intuition, for her it's all black and white, logical and factual. But I have a bad feeling about Mel.'

'We shouldn't ignore intuition,' Dorothy said. 'It's just a kind of knowledge we don't fully understand yet.'

The phone rang out at reception and Indy left to deal with it.

Dorothy straightened one of Gina's feet, which was pointing out a little, turned her leg slightly, then rested her hand on Gina's hands. She stared at her for a long time then eventually turned away and pulled her phone out of her pocket. She pressed call and waited. She'd looked up 'byde' in her Scots dictionary when she came home from Craigentinny, as well as 'live' it meant 'endure'. So Natalie's school motto was 'I endure it'. That seemed about right.

'Hello, Royal Bank of Scotland, Hardeep speaking, how can I help?'

'I want to cancel a direct debit from my business account,' Dorothy said.

It was done in less than a minute and Dorothy hung up. So easy to sever a link to the past.

Indy popped her head round the door. 'There's a Jacob Glassman on the phone, insisting on speaking to Jim about a case.'

Dorothy went to reception and picked up the phone.

'Hello?'

'To whom am I speaking?'

'This is Dorothy Skelf.'

'I want to speak to Mr Skelf.'

Dorothy swallowed. 'Mr Skelf is no longer with us.'

'How do you mean?'

'He's dead.'

'Oh.' His voice was posh Edinburgh with a tiny hint of Eastern Europe, and he sounded old.

'Can I help?' Dorothy said.

'Mr Skelf had an appointment to visit me yesterday.'

Dorothy remembered something, Jacob Glassman's name on the PI whiteboard upstairs, alongside another name she couldn't remember.

'I'm sorry,' she said. 'I'm taking over all Jim's cases, how can I help?'

'It's rather delicate,' Jacob said, lowering his voice. 'I can't talk about it just now, she's here.'

'Who is?'

'Susan, of course.' This was a whisper.

The other name on the board, Susan Somebody.

She heard him clear his throat down the line. 'Perhaps you could visit me later today?'

'I'm not sure,' Dorothy said.

'Mr Skelf already cashed my first cheque as down payment.'

She hoped there was a file upstairs in the office with a few details written down.

He coughed again. 'She'll be out at 2 p.m., is that convenient?'

Dorothy touched her forehead, caught the scent of the chrysanthemums on the desk. 'Remind me of your address?'

15
Jenny

St Leonards Police Station was an eighties-built, orange-brick block crouching in the shadow of Salisbury Crags. It formed an L shape along two intersecting roads, large glass frontage, revolving doors and dark-blue trim everywhere. Jenny wondered how many people were in the cells right now, what they'd done, if they felt hard done by. She'd visited the police station once before when she was a Napier student in the mid-nineties. She was groped in the queue for an indie club at Espionage on Victoria Street at two in the morning, a hand up her skirt and into her pants, and when she kicked up a fuss she was punched in the face by one of the guy's mates. The bouncers made sure they hadn't seen anything. When she got to the station the officers on duty struggled to hide smug smiles. Dressed like that, you deserve what you get. The disgust was palpable. She hoped things would be different now if Hannah had to report abuse, but she doubted it.

'Shall we?' Dorothy said.

Jenny followed her mum through the doors into reception. Dorothy asked for Thomas Olsson at the desk then stood playing with the strap of her leather handbag. It was more of a satchel really, a practical thing with buckles.

'Are you OK?' Jenny said.

Dorothy nodded but she looked worried. Jenny felt something powerful, seeing her mum like that. It was never easy, seeing your parents' power diminish, realising all their frailties and foibles. Realising that they're just ordinary people struggling to get by like the rest of us.

Jenny had returned to Greenhill Gardens earlier, still shaking with adrenaline from her encounter with Bradley. What the hell was happening to her? If that had been the other way round, she would've been shouting about sexual assault. But there was something about his attitude that made the red mist descend. It didn't take the world's best shrink to realise Craig had fucked up her attitude to men, but that was so long ago, why was it rearing up again now? She had to keep a lid on it.

When she'd got home from Kings Buildings, she found Mum in the garden staring at the charred site of the funeral pyre. Dorothy explained about the payments, Rebecca in Craigentinny, her daughter. The implication was clear, either Jim was involved with Rebecca, or Rebecca was his daughter, or maybe Natalie was his daughter. Maybe he had something to do with Simon's disappearance. Either way, he was a liar. He'd lied to his wife, kept secrets from his family, and given away thousands of pounds of their money. Of course, with Dorothy's unfaithful past, she couldn't claim too much moral high ground. But at least she hadn't lied, Jenny supposed. As far as Jenny knew.

Dorothy was playing with a bracelet on her wrist, three colourful strands intertwined and held together by a small button with an eye on it. Hannah made it for her years ago, and Jenny couldn't believe Dorothy still had it. She tried to think if she had anything Hannah made at school, the necklaces and keychains, paintings, random collections of stones and sticks, painted and stuck together in the name of art.

Two police officers in bulky stab-proof vests came in through the revolving door carrying coffees and went through to the back. The woman at the front desk smiled at them.

Jenny spoke to Dorothy. 'Remind me how you met Thomas?'

Dorothy smiled. 'Same way we meet anyone, we did his wife's funeral.'

'But you knew him from yoga before that.'

'He comes to class on a Tuesday.'

'A cop doing yoga?'

'What of it?'

'Did Dad know you were friends?'

Dorothy paused at that. 'What are you implying?'

Jenny shook her head. 'Nothing, I just wondered.'

'What century is this?' Dorothy said. 'A woman can be friends with a man.'

'Sure.'

Dorothy shook her head. 'Not that it's any of your business, but yes, your dad knew I was friends with Thomas. He didn't have a problem with it.'

The door from the back office opened and a tall black man in a fitted suit appeared.

'Dorothy, good to see you,' he said, his accent a mishmash of Scottish and Nordic. 'Come on through.'

'This is my daughter, Jenny.' She turned to Jenny. 'And this is Thomas.'

Jenny shook his hand, he had a firm grip but soft skin.

'Dorothy has told me a lot about you,' Thomas said.

'I wish I could say the same,' Jenny said.

The meeting room on the first floor had great views of Salisbury Crags and Arthur's Seat. The summits of both were peppered with tourists and walkers, little dots on the skyline.

Thomas had a brown folder open in front of him. Jenny studied him as he flicked through some papers. Mid-fifties, fit, smartly presented, widowed. He was a catch.

He shook his head. 'There's not much here, to be honest.'

He flicked a page over, some handwritten notes, an official-looking form.

'Simple missing-person case, never resolved. He was reported missing by his wife, but we did nothing at first. Then she called again two days later, still no sign, so an officer was assigned the case. They checked his bank and phone, no activity. Nothing on his email, and this was before social media.'

'How did I not know about this if he was working for us?' Dorothy said.

Thomas ran a finger along a page. 'Officer Daniels spoke to Jim and Archie, they said they didn't know anything, there was nothing suspicious.'

'The police interviewed Archie?'

'Not an interview, just a chat.'

Dorothy turned to Jenny. 'I asked Archie, he never mentioned it.'

'Maybe he forgot.'

Dorothy shook her head. 'Officer Daniels, is he still here?'

'She,' Thomas said. 'Lorna Daniels went on maternity five years ago, never came back.'

Jenny looked out of the window, someone was flying a kite on the grass below the cliffs. 'Do you have contact information for her?'

Thomas put the paper down. 'I can get it but I'm not sure she'll be any use. We deal with hundreds of cases, this was a long time ago. She would've only spent a few hours on it, given our workloads.'

'Nevertheless,' Jenny said.

Dorothy sighed. 'I need to speak to Archie again.'

'You think he's involved?'

Dorothy tucked her hair behind her ear. Thomas watched her, and Jenny watched Thomas. They were friends for sure, but maybe more. Jenny tried to picture her mum sneaking around behind Dad's back with this guy. Given her history, it wasn't impossible.

'I don't know what to think,' Dorothy said.

Thomas closed the folder and slid it across. Dorothy placed her fingers on it and closed her eyes as if trying to divine deeper meaning from it, some inner truth.

'I'm sorry there's not more here,' Thomas said. 'But if there's anything else I can do, please ask.'

Dorothy opened her eyes. It took a moment for her to focus on the room.

Jenny cleared her throat. 'Actually, there's another missing person you could look into for us.'

Thomas frowned and looked from Jenny to Dorothy, who nodded.

16
DOROTHY

Hermitage Drive was a line of large, sturdy Victorian houses on the shoulder of Blackford Hill, with views south over to the Braids. Number eleven appeared a little dishevelled compared to some of its neighbours, but it was still an impressive beast.

Dorothy rang the bell and waited. Eventually she saw motion through the frosted glass, then the door opened. Jacob Glassman was short and hunched over, maybe around ninety, walking with a frame. His hair needed cutting and he'd recently had a bad shave, leaving blood spots and missed bits at his nose and under his chin. But his eyes were clear as he waved her inside, checking the street behind her.

'Mrs Skelf,' he said.

'Dorothy.'

He extended a hand. 'And I'm Jacob, thank you for coming.'

He shuffled towards a room at the back of the house and she followed. It was a large, open-plan dining room and kitchen, bookshelves lined with old, leather-bound volumes along one wall, bright abstract paintings above. There was a remarkable view out the window down to the Braid Burn in the valley below the house.

Jacob settled in a seat at the dining table, pushing his frame to the side. 'Did you bring the cameras?'

He waved for her to sit down, so she pulled out a chair opposite.

'What?'

'The spy cameras, Mr Skelf was supposed to install them yesterday.'

There was a rattle in his voice, a heaviness to each breath.

'I'm sorry, there's been quite a lot of upheaval with Jim's passing,' Dorothy said. 'I couldn't find his notes on you. Perhaps you could remind me?'

He frowned, looked agitated. 'I told your husband all this.'

'And again, I'm sorry.'

'It's very simple,' Jacob said. 'She's stealing from me, moving my stuff about too.'

'Susan?'

His eyes widened. 'Yes.'

'And who is she?'

'She's my carer.' He said this last word with disdain. 'That's what they call themselves these days. Not nurses. Not that I need anyone to care for me.'

Dorothy had checked the whiteboard. 'Susan Raymond, is that right?'

'Yes, yes. My delightful daughter-in-law hired her, so that her and my son wouldn't have to visit. Not that they ever did that anyway, of course.'

'So she's from a private company.'

Jacob lifted a trembling hand to his cardigan pocket, pulled out a card, handed it over. Bright Life Care, a website and telephone number. 'But she's no good.'

'What makes you think she's stealing from you?'

He got annoyed. 'Because things have gone missing, of course. I'm not stupid.'

'OK.'

'Just because I'm old, doesn't mean I'm senile. People treat you like an imbecile half the time, just because your body's fucked.'

Dorothy raised her eyebrows.

He cleared his throat. 'Oh, the old man can swear? Whoopee. Fuck, shit, bollocks. I lectured on linguistics for forty years, I know all about the power of language. And I came over as a teenager on the Kindertransport, so I've had plenty to swear about in my time. My wife has been dead for fifteen years, my children don't want to spend any time with me, and my nurse is stealing my shit. So forgive me if the odd swearword slips out.'

Dorothy smiled. 'Not a problem.'

He narrowed his eyes. 'Where are you from?'

'What do you mean?'

'Your accent,' he said. 'America?'

'California originally,' she said. 'But I've been here fifty years.'

He nodded. 'But they never leave you, do they? Those formative years.'

His stare seemed to burrow into her, and she found herself picturing the waves crashing against the pier on Pismo Beach all those years ago. 'No, I suppose they don't.'

'My wife was Ukrainian,' he said, nodding at the pictures on the wall. 'She painted them. She lived through Stalin's famine as a small child. Incredible, really.'

He coughed again, brought a thin hand to his mouth. 'So you'll bring the cameras?'

Dorothy knew they had motion-activated cameras in Jim's office, but she'd never had to set them up or use them.

'Tell me more about what's gone missing.'

He shook his head. 'Mostly money, but other things too. An old television that was in one of the upstairs rooms. I had an iPad that I can't find anywhere. Even some books, first editions. And food.'

'Why would she take your food?'

'I don't know.'

'Have you confronted her about it?'

'I want evidence first. So you'll bring the cameras?'

He was anxious, the tremor in his hand worse.

'OK,' Dorothy said, wondering if she'd be able to figure out how they worked.

There was a sound from the hall, a key in the front door, then it opened.

'Hello, Mr Glassman.'

Jacob tensed up, eyes wide. 'That's her. She's not supposed to be back.'

'She has a key, how did that happen?'

Jacob shrugged. 'My daughter-in-law.'

A round young woman wearing lots of make-up and large hoop earrings came into the room and stopped when she saw Dorothy.

'Hello, there,' she said.

'Hi.'

Jacob's hand shook as he reached for his walking frame and stood. 'I wasn't expecting you back.'

'Forgot my phone,' Susan said, nodding at it on the kitchen worktop. She scoped Dorothy. 'We don't get many visitors, do we Mr Glassman?'

Her voice was too loud, as if Jacob was deaf.

Dorothy stood. 'I'm Dorothy, a former colleague of Jacob's. At the linguistics department.'

'Right.'

'I was just passing, thought I'd pop in and say hello. But I'll get out of your hair.'

Jacob was shuffling towards the front door now, and Dorothy smiled at Susan as she passed, got a tight smile in response. She could feel Susan's eyes on her all the way to the front door. She noticed a stairlift fitted on the stairs as she reached the front door and slid past Jacob.

He raised his eyebrows and spoke softly. 'Is she still watching?'

Dorothy nodded.

'She's not in tomorrow morning, can you come back then?'

Dorothy thought about her own daughter back living with her again, her granddaughter just down the road, a strong network of women supporting each other. She thought about Jacob, alone in his big house.

'Of course,' she said.

Judging by the numbers of cars parked on the road outside and along the paths in the graveyard, this was going to be a busy one. As Archie drove the hearse to the crematorium entrance, Dorothy saw a few smokers sucking on cigarettes and stubbing them out. They scuttled inside as the funeral car pulled up behind the hearse.

Seafield Crem was a chunky art deco 1930s build, tall thin windows and columns, half covered in spreading vines like it was partly organic. Dorothy took a breath and got out, smoothing her skirt and tugging on the hem of her jacket. Archie opened the rear of the hearse as the family spilled out of the car behind, three men arching their backs, a woman keeping her head down, nose pressed into a tissue. This was Gina O'Donnell's family – dad, brother, sister and her husband. The sister, Orla, had organised the funeral, her dad too distraught to handle the details. She was brunette with green eyes and a sharp tongue, a hard look on her face, but then that was probably the circumstances. Dorothy was a little surprised they hadn't gone bigger on the viewing and ceremony, being Irish, but no two funerals were the same, no two people experienced grief the same way.

Dorothy went to Orla as the men and Archie pulled the coffin along the rollers in the hearse and eased it onto their shoulders. At least they had enough people. Dorothy would have to think about that for future services, with Jim gone they had one less person to shoulder the weight. Dorothy had done it occasionally when she had to, but she was seventy now, she couldn't carry the weight of the dead forever.

Orla let out a gasp when she saw the coffin. Dorothy put her hand on Orla's arm then felt a sudden, overwhelming wave of emptiness sweep through her. She pictured Jim's burning body in the garden then flashed to an imaginary funeral, all the people they'd buried and burned in the last five decades standing in a colossal cathedral, smiling and applauding as the man who committed them to death was carried into the place in a bright-red coffin on the shoulders of the babies they'd buried, the foetuses, the stillborn, the teenage suicides and car-crash victims and overdoses and murders and stupid mistakes and even more stupid accidents, drownings, electrocutions, stabbings, decapitations, bodies crushed and impaled, bloated and dismembered, scooping up the pieces from a railway line or an industrial blender, skulls flattened by concrete blocks or masonry, rib cages and pelvises crushed by articulated lorries, a never-ending sea of death and destruction, and Jim was at the head of it all, had dealt with it his whole life and now it was Dorothy's turn.

She felt her legs go from under her and collapsed, stroking the fabric of Orla's skirt as she went down. She lay on the hard ground, the palms of her hands scraped and sticky with flecks of gravel where she'd put them out to protect herself.

The four men with the coffin stared. Archie clearly wanted to run over and help but if he released his corner of Gina's coffin, the whole thing would unbalance.

'Are you all right?' Orla said, rolling vowels in a Cork accent.

Dorothy blinked and brushed at her hands, which stung. The sun seemed too bright in the sky. She looked at the crematorium and thought she saw the vines moving, reaching out to wrap around her, pull her into the vegetation, make her one with the earth, reduce her to constituent molecules, just like her dead husband. She could smell the dirt and trees, pollen sucked into her lungs, and she could smell the sewage plant across the road, imagined the atoms of people's excrement mingling with her own to form a new kind of life. Somewhere in the trees behind her sparrows were chattering, the trill of wings flapping as they scuttled from branch to branch, and she longed to be up there with them.

'I'm fine,' she said, getting to her knees, which ached. She was an old woman now. She accepted that as the way of the world, but right now she despised her body, the wreck it had become, a collection of failing parts waiting to end. And at her core was a hole where her love had been, where her husband had been, where everything she invested in their relationship was lost because he hadn't been truthful.

'I'm fine,' she said again.

She pushed herself up to standing, felt the weight of her skull, throbbing pressure through her body.

'Are you sure?' Orla said.

The men were still watching her, holding the coffin, as Dorothy had a breakdown or whatever it was.

She nodded and the men shuffled into the building. Archie threw her a worried look, lines across his forehead, eyes narrow.

She brushed the lap of her skirt as Orla offered the crook of her elbow to take.

'Thank you,' Dorothy said, and let herself be led inside by a woman she didn't know, to the funeral of another woman she didn't know. But as Dorothy was realising, she didn't really know anyone.

17
HANNAH

She looked at the menu, full of ham hocks and fish she'd never heard of. Montpelier's wasn't cheap but Dad was paying, Hannah liked to choose somewhere decent for his guilt lunch. Montpelier's was a magnet for the rich Morningside brigade, full of old money and aspiring Tories, posh students who didn't make it to Oxbridge. There were hunt paintings on the wall and a sense of extreme deference from the white-clad staff. Hannah sipped her Malbec. She had no idea if it was a good wine but it was £38 a bottle.

'Here's to a lovely guilt lunch,' she said.

Craig smiled and raised his glass. 'Cheers.'

'Guilt lunch' was a joke they shared. They'd established a weekly get-together not long after Craig left Jenny to shack up with Fiona, graduating over the years from Maccy Ds and KFC to pub food and now this. Maybe in a couple of years the guilt lunch would stretch to a Michelin star or two.

'So how are you coping?' Craig said.

It took a moment for Hannah to realise he was referring to Grandpa.

'Fine.'

'And your mum?'

'She's OK.'

'It can't be easy for any of you.'

Hannah nodded. 'We're keeping busy, funerals to deal with. And a case.'

'For the private investigator's?'

Hannah took a drink and sucked her teeth as the wine went down. She swirled the glass, watched the legs drag down the side.

'Mel is missing,' she said.
'Your flatmate?'
'Yeah.'
Craig had met her once or twice at the flat in passing, Hannah remembered, and one day months ago when their guilt lunch spread into the afternoon, Indy and Mel coming to meet her just as Craig was leaving.
'Maybe she went to her parents,' Craig said. 'Or a boyfriend.'
Hannah shook her head. 'We tried all that.'
'We?'
'Me and Mum.'
'The pair of you are looking into it?'
'Sure.'
'Do you know how to do that?'
'As much as anyone.'
'So where have you got to?'
'I talked to her boyfriend and Mum spoke to a tutor. I had lunch with her brother yesterday.'
'Anything?'
'She had a secret phone. I have her regular phone, but she was getting messages on another one.'
'Are you sure this is a good idea?'
'How do you mean?'
'You and your mum are both grieving, your mum especially. Her dad has just died, remember.'
'So?'
'It's a stressful time.'
She wondered how she would feel if Craig died suddenly. But that was different, he was in his forties, Jim was seventy. His death wasn't expected, but he'd had a good life. Indy was always coming back home from the funerals of kids, teenagers, young parents, crying about the loss of potential. That's what hurt most, the death of hope that the next generation will be better than the last.
'I think Mel's case is keeping her mind off that.'

'That's living in denial.'

'Maybe,' Hannah said. 'But what's the alternative, let it overwhelm you?'

Their starters came, terrine for him, scallops for her. The place was busy and Hannah let herself get lost in the hubbub, enjoyed being in a communal space, part of the human ritual of eating together that went back millennia. She was a little drunk, she wasn't used to wine. The plates went away and mains arrived, lamb tagine and the famous ham hock. They made small talk, a distance between them, ten years of living apart that a weekly guilt lunch couldn't hide. She asked about her cute half-sister and Craig talked glowingly. Hannah wondered if he was a different dad this time round. Why do guys get a second chance? She should hate him for the way he treated Mum, the way he left them, but ten years made a difference. She felt older than she was, more mature, something forced on her by circumstance. She had a sudden realisation that she didn't need her dad in her life, but still wanted him somehow. That made her happy and sad. She really had drunk too much wine.

She realised the time as the plates were cleared.

'Shit, I'm supposed to be along the road, there's a wake at the house. I said I would help Indy prep the room. There's catering.'

'Business as usual, eh?'

Hannah drank the last of her wine and placed the glass heavily on the table. 'It's the first funeral since Grandpa, we all have to muck in.'

Craig narrowed his eyes, taking her in. 'I worry about you.'

'How do you mean?'

'It can't be good for any of you, surrounded by death all the time.'

Hannah shrugged. 'It's other people's grief, not ours.'

Craig shook his head and scratched at the tablecloth. 'But it's not, it's your grief too. How can you do funerals when you've just lost someone?'

Hannah stared at her dad for a moment then pushed her chair back and stood up, a little unsteady. 'What choice do we have?'

18
JENNY

She tugged at her collar, itchy at the neck. Jenny had borrowed one of Dorothy's blouses because she didn't have anything in her wardrobe suitable for a wake. She looked round the reception room. There were forty mourners milling about, looking as uncomfortable as she felt, nibbling on triangle sandwiches and sipping wine from small glasses. The décor was demure pastel shades, a mirror over the marble fireplace, abstract seascapes on the walls. The patio doors were open, a handful of people outside. The doors opened out to the back garden, and Jenny saw the blackened remains of her dad's funeral pyre out there, like they'd been roasting a pig on a spit.

She remembered kicking a football out there with Dad, four decades ago. It had been strange having a funeral director for a dad, but not for the reason most people thought. There was no delineation between home and work because, for Jim, home was work. He was on call twenty-four hours a day, seven days a week, always answering the phones and heading out at odd times to pick up a body or comfort a widow or brother. But that meant she got time with him at surprise moments when he wasn't busy. She had memories of him dribbling the ball between the two oaks in his full undertaker get up, playing hide-and-seek amongst the second-floor cubbyholes, helping her to build a jewellery box as a school project in the workshop, amongst the coffins and the sweet smell of wood shavings. Jenny felt a wave of sadness make her heart flutter, and she breathed deeply.

'It was a lovely service,' an old woman said as she entered.

Jenny returned a flat smile. The flat smile was a staple for funeral workers, acknowledgement of what was said with a tinge of sadness. She didn't have a role here, really, just keeping an eye on things while people hovered and swapped stories about the deceased. Given that Gina had hanged herself at home alone, there was an edge, a sense of life wasted, potential destroyed.

Jenny and Indy were holding the fort after Dorothy had come in ashen-faced and headed upstairs to lie down. Archie said she'd collapsed outside the crem but refused to see a doctor. Just stress, she told Jenny as she waved away a helping hand, clinging to the banister like a crutch.

Indy was so good at small talk with the bereaved. They were drawn to her, because of her bright hair, dark skin, beaming grin. No flat smile for her, she seemed full of life, but never in a disrespectful way, like she was in tune with the universe. Jenny couldn't get a handle on it, the whole thing made her feel ill.

She saw the deceased's sister approach Indy, start talking, but not platitudes or small talk. Indy indicated Jenny with a nod of her head and a surprised look. Her eyes widened in warning as the sister came towards Jenny.

'Are you a Skelf?'

Jenny nodded. 'I'm Jenny.'

'I'm Orla, Gina's sister. What happened to the old guy I arranged the funeral with, is he not here today? I expected him to handle everything.'

Jenny rubbed at her eyelid, blinked heavily. 'That was my dad. He died.'

'Shit, I'm sorry.'

Jenny shook her head, it felt awkward talking about her dad's death at someone else's funeral, like she was muscling in on their grief.

'So,' Orla said. 'You work for the family company?'

Jenny thought about Dorothy upstairs. 'Yes.'

'I need to speak to you about something.' She looked at the room full of people. 'Do you have somewhere private?'

Jenny led her across the hall to one of the empty viewing rooms, the table set up in the middle. She offered Orla one of the leather armchairs but the woman shook her head.

'I like to stand.'

Jenny waited.

'This is a bit weird,' Orla said eventually.

'It's a hard time,' Jenny said.

Orla shook her head. Jenny caught a whiff of acidic perfume.

'I don't mean that,' Orla said, waving at the wake beyond the closed door. She rubbed at her brow, looked round the room for inspiration. 'So you work for the family business?'

She was repeating herself, stalling.

'Yes.'

'Both parts?'

'How do you mean?'

Orla pointed at the closed door again. 'It said on the side entrance that you're a private investigator's as well as a funeral director's.'

'Yes.'

Orla looked at Jenny. 'And you do that, the investigating, like?'

Jenny paused for a moment. 'Sure.'

'Then I have a case for you.'

'What?'

'That's what you call it, a case? I have a job for a private investigator.' She laughed, a self-mocking sound. 'I can't believe I'm doing this.'

'Are you sure you don't want to sit down?'

'At a funeral,' Orla said. 'I mean, it's disrespectful, isn't it? But I don't know if I'll have the guts to come back another time.'

Jenny resisted the urge to tug at her blouse collar again, but she could feel the skin on her neck was raw. She thought of Gina's neck, the marks from the belt that Archie covered up.

Orla touched her hair. 'It's such a fucking cliché.' She rubbed at her elbow and breathed deeply. 'I think my husband is cheating on me.

Liam Hook. He's through there right now, being all caring and sensitive, a shoulder to cry on. But he's having an affair. I want you to get some evidence and when you do I'm going to divorce the bastard.'

'What makes you think he's cheating on you?'

Orla threw a stare at Jenny, eyes on fire. 'You're not wearing a ring, are you married?'

'Divorced.' Even after all this time the word felt shameful, an admission of defeat.

'Why did you get divorced?'

'He met someone else.'

Orla nodded. 'So you know what I'm talking about. Did you realise he was cheating on you?'

How had this become about Jenny? 'I had no clue.'

Orla's eyebrows went up. 'Wow, OK. He must be a fucking good liar.'

Jenny shrugged, looked away.

'Liam is not a good liar,' Orla said. 'Says he's working late, if you can believe it. But when I call the office he doesn't pick up. On his mobile it doesn't sound the same as the office, the acoustics are different.'

'Have you asked him about it?' Jenny said.

Orla shook her head. 'I want proof, that's where you come in.'

Jenny swallowed and tugged at her collar. 'I don't know.'

Orla narrowed her eyes. 'You're a private investigator, aren't you?'

Jenny didn't answer straight away. Was she? She remembered grabbing Bradley at the uni campus, how she lost control of herself. She thought about her mum upstairs, ill with stress and grief. She thought about the money her dad paid out, the missing former employee. She thought about Mel, another vanished person. If they didn't solve these mysteries, who would?

Orla was waiting for an answer. 'Well?'

'Yes, I'm a private investigator.'

'So you'll take the case?'

'I'll take it.'

19

HANNAH

Everything was too bright. The long strip lights overhead, their electric buzz rattling her brain, the spotlights on the whiteboard she was staring at, even the logo on Dr Longhorn's MacBook seemed to throb with her headache. She never normally drank much and there was confusion mixed with the pain. After the wine with Dad she'd turned up at Skelf's to help, but instead drank more wine in a little plastic cup before having to lie down. Her mum and Indy helped her upstairs and put her in Jenny's old bedroom. That was late afternoon and she slept right through, waking this morning with Schrödinger licking her face in the morning light.

Mel's disappearance was getting to her. She was aware of a black fog in the back of her mind, and knew what that could lead to. One of the reasons she didn't drink much alcohol was the effect it had on her teenage brain a few years ago, bringing on anxiety then depression, her fifteen-year-old self trying combinations of medication, finally settling on something that didn't make her feel like she was living in cotton wool. Then months of gradually reducing the dose plus meditation learned from Dorothy, the odd bit of yoga, and a brief obsession with running. The occasional glass of wine had been reintroduced, but yesterday was way over. Her dad wasn't to blame, she'd kept the anxiety and depression from him, worried he would see her as a cause to be fixed.

So there was guilt to go with today's hangover. Waking up in her mum's old room didn't help. She'd crept out before anyone was awake, then had to face Indy at the flat. But she didn't judge, just a sympathetic hug and a worried look, which made the guilt worse.

She'd arrived late at the lecture and sat at the back. She could see Xander and a couple of his mates over the other side, a nod of acknowledgement when she tried to slide in unnoticed.

Peter Longhorn was talking about quantum entanglement but she couldn't take it in. Her body vibrated with the buzz from the lights and it made her feel exposed, as if her hangover had worn away her skin, dissolved the border between her and the universe so that she might float apart any second and join the great mess of chemical existence.

Entanglement was the kind of mindfuck she usually loved in physics, that entangled pairs of subatomic particles were intrinsically linked by their quantum state even when separated. Measurement of one particle's state collapsed the function and gave information on the other's state instantaneously, breaking the rule that limited transfer of information to the speed of light. And that was just the start. Digging into the maths there were caveats and inconsistencies, violations and arguments about what rival theories meant, even the idea that time could be a side-effect of entanglement. It was all about perspective, where you viewed the universe from, how you observed it and interacted with it, how cause and effect played out on every level, from quarks to galaxies.

Right now, her perspective was that if she didn't get some Irn Bru soon she might pass out.

She watched Longhorn with narrow eyes. He was tall with an air of authority, but without being a dick about it. He had a navy shirt tucked into dark jeans, pointy leather shoes, a cut above the sartorial elegance of other staff who wore mostly *Star Trek* T-shirts and trainers. He was mid-thirties, short blond hair and clean-shaven. And he was Mel's Director of Studies, a token role in her case, since the DoS only got involved if a student was skipping classes or failing.

The class ended and everyone shuffled out, Xander nodding again at Hannah. He was about to come over and speak to her but seemed to have second thoughts, turning away through the doors.

Dr Longhorn shuffled papers together and closed his laptop as she approached. Her head was thumping and her eyes were heavy.

'Dr Longhorn,' she said, swinging her rucksack onto her shoulder.

'Peter, please.'

She nodded even though it made her cringe. 'I was wondering if you'd seen Melanie Cheng recently?'

'I could ask you the same question.'

'Really?'

'She had an appointment to see me the other day, never showed up.'

Hannah noticed his wedding ring, how long and thin his fingers were.

'What was the appointment about, if you don't mind me asking?'

'I have no idea. She emailed to set it up but didn't say why.'

'She emailed you?'

'Is something the matter?'

Hannah tried to quell her stomach, she felt hungry and sick at the same time. 'She's gone missing.'

Peter stopped tidying. 'What do you mean?'

'No one has seen her for three days.'

'Did she go back home?'

'When I say no one, I mean no one.'

He took something from her tone. 'Have you contacted the police?'

'They're not interested, there's no law against going missing.'

Peter began putting his belongings into his leather briefcase. 'I'm sure she'll turn up.'

'You don't seem that bothered.'

'If I had a pound for every student who didn't turn up to classes for a few days.'

'This is more than that,' Hannah said. 'She made an appointment with you, maybe she was worried about something?'

'Maybe,' Peter said. 'But her grades and lab work are fine, she's a model student.'

'Exactly,' Hannah said. 'So where is she?'

'I'm sorry I can't be more help,' he said, looking at his watch. 'I have a faculty meeting I'm already late for.'

Students were filing in for the next lecture, backpacks and water bottles, T-shirts and jeans, young men and women all present and correct, not missing from their lives. Hannah rubbed at her temple, tried to ease the pain. But throbbing behind it was something she was sure about. She'd checked Mel's emails a hundred times, there was nothing in them asking Peter Longhorn for a meeting.

'This is my granddaughter, Hannah.'

Hannah shook hands with the old man in the doorway, the skin on his hands rough and gnarly.

'Hi, there.'

They were at one of the swanky houses on Hermitage Drive, round the corner from the allotments.

'Jacob,' the old man said, and waved them inside.

Dorothy and Hannah followed him through to the living room. Hannah had a small, black canvas bag full of camera equipment over her shoulder. Her hangover was clearing nicely, but she was still chewing over what Longhorn had said about an email. It didn't make sense.

She'd been on her way home after classes when she got a call from Gran, asking her to come over and help explain how the spy cameras worked. She was glad of the distraction, to be honest, and she got to see Indy at Greenhill Gardens too. The cameras were pretty simple, small black cubes that could take snaps or record video when activated by motion in their field of view. But they were pretty old, didn't have cloud backup, just SD cards that had to be removed and viewed on a laptop.

'Hannah is our tech expert,' Dorothy said, as Jacob hovered over a hard seat then lowered himself carefully.

Hannah guessed that it would be too much effort to get in and out of a sofa without some help, and Jacob didn't seem like the kind of person to ask for assistance.

She unzipped the bag and took out one of the cameras. It looked innocuous, which was kind of the point. She explained how they worked to Jacob, talked about the best place to set them up. An hour ago she hadn't known any of this shit, had just Googled it before they came round. She talked about image resolution, battery power. How often they'd have to replace batteries and SD cards depended on how much activity there was during the day.

He smiled. 'You're talking to me like an adult.'

'You are an adult.' Hannah stood up. 'So we have five cameras, where shall I put them? Is it just downstairs, or do you want some of upstairs covered too?'

He thought about it for a moment. 'Mostly downstairs. One in here somewhere, one in the kitchen and one in the study through there.' He waved a hand behind him.

Dorothy held her hands out. 'Of course, the more cameras we use, the longer it will take us to go through the footage from them all.'

'I want her caught,' Jacob said, with a firmness that surprised Hannah.

'Of course,' Dorothy said.

'So, the other two cameras?' Hannah said.

Jacob nodded to himself. 'I have some things in my bedroom that I think she's been going through, so one in there. It's straight ahead of you at the top of the stairs. But there's nothing much in the other bedrooms now, so maybe just put the last one in the upstairs hall? Susan shouldn't really be up there at all, so if it picks up anything, I can speak to her.'

Hannah began looking around the living room for a place to hide the camera. It had a 150-degree angle spread, so anywhere would do, really, the main thing was to keep it hidden.

Dorothy spoke to Jacob about Susan's schedule, and he wrote down with a shaky hand when she was due over the next few days. This would help them to decide when to come and replace the SD cards and batteries, and also give them a better idea of which time stamps to look at on the footage. That way they could eliminate the footage of Jacob on his own moving around the house, although looking at him, he probably wasn't doing handsprings across the Persian rug.

The décor in the living room hadn't been updated in decades, a lot of orange and browns, swirling patterns on the heavy curtains and rugs. But it was dust-free, which made Hannah think.

'Does Susan clean the place too?'

'No, I have a cleaner,' Jacob said. 'A young girl, very efficient.'

'What makes you think Susan is behind the missing stuff and not her?' Dorothy said.

'Because Monika is lovely, and Susan isn't.'

Hannah frowned at that piece of impeccable logic.

Dorothy nodded. 'Well, we might have to widen the search times if we don't find anything with Susan.'

'Fine,' Jacob said.

Hannah found a spot in the corner of a bookshelf, pushed the camera cube into the shadows, shifted the angle slightly until she was happy.

In the kitchen she placed one on the underside of the extraction fan hood above the cooker, then in the study she propped one up inside the grate of the unused fireplace. Upstairs she went into Jacob's bedroom, another dowdy space with little light. She wondered about that for the clarity of pictures on the camera footage, but nothing could be done. There were sliding mirrored doors on a wardrobe, left open, and she placed the camera on a high shelf, obscured from below by a scarf.

Out in the hall there weren't many places to choose from, but she eventually settled on the top of the curtain pole across the window that looked over the green expanse of the Braids.

She looked around. This was a big house with five bedrooms, this floor on its own was bigger than her flat. Totally wasted on a single old man, but there you go. It was his home and his right to live wherever the hell he wanted.

She listened to Dorothy and Jacob's voices drifting up the stairs. It reminded her of being a kid, hearing her mum and dad talk through the wall as she lay in bed cuddling a teddy. The security of that murmur, the realisation that they were there for her.

But of course they weren't. Not really, in the end. They had split up and she had grown up, and everything changed. And here she was, spying on an old man's carer to see if she was betraying him. She wondered about Peter and Mel and the email he mentioned. Maybe more betrayal. Then she slowly walked down the stairs, imagined herself back in time, her mum and dad together on their sofa downstairs, the world still comforting and reliable.

20

DOROTHY

Dorothy stared out of the window. Three teenagers were flipping a Frisbee to each other across the park, unnervingly accurate. Who has the time to get good at Frisbee? They wore clothes that looked like they were from the 1980s, mismatched, flammable primary colours and patterns. She had the phone pressed to her ear as she listened to the ring. She knew the address was on the shore at Newhaven and pictured a seascape, choppy waters all the way to Fife.

'Hello, what do you want?'

The voice was working-class Edinburgh, impatient and tired. Dorothy heard kids' television in the background. Lorna Daniels left the police to become a mum and never returned.

'Hi, sorry to bother you.'

'Are you?'

Dorothy wished she'd gone to visit the woman, maybe face-to-face would get a better result. The address was one of the new apartments on Sandpiper Road, no sense of community, thrown up next to holiday rentals and cheap hotels, spread amongst waste ground and disused dockland on the edge of Leith. She could imagine how you might feel isolated, stuck there all day.

'My name is Dorothy Skelf, are you Lorna Daniels?'

'Whatever you're selling, I'm not interested.'

'I was given your number by Thomas Olsson at the Pleasance Police Station.'

'Thomas gave you my number?'

'He's a friend of mine and he thought you might be able to help me.'

Dorothy heard a child whine in the background, something about a sweetie. The sound went muffled at the other end then came back.

'How?'

'Maybe it would be better if we met up?'

The woman laughed, an exasperated sound. 'Do I sound like I've got time to meet you for a latte?'

'I'm sorry, I'll get to the point. It's about a case you worked on.'

'I'm not supposed to talk about that stuff.'

'I understand, but this wouldn't betray any confidences.'

'Which case?'

'A missing person, Simon Lawrence.'

A pause down the line. The sound of a cigarette being sucked?

'Doesn't ring any bells, when was this?'

'July 2010.'

This time the laugh was full-throated. Outside Dorothy's window a dog had leapt into the air and intercepted the Frisbee and was teasing the students with it, darting out of reach.

'Christ, that's ten years ago,' Lorna said.

'I realise that, but you'd be doing me a favour if you could remember something, anything at all.'

'Lady, I can't remember what I was doing two hours ago, motherhood brain melt. There's no way I remember a missing-person case from a decade ago.'

Schrödinger sloped into the room and wandered around the far wall, not looking at Dorothy. She watched him pace across the floor.

'He had a pregnant wife, Rebecca, lived in Craigentinny.'

'What was your name again?'

'Dorothy Skelf.'

Another pause, another drag on the cigarette.

'As in the undertakers?' Lorna said eventually.

'That's right,' Dorothy said. Schrödinger was at the bay window now, head still turned away as if hiding something. 'Simon Lawrence used to work here.'

'I remember.'

Schrödinger turned. He had something in his mouth. He took a few steps forwards and placed it at Dorothy's feet. Another bird, goddamn it. This time a sparrow, one of the knot that flurried around the feeders in the garden. They were placed high so he couldn't reach them, but this one must've been a straggler.

Dorothy stuck out her foot to scoot the cat away, and he slunk behind a chair, turned and stared at her.

'What exactly do you remember?' she said.

'The wife was up to high doh about it.'

Dorothy hadn't heard that in a while, meaning anxious and exasperated. One of the Scottish phrases she had to get used to when she first arrived.

'And?'

An exhale down the phone, definitely smoking. 'And nothing. I did all the usual stuff, spoke to friends and family, checked his phone and bank account. No trace.'

'What about at work?'

'I went to the funeral home. Do you work there?'

Dorothy stared at the dead sparrow on the floor. Its chest punctured with teeth marks, loose plumage drifting in the swirls of air caused by Dorothy's movement. 'Yes, it's my business now.'

'I spoke to the owner, nice old guy.'

'Jim.'

'And a younger guy who did odd jobs.'

'Do you remember what they said?'

'If there was anything suspicious it would be in my notes. Did Thomas show you them?'

'Yes.'

'Well, that's all there is.'

'But how did they seem, the men at the funeral home?'

'How do you mean?'

'What were they like when you spoke to them?'

Dorothy wanted a corner to pick at.

'They were just regular guys,' Lorna said. 'You work with them, right?'

Schrödinger approached on his haunches, like it was a game. Dorothy thought she saw the sparrow's chest rise, but maybe it was just a shimmer of feathers.

'So what was your hunch about Simon?'

Lorna laughed, a friendlier sound than before. 'It's not about hunches.'

'You must've had some opinion about what happened.'

A pause, no sound of inhalation, maybe the cigarette was finished. 'Honestly, I can't remember. But if you're asking me now, with his pregnant wife and all, I think he just panicked and left, changed his name and started over somewhere else. Maybe he's got another wife and kid now.'

Another wife and kid. Dorothy let that roll around her head.

There was a clatter in the background down the phone and a child's wail.

'To be honest,' Lorna said, 'I wouldn't mind that myself, disappearing and starting again. Who doesn't dream of that?'

Dorothy glanced out of the window. The kids had got the Frisbee back from the dog and had stretched into a wider triangle. They were hurling it fifty yards, still landing it in each other's hands.

'I have to go,' Lorna said.

'Thank you,' Dorothy said. 'I really appreciate it.'

'I hope you find what you're looking for, whatever that is.'

Then she was gone, just the dial tone.

Another wife and kid. A secret life. Starting over again.

Dorothy stared at Schrödinger, who was sitting in a strip of sunlight on the chair. She picked up the sparrow from the floor, felt the tiny weight of it in her hand. She wanted to sense life, breathing, but there was nothing.

'Goddamn cat,' she said, putting the sparrow in the bin.

She went to the sink and washed her hands, rubbing for longer than necessary, trying to scrub the death from her fingertips. Then she headed downstairs and through to the embalming room.

Archie was wearing blue plastic gloves, and holding a scalpel over an elderly man with his chest bared. He made a deep vertical incision in the chest, just below the left side of the collarbone. He looked up and nodded at the corpse.

'William Baxter,' he said. 'Pacemaker.'

They had to remove pacemakers by law in case they exploded in the crem furnace. Dorothy always wondered about the first time that happened, if anyone was injured or even killed. A last revenge from beyond the grave. She answered questions about it all the time at funerals because of a famous Scottish novel that opened with someone's grandmother exploding that way.

Archie kept going over the same incision, making it longer and deeper. He pulled the skin apart to expose the flesh beneath. It moved under his fingers like a joint of meat in a butcher's hands, nothing more. But this was something more, this was William with his dodgy heart, beloved by family and friends.

'I want to ask you something,' Dorothy said.

Archie picked up the scalpel again and widened the cut. Dorothy saw a glint of metal in the wound.

'Yeah?'

'About Simon Lawrence.'

Archie pulled the skin at either side of the cut and Dorothy saw more of the brushed-metal disc inside.

'You already asked me about him,' Archie said, head down in concentration. His fingers probed inside, peeling back layers and digging in.

'I thought you might have forgotten something.'

She came closer, staring at the top of Archie's head, watching his movements. She glanced at the body on the slab, sunken cheeks and chest, withered arms, wispy white hair on his chest, stubble on his chin. It was a myth that hair and nails kept growing on a body after death. The body starts to dehydrate as soon as you die and the skin shrinks and tightens around the corpse, exposing hair that was under the surface.

Archie stuck the scalpel in the hole, severing the sutures that kept the pacemaker in place, then he flipped his fingers and the disc popped out. It was an old one, the size of a flattened yo-yo, and must've felt obvious to the touch. It was linked via two wires at a clunky connector, the wires disappearing into the body, through the ribs into the heart. Archie snipped the wires and pushed the ends into the wound, squidging the flesh together and placing the pacemaker on a tray by his side.

He looked up. 'Forgotten something?'

Dorothy thought there was something in his eyes, a guardedness. 'Tell me again what you remember.'

'He was working here when I started,' Archie said, dropping the scalpel and picking up a surgical needle and thread. 'Doing the same as me, really. Driving, putting the coffins together, picking up bodies.'

'What else?'

'He was quiet, didn't say much.'

'What do you remember about him stopping working here?'

Archie made a couple of loops through, drawing the flesh together at the bottom of the cut, tugging it tight. It didn't have to be neat, no one was going to see it, but Archie did a tidy job all the same.

'What's this about?' he said. 'There's something you're not telling me.'

'Did you speak to the police?'

Archie looked puzzled. 'Why would I talk to the police?'

'Simon Lawrence disappeared.'

'What?'

'He didn't get a job in an office.'

Archie shook his head. 'That's just what I assumed, maybe Jim told me.'

'He just vanished.'

'After he quit here, you mean?'

Dorothy looked at the needle in Archie's hand, the half-closed wound on the body. 'I don't think he quit, I think he went missing.'

'But you would've known about that, wouldn't you?'

Dorothy put her hand out to touch the metal table, the cold of it reassuring. 'I didn't know anything about it.'

'Well, then.'

'You don't understand, Jim lied about it.'

'Why would he?'

'That's what I'm trying to find out.'

Archie made another stitch in the skin.

Dorothy leaned in. 'What I'm trying to work out is whether you're lying to me too.'

Archie straightened up. 'I'm not lying.'

Dorothy pressed her lips together, pushed herself away from the table. 'I talked to the police officer who looked into the case. She said she spoke to two people here about Simon.'

Archie held the needle tight in his gloved hand. 'I never spoke to the police, I would remember that.'

'Either you're lying or she's lying.'

Archie stood there, his hands resting on William's chest. 'This is, what, ten years ago? Maybe the officer remembered wrongly. Maybe she spoke to Jim and someone else.'

'There was no one else here back then.'

'Well, maybe she spoke to someone somewhere else and she's conflating the two.'

Archie looked at her and she held his gaze. She wanted to tell something from his expression, but she wasn't sure at all.

Archie rolled his tongue inside his cheek. 'Why do you care anyway? It's ancient history.'

Dorothy thought about the bank account, the money. She thought about Rebecca in Craigentinny bringing up her daughter, no husband to help. She thought about Jim's life assurance lie,

Rebecca accepting the money without caring. She thought about Jim talking to the police about Simon but never mentioning it, she thought about an employee vanishing, ceasing to exist, just like William Baxter here.

'It's not ancient history at all,' she said.

Archie waited for her to elaborate, but she couldn't think what to say. If Jim lied then nothing was certain. Her life was built on sand and she didn't know how to cope.

She shook her head.

Archie went back to work, sewing up William's chest, repairing the wound even though there was no need.

21
Jenny

Liam Hook was senior communications manager in the statistics department of the Scottish government, whatever that entailed. Orla had emailed Jenny a bunch of information about him, but the work stuff was written in management speak, impossible to penetrate.

Jenny sat in the body-collection van in a cobbled lane round the back of Commercial Street in Leith. She could see the main entrance of the government building on Victoria Quay, a giant office block that had kick-started Leith's regeneration a while back. She was in a private permit space and looked around nervously. Tailing someone was hard. She'd parked outside Orla and Liam's house in Craigleith this morning, but he left for work on foot then got a bus. You never saw that in American movies, someone trailing a bus in a body van. He'd gone to work as expected, so she didn't know what to do then. She'd parked legitimately and walked to a café along the road, taken her laptop and gone over some of Orla's information, but the price of parking was crazy and she had to return to the van to move it.

Liam didn't emerge at lunchtime, at least not from the front entrance. There were other ways out of the building, he could head towards Ocean Terminal or the restaurants along the Water of Leith. So really, Jenny was on a hiding to nothing.

She drove around in the afternoon bored out of her skull then returned at half past four. Orla told her that he normally finished at five but was planning to work late. If he really was working late Jenny could sit here forever, but if he went somewhere else she might have a chance. Although he'd seen her at the funeral, she hoped he wouldn't recognise her. In these circumstances, different clothes, her hair tucked into a beanie, she might get away with it. Of course he might've already left, in which case she'd wasted a day. Being a private investigator was so annoying.

At five, a rush of workers spilled from the building, heading to cars or the bus, a few stopping at the outside tables of bars, ready to drown their sorrows. The crowds petered out and Jenny looked along the road for a traffic warden or nosy local ready to give her grief for not having a permit.

She was wondering if this was a waste of time when she spotted him coming out of the office. He was tall and broad, not muscle-bound but solid all the same, wavy black hair and a black suit that fit his body well. The suit looked more expensive than your typical civil-service outfit.

She shrank down in the car as he passed then watched as he turned along the lane. She got out, looked again for traffic wardens, then followed. Finally she felt like a PI, collar up, following some guy wherever he went. She had no plan, but maybe that's all this job was, following people until something interesting happened.

He didn't look round, didn't suspect. He went over the Water of Leith and along Bernard Street then turned into the narrow lane of Maritime Street. This was old Leith, ancient bonded warehouses, some turned into hipster offices, others still derelict. There were fewer people in the street now and she saw him disappear into a tiny vennel. She reached the vennel moments later, slowed but didn't stop, glanced in. Just a little square, a dead end flanked by terraced buildings, old brick and thick walls, low doorways set back from the cobbles.

She couldn't see Liam, which meant he'd gone into one of the buildings.

She hesitated then entered the square. The windows were small on all sides, and she hoped he wasn't looking out of one. She got her phone out and pretended to be absorbed by it, checking a map having taken a wrong turn. She went to the first door and took a photo of the name, Red Box Design. Then she wandered to the other door and took a picture of the sign without breaking stride. It was cheap metal, bolted to the stone, Maritime Artist Studios. She walked out of the vennel then along the street and into a café thirty yards back down the road. She ordered a black coffee and sat at the window, glancing through the glass and Googling both names. The first place had a snazzy website, bespoke graphic design for trendy clients. Maritime Artist Studios just came up with a link to the map on her phone. No phone number or website, just a couple of mentions on a sculptor's blog, some pics of recycled metal installations in a small studio.

She drank coffee and waited. Being an investigator was boring ninety-five percent of the time, sure, but she had the bug now, she needed to find out what this was about.

Over the next couple of hours a handful of people came out of the vennel entrance, presumably employees of Red Box or people from the studio. No Liam, though. She searched more online, didn't find anything useful. She was jittery from the coffee and wondered if she'd missed him while looking at her phone. She was about to go around the square again when Liam appeared and walked briskly past the café. She turned away as he passed then got her things and left, following him back the way he'd come. He got to the corner of Bernard Street then turned into The King's Wark, a pub on the corner.

She waited a full minute then approached, pulling the door open. She'd drunk in here before, a woman her age had drunk in most pubs in Edinburgh and Leith. According to the plaque on the wall, this place had been around for 600 years, since some royal guy needed a place for a quick pint before getting on his ship at Leith Docks.

Liam was sitting at the bar drinking craft lager and looking at his phone. She went to the other end of the bar, faced away from him and ordered a double gin and tonic from a young guy with sculpted pecs and oversized glasses. The place was busy with office stragglers and early-evening diners. It was dingy, blackened stone walls, small windows, candles on the dinner tables. The layout was labyrinthine and she found a cubbyhole table where she had a view of Liam.

He smiled at a barmaid. They chatted, the body language suggesting this wasn't the first time. He said something and she laughed. She was early twenties, tall and plain-faced, with a tight body in bar T-shirt and leggings. She might be flattered by his attention, and he would definitely be flattered by hers. They talked for a few minutes then she went to serve someone. His gaze lingered on her arse as she walked away, then he went back to his phone.

Was this it, the barmaid? Then what was the stuff at the studio? Maybe the two were connected somehow. She thought about men looking at women the way Liam looked at the barmaid. Hardly a crime, men would argue, but it built a bigger picture, a culture of objectification that changed the dynamic. Jenny had internalised it all her life, taken part in it, she maybe even enjoyed the attention when it wasn't knuckle-dragging or harassing. But wasn't that just a kind of Stockholm syndrome? Men treat you like shit so often that when you find one who's not a complete bastard you're so grateful you jump into bed with him. But that line of thinking turned it into a war. She'd felt confrontational for a long time after Craig left, men were the fucking enemy, their bad behaviour excused by society, women going along with it.

That anger wasn't sustainable. It ate away at her for the first few years, though she didn't want Craig or Hannah to see it, because then the victory was his. But that was the language of a war again. She wondered how she would feel if she was watching a middle-aged, married woman flirting with the young barman with the muscles. She would cheer her on, waving pom-poms from her cubbyhole.

Maybe it was just her age. Hannah's generation were so much more sorted about gender, misogyny, patriarchy and the rest.

Jenny always thought of herself as a feminist but maybe that was a lie, because she didn't call out the daily bullshit of catcalling, stalkerish behaviour, aggressive flirtation. She used to get groped at grunge gigs and just accepted it as part of the experience. There was that guy Dale who she slept with then dumped, and he stood across the street every night for a month, staring at her bedroom window for hours. Hannah's generation was flagging this shit up, and that seemed to percolate through society.

At least Hannah would never be cheated on by a boyfriend or husband, but was it any better if she was betrayed by a girlfriend? What if Indy slept around behind her back, or if Hannah did it to Indy? Relationships were a mess, Jenny knew that well enough.

Liam began talking to the barmaid again. It looked like she was flirting with him, but her job was to keep drunk people sweet. Jenny thought about Craig, wondered how he was able to fuck Fiona at the office or in a hotel when he had a wife and daughter at home. But we all compartmentalise, we make excuses to ourselves, justify decisions, ignore the awful things we do because the alternative is to accept that we're bastards.

Christ, this case wasn't doing her head any good.

Her phone rang, and she panicked and pressed answer, worried the noise would make Liam turn round.

'Hi, Jen.'

Craig. A message from the universe.

'Craig.' She kept her voice down, hand over her mouth. There was enough noise in the place to cover her, but it felt weird. 'What do you want?'

'Are you OK?'

'Fine.'

'I'm not interrupting anything?'

She looked at Liam, nearing the end of his pint. He hadn't ordered another one yet, was still talking to the barmaid, who was playing with her ponytail.

'Not really, what do you want?'

'Just phoning for a chat.'

'Come on.'

A pause on the other end. 'OK, I had lunch with Hannah yesterday.'

'I know. And?'

'She said you're looking into her flatmate going missing, as an investigator.'

Liam had almost finished his pint now. The barmaid was serving someone a complicated cocktail, and he flicked through the back pages of a tabloid. Just a guy in the pub doing guy stuff.

'Yes,' Jenny said.

'Do you think that's a good idea?'

'Why not?'

'Shouldn't you leave it to the police?'

'The police aren't bothered, that's why I'm doing it.'

'And Hannah is helping too?'

'She knows Mel best.'

'Doesn't she have exams?'

'Exams aren't for ages,' Jenny said. She resisted the urge to say that he should know that.

'I just think, with Jim passing and everything, I don't know if you and our daughter should be getting involved in this.'

That use of 'our daughter' really got to Jenny. A way to apply pressure and link himself to her and Hannah.

Liam tipped up his glass and finished his beer, folded the paper and laid it on the bar. Jenny thought of Hannah asking around about Mel, Dorothy asking about Jim and the money, the pair of them at that old man's house with the spy cameras. She scooped her G&T as Liam said goodbye to his barmaid. So he wasn't waiting for her to come off shift, take her back to his studio and fuck her brains out. Or maybe he was heading there now to get the place ready for her. Either way, Jenny had to find out.

'It's none of your business what me and Hannah get involved in,' she said.

Liam was at the door of the pub, a blast of traffic noise and splash of evening light as he opened it and was gone.

Craig cleared his throat down the line. 'I just think—'

'Sorry,' Jenny said, getting up. 'I don't give a shit what you think and I have to go.'

She hung up, put her phone away and followed Liam out of the pub.

22
HANNAH

The Old Bell was dead and the Quantum Club were in their usual corner around two small tables at the far end of the bar. It was gloomy, dark-burgundy leatherette seats and black beams across a low ceiling. In winter it might've been cosy, but with autumn sunshine outside it seemed perverse to be cowering in the darkness.

Hannah was ready to get stuck in as she walked towards them. There were seven of them, two girls and five guys, including Xander and Bradley. All of them had frothy brown drinks in front of them, Deuchars eighty shilling or IPA. Louise and Ayesha had halves, the rest pints. Lovely bit of conforming to gender stereotypes, Hannah thought.

She caught Xander's eye and he looked away. He was boxed into the corner by Louise, who was sitting close to him, legs almost touching.

'Have you heard from Mel?' Xander said as she reached the table.

Louise reached for her drink and sipped, eyes averted.

Hannah shook her head, partly answering his question, partly in disgust at him sitting here drinking with the rest of them when Mel was gone.

'What the hell do you care?' Hannah said, which made them all stare.

'What?' Xander said. He looked uncomfortable and Hannah was glad.

'If you gave any kind of a shit, you'd be helping me find her.' She looked round the table. 'That goes for all of you. This is serious, don't you get it?'

They all looked at their drinks or down at their laps.

'Just a minute,' Bradley said. He was on the nearest stool, and he stood up and towered over her. 'We all care about Mel, but what can we do?'

Hannah turned to him. 'I think you've done enough.'

'What's that supposed to mean?' His fists were at his sides, but he was wavering.

'You really want to go there?'

Bradley seemed to get a second wind. 'Was that your mum came to see me the other day? Are you crazy, sending your mother to harass innocent people?'

'Innocent?'

She turned to Xander, pointed a thumb at Bradley. 'Did you know he sent dick pics to Mel?'

Xander's face flushed and he pushed past Louise's legs as he came round the table. 'What?'

'That's bullshit,' Bradley said, standing his ground.

Hannah spoke to Xander. 'He admitted it to Mum, said he fancied her and thought he would try it on.'

Xander frowned. 'What's your mum got to do with this?'

Bradley lifted his chin up. 'She sent her psycho mother round to threaten me.'

Hannah laughed. 'Intimidated by a middle-aged woman?'

'Obviously being a nutter runs in the family,' Bradley said.

Hannah ignored that, turned back to Xander. 'Mum's helping me with the investigation.'

'What investigation?' Bradley said. 'You're not a fucking cop.'

'No, but I'm going to find Mel, even if morons like you don't give a shit.'

'I give a shit,' Xander said.

Hannah raised her eyebrows at him. 'You've got a funny way of showing it.' She pointed at Bradley. 'This arsehole sent photographs of his penis to your girlfriend, don't you have anything to say?'

Xander took a step towards Bradley, Hannah in between staring up at the two of them.

'Is that true?' Xander said.

'Of course not.'

Xander turned to Hannah. 'He says he didn't do it.'

'He would, wouldn't he?'

'Do you have any proof?'

Hannah held her hands out. 'He admitted it.'

'You have the pictures?'

'No.'

'I thought you had Mel's phone?'

Hannah wrinkled her nose. 'She had another phone.'

Xander stood down from high alert. 'I didn't know about another phone.'

'Vic told me,' Hannah said. 'She got disturbing messages on it.'

She looked at Bradley for that last bit.

'Do you have that phone?' Xander said.

Hannah looked from one to the other, then at the rest of the group watching slack-jawed in their seats. 'No.'

All energy seemed to leave her. She wanted to confront these dickheads and their lack of compassion. She wanted to trick them into something, a slip-up or a fight, rolling around on the floor punching each other. She just wanted people to give a shit about a missing young woman, all the millions of missing girls across the planet that men didn't give two fucks about. Here were two well-educated young guys acting like cavemen, chatting up girls in bars when their girlfriend was missing or sending photos of their genitals on the off chance they would get lucky. There was no concern here and that just made her more angry, more determined to find Mel and return the world to the way it was before her grandpa died and her friend disappeared.

23
DOROTHY

She was young again, her skin tight and smooth, the muscles of her legs toned and firm. She rubbed sun cream into them and looked around. Pismo Beach didn't have the tourist appeal of Santa Barbara or Malibu, but the sand was still golden and the surf was high. Jim sat next to her on the towel watching the surfers glide on the breakers. Jim was young and strong too, thick arms and solid chest. They had their whole lives to come.

It was Easter Sunday and the beach was full of Hispanic families barbecuing, large groups spread out on blankets, chairs, even benches carried down from front porches. Beer in the coolers, a game of catch, kids kicking a soccer ball. The sun was high and Dorothy felt it soak into her bones.

Jim watched two young women in bikinis walk past, kicking up spurts of sand. A flicker of irritation passed through her then slipped away. Men will be men, it was only looking, Dorothy had his heart. They were in love and he made her feel beautiful. He was attentive in the bedroom, gave her gifts and compliments, was devoted to her. He'd never met anyone like her, she was sure of that, back in gloomy Scotland with its rain and inhibitions. He told her all about it, how depressing the place was, yet something in his voice spoke of his love for the place, as if he carried some of that dourness in his DNA.

Jim turned from the girls and their jiggling asses, saw that Dorothy had been watching him, and leaned over to kiss her, lingering, his hand on her thigh, fingers touching the strap of her bikini. She felt the heat rise in him and herself, as if their bodies were communicating with each other directly.

She woke in the grey-striped dawn in her bedroom, still on her side of the bed, next to empty space. She remembered finding Jim on the toilet floor lying in his own piss, his skin already shrinking, lips a lighter colour, eyes wide open.

The warmth of her dream faded, replaced by the chill of Scottish autumn. She hated dreams of California, they made her miss her childhood home in a visceral way. And now she hated dreams of Jim too, a reminder of what she'd lost.

Men will be men.

But what if he didn't just look at other women?

She sat in the body van and looked at Rebecca's house. Archie needed the van for a pick-up later this morning so she had to be quick. It was obviously better to bring the anonymous white van rather than the silver hearse. Park a hearse anywhere and people will start talking. She breathed deeply, reciting a simple mantra in her head to stay calm. She wasn't sure why she was here but she had to speak to Rebecca again. Her car was in the drive, so she wasn't at work yet.

Dorothy got out and walked across the road. It was dreich today, a good Scots word for it, low cloud and cold mizzle hanging in the air, Arthur's Seat vanished in the mist. She pulled her collar up against it, went up the path and rang the doorbell. Waited. Breathed in and out.

She heard the clumping footsteps of the girl inside, then Natalie opened the door. She was in a white polo shirt and black leggings, bare feet. The smell of burnt toast lingered and she had a smudge of chocolate spread at the corner of her mouth.

'Hi, Natalie,' Dorothy said. 'Remember me?'

Natalie nodded but didn't speak.

'Is your mum around?'

Natalie looked nervous. 'She's upstairs.'

Dorothy nodded, leaning forwards. 'Could you get her, please? Tell her Dorothy Skelf is here to see her.'

She could hear the sound of the shower running as Natalie thudded up the stairs with flat feet.

'Mum?'

She heard Natalie walking across the upstairs landing. There was a muffled reply through a door.

Dorothy stood in the doorway and looked down the hall. The detritus of an ordinary life, shoes piled on a rack, an umbrella, bike helmets. On the banister were jackets hung by hoods, and on top was Natalie's school sweatshirt, the burgundy one with the school crest on it. Dorothy stepped forwards and saw something on the sweatshirt, several of the girl's black hairs clinging to the material. She stared at them for a few moments, listening to Natalie upstairs talking through the door to her mum, the smell of toast still in her nose, cartoons on the television in the living room. Then she carefully picked as many of the girl's hairs from the sweatshirt as she could see, took out an old receipt, folded the hairs inside the piece of paper and placed it in her pocket. She heard the bathroom door open upstairs as she turned and left, striding down the path and breaking into a jog as she crossed the road to the van. She got in, started the engine and pulled out, not looking in the rear-view mirror as she drove away.

Archie and Dorothy sat in the van waiting for the council waste lorry to pull away from the large commercial bins round the back of St Columba's. Archie waved to the lorry driver as they passed, and Dorothy felt bad as she thought about their two services picking up different kinds of refuse from the hospice.

They reversed the van to the corrugated metal door and Archie killed the engine. He lifted a rolled-up body bag from the back seat and they got out and went to the buzzer next to the gate.

'Hi,' Archie said. 'Skelf's to pick up Mr Duggan.'

They were buzzed into the nondescript foyer, concrete and pastel paint, linoleum floor. No need to make this appealing to prospective clients, this was the way out in every sense of the word.

A middle-aged woman in blue scrubs emerged from a door.

'Hey, Archie,' she said.

'Moira.'

She saw Dorothy, who never did pick-ups while Jim was still around. You could see her putting it together.

'I was sorry to hear about Jim,' she said.

'Thank you.'

'He was lovely,' Moira said. 'Just a lovely man.'

Dorothy reckoned this woman was maybe twenty years younger than Jim, still attractive, a sparkle in her smile, plenty of ass to hold on to, didn't men like that? Damn, she had to pull herself together.

'Thank you,' she said again, and felt stupid.

A long, awkward silence.

Archie cleared his throat. 'We're here for John Duggan?'

'Of course,' Moira said, 'this way.'

She led them to an open space, a couple of gurneys parked in the corner, industrial-sized fridge taking up the opposite wall. She and Archie wheeled the gurney to the fridge and she opened the door. There were nine slots arranged three by three. She pulled one out as Archie unfurled the body bag onto the gurney, unzipped it and lined the gurney up.

Moira and Archie exchanged a glance then looked at Dorothy. She stood there thinking about Jim's skin crisping on the pyre, then about the sunburn he always got on the beach, his pale Scottish skin unprepared for Californian sunshine. They used to joke about it, how he burnt in five minutes.

She didn't step any closer to the body in front of her.

Moira took John Duggan's feet while Archie put his hands under the armpits, then they counted to three and shifted him onto the body bag, tucked him inside then zipped up.

The cold air from the fridge made the skin prickle on Dorothy's arms and neck.

'Got any holidays planned?' Archie said.

'Tenerife in October,' Moira said. 'I need it.'

'Sounds nice.'

They sorted paperwork and swapped small talk as Dorothy watched, feeling dislocated, as if she was the corpse here. She had an inkling of how Archie felt before his medication stabilised, what point was there in interacting with the world if you were already dead? How could you expect others to take you seriously when you weren't here at all?

She touched the folded piece of paper in her pocket with Natalie's hairs inside and felt like she was a ghost, walking invisibly through the world.

What use was a funeral director who couldn't touch dead bodies?

She sat on the bed and looked out of the window. All she could see from here was the top of the high wall between their house and the neighbour's, white clouds scudding across blue sky like they were racing each other. The uppermost branches of an oak, waggling its fingers towards heaven in the breeze.

She lowered her head until it was in her hands. She pressed her face into her fingers, pushing at her eyeballs until it hurt. She felt something rising inside her then sobs came out, shaking her shoulders, tears dampening her palms, snot suddenly in her nostrils that she had to sniff back. She gasped in air and sat up, arching her back.

'My God,' she said. 'Get a grip.'

She shook as she wiped at her cheeks with the backs of her hands, breathing with jerky movements of her chest.

She swallowed and pulled the piece of paper from her pocket, unfolded it carefully. Four hairs, two with the root still attached. Was it illegal to take someone's hair without consent? It certainly felt wrong. But she appeared to be that kind of woman now. She sat staring at the hairs for a while then folded them away.

She reached over to the bedside table and opened the drawer. Pills for Jim's prostate, a book about the history of Bruntsfield with a receipt halfway as a bookmark. A book that would never be finished. A packet of tissues, a tape measure for some reason, and then what she was looking for, his comb. So old-fashioned, no one used combs anymore, but he had. She picked it up and squinted at it. Several short white hairs. She lifted them from the comb and placed them into a small plastic bag she'd brought from the kitchen and sealed it up.

She sat with the bag and the folded paper in her lap then she remembered something and reached into her pocket. The bone. The piece of Jim she was carrying with her all the time. The sharp edge was still darkened with a smudge of her own blood.

She reached for her phone.

'Are you sure you want to do it this way?' Thomas said.

Students and tourists slid up and down the street past their table outside Söderberg like twigs in a river after the first thaw of spring, full of promise but destined to be spat into the sea eventually. Dorothy watched them and tried to shake the feeling she was a malevolent spirit, bent on evil.

'I need to know,' she said.

Thomas held the two hair samples in his fingers like they were from a nuclear reactor meltdown.

'You know you can send off for a DNA testing kit, do this online.'

Dorothy ran her tongue around her top teeth. 'I looked it up. They generally need mouth swabs, hair is much harder. I figured a proper forensics lab might do better.'

Thomas's eyebrows went up. 'And how am I supposed to swing this? We have procedures, resources have to be accounted for. It's not like I just drop by the lab and bang these on the table.'

'Sure, but someone of your stature.' Dorothy smiled to let him know she was trailing sarcasm, but also buttering him up at the same time.

'Flattery will get you everywhere.' He rolled his eyes. He was still toying with the samples, rubbing them between his fingers. 'Do you want to tell me what this is about?'

Dorothy took a sip of her tea. 'I think you know what it's about.'

Thomas nodded. 'Jim and the money.'

He waited for her to speak but she didn't.

'How about you lay it out for me?' Thomas said.

'I don't know.'

'I might be able to help. A police officer of my stature.'

She smiled. It was good to be understood by someone, to be seen. That's what she missed most about Jim, that he really saw her for who she was, he knew her at her best and worst, through the miscarriages and the deaths of her parents, the depression in the aftermath, the cancer scare that turned out benign, the time Jenny had an emergency appendectomy, all of it. Even the spell when she lost her mind, hooked up with Lenny Turner again after twenty years, scared of domesticity and Scottish life and motherhood and a life surrounded by death, stupidly mesmerised by Californian sunshine and an old lover who still viewed her with lust. Even through that, Jim had understood. He was heartbroken, of course, but he seemed to sincerely forgive her, and that was the most amazing gift.

No one else would ever have that level of shared experience with her, the knowledge of life's mundane elements, the quirks and foibles, the likes and dislikes. She was seventy now, had spent fifty years with him, nothing would even come close.

But Thomas did see her, he understood her. It was like paddling in the shallows compared to the deep dive of a lifetime of experience, but sometimes splashing in the shallows was enjoyable all the same.

She pointed across the table. 'The bag is Jim's hair.'

'OK.'

She wondered what to say that would not make her seem crazy. 'The other sample is Rebecca Lawrence's daughter.'

Thomas pressed his lips together. 'And how did you get a sample of her hair?'

Dorothy watched two teenage boys clatter past on skateboards down the slope towards the Meadows. They were weaving between walkers with panache, showing off skills, full of energy.

She didn't answer.

Thomas shook his head. 'Was it legal?'

'Technically?' Dorothy said.

Thomas stared at her.

'I don't know,' she said.

'O–K,' he said, stretching the letters out. He put the samples down and rubbed his face like he was tired. 'What do you hope to achieve with this?'

Dorothy sipped her tea, caught a whiff of something fishy from a nearby table, salmon or tuna. She was suddenly aware of the rustling leaves on the trees.

Saying it out loud would make it more real and she didn't want that. It would also be obvious how stupid this was. But she leaned forwards anyway, touched her finger to Natalie's sample on the table.

'I want to know if Natalie is Jim's daughter. Or maybe his granddaughter, maybe Rebecca is Jim's daughter. Maybe she got in touch with him when she was pregnant with her own kid.'

Thomas put his hands out wide. 'But how would that tie in with Simon's disappearance? Or the fact Jim was paying her money?'

'I don't know,' she said. 'But Jim lied to me about Simon's disappearance and I think Archie is lying too. Rebecca was pregnant with Natalie when Simon disappeared and Jim started paying her. It all stinks.'

Thomas frowned. 'Are you saying Jim was sleeping with Rebecca, she got pregnant, and between them they got rid of Simon? Or he had an affair decades ago and a daughter he never knew about? But then Simon working for you is a crazy coincidence.'

'Maybe it wasn't a coincidence, maybe Simon came to us on purpose.'

'Why?'

Dorothy rubbed at the table. 'I don't know.'

'You realise how insane this sounds.'

Dorothy touched her eyebrows. 'Yes.'

'He would've been sixty years old when he was sleeping with Rebecca – if he did.'

She stared at him. 'Sixty-year-olds can't have sex?'

'She would've been in her mid-thirties then.'

'So?'

'In a happy marriage.'

'We don't know that. Maybe Natalie isn't his, maybe Jim bonded with Rebecca over her missing husband, took advantage of a distressed pregnant woman.'

'Then this DNA test is pointless.'

'It's just one possibility.'

'Jim was a good man, Dorothy. He loved you, that was obvious.'

'That's right, men who are in love with their wives never have affairs.'

'Not Jim.'

'Especially when those wives are old and wrinkled and dried up.'

Thomas paused and held her gaze. 'You're none of those things.'

She looked away, embarrassed that she'd fished for the compliment. This wasn't about that.

A young woman walked past pushing a girl in a buggy. The toddler had a banana squished in her fist, chewing at the fruit from the edge of her fingers. Her mum was on the phone, talking loudly about booking a holiday.

Dorothy turned back to Thomas and lifted the two hair samples off the table.

'Can you do it or not?' she said, holding them out.

He looked at the samples then at her. Eventually he took them and put them in his pocket.

'It'll take as long as it takes,' he says. 'It depends how busy they are and the quality of the sample.'

Dorothy exhaled. 'Thank you.'

Thomas finished his coffee and placed the cup in the saucer. 'What happens if it comes back negative?'

'I don't know.'

'What happens if it comes back positive?'

She looked at the stream of people, hundreds of them getting on with their lives, talking and eating and breathing and laughing and crying like regular people. She felt disconnected from it all.

'I don't know that either,' she said.

24
JENNY

Jenny stared at the bubbles clinging to the lime in her gin and tonic. Lunchtime back at The King's Wark, this time she was sitting at the bar, her back to the diners and the door. Tiny shards of sunshine cut through the windows as the same barmaid from last night poured pints of Italian lager for two guys in suits. Jenny looked at the receipt she got with her drink, 'You Were Served Today By Sam'. She'd already Googled the name and the pub, tracked her down on LinkedIn. Sam Evans. She made a mental note to follow up on that later. When Sam was done serving, Jenny stared at her watch and sighed dramatically. Sam turned and Jenny tapped her watch.

'Men, eh? He's half an hour late.'

The barmaid made a sympathetic face. She looked prettier up close, freckles and dark eyes. Jenny could see why guys might drink in here because of her.

Jenny twirled the stirrer in her drink, swished the lime around. 'You got a boyfriend?'

Sam looked across the pub for something else to do but then took a step closer anyway. 'Yeah.'

'So you know, right?'

'I suppose so.'

Jenny followed her gaze around the place. The barman who served her last night wasn't in, so she took a punt.

'I haven't been here before,' she said. 'Nice place.'

Sam shrugged. 'It's OK.'

'Different if you're working.'

That got a tiny smile. 'Yeah.'

'Actually, a friend recommended it, I think he drinks here quite a lot. You might know him?'

She got a shrug for that.

'Liam Hook.'

She watched for a reaction but Sam shook her head.

'Tall, dark and handsome,' Jenny said, forcing a laugh at her own cliché. 'Forty years old. Comes in after work sometimes, so I guess he'd be wearing a suit.'

Another shake of the head. 'Get a lot of guys in here like that.'

When Jenny was twenty, forty-year-old men were invisible to her, especially if they wore a suit. But her experience wasn't universal, she knew younger women who went for the sugar-daddy thing, the flattery of a guy with experience and cash in his pocket.

She tried to read Sam's body language. She looked very at home behind the bar.

'Fuck this guy,' she said to Sam, touching her watch. 'He doesn't know what he's missing.'

She downed her drink and got up, the barmaid watching as she walked squinting into the daylight outside.

She went to Maritime Street, feeling the alcohol in her system accelerated by sunshine. She couldn't handle her drink now like she could when she was younger, found herself buzzing as she strode across the cobbles to the vennel and the studio. She walked up and tried the door, and to her surprise it opened. She went into an empty foyer, narrow corridors in both directions. She noticed that the buzzer system and lock on the door were both busted. A beer crate acting as a coffee table had a spread of community flyers and notices, exhibitions, drop-in workshops, some crap about tribal drumming, chakra realignment. On the walls were posters for local gigs, galleries and clubs, all cheap, lo-fi stuff.

She hesitated then went right. She could smell burning plastic, other kinds of industrial smells she couldn't identify. The corridor had three doors off to the left, all unmarked, cheap plywood. She walked to the end and back, then along the other corridor, which was the same except with a scabby toilet at the end. She knocked on the nearest door, no answer, then tried the handle. Locked. Same at the next one. Knocked on the third and got 'Just a minute.'

A woman in her late twenties opened the door, a lit blowtorch in one hand, goggles pushed into her mess of curly red hair, wearing orange overalls that made her look like a terrorist prisoner. She stuck her chin out.

'Yeah?'

'Hi, I was thinking of renting one of these studios, do you know if any are free at the moment?'

The blue flame of the blowtorch flickered as the woman moved her hands about. 'Maybe, I think Derek committed himself to the psych ward again. In and out of that place. He struggled to pay rent anyway, so I reckon the owner would be happy to see someone else.'

'Could I have a look at it?' Jenny said.

'Mohammed will have a spare key but he's not around.'

'Are they all the same?'

'More or less.'

'Could I check out yours, just for two secs?'

The woman thought for a moment then opened the door.

Jenny walked in, the smell of welding strong. The room was dominated by a six-foot sculpture made from rusty scrap, shaped into an embracing couple, two naked women. A cut-down car door panel had been beaten into the shape of a leg and lay on the floor beneath the sculpture, as if the woman in the embrace had just been in an accident. The rest of the room was cluttered with old metal junk, bigger pieces on the floor, smaller ones on a long table. A large sink, a corkboard, posters everywhere. The room was surprisingly light, much bigger windows on this side of the building flooding the space.

Jenny chewed her lip. 'Have you got a number for Mohammed?'

The woman went to the table and lifted a bent business card. 'He's more likely to answer in the evenings.'

Jenny took the card. 'Thanks.'

Back at the door, she turned. 'It was a friend of mine suggested this place. Liam Hook?'

The woman nodded in acknowledgement.

Jenny waved along the corridor. 'Which one is his, out of interest?'

The woman pointed with her chin. 'Last one down the other end.'

'Thanks.'

And the door closed.

Jenny walked to Liam's studio, knocked, nothing. She looked around then stepped back and kicked her boot against the handle. The door juddered in the frame. She booted it again and again, pausing after each time to look along the corridor. Then a fourth kick and the wood of the frame splintered around the lock. Two more hefty boots and the door swung open. She looked around then went in.

The room was full of large canvases, racks of them stacked against the walls, two on easels in the middle of the room, another two laid flat on the floor. There was a table full of paints and brushes along one wall, a sink and draining board covered in paint splatters, cups and jars, dirty rags and towels. Jenny approached the easels. The paintings were six feet by four, swirling abstracts with recognisable elements, skulls and flowers, spines intertwined with vines, animal body parts intermingled with tree roots, soil and earth. She touched a canvas in the corner, rubbed her thumb against the material. She wandered round, soaking it in. The two on the floor were similar, brighter, more blooms and petals blending into hair and fur. She flicked through the stacked canvases, more of the same, strong shapes disappearing into shimmering backgrounds.

She walked round the sink and table, inhaling the turps and paint fumes which reminded her of DIY, doing up the flat in

Porty with Craig before Hannah was born, sheets covering the floorboards, the pair of them full of optimism.

She returned to the pictures in the middle of the room. They were very good. She looked around. There was nothing in here but painting equipment, no desk or drawers, no laptop, nothing perverse. So this was it, his dirty secret was that he was a talented artist? It didn't make sense. She looked at the damaged door, sucked in the paint smell one last time, then turned and left.

25

HANNAH

She stared at the name on his door. 'Longhorn' made her think of someone boasting about his big dick, and she tried to shake an image of a naked Peter Longhorn, massive penis hanging down to his knees.

She knocked on the door, no answer. She knocked again just in case, cleared her throat. She tried the handle and the door opened. She breathed then went inside and closed the door behind her.

The trusting nature of academia. She imagined burglars walking into the building and going through the offices like locusts, stripping the place of everything electrical, phones, laptops, Kindles, iPads, all into a giant van.

Peter Longhorn's office was small and tidy, a narrow window with a view west of grey brick and white-framed windowpanes. Posters for symposiums and conferences on the walls, a framed picture on the desk of a woman in her early thirties smiling and holding a baby who was fumbling with a melting ice-cream cone, bib around her neck and sunhat on. The woman in the picture was pretty, blonde hair in a mess, flowery blouse askew with one hand tight on the baby's rump.

Hannah scanned the room – piles of papers, textbooks, journals, scientific dictionaries. She went to his desk, cheap chipboard and plastic moulded corners. There were locks on each drawer but they all opened.

The top drawers were full of pens and Post-its, other people's business cards. She went through them, doctors and professors from other institutions, nothing obviously weird. She flipped through notebooks full of equations and diagrams. Next drawer down was more paperwork, brown folders full of essays and exam scripts, all marked. She lifted them out and felt around at the back of the drawer space, nothing. Put them back. The final drawer had conference and laboratory brochures, ranging from pamphlets to thick, glossy prospectuses. She pulled them out and riffled the pages, seeing if anything fell out. Nothing. She shoved her hand into the empty drawer, her fingers shifting dust as she felt around. And touched something.

She pulled them out. Three photographs with wide white borders, like from those retro instant cameras. She flipped them over in a trembling hand and stared. The first was a picture of Melanie lying on a hotel bed wearing black lingerie that Hannah hadn't seen before. It wasn't in her drawer back at the flat. Mel was smiling at the camera, propped on an elbow, her other hand on her smooth thigh. Hannah stared, tried to make sense of it, then she looked at the next one. Mel naked in a shower, hands running through her hair, eyes wide and grinning, eyebrows raised as if asking the photographer what they thought they were playing at. The shower was standard hotel décor, grey tiles and white surrounds. Hannah stared at the mole under Mel's left breast then back at her face. She turned to the third picture. A selfie. Mel and Peter Longhorn, cheeks pushed together, faces filling the frame, relaxed and happy, a slight pout on Mel's lips, a look of contentment in both their eyes. All Hannah could see in the background was a sliver of white tablecloth and the glare of a candle. A restaurant somewhere.

Hannah sat down in Peter's chair and stared at the pictures, thinking. Then she shook her head, pocketed them, put the brochures back and left.

'Holy crap,' Indy said.

'I know, right?'

They stood in the kitchenette of the flat, the smell of veggie lasagne coming from the oven. Indy held the photos in her hand, switching between them.

'This is crazy,' she said.

'Yep.'

'How did we not know?'

Hannah shook her head.

'I mean, she was either here or with Xander or studying, right?' Indy said.

'Apparently not.' Hannah took the photos from her.

'He's her lecturer.'

'And mine.'

Indy touched Hannah's arm. 'So where do you think she is?'

'I don't know.' Hannah felt bad that the naked picture was at the top, so she switched it for the selfie.

Indy pointed at the pictures. 'This guy must know.'

'I tried to find him but he wasn't anywhere. He was supposed to have a first-year lecture this afternoon, never showed.'

'You think he's done a runner?'

'He's got a wife and baby.'

'All the more reason to hide, if he has something to do with Mel going missing.'

'He has to be behind it.'

'So you need to go to the police.'

Hannah sighed. 'I didn't exactly get these legitimately.'

Indy rubbed her arm. 'That doesn't matter, it's evidence.'

'Not evidence they can use in court.'

'They can use it to squeeze him.'

Hannah pursed her lips. 'It's only proof that he was seeing her, nothing more.'

'Come on,' Indy said.

'That's what he'll say, what the police will say.'

Indy leaned over and switched the oven off, reached for the oven gloves. She lifted the lasagne onto the worktop then dropped the gloves. It smelled beautiful but Hannah felt sick at the thought of eating.

Indy nodded at the pictures again.

'So go to a friendly cop,' she said. 'Speak to Dorothy's friend.'

26
Jenny

It was only four days ago they sat at this table drinking whisky for her dead dad, but it felt like weeks, months. A totally different life now, this was home. She'd had several angry phone messages from her ex-landlord in Portobello. She was living back at her childhood home, working as a funeral director and private investigator, how the hell had that happened? But she knew why, the reasons were in the room with her.

Hannah stood at the PI whiteboard, now covered in scribbles, lines, queries and pictures. She'd printed out pictures of Mel, Vic and Xander that she got from Mel's phone, then mugshots of Bradley and Peter from the physics department website. The lines between Melanie's photo at the top and the others below were marked with phrases like 'dick pics', 'quantum club', 'second phone'. Hannah held the three Polaroid pictures in her fist, fanned out like playing cards.

'It's enough for the police to get involved.' She looked at Dorothy.

Dorothy eased out of her chair and walked to the board, whisky glass held lazily in her hand like it was too heavy. Amber liquid sloshed to the rim then settled as she lifted it and sipped. Jenny had never seen her mum drink like this, it wasn't a good sign.

Dorothy squinted at the whiteboard then took the pictures from Hannah. She flicked through them, stopping at the shower one the longest, then handed them back.

'I'll speak to Thomas,' she said.

Hannah raised her eyebrows. 'I want to talk to him, it's my case.'

Her case, thought Jenny, this is who they were now.

Dorothy nodded like it was the most normal thing in the world. 'I'll set it up.'

Jenny felt the burn as she sipped her whisky. 'You think this lecturer knows where Mel is?'

Hannah waved the pictures. 'He knows more than he's telling, that's for sure, it's too big of a coincidence.'

Jenny blinked, felt the heaviness of her eyelids. 'And she never said anything to you about seeing him?'

'Nothing,' Hannah said, shaking her head.

'What about the others?'

Hannah turned to the board, pointed at Bradley. 'We know this guy's a perv.' She tapped Xander. 'And this guy's kind of sleazy.' Then she waved the Polaroids again. 'But this is something else.'

Jenny looked out of the window. It was dark, just the trail of footpath lights stretching across the park. A couple were walking close, hugging each other, two lads coming the other way passing a beer can back and forth. An old man shuffled along with a Labrador beside him.

'Mel has some lovely men around her,' she said.

Dorothy turned and wavered. She seemed drunk. 'Don't we all.'

Jenny stared at her.

'What does that mean?' Hannah said.

Dorothy waved her drink around. 'Your grandpa was lying to me for years.'

Jenny stared at the table as Dorothy explained to Hannah about the money, Rebecca and her daughter, Simon missing for years.

Silence as Jenny dug her fingernail into the grain of the wood.

'So Grandpa was sleeping with her?'

Dorothy gave an exaggerated shrug. 'It certainly puts one's grief into perspective.'

Jenny stretched her neck. 'We don't know anything for sure.'

'We know he lied.' Dorothy fixed her eyes on Jenny. 'It's hard for you, he's your dad, and he was my husband. But we can't be blind to these things.'

'Don't you think you've had enough to drink?' Jenny said.

Dorothy swallowed hard. 'I'm your mother.'

'I'm just saying.'

'The number of times I had to pick you up off the floor as a teenager, off your head.'

'That's a long time ago, Mum.'

'I never understood your constant need to fuck yourself up,' Dorothy said.

'Gran,' Hannah said.

Silence in the room.

Eventually Jenny spoke. 'Anyway, like I said, we don't know anything about Dad for sure.'

'We will,' Dorothy said.

Hannah frowned. 'How do you mean?'

Dorothy looked from one to the other of them. 'I gave Thomas DNA samples to compare.'

Jenny sat up. 'Samples from who?'

'Your dad and the Lawrence girl.'

Hannah sucked her teeth. 'How did you get a DNA sample from a girl you've only met once?'

Dorothy finished her drink. 'I went back and got it.'

'How?' Jenny said.

Dorothy turned, her gaze steely this time. 'I just did.'

Jenny drank. 'Christ.'

Silence for a moment broken by Schrödinger purring as he came in the room. He approached Dorothy then went to play with the bottom of the curtains.

Hannah spoke to Jenny. 'Speaking of lovely men, how's your adultery case?'

Jenny stared at her drink then smiled. 'He's an artist.'

'What?'

She pulled her phone out of her pocket and went to the camera roll. She got up and handed it to Hannah, who flicked through them.

'He goes to a studio after work,' Jenny said. 'And paints these.'

'How did you get into his studio?' Dorothy said.

Jenny pictured kicking the door in and felt a twinge of shame, heat rushing to her face. Was this who she was now? Angry and violent, barrelling her way through life.

'A sculptor let me in to look around. I said I was interested in renting a space.'

'They're cool,' Hannah said, tapping Jenny's phone screen.

'I know.'

Hannah passed the phone to Dorothy. 'And that's it?'

'So far. He goes for a drink afterwards at the shore in Leith. Chats to the barmaid, but not chatting her up as far as I can tell.'

'And his wife doesn't know?' Dorothy said.

'This is his dirty little secret, apparently.'

'Why would he not tell his wife?' Dorothy said.

Jenny took the phone back and looked through the paintings. A tree made of spinal vertebrae, fingers for fronds, merging into alien floral structures.

'Maybe he's shy,' she said. 'Or scared of ridicule.'

'Are you going to tell her?' Dorothy said.

'I haven't decided yet,' Jenny said. 'I want to stay on him a bit more, see if there's anything else.'

It was only as she said it that she realised it was true. There was something about Liam that interested her, apart from the paintings. She thought about all the men in Mel's life, her own ex-husband cheating on her. Liam was just another guy, of course. But maybe he wasn't. If you think every guy is the same, doesn't that condemn them to being so in your eyes? She was going round in circles. And if you dug deep enough couldn't you find some dirt, something you didn't like about anyone, including yourself?

She thought about her dad, the lies Dorothy thought he'd told. She remembered once when she was ten, she was playing aimlessly in the storeroom out back when she knocked over one of the boxes of unclaimed cremation remains. She stood and stared at the ashes spread across the floor, then walked out to the garden and kept playing, cartwheels on the grass, a skipping game. Later her dad wandered out and confronted her about the mess and she lied, felt the rush of blood to her cheeks, such a giveaway. Instead of shouting at her, he lowered his voice, always a bad sign, and gave her a pep talk about the importance of honesty and taking responsibility for your mistakes. She felt her cheeks flush again now as she remembered it, and thought about Jim's honesty, whether he had taken responsibility for his actions.

She looked up. 'What about your old guy in the Hermitage?'

Dorothy shrugged. 'We'll see what the cameras throw up but I'm not convinced. My gut tells me he's imagining it.'

Hannah frowned. 'He seemed pretty sharp to me.'

'Maybe.'

Dorothy went to the other whiteboard and looked at the funeral jobs. Gina O'Donnell had been wiped away, cremated and gone. There were still four names up there, one body to pick up, two in the fridges downstairs and a fourth in the viewing room, ready for tomorrow's ceremony.

Jenny saw William Baxter's name, the call she'd taken. He was in the fridge. She thought of him, cold and naked. She pictured herself crawling into the adjacent slot in the fridge, lying down in the cool air, slowing her metabolism until there was nothing to measure, no heartbeat or pulse, no brainwaves or thoughts, nothing left of her except dead cells and lifeless matter.

27
Dorothy

The Church of Scotland minister didn't seem to know anything about William Baxter. Dorothy knew more from Jenny's scribbled notes a few days ago. There were two dozen people at the service in the Skelfs' chapel, William's widow stoic and quiet at the front, flanked by two sons, their wives and three grandchildren. The rest were elderly, in various states of decay, many walking sticks and a mobility scooter parked at the back. Dorothy felt the age of her bones. She closed her eyes and thought of those Pismo barbecues, school dances, picnics and fairgrounds, car trips and flirtations with boys, then Jim, her big, daft Scottish boy appearing and changing everything. She looked out of the window to where they'd burned his body, not even a week ago.

She stared at the back of Mrs Baxter's head. They had this in common, left behind by the men they loved, the men they thought loved them. Left behind to find out all the nasty secrets, to float rudderless on a sea of grief, lies and bullshit. Dorothy swallowed and took a deep breath, looked at the leaves shimmering in the breeze outside.

There was a disturbance outside the chapel door, voices raised. The minister hesitated, looked up from his notes. Mrs Baxter turned to her son, who shrugged then gave Dorothy a hard stare. Dorothy moved towards the door. Her hand was almost on the handle when the door flew open and clattered against the wall, denting the plaster.

'How fucking dare you.'

Rebecca Lawrence was hard-faced and fuming, shaking off an apologetic Indy as she gripped the door handle with red knuckles.

'I'm so sorry,' Indy said.

'It's OK,' Dorothy said. She turned to Rebecca, nodding behind her at the Baxter funeral service. 'Maybe we could go somewhere private.'

Rebecca let go of the door handle and came into the room, pushing past Dorothy.

'No,' she said. 'I want everyone to know what a nasty piece of work you are.'

'This isn't appropriate,' Dorothy said.

The Baxters and friends were staring, William's widow confused, the sons with faces like thunder.

'I'll tell you what's not appropriate,' Rebecca said. 'Coming to my house and raking over my husband's death. I grieved for that bastard twice, when he went missing and when I had to declare him dead. And now you come round making accusations, suggesting I'm screwing you out of money.'

'I never said that.'

'You said I wasn't due anything from my husband's life assurance.'

'There was no life assurance,' Dorothy said.

She reached out and tried to touch Rebecca on the elbow but the other woman shook her off.

'And now my bank tells me you've cancelled the payments.'

'I'm sorry.'

'I'm a single parent with a ten-year-old daughter, what am I supposed to do?'

'Please leave.'

The voice from the doorway made Dorothy turn. Jenny was in her funeral outfit, her fists balled, strands of hair falling from her ponytail.

Rebecca turned, wide-eyed. 'What did you say?'

'You heard me,' Jenny said, stepping into the room.

'Who the hell are you?'

'I'm Jenny Skelf, I help run this business. And we don't owe you anything, not a penny.'

Rebecca was shaking, her head angled to the side. 'It was your father who made me sign the paperwork, who set up the payments.'

'Do you have any of that paperwork?'

Rebecca smiled and reached into her handbag, pulled out some crumpled pages. 'Too right I do.'

Dorothy took a step towards her. 'Can I see that?'

Rebecca snatched the papers away. 'My lawyer will be in touch. I'm going to sue, I'm going to put this place out of business. You won't even stick to an agreement your dad made. That's how you honour him.'

'Don't you dare speak about honour,' Jenny said.

'He promised me.'

'He lied to you,' Dorothy said, finding her voice. She looked at Jenny, Indy still hovering in the hallway behind. She avoided looking at the Baxter party, the minister's face. 'He lied to all of us.'

Rebecca looked from Jenny to Dorothy and back again. She swallowed hard and spoke to Dorothy. 'Why did you come back round?'

Dorothy frowned. 'What?'

'You came to our house yesterday morning, spoke to my daughter then left. Natalie is traumatised by all this, people talking about her dad.'

'I'm sorry,' Dorothy said. She thought about Natalie's hair fibres in the police lab. 'I wanted to explain to you in person, but I lost my nerve.'

Jenny narrowed her eyes at Dorothy.

Rebecca lowered her head. 'Do you know what it's like?' She seemed to be talking to herself. 'To have someone just disappear? Your husband, gone forever.'

Dorothy didn't know what to say.

Rebecca's shoulders slumped, all fight gone.

'A girl needs a father,' she said.

Dorothy shared a look with Jenny, then reached out and touched Rebecca's elbow. This time she let herself be led away. Dorothy closed her eyes as she passed Jenny and thought about husbands and wives, fathers and daughters.

28
Jenny

Sunshine and traffic noise, the chatter of Spanish students at the next table. They were sitting outside a Brazilian restaurant on Lothian Street, green-and-yellow flags everywhere, boards advertising cheap tapas and pints of Brahma from Sunday to Wednesday. Orla Hook had a large glass of Shiraz in front of her as she fiddled with her wedding ring. It was lunchtime and the place was busy. Jenny would always know this place as Negotiants, a late-night café in her student days, and an even later club downstairs. It had been one of the few places in town open till 3 a.m. where you didn't have to pay entry. All the pubs and clubs had changed since she was a teenager, the turnover of styles and décor rolling onward all the time. Across the road was Bristo Square, which had also been transformed and gentrified, surrounded by Edinburgh Uni buildings and full of students soaking up the last sunshine of late summer.

'Students,' Orla said, rolling her eyes.

Jenny examined her. Orla was too young to remember the comedy character who used to rage against students. So maybe there was no irony, maybe she just really hated students. Which was interesting, given that she worked in the payroll department of the university on Chambers Street.

'Don't you have to work with them all day?'

Orla shook her head. 'I deal with staff.' She was hunched forwards, supping her wine like it was bedtime cocoa. 'You should see what some of these professors get paid for working five hours a week. And the pensions and perks, it's unbelievable.'

She took another hit of wine as a row of maroon buses went

past on the road, blocking their light for a moment. Obviously Edinburgh Uni payroll didn't mind you working the afternoon half-pissed.

'So where's the brown envelope?' Orla said.

'What?'

Orla nodded at Jenny's bag. 'You're supposed to give me evidence in a brown envelope, isn't that how these things work?'

Jenny suddenly realised how nervous Orla must've been. Jenny had phoned her at work earlier and Orla arranged this lunchtime meeting. Maybe she was expecting the worst, wanted to get some Dutch courage, as well as time to compose herself.

'That's just old movies,' Jenny said.

Orla's leg was twitching. 'Give me the bad news.'

Jenny sipped her gin and tonic. 'It's not what you think.'

'Then what is it?'

'I followed him. You're right that he's not working late.'

Orla glugged wine. 'Come on.'

'He left the office on time and went to a studio off Maritime Street.'

'A studio?'

'An artists' studio.'

Orla made a face. 'I don't think so.'

'He stayed there for two hours then went for a drink in The King's Wark.'

'Alone?'

Jenny nodded. 'He spoke to the barmaid for a while.'

'Like, chatted up?'

Jenny pressed her lips together. 'No. I went back the next day and spoke to her, she doesn't know him.'

'Was he waiting for someone maybe, someone who didn't show?'

'It didn't look like it. He had a drink then left, I followed him to your place around nine o'clock.'

A group of male students strutted past, shoving each other and laughing, one of them swinging a backpack over his head. Kids in sunshine. Orla watched them until they passed.

'So what is this about a studio?'

Jenny leaned forwards. 'I went back there yesterday and asked around. Someone knew him.'

'A woman?'

'Yes, but I don't think that's it.'

'How do you know?'

'He has his own room in the place.'

'I don't understand.'

Jenny reached into her bag and pulled out the printouts. She'd printed off a few snaps of the paintings. She slid them across the metal table and Orla stared at them.

'What am I looking at?'

'Liam's a painter.'

Orla looked up, eyebrows raised, then down at the printouts. She shuffled between them and Jenny saw some of the shapes, a distorted spine, red and yellow blossoms spindling from either side.

'You've made a mistake.'

'I don't think so.'

'Liam does not have a creative bone in his body.'

Jenny pointed at the pieces of paper. 'There's the evidence.'

'I have never seen him paint in my life.'

'Nevertheless.' Jenny sipped her drink.

'Are you sure he did these?'

Jenny nodded. 'Pretty sure.'

Orla looked at each of the printouts in turn, gripping them too tight, creasing the paper in the corners. Eventually she put them down and lifted her drink, took a large swig. 'You're wrong.'

Jenny reached out and touched the corner of the nearest printout. 'Why is it so hard for you to believe your husband painted these?'

Orla's eyes hardened, her body stiff. 'Have you ever spoken to him?'

'No.'

'If you had, you'd know he's not that kind of man.'

Jenny held her hands out. 'I don't know what else to tell you.'

Orla looked at the flow of people along the pavement. The vans and cars, trucks and buses, streaming in and out of town.

'I want you to keep following him,' she said eventually.

'I don't think there's much point.'

'It's only been two days,' Orla said. 'Talk to the barmaid again. Or the other people in this studio, maybe he's fucking one of them.'

Jenny collected up the printouts as Orla downed the remains of her wine. Her teeth and lips were stained red as she stroked her fringe away from her eyes.

'I know there's something else going on,' she said. 'This isn't it.'

Jenny wondered if all her clients would be like this. Then she wondered at herself for thinking she would have future clients. Then she pictured herself in a mac and hat, passing unmarked envelopes to clients in dark alleyways and dingy bars.

'OK,' she said finally. 'It's your money.'

'That's right,' Orla said. 'It's my money.'

29
HANNAH

East Fettes Avenue was a nice part of town, north of Stockbridge and New Town, wide road, a couple of big churches nearby, Broughton High School across the road and Inverleith Park round the corner. The terraced houses that Hannah parked the hearse outside were expensive for a lecturer's salary, so his wife had to do something that earned proper money.

She and Dorothy had taken the pictures of Mel to Thomas, who said he would send someone to speak to Peter Longhorn. Hannah asked to tag along but Thomas said that was ridiculous. So she'd dropped Dorothy off, phoned uni payroll pretending to be from HMRC, and got Peter's address from a nervous lackey.

And here she was. The hearse was noticeable but she didn't care. About half an hour after she arrived, a police car turned up. Two men got out, one plainclothes the other in uniform, and were invited inside by the pretty wife with the baby cradled in her arm.

That was forty minutes ago. She wondered about the wife and baby. Sleepless nights, loss of sex drive, breast feeding, nappy changes, tantrums and the sudden lack of freedom. Enough to turn a guy away from his exhausted wife to a twenty-year-old student. It didn't take much for men to fuck around. Hannah thought about all the times some married guy had chatted her up in a bar, even when she was there with Indy, obviously a couple. Oh, to have the confidence of a middle-aged white man, honestly, these guys acted like the world belonged to them.

It was afternoon and the high school was coming out, streams of teenagers in black and white, just the red flashes of their ties marking them out from any other kids in the city. Boys were mucking about and jumping into the road, girls pulling on short skirts and covering their mouths at something outrageous one of their mates said. They all gave the hearse a wide berth, some peeking in wide-eyed and turning away when Hannah held their gaze.

She thought of her own school days, the safety in finding your own small group of friends, bolstering yourselves against the hard world. Hannah's coming-out was relatively painless and she was grateful for that. Her three best friends were all straight and fine with it, but there was a slight distance afterwards, like they couldn't talk about boys in front of her, or maybe they worried she was about to jump their bones. On the surface all was fine, she socialised, hung out, went to prom, but she was glad when uni came around and she could start from scratch. Maybe life needed that, the chance every few years to start somewhere new, where no one knows you and you can redefine yourself, untied to the past.

The school kids had thinned out, but still no one came out of the Longhorn house. The front garden was tiny, a lot of them in the row were converted to parking spaces. Somewhere to park your car was prime real estate in this city, Hannah had already pumped umpteen coins into the meter for the privilege of sitting here.

The door of Peter's house opened and the two cops stepped out. They turned on the doorstep, Peter in the doorway holding the frame, and the three of them smiled, sharing a joke. They talked for a few moments, the body language of new friends, then Peter reached out and shook both their hands.

Hannah got out of the hearse and strode to the house.

'Hey.'

All of them turned. She could see now that Peter's wife was in the doorway too, behind him and to the side, supporting him all the way. When Peter saw Hannah he tried to usher his wife inside, but she stood her ground. She was still carrying that bloody baby on her hip.

Hannah turned her attention to the cops. 'Are you not arresting him?'

The plainclothes guy adjusted his stance. He was about the same age as Longhorn, shorter, broader, his hair already receded from his forehead.

'Can I help you, Miss?'

'Why aren't you arresting him?' Hannah said, reaching the garden.

'This is none of your business,' the cop said.

'My friend is missing and he had naked pictures of her in his desk.' She pulled the photographs out of her pocket and waved them as she walked up the path.

The uniformed officer took a step towards her, puffing out his chest. He was in a stab vest, and she imagined picking up a rock from the side of the path and hurling it at his head. Instead she sidestepped him and darted up the steps to the front door.

'You,' she said, in Peter's face now. 'What do you have to say?'

'You've got a nerve.' This was his wife, stepping forwards. 'You broke into his office.'

Peter turned. 'Emilia, please.'

Hannah thrust the pictures in front of Emilia, the naked one on top. 'Look.'

Emilia shook her head. The baby in her arms looked like it was about to start crying.

'He's explained it to the police,' Emilia said. 'She was obsessed with him, stalking him.'

'And you believe that?'

The woman held her gaze as if testing herself. 'He wouldn't lie.'

Peter shifted his weight and put his hands out to take the heat out of everything.

'What about this?' Hannah flipped through the pictures, came to the selfie of Peter and Mel.

Peter shook his head. 'She surprised me with a camera one day in the cafeteria. I couldn't exactly say no.'

'You're on a date,' Hannah said, pointing.

'No.'

Hannah waved the pictures. 'Why did you have these?'

Peter looked embarrassed. 'She sent them to me, I didn't know what to do with them.'

Emilia leaned out of the house.

'Get away from my family,' she said under her breath.

'I think we've had quite enough.' This was the plainclothes guy.

Hannah turned to him. 'I can't fucking believe this.'

The cop nodded at the pictures in her hand. 'Those don't prove anything and they were obtained illegally.'

'But they're suspicious as hell.'

Emilia spoke to the cops. 'Get this bitch away from our house, she's dangerous.'

'Emilia, please,' Peter said.

'She's probably obsessed with Peter too.'

Hannah took a step towards her. 'I beg your pardon.'

She felt the uniform cop holding her arm, pulling at her.

'Get the fuck off me,' she hissed behind her. She tried to shake him off but he held firm.

Emilia was in her face now. 'Just another silly student with a crush.'

Hannah raised her hand and brought it down on Emilia's cheek so hard that the woman almost lost balance, bumping into the doorframe with the baby, who screamed, tears in her eyes and snot from her nose.

Hannah stood there breathing heavily, her body shaking with adrenaline.

Emilia slowly righted herself, put her hand to her reddened cheek, then smiled at Hannah.

'I want her arrested for assault,' she said.

Hannah felt her other arm being grabbed by the uniformed cop and pulled behind her. She looked at the faces in front of her and tried to think of a time before all this, as the cop shoved her down the steps towards the police car.

30
JENNY

'Cheers.'

She smiled at Craig across the table. She was mad at herself for being here but it also felt comfortable. She looked round the beer garden of The Pear Tree, full of students, leftover tourists and what she would've called crusties back in the day, not homeless exactly, but happy living on the edge of things. There were a lot fewer crusties than there used to be, the subculture either moving on or disappearing altogether as the world became more uniform.

She turned back to Craig.

'What are we doing, Mr McNamara?' she said.

'Just having a drink, Ms Skelf.' He sipped his pint.

She drank from her double gin. 'Really?'

He bowed his head in mock reverence. 'And I'm saying sorry by buying the drinks.'

She shook her head.

After meeting Orla she'd wandered around Teviot and Southside wired from the lunchtime booze, soaking up the sun, watching the students. In her head she was still Hannah's age, but that delusion was busted every time she caught her reflection in a shop window. Walking amongst the energy of these kids, Hannah's contemporaries, made her feel young again.

She'd sat in the Meadows, the grass still a little damp despite the sunshine, and watched young parents with toddlers in the play park. So now she was the creepy middle-aged woman hanging around the play park. She missed that time with Hannah, being needed. Larkin got it wrong, it wasn't your parents who fucked you up, it was your kids. They need you for everything, make themselves the focus of your entire world, then the years slip away and they don't need you anymore, and you have a gaping hole in your heart where your life used to be. And she didn't even have a husband to share that emptiness with.

She'd walked back to the house and there was Craig standing at the front door, about to knock, with a beautiful orange orchid in his hand.

So here they were, drinking in the late afternoon as a wasp sniffed around the sticky rings their drinks made on the table.

'Shouldn't you be at work?' Jenny said.

'I left early.'

'What about Fiona?'

'What about her?'

'The two of you work together, where did you say you were going?'

He frowned as if the question was stupid. 'I told her I was coming to see you.'

'Really?'

'We don't keep secrets from each other.'

As soon as he said it he looked sheepish. He and Fiona sure as hell kept their affair secret when he was still married to Jenny. He lifted his Stella to his lips to cover his embarrassment.

She couldn't help it. 'That must be nice for the two of you.'

'I'm sorry, I didn't mean anything.'

She drank her gin, ice clacking against her teeth, the lime sharp on her lips. 'And why did you say you were coming to see me?'

'To say sorry. I was a dick on the phone the other night. You and Hannah are going through a hard time, I should've been more supportive.'

'Thank you.'

'I think it's great you're helping Dorothy, she must love having you close.'

'I hope so.'

'How is she coping?'

The truth was Jenny didn't know how her mum was coping. The business with the money and Dad's lies, and the Lawrence woman, what was that? A diversion, something to focus on that wasn't Jim's death, or was it a real mystery to be solved? And the Glassman case, just another diversion? Maybe life is just a succession of diversion tactics, moments to keep you busy, stop you thinking about the big stuff. But death brings the big stuff into focus.

'She's OK, considering.'

'And you?'

'Fine.'

'And Hannah?'

Jenny spotted two women Hannah's age at a nearby table. They looked Scandinavian, good bone structure, blonde hair, tanned skin. She was aware Craig hadn't looked at them, not even a glance. Was he deliberately not looking or had he really not noticed? She was annoyed at herself for noticing he hadn't noticed, which made her smile.

'Hannah is more sorted than any of us,' she said.

'True dat.' Craig's tone was self-mocking, using a phrase too young for him. There was so much history between Craig and Jenny, so many in-jokes, insignificant knowledge that no one else shared with her. That was the worst thing about divorce, not the separation or loneliness or stepping back into the putrid swamp of dating, but the little shared quirks and foibles, the things that only one other person knew about you, the stuff that would be gone when you both died. She thought 'like tears in rain', just like Rutger Hauer at the end of *Bladerunner*, and she knew Craig would get that reference because they watched that movie lying in bed post-sex, eating chow mein, drinking some dreadful schnapps they'd picked up somewhere, quoting lines to each other and marvelling over Daryl Hannah's hair and that other actor's pockmarked face.

Craig smiled. 'I don't know how we managed to make such an amazing human between us.'

'They fuck you up, your mum and dad.'

He smiled in recognition. 'We tried our best to do that, for sure.'

'Yet look how she turned out.'

A cloud flirted with the sun in the west.

'Any news about her flatmate?' Craig said.

Jenny thought about those pictures. The police would have spoken to Longhorn by now. She thought about Xander and Bradley.

'She hasn't shown up,' she said.

'It's not just a student bender?'

Jenny shook her head. 'Kids don't do that anymore, not like we did. They don't go on drug-fuelled adventures for days, especially not young women. They can't afford to, for a start, every day at uni costs hundreds of pounds. And the world is a more dangerous place now for women.'

'You think?'

'Definitely.'

The Scandi girls were checking Tinder profiles on their phones and giggling, swiping away the arseholes one by one. If only it was that easy in real life. Craig looked at them laughing and Jenny was happy he'd finally acknowledged them. When she and Craig were together he would've commented on them, something innocuous, to let her know he was a man who noticed pretty girls, but that they weren't a threat to Jenny. But that turned out to be another lie, of course. Once you know a man is capable of sleeping around, you just presume he is sleeping around. She wondered how Fiona dealt with that.

'Well,' Craig said. 'I hope she turns up soon.'

'Me too.'

Craig's pint glass was empty and his hands were flat on the table in front of him. Jenny leaned forwards and placed her hands on top of his. He didn't flinch, looked up and gave her a quizzical look.

'Thanks for being here,' she said.

He shrugged like it was nothing.

She squeezed his hands then lifted her glass and finished her drink.

'And I'll have another double, thanks,' she said.

31
DOROTHY

She pushed her glasses onto the top of her head and rubbed at the bridge of her nose. Her eyes ached from staring at the laptop screen so long and she was bored rigid from watching the mundanity of Jacob Glassman's contained life. She thanked whatever higher powers existed that she still had her health and mobility at the age of seventy, and she worried like hell that she would live to ninety and be housebound and dependent on help.

She and Hannah had gone to visit Jacob first thing that morning, swapping SD cards and batteries on all the cameras. Jacob seemed more vague about the whole business than he had been two days ago when they fitted the cameras, which made Dorothy worry. He said that he hadn't noticed anything odd around the house, or going missing, in the last forty-eight hours, which didn't add to Dorothy's confidence that anything was even happening in Hermitage Drive at all.

Back at home, Hannah had showed her how to access the files on the cards, which filename related to which camera at which time. There was a lot of material to go through. This surveillance stuff was the bread and butter of the investigation business, Jim had told her more than once, but it was long, boring work. At least she didn't have to sit in a car all day outside a home or office, waiting to catch sight of someone up to no good. But she still had to trawl through hours of this footage, even with motion-activated cameras.

She'd started checking the footage from the kitchen and study for the time periods Susan had been in the house, but there was nothing obviously suspicious. She then checked the living-room camera and the upstairs ones for the same time period. The downstairs cameras had a lot of footage for that time slot, but it was standard occupational-therapy stuff, exercises and so on, as well as boring things like Susan putting the kettle on, Jacob flicking through an old book. He had to go to the toilet often, and Dorothy would see him shuffling off screen with his walker, returning ten minutes later, sometimes with his fly still down. She was glad there wasn't a camera in the downstairs bathroom.

For the same time period, the upstairs cameras had nothing, so it looked as if no one had been up there. Dorothy thought about what Jacob said, that an old television had gone missing from an upstairs bedroom. She should've checked to see if there was a dust shadow where the TV had been when she was at the house, but maybe the cleaner had been in since. That's if it was even stolen in the first place. Dorothy wondered about the cleaner.

She paused the screen and closed her eyes. Tried to centre herself and opened them again. She picked up the two sheets of paper Hannah had printed off for her earlier, research on Susan Raymond. There was her LinkedIn profile, lots of praise and an apparently exemplary record as an occupational therapist since she graduated five years ago from Queen Margaret University and finished her training. A pretty normal Facebook profile and no presence on Twitter or Instagram, according to Hannah. But then, Dorothy was learning that people who seemed simple and innocent on the surface could have all sorts of hidden secrets.

She made a mental note to ask Jacob when the cleaner would next be in. She still had to check each of these cameras for other times of day, and there would soon be more footage from the new SD cards. She didn't know how she was going to keep on top of it, as well as everything else.

There was a soft tap on the door to the office, and Archie was standing there.

'Are you all right?' he said.

Dorothy rubbed at her face and nodded.

'What are you doing?' Archie said, nodding at the laptop screen. There was a frozen image of Jacob, book open on his lap, eyes closed.

'Just spying on an old man,' she said.

'OK.' Archie straightened up in the doorway. 'I'm heading out on a pick-up and I could use the help. Do you want to come?'

Dorothy closed the laptop screen and threw the printouts onto the desk.

'Yes, I do.'

There was nothing left of Erin Underwood. Dorothy wanted to bundle her emaciated body in her arms and hug her, but she feared the bones might break under the pressure. Leukaemia, surgery, chemo and radiotherapy had left the teenager a human husk, hairless and with skin like rice paper, shrunken into herself like a voodoo doll.

They were in the mortuary at the ERI. Really Erin should've been in a hospice or at home for the last stretch, but sometimes there wasn't time, sometimes people just gave up in front of your eyes. There were big banks of body fridges here, a phalanx of gurneys laid out like dead soldiers on a battlefield, post-mortem tables and toolkits, plus all the paperwork that went with the NHS.

Archie was sorting that paperwork and swapping small talk with the young mortuary worker in his overalls, tall and skinny with a goofball smile and wild, curly hair. Dorothy imagined this kid in the pub tonight, talking about what he did at work. It was hard for anyone in this industry to socialise outside of it. It often didn't go down well when people found out what you did for a living. They either presumed you were morbid or they had their own creepy questions about how it all worked. Or they recoiled from conversation completely, refusing to think about mortality. She tried to imagine this affable lad dropping it into conversation as he chatted up someone at the bar.

Jim hadn't been working in the funeral business when she met him, he was a young lad himself, carefree and enjoying life, only to get sucked into working with the dead after his father had died. But he hadn't resented it, had found his calling, and so had Dorothy, although she wondered about that now. She'd allowed her life to be subsumed by her husband's. Such a common story for her generation, but what do you do once that's gone? Disconnected from Jim's influence and with everything she was discovering, she wondered whether she was ever cut out for this in the first place. What if she'd got together with Isaac instead, who now worked as a movie producer, or Adrian who retired recently from his hotshot legal firm. Or if she hadn't allowed Jim to talk her back to Scotland, if she'd stayed in a duplex in Pismo Beach with divorced Lenny, surfing in the mornings and barbecues in the evenings. There were an infinite number of pathways your life could take. How do any of us really know what to do with our lives? And how, after seventy years, do we know whether it was all a waste of time?

She looked at Erin's face, framed by the body bag. How little time we have. These were the hardest ones, teenagers and kids, the death of potential, the death of possibility. Erin was younger than Hannah, would never go to university or get a job, never find a husband or wife or go travelling or sleep with a hundred men or women, she would never just sit in a quiet room with a book, staring at the sunlight coming through the window for a moment and realise how lucky she was to be alive.

Dorothy swallowed hard and zipped up the body bag just as her phone rang. She pulled it out. Thomas, the DNA results.

'Hi,' she said, her voice catching.

'Hello Dorothy, I tried calling Jenny first but she didn't answer.'

'Jenny?' Dorothy was confused. 'What's this about?'

Thomas cleared his throat. 'I'm afraid I have Hannah here, she's being detained on possible assault charges.'

Dorothy put a hand out to steady herself and touched the chilled arm of Erin Underwood through the body bag, so thin it felt like a twig ready to snap.

She paced around the reception of St Leonard's Police Station feeling Jim's bone in her cardigan pocket, pushing her thumb against the point like it was a tattooing tool. She imagined inking her body with elaborate Maori shapes and curls, testaments to ancestors, a link to the dead. But what if your dead didn't deserve their stories told, what if they were disgraceful?

The door to the business part of the station swung open and Thomas held it with a spread palm as Hannah ducked out.

'Thanks,' she said, then spotted Dorothy and came in for a hug.

She smelt of sweat and adrenaline, mingled with her shampoo, apples and something sharper.

'Where's Mum?' she said, stepping back.

Dorothy shook her head. 'She's not answering her phone.'

Thomas stood behind Hannah, waiting to engage.

'What's the story?' Dorothy said to him.

Thomas nodded to Hannah as if to say it was her story to tell.

'I was stupid,' she said, shaking her head.

Dorothy rubbed her arm. 'I guessed that.'

That brought a smile.

'I went to Longhorn's house and waited while the police spoke to him. They didn't arrest him and I kind of flipped. I hit his wife.'

She swallowed and tears came, her shoulders shaking as she wiped at her nose with a tissue.

'I don't know who I am at the moment,' she said between breaths.

Dorothy hugged her again. It was painful seeing her granddaughter like this, it scratched at her heart.

'I've spoken to the Longhorns and squared it away,' Thomas said. 'Hannah's only getting a warning this time, but she needs to stay away from them.'

'Of course,' Dorothy said.

'I'm sorry,' Hannah said.

Dorothy held her. 'It's stress. This is a hard time for everyone.'

She looked at Thomas. 'What did the officers say?'

Thomas shook his head. 'There's just no evidence, the pictures don't count because of how Hannah got them. They have good cause to say Hannah is pestering them, and they say that's what Melanie was doing too.'

'It doesn't seem likely,' Dorothy said.

'I know,' Thomas said. 'But until we have more to go on, that's all we can do.'

Hannah released herself from Dorothy's embrace and straightened her collar, put her tissue away.

Thomas raised his hand and Dorothy saw a piece of typed paper. His look confirmed what it was.

'The results,' she said.

'I was about to call you anyway.'

'And?'

'It's not a match,' Thomas said, handing the paper over. 'There's no DNA connection between Jim and the Lawrence girl.'

Dorothy stared at the paper. Technical phrases, a line graph, some numbers, it might as well be hieroglyphs.

Hannah looked from Dorothy to Thomas. 'What does that mean?'

Thomas deferred to Dorothy. He always let her speak, such a small thing but an important one.

The paper quivered in her hand.

'I don't know,' she said.

32
JENNY

They leaned against the wall, body language like teenagers after a nervous first date. She was reminded of that, being walked home from pubs by boys while still at school, snogging their faces off out of sight of the house. Not that she would've cared what Dorothy and Jim thought back then, grunge nihilist that she was. Stumbling through the door in the early hours, sometimes staggering into the viewing rooms to chat to one of the bodies about the meaning of life, once or twice going through to the workshop and climbing into an empty coffin just to see what it was like. And once, really hammered, climbing onto a tray of the body fridge and sliding herself in.

She was drunk enough now, energised by the booze and the familiarity of easy conversation with her ex-husband. It was painful being reminded of the best friend she'd lost when they split. Husbands and lovers come and go, but she and Craig were friends back then, comfortable knowledge built up between them, and he threw that away. She tried to remind herself of that as he stood here smiling. It was his fault. But she found herself softening as they shared a joke about a slouching emo kid passing by, then an elderly man in red cords, beige jacket and fedora.

'This is me,' she said, angling her head towards the house over the wall.

'It is,' he said, swaying a little.

She wondered how drunk he was.

Woodpigeons cooed at each other in the pine tree looming over the wall, flapping wings as they flitted from branch to branch, one following the other as they moved in a coy dance.

'Will you get in trouble?' she said.

He frowned. 'From who?'

'Fiona.'

'For what?'

Jenny splayed her hands out. 'For getting drunk with your ex-wife.'

Craig smiled and shook his head. 'She'll understand.'

Jenny raised her eyebrows. 'Must be a change for you, having a nice doormat to get back to.'

He gave her a look as if to say, *come on*. 'That's not fair.'

'Hey, I don't know anything about your current marriage and I want to keep it that way.'

'Fine by me.'

The woodpigeons flew out of the tree and onto the wall above them, one strutting after the other, the female flapping, edging away in small bursts, keeping a short distance between herself and the male bird. Schrödinger appeared at the end of the wall having leapt up from the other side. He hunkered down and began stalking the birds, but they spotted him and fluttered into the top of the tree, making the uppermost branches sway. Schrödinger skulked along the wall then disappeared back into the garden.

'That your cat?'

'Mum's. It's called Schrödinger, Hannah's idea.'

'She's some girl.'

'She is.'

Jenny closed her eyes for a moment longer than a blink, felt her head spin.

'I better go inside,' she said eventually. 'Find out how the dead are doing.'

Craig leaned his weight into the wall. 'Are you really a funeral director now?'

'Someone has to help Mum.'

'You're a good daughter.'

'I don't know about that.'

'And a really good mum.'

Jenny laughed. 'How drunk are you?'

Craig shifted his weight from one foot to the other, that old nervous energy still trilling through his muscles. 'I'm just trying to imagine you as one of the coffin bearers. Have you been working out?'

He reached out and pretended to squeeze her bicep. She thought about coffins, then her dad on the funeral pyre, his flesh melting away and his body fluids evaporating, the meat of him dissolving into ash and dust and blown away. She felt a knot in her belly then suddenly she was crying, covering her face with her hands, ashamed.

'Hey,' Craig said.

He wrapped his arms around her and she pushed into his shoulder, could smell the CK One he still wore after all these years, and the familiar smell of his sweat underneath. The combination made her dizzy as she sobbed and imagined her tears falling on stony ground, being evaporated by sunshine into the clouds to mingle with her dad's atoms, combined forever in the water cycle, keeping plants and animals alive, keeping ocean currents flowing, passing through the bodies of whales and sharks and giant squids.

She lifted her head away from his shoulder, eyes still closed, and felt the stubble of his chin and his lips against hers, and she pressed against him, suddenly years younger, and he kissed her back and she pushed her tongue into his mouth and leaned her body into his and tasted her own tears which had slipped down her cheek and she was twenty years old and had her whole life ahead of her and she was kissing a boy and her dad was still alive and she had nothing to worry about, not a care in the world and everyone she loved would live forever.

After too long, she pulled away and stepped back. She looked at her feet.

'That was a mistake.' She couldn't look straight at him, like he was the sun low in the sky.

'Sure.'

'I should go.'

'Yeah.'

She nodded to herself, still tasting him on her lips, the echoes of his touch on her back, tear stains on her cheeks. She turned and went inside to see how the dead were doing.

33
HANNAH

'Babes, you're crazy,' Indy said.

Hannah rubbed the back of her neck then ran a finger along the reception desk.

'I lost it,' she said. 'He has to know something about Mel but the police don't seem bothered.'

Indy came from behind the desk and hugged her. She felt Indy's body against her own, smelled her perfume and the scent of lilies on the desk. Why do people associate cut flowers with funerals? They die a few days after, just to rub it in, the fact that nothing lasts forever. Memento mori and all that. She saw the catalogue on Indy's desk for memorial jewellery, lockets and pendants holding a pinch of your loved one's ashes round your neck. But what if you lost the necklace? She'd heard of people getting the deceased's ashes tattooed into their skin and she liked that, making them a part of you. And there were also stories of people snorting the dead up with a line of coke, or having them fired into space in a rocket.

She pulled away from Indy's embrace and looked at her tattoos, beautiful Hindu designs up her arms, snaking down and around her hands. She wanted to be a part of that one day, embedded in her lover's skin forever. But nothing was forever except the elemental particles. All that 'made of stardust' stuff was true but meaningless. Better to think of it the other way – that future stars and planets would be made from you. Maybe one day some of her atoms would be part of a meteor that crashed into the home planet of an advanced civilisation, wiping them out. Maybe molecules from her and Indy would be part of a giant black hole, consuming its corner of the galaxy like a greedy baby, swallowing up gas giants and brown dwarves and neutron stars like spoonfuls of mushy peas.

'I'm worried about you,' Indy said.

'There's no need to be.'

'I think it's great you're trying to find Mel, but you have to stay sane in the process. You know you can get obsessive about stuff.'

Hannah frowned, but that was true. She was the intense one in their couple. It was funny how relationships worked, you both start out as the exciting, spontaneous ones, but once the façades begin to drop you fall into more natural behaviour, like particles in a collider experiment, unable to act any way other than how the laws of physics dictate, a blend of your own innate properties and the forces applied to you. So Hannah became the organised and obsessive one, and Indy became the laid-back one, the emotional supporter.

They heard a clatter from the direction of the workshop, something large hitting the floor.

'Archie's gone home, hasn't he?' Hannah said.

Indy nodded. 'And Dorothy's upstairs.'

They shared a look then headed through the back, Hannah pushing the door open. She saw her mum's arse in the air, Jenny bending over and trying to pick up a coffin lid from the ground.

'Mum?' Hannah said.

Jenny righted herself with the lid in front of her like a shield. 'Sorry, I bumped into this a tiny bit.'

Indy went over and touched the edge of the lid where the wood had split.

'This is useless now,' she said.

'It was an accident,' Jenny said.

'What were you doing?' Hannah said.

Jenny looked around for an answer, then down at the lidless coffin on the workbench. She put a hand in and touched the lining as if stroking a cat. 'Nothing, just thinking.'

'And mucking about with the coffins,' Indy said, taking the lid and resting it against the wall.

Jenny went wide-eyed with sarcasm. 'Sorry.'

'Are you drunk?' Hannah said, stepping closer.

Jenny rubbed at her forehead. 'I've had a couple.'

'Is that why you didn't answer your phone?'

'What do you mean?'

Jenny fumbled her phone out of her pocket, took a second to key in the passcode, then raised her eyebrows. 'Sorry.'

'Hannah was arrested,' Indy said with a smile.

'What?'

'I wasn't,' Hannah said. 'I was detained then given a warning, it's not the same thing.'

'She hit Peter Longhorn's wife in the face.'

Hannah gave Indy a stare. 'It wasn't like that.'

Jenny shook her head as if trying to dislodge something. 'What am I missing?'

Hannah sighed. 'It doesn't matter, we'll catch you up when you're sober. Who were you drinking with?'

Jenny pulled at her earlobe. 'The Hook woman. She doesn't believe her husband is an artist. She thinks he's up to something and wants to keep paying us to follow him.'

Indy went to the back door, which Jenny had left open, and locked it. 'People are weird.'

Jenny lifted a finger. 'That is so true.' She turned to Hannah. 'I'm sorry I didn't get your calls.'

Hannah rubbed her hands together. She wondered how Emilia Longhorn's face felt.

'Probably just as well, in this state.'

Jenny pushed herself away from the workbench and the coffin. 'I'm not in any state.'

'OK, whatever,' Hannah said. 'You know, maybe Gran was right about you, Mum.'

Jenny looked confused. 'What about me?'

'You always need to be fucking yourself up.'

'I'm not fucking myself up.'

'Han,' Indy said.

Jenny took an unsteady step forwards, waving a hand. 'No, let's hear it. Let's hear what the prodigal daughter has to say about her drunken mum.'

Hannah shook her head. 'Forget it.'

'What?'

'I said forget it,' Hannah said. 'There's no point talking to you like this.'

Jenny moved her head and hands, exaggerated movements. 'I'll have you know I was just talking to your dad about you.'

Hannah stopped at that. 'And?'

Jenny placed a finger to her lips and made a shushing sound.

Hannah sighed.

'I'll put the kettle on,' Indy said.

'Hannah.'

This was Dorothy standing in the workshop doorway. She had her phone in her hand and a look on her face that wasn't good.

'What?' Hannah said.

Dorothy nodded at the phone. 'It's Thomas, the police have found Melanie. I mean they've found her body. I'm so sorry.'

34
Hannah

The sun was bright and she hadn't slept. The fact people were walking up and down Middle Meadow Walk as if nothing was wrong was an insult. How can everyone go about their business when the world has stopped? Hannah pinched the bridge of her nose and swallowed hard. She felt Indy rubbing her arm.

'Babes,' Indy said, voice full of hurt.

Hannah could smell the coffee on the table in front of them, and the almond pastries, and she caught a sniff of last night's pizza and stale lager from the bin down the road from Söderberg.

'I can't get over it,' she said.

'I know.'

'I thought she would turn up, I thought this was all a game, like she was playing hide-and-seek or something. I never thought...'

They'd been round and round it between them into the early hours lying in bed together. But they had nothing, which was why they were here. Thomas had agreed to meet them for breakfast and fill them in on the case. Hannah had passed over Mel's parents' number, and she was selfishly relieved she didn't have to make that call. She didn't know how Indy or Gran ever got used to it with the funeral work, speaking to people in that moment of grief and shock. Dealing with death every day had to take its toll on your psyche, all that distress and emptiness and loss.

She saw Dorothy and Jenny walking from the park, sunglasses on, then she spotted Thomas appearing from between the uni buildings on George Square. She stood up and walked across the path without checking for cyclists.

'Well?'

Thomas waved her back towards the café table. 'I'm sorry.'

'Never mind that,' Hannah said. She was aware of Dorothy and Jenny arriving, Indy watching her with a cup in her hand. 'I need to know details.'

'Please sit,' Thomas said, then indicated the other two. 'All of you.'

They ordered tea and more things to eat, although Hannah wanted to slap the pastries off the table in disgust. The stench of them made her sick.

'Where was she found?'

'Hannah.' This was Jenny, hungover.

'I need to know,' she said, turning on her mum.

'I promised Dorothy I would tell you all I know and I will,' Thomas said. 'Melanie's body was found at seven-forty p.m. last night in the thick undergrowth at Craigmillar Park Golf Course.'

Hannah sat up. 'That's next to the James Clerk Maxwell Building.'

Thomas nodded.

'So it was probably Peter,' Hannah said.

'Hang on,' Jenny said. 'What about Bradley?'

'And Xander,' Indy said.

Hannah frowned. 'How was she killed?'

'Initial signs suggest strangulation,' Thomas said.

'Any sign of sexual assault?' Hannah said.

Jenny touched her head. 'Hannah.'

'What?'

Thomas shook his head. 'No evidence of rape.'

'So what now?' Dorothy said, voice calm.

Thomas waved a hand around the table. 'We formally interview the people you've already spoken to.'

'What about forensics?' Hannah said.

'There's a team on the scene collecting evidence. Once they're finished there, they'll need to go through Melanie's room in your flat. We'll ask all our suspects for swabs, look for a match. Not just for crime-scene evidence, there's something else.'

Hannah felt a thrum in her fingers as if the Earth was trying to send her a message.

Thomas looked around the table then lowered his eyes.

'Melanie was pregnant.'

Hannah was turning the key in the lock when her phone rang. She bundled through the door, Indy following behind, and looked at the screen. Vic, shit. She stared at it for a long time then pressed answer as Indy disappeared into the kitchen.

'Have you heard?' Vic said. His voice was on the edge.

'I'm so sorry, Vic.'

'I can't believe it.'

'I know.'

A long gap. 'She had a baby.' Vic was crying now. 'Mum and Dad, my God, I don't know how they'll cope.'

'I'm so sorry.' Hannah could only think to keep saying the same thing over and over until the end of time.

'I need to find who did this,' Vic said. 'Do you understand me?'

'Yes.'

'Do the police know anything?'

'They're following leads.'

'What does that mean?'

Hannah looked at the door to Mel's room. She ran her finger along the wood. 'We spoke to some people and passed our information on.'

'Tell me.'

'You can't just bully them,' Hannah said. She thought about the slap she gave Peter's wife. 'You need to let the police handle it.'

'Is that what you did when you were investigating?'

'It's different.' For the life of her, she couldn't think how it was different.

Vic sighed, composing himself. 'What about the second phone, did you find it?'

Hannah pushed open Mel's bedroom door, the same layout of furniture, all her things still sitting where she left them. 'No, I never did.'

'That's the key,' Vic said.

'I don't know.'

Vic was in tears again, his voice a ragged mess.

'Just find out,' he said, sobbing. 'Please find out who killed my sister.'

Hannah stared at Mel's bed, her desk and wardrobe.

'I will,' she said.

She hung up and stood in Mel's doorway. Then she heard something coming from the kitchen. Crying.

She went through and Indy was standing at the sink with the kettle in her hand and the tap running, her shoulders shaking. She wiped at her cheeks with the back of her other hand and breathed deeply.

'Indy.'

She turned.

Hannah was in such a mess about this, she hadn't stopped to think about Indy. Her parents already dead, now another death up close. Maybe it was because Indy now worked at Skelf's, Hannah always subconsciously assumed she could handle anything. But the death and grief of strangers is so different to your own, that's what Dorothy always told her.

Hannah remembered the first time she laid eyes on Indy, a month after her parents' funeral. She'd been answering the phones at Skelf's when Hannah popped by to see Gran and Grandpa. It wasn't exactly a thunderbolt of attraction, but she was so easy to talk to, God, that big smile, those dark eyes. She radiated something, a kind of self-respect and self-worth, which was easy to fall in love with. Which is precisely what Hannah did.

That smile and confidence made it all the harder to see her like this.

Hannah went over and took the kettle from Indy's hand, placed it on the draining board and switched the tap off. She wrapped her arms around her and held on tight.

'I'm sorry,' she said.

She felt Indy swallow. 'You don't have anything to be sorry for.'

'Yes, I do,' Hannah said. 'I take you for granted all the time.'

Indy pulled back and nodded.

'You do,' she laughed. 'But it's nice having someone who relies on you.'

'Christ, do I rely on you.'

Indy sniffed and wiped her eyes, caught sight of the time. 'Shit, I'd better get to work.'

'Dorothy won't mind,' Hannah said.

'No,' Indy said with a smile. 'She needs me.'

'I need you.'

'It's nice to be needed, eh?'

Indy kissed her and pushed away. She gathered her stuff together as Hannah watched, then left the flat.

Hannah looked out of the window for a time then went along the hall to Mel's room. She stood there for a long time.

When she finally stepped over the threshold it felt disrespectful. Why should it feel different now that Mel was dead? The same room, the same view out of the window, the same pictures pinned to the noticeboard, the same neat bed with the plain bedspread, the same teddy bear Mel insisted on having in bed with her. Hannah had never seen Mel cuddle it or interact with it in any way. But maybe that wasn't the point, maybe it was just good to know there was something familiar in your life you could rely on.

Hannah didn't feel she could rely on anything at the moment. Indy had gone back to work, sitting at that desk dealing with death notices and flower arrangements and music for services and all the mundane pain and trauma. And then there was this, one of your friends dead, just like Grandpa. How many more people in her life would die? But that was selfish, making it about her. She tried to imagine Yu and Bolin, how they felt, but she couldn't get her head around it.

She couldn't catch her breath, anxiety creeping up from her stomach, freezing her heart and lungs, closing her throat, making it impossible to swallow. She put a hand against the door jamb and sucked in air, felt her legs weaken, leaned against the wall, blinked to get rid of the spots drifting across her vision.

The second phone was key, that's what Vic said. She had no idea if that was true but it was an anchor to stop her being cast adrift. She walked to Mel's bed, threw the teddy on the floor then the bedding, stripping the sheet from the mattress and the pillow cases too, shaking everything down, throwing it all into a pile in the middle of the room like a crumpled carcass. She threw the pillows down too, then flipped the mattress onto the floor, checking underneath the slats on the frame. She pulled the bedframe away from the wall, stuffing her hand into the dusty gap. She came out with tissues, a bookmark, a postcard from her parents in Venice that must've slipped down there. The bed had a low base and she heaved it onto its side, found some old running shoes under there, an empty suitcase, some boxes of first-year physics and maths notes. She flipped through the pages, hoping to find something, but it was all just handwritten equations and diagrams, study schedules, boring stuff.

She went to the desk, pulled out the drawers and dumped them on the floor, sifted her hands through the stationery, not even thinking what she might find, just hoping the universe would guide her fingers, though she knew that was ridiculous. She was frantic, throwing junk behind her, getting her fingers into the corners of the drawers, tipping them over to check underneath because she'd seen a TV show once where someone had a secret key taped under their desk drawer. But there was nothing, just a crude drawing of a cock and balls that some moron must've done years ago.

She went to the wardrobe, flicked through dresses and blouses, taking each off the hanger and frisking it down like an airport security guard, throwing it onto the pile in the middle of the room. Skirts and trousers next, then shoes, checking nothing was hidden inside. She imagined using the Force like in *Star Wars*, closing her eyes and having a crucial clue drift across the room from a secret hiding place and into her hand. She closed her eyes for a moment and put her arms out, then felt immensely stupid when she opened them and looked at her empty hands.

She looked around the chaos of the room. Just the chest of drawers left. She pulled all three drawers out and threw them on the floor. Tights and bras, T-shirts and pyjamas, hoodies, leggings and jumpers, nothing unusual or out of place. All of it dumped behind her in the mound with bedding and other clothes, trainers and heels, everything Mel owned in a pile of pointless nothing. Hannah sat on the edge of the pile and imagined turning it into a funeral pyre, placing a lit match against the flimsiest blouse, lighting up all of Mel's life and burning down the flat in the process.

She stared around her for a long time, thinking. Then she spotted something, a small piece of paper poking from underneath the empty suitcase that had been under the bed. She closed her eyes, breathed, opened them and reached for the paper. She unfolded it carefully. It was a receipt for a pay-as-you-go phone, purchased from Carphone Warehouse on Princes Street two months ago.

Hannah looked at the paper then around at the mess.

The Force is strong in this one, she thought.

35
DOROTHY

Jim always told her that sun-drenched funerals didn't feel right, especially in Scotland, but any chance to have warmth on her skin was bliss for Dorothy. Craigmillar Castle Park Cemetery was the newest in the city, a languorous spread of gentle slopes hiding between the Inch Park football pitches and the fourteenth-century castle at the top of the hill. It was neatly mown with some fenced-off tree nurseries, the sapling beech trees already bent over from the wind that ripped over the hill most days.

Today was breezy and warm, bees sniffing at the flowers on the graves, a pair of rabbits with their tails bobbing in the long grass of the adjacent field. At the bottom of the slope was the area set aside for children's graves, including those who were stillborn or died soon after birth. Dorothy had done a few of those funerals, heartbreaking for everyone, and she never felt she managed to help the bereaved parents. One grave down there had a scan photo pinned to the gravestone next to a cuddly duck that the kid never got to cuddle.

But they were up the hill today, halfway along a new row of plots, for Ursula Bonetti's send off. Her brother arranged the funeral, and by his account she was a terrific lady, full of vitality, from the deli she ran in the West End to the amateur opera and musical theatre, a long line of lovers into her elderly years, but never settled down. So what? Dorothy had the opposite life and where had it got her?

The open grave was surrounded by more than a hundred people, mostly Italian Scots but others too, and many of the women wore brightly coloured dresses. Ursula had requested it, refusing to make this a downbeat affair, and she left money for a huge party later at The Balmoral, pricey at the best of times. She'd lived with cancer without treatment for just two months before giving up in her sleep. It was a brave way to live and die, and Dorothy had a pang of envy.

Archie organised the Bonetti brother and the rest of the pall-bearers. He was keeping an eye on Dorothy after the incident at Seafield, but she was fine. She felt a kind of detachment, this wasn't her grief, it was Gianluca Bonetti's and the rest of Ursula's family and friends.

The priest intoned over the hole in the ground, the ornate white coffin sitting alongside on the carpet of fake grass the council provided. People rarely did open burials with everyone invited these days, but Dorothy liked it. It was more real, the smell of the earth, the gulls flapping overhead, gusts of wind making a couple of older ladies hold on to their hats. People had been honouring their dead this way for thousands of years, and that thread connected all of humanity.

Dorothy was the driver today so she let Archie orchestrate the service. Not that anything really needed taking care of, if they did their preparation a funeral almost ran itself on the day. She turned her face towards the sun, thin wisps of cotton clouds straggling across the sky.

She thought about Melanie. She wondered if the Chengs would bring the funeral to her. She would be honoured to handle it even though it would be difficult. Dorothy thought about the secrets Melanie's body might hold for forensics and the pathologist at the Cowgate mortuary. If she would give anything up or if she would be buried with those secrets. Because sometimes we don't get answers, sometimes we never see the connections that lie under the surface. She looked at Ursula's coffin surrounded by people. What secrets did Ursula die with? Everyone has an interior life that's winked out when they die, where does that knowledge go?

What secrets went up in smoke with Jim's body? She thought about DNA, just molecules bound together, yet they hold so much information, so much that connects us. Or doesn't, in the case of Jim, Rebecca and Natalie. But just because Natalie wasn't related to Jim, didn't mean Jim and Rebecca weren't lovers.

And she thought about Jacob Glassman alone in his big house, if there were secrets hidden in the camera footage, if he would ever have an answer.

The priest stopped talking and Ursula was lowered into the ground. Gianluca Bonetti threw a handful of damp dirt onto the white wood, followed by others, each standing for a moment then moving on. Archie watched them reverently, hands together in front of him. He had secrets, secrets that weren't buried forever or burned. More earth went on top of Ursula's body as Archie looked at Dorothy then turned back to the grave.

Staring at the grave, something occurred to Dorothy and the obvious nature of it made her cheeks flush. She'd always assumed Simon Lawrence walked away from his family responsibilities. But what if he didn't have a choice, what if someone got rid of him? It was hard to get rid of a person, to get rid of their body. Unless.

She stared at Archie by the open grave for a long time, then realised what she had to do next.

36

JENNY

The hangover was lifting but the sense of shame lingered. Jenny had spent the last hour wandering around the funeral home like a ghost. Hannah had gone home, and Mum and Archie were on a funeral, there was just Indy on reception as Jenny pitched up there like a shipwreck victim on shore.

'How are you holding up?' Jenny said.

Indy smiled. 'I could ask you the same thing.'

Jenny nodded. 'Mine is self-inflicted. No sympathy.'

The silence was awkward before Jenny spoke again. 'I still can't really believe it, about Mel.'

Indy swallowed hard, then her head went down and she started crying.

'Oh, hey,' Jenny said. She went round behind the desk and put her hand on Indy's arm. Indy stood up and moved into a hug, wrapping her arms around her and holding tight. Jenny rubbed at her back, feeling the shudders of Indy's breath against her chest.

'It's OK,' she said. She knew it wasn't OK, but what else could you say? She had a flash of memory, holding Hannah as a toddler with a scraped knee, inconsolable at the pain and indignant at the way the world had conspired to hurt her. Then again, years later, when she had to break the news that Craig was leaving them, that mix of hurt and anger, so easy to understand.

'Shhh,' Jenny said. She thought about Indy's life, so hard compared to her own, her parents already dead, an orphan and barely even an adult. And yet she was always the more mature one in her relationship with Hannah, always the sensible one, the strong one.

'I'm sorry,' Indy said.

'Don't be silly.'

Indy pulled away and took a huge breath, wiped at her face. 'I don't know what's wrong with me.'

'You have every right to be upset,' Jenny said.

Mel was Indy's friend as much as Hannah's. Hannah's obsession had railroaded everyone else out of the way, but the quiet ones like Indy still grieved, they just didn't kick up a stink about it.

'It's just,' Indy said, sniffing, 'this is bringing up a lot of stuff. About my mum and dad.'

'Of course it is.' Jenny tried to keep her voice calm. 'You must miss them.'

Indy nodded. 'More than I ever say to Han. It's difficult.'

'I know.'

Jenny wondered how Indy saw her. Indy and Hannah weren't married, but Jenny was more or less a mother-in-law. She hoped she didn't come with the baggage that title suggested.

'You can talk to me anytime,' she said. 'About anything.'

'I just get so angry sometimes,' Indy said, touching the back of the chair. 'That they left me alone. But that's selfish.'

'It's totally understandable.' Jenny thought for a moment. 'Did you ever speak to anyone about them? I mean counselling or something?'

Indy shook her head. 'Everyone thinks I'm so strong. No one suggested it.'

'Everyone needs someone to talk to,' Jenny said, wondering who *she* had to talk to. She was the same when Craig left, OK that wasn't a bereavement, but she felt a whirlwind of fury and emotion, and never spoke to anyone about it. Who could she have gone to?

The phone rang, and Indy fanned at her face and breathed again.

'Are you sure you're OK?' Jenny said.

Indy nodded and took the call.

Jenny watched for a few moments, listening to Indy's calm reassurances to someone else going through trauma, it was amazing she was strong enough to do that. Hannah was lucky.

Jenny wandered to the embalming room. She stood staring at the instruments on the tray next to the empty body table. She ran a hand along the metal. This was the coldest place in the house, the air conditioning running high to reduce decomposition, and the blast of cool air seemed to sooth her hangover. She couldn't handle drinking during the day, not at her age. Christ, while poor Mel was lying in a bush somewhere and Hannah was getting bailed out of the station, she was kissing her ex-husband against the wall like a fucking teenager. She was mortified. But, if she was being honest, also a little thrilled about that.

It came down to the basic human desire to be wanted. She knew she had some power over Craig, she could still turn him on. She was still an attractive woman. She'd got used to being invisible to younger men, as if they saw right through her, as if she was a ghost. That was partly liberating, no longer getting hassle or abuse, not having to put on a show. But at the same time there was a niggle at the back of her mind. She didn't want to be done with all that, because that meant giving up on love, which meant giving up on life.

She walked over to the fridges and looked at the names written there. Each one a life lived, larger or smaller, better or worse, none of it mattered now. Ashes to ashes, and all that. She thought about her own funeral, how she might be summed up. Who would even be there? She was a ghost already. God, no one ever warns you about the existential angst that comes with hangovers in your forties.

She thought about Mel, down on the slab at the city mortuary. Her devastated parents and brother. She thought about how she would feel if it was Hannah, and felt tears come to her eyes almost immediately. She swallowed hard and rested her head against one of the fridge doors. The cool metal against her forehead was calming, and she was aware of the weight of her own eyelids. Her body sagged, gravity pulling her down into the earth, where she would be one day, sooner or later.

She had to get out of this fucking funeral home.

She had an idea, and walked through the workshop to the garage, picking up the key for the body van on the way, then got in and started driving. It was fifteen minutes to Inverleith, but she got snarled in the usual traffic on Lothian Road and Charlotte Square.

She parked in East Fettes Avenue outside Peter Longhorn's house. She knew the number from the whiteboard back home. She sat for ten minutes wondering why she came here, what she should do. She had to feel useful, had to do something, but Thomas had made it clear the police were handling the investigation now, since they found Mel.

She was about to go and ring the doorbell and wing it when a taxi pulled up next to her and Peter got out, handing over money. He went straight up the path to the house. The taxi drove away as he put his key in the door, but it didn't open. He looked confused for a second, tried again, then removed it and took a step back, looked the house up and down as if it had insulted him. He rang the bell and knocked too. Waited. Tried them both again. Stepped back again.

'Emilia,' he shouted.

No response.

'Emilia.'

Doorbell again, this time constant, *ding-dong, ding-dong, ding-dong*.

His phone went in his pocket and he got angry at the name on the screen. Answered it and looked at the upstairs windows. It was obviously his wife, it was clear what was happening.

His body language was furious as he spoke, the wronged man. His voice was soft as he pointed and gestured, shaking his head, explaining his story. But it was clear he was getting nowhere.

After a few minutes, an upstairs window opened, and Emilia

heaved a holdall out, which thumped on the ground by Peter's feet.

'Emilia, this is crazy,' he said, waving his phone at her.

'Don't ever speak to me again,' Emilia said. 'Except through my solicitor.'

Her voice was calm, stony, her arms folded.

'Just let me in and we can talk,' Peter said. 'It's all a misunderstanding, the police let me go.'

'I don't care about the police,' Emilia said. 'I have to protect our daughter.'

She closed the window and stepped out of sight.

'Em,' Peter shouted. 'Fuck's sake, Em.'

He tried calling her, no answer. He went back and banged the front door some more, but ran out of steam.

Jenny got out of the van and walked to the front gate, up the path.

'How did it go at the police station?'

Peter turned and frowned. 'Who the hell are you?'

'Jenny Skelf.'

He stared at her while he put it together. 'Hannah's mum? What do you want?'

'I'm investigating Melanie Cheng's death.'

He looked confused by that, but let it slide. 'Your bitch of a daughter got me into this mess.'

'You got yourself into it.'

He squared up to her. He was tall but not heavy-set, but any guy could be threatening given enough anger.

'I haven't done anything wrong,' Peter said.

'You were sleeping with Mel. You got her pregnant. She was going to tell your wife so you strangled her.'

'How fucking dare you,' Peter said, gripping his phone like a weapon. 'The police let me go.'

Jenny nodded at the holdall on the ground between them. 'I think your wife needs a little more convincing.'

Peter pressed his lips together. 'I am going to sue your daughter once this is all over. She broke into my office.'

'And found valuable evidence.'

'And I'm going to sue the university too.'

'Why?'

Peter frowned, looked back at the house. 'Those bastards have suspended me without pay.'

'So you admitted seeing Mel?'

Peter took a step forwards. 'I told the police the truth. We had a thing, yes, but I didn't know she was pregnant, and I certainly didn't kill her.'

'What kind of thing?'

Peter didn't speak.

'I can see why you would go for her,' Jenny said. 'But, no offence, what did she see in you?'

Peter chewed on his lip. 'She said she liked older men. I didn't ask too many questions.'

He stared at the holdall and all the life seemed to go out of him. He looked at the house, no sign of Emilia, then he looked at the phone in his hand.

'I'm going to destroy your family, like you've destroyed mine,' he said eventually, but it sounded weak, a comeback delivered too late.

Jenny almost felt sorry for him in that moment, but then she remembered Mel's body down at the city mortuary.

'You'll get what you deserve,' she said.

He shook his head, picked up the holdall and shouldered it. Took a last look at the house then pushed past Jenny and down the street.

As she watched him go, her phone rang. She pulled it out. Orla.

'He just called me,' Orla said. She sounded hyped. 'Says he has to do a training thing, he'll be home really late. I think this is something.'

Jenny was still pumped with adrenaline.

'I told you,' she said. 'I don't think—'

'And I told you I don't believe he's fucking Picasso or whatever. Just find out what the hell my husband is up to.'

Jenny hung up. She had a flash of memory, looking at a coffin last night, thinking about climbing in. Standing in the low sunshine with Craig, the smell of him and the fuzz of booze taking her back twenty-five years. Feeling alive again, something that didn't happen often. And she thought about Liam throwing paint onto a canvas, making something out of nothing, and wondered if that's how he felt when he did it, if he felt alive.

She drove the van through rush hour, took ages to get across to Leith, managed to find a parking space on Constitution Street and walked along Bernard Street. She checked The King's Wark first, no sign, then doubled back. The streets were full of office workers walking home, another day nearer the grave for every one of them. But they were smiling in the sunshine, wearing shades like it was Paris or Milan, the terror of a Scottish winter banished from their minds.

She walked up Maritime Street and into the vennel, didn't stop, just pushed at the door to the studios. Security for this place was woeful. She crept to Liam's studio and stood outside breathing. The door had been patched together at the lock where she'd booted it in. She cocked her head and listened. A shuffle of feet inside, then a few moments later she heard him clear his throat.

She retreated to the café on the street, got a black coffee, poured in three sugars and waited. She thought about Melanie. Was it Longhorn? Or this Bradley tutor guy, or the boyfriend? Dick pics, naked pictures and God knows what else. So she had a boyfriend and was seeing her lecturer, if either of them found out about the other that might mean something. The tutor was less likely, but maybe he was jealous of others getting a piece of her.

An hour later Liam came out of the vennel and walked along the road. Déjà vu. Jenny gulped down her third coffee and followed at a distance, her trainers scuffing the gutter. She followed him to The King's Wark. This time she walked round to the other entrance on The Shore and went in. And there he was at the bar, smiling, chatting to the same barmaid, sipping his pint, looking at the crossword. Maybe Jenny would follow him forever, paid by Orla, end up having a symbiotic relationship with them, going wherever Liam went, taking money from Orla, reliant on their affluence and secrets for her livelihood.

A woman from a corner table got up and went to the bar next to Liam. She was dressed in a short skirt and skimpy top, like she was out on the pull along Lothian Road on a Friday night. Nobody went out on the pull in The King's Wark on a Wednesday. Maybe she was meeting friends and heading to town later, but still. She was tall and slim, black hair in silky waves, a perfect arse in that black skirt, damn it, tanned legs that ended on big heels as she placed her tiny handbag on the bar and ordered from the cocktail menu.

She turned and smiled at Liam, and he smiled back. Jenny shrank into her dark corner and widened her eyes. The bombshell started a conversation and Liam joined in, Christ, what man in the world wouldn't. She was mid-twenties, not a baby but far too young for him. The body language said they didn't know each other, but Jenny was no expert and maybe that was part of what was going on.

The woman touched her hair then tucked it behind her ear, and Liam straightened his posture in response, paying attention. She wore a lot of lip gloss, eyelash extensions fluttering. Jenny couldn't work out whether she was genuinely interested in him or just liked attention.

Liam leaned forwards when the woman's mojito arrived and offered to pay for it. She accepted. That meant a longer conversation, and the barmaid poured Liam another pint with raised eyebrows that Jenny understood. The woman was making a play for him. It wasn't completely unbelievable, Liam was handsome and well put together, but he was at least ten years older than her, and hadn't been on the lookout, was just sitting nursing his lager. This never happened, except it was happening in front of Jenny's eyes.

Jenny got her phone out and pretended to check social media as she zoomed in and took a few pictures of them chatting. The woman sat on the barstool next to him and faced him. The way her skirt rode up her thighs when she leaned towards him drew the eye.

She was mirroring his body movements, touching her ear, lifting her drink, chin resting on the heel of her hand. This was what pick-up artists did, why was she pulling this stuff on a guy in a Leith pub?

They kept talking, drinking, mirroring, occasionally a laugh, but something was off. Liam wasn't responding the way she wanted, she had to reignite the conversation while he glanced down at his crossword. The barmaid went to serve someone and Liam's attention was grabbed for a moment before the dolly brought him back to her with a swish of hair and a waft of perfume. He responded, but his smile was more polite than predatory.

She finished her mojito with a flourish and put the empty glass down like a challenge. He finished his pint, smiled warmly and stood up to leave. She put a hand on his arm and he stood and listened while she leaned forwards and talked in his ear, then he calmly replied, removed her hand from his arm and walked away, out of the pub and into the evening sunshine.

The woman had a face like fizz as she waved her empty mojito glass at the barmaid, who went to make another.

Jenny went to the bar, sat in the seat Liam had just been in. She made a show of checking the woman up and down, and she eventually turned.

'Can I help you?' she said. Soft English accent, home counties.

'What was that about?' Jenny said.

'What?'

'With that guy.'

'What guy?'

Jenny bit her lip. 'The guy you were just trying to pull.'

The woman frowned as the barmaid brought the fresh drink.

'I'll get that,' Jenny said, handing over her bankcard to the barmaid. 'And a double gin and tonic.'

That got the woman's attention.

'What's it to you?' the woman said.

Jenny stuck out her hand. 'I'm Jenny.'

The woman stared at her, then at the mojito, then at the barmaid who was fixing the gin and handing the card reader over.

'Darcy,' she said eventually.

'Nice to meet you.'

Darcy took a sip of her cocktail and smacked her lips. 'You never answered my question. And why were you watching us?'

Jenny wondered how much to say. 'I'm interested in him.'

Darcy scoffed. 'Good luck.'

'Not like that.'

'Me neither.'

'Then why were you all over him?'

The woman shook her head. 'I wasn't.'

'Come on,' Jenny said, sipping her drink.

Darcy stroked at her skirt and Jenny mirrored her. Darcy looked at the gesture and shook her head.

'I know all about that,' she said, putting her hand on Jenny's hand and leaning in. Her perfume was sharp and classy, her make-up perfect smoky tones that matched her eyes and hair. 'So unless you really want to get it on with me, cut it out.'

She leaned back and picked up her drink. Sipped from the glass.

Jenny watched for a moment, putting it together.

'You're an escort,' she said.

The woman raised her eyebrows in a conspiracy. 'No I'm not, that's outrageous.' Her deadpan tone didn't match her words.

'You were trying to pick him up for work?'

'No.'

'But why here? You won't get any work around here.'

'You've got me all wrong, lady.'

Jenny drank her gin and opened her bag, got out her purse. 'I don't think so.' She made a show of peeling off three twenty-pound notes and placing them on the bar.

Darcy waited a moment and looked at the money. Then shook her head.

'I want to know what this is about,' Jenny said.

'Me too,' Darcy said.

'How do you mean?'

Darcy raised her eyebrows at the money and Jenny added another two twenties. Darcy picked the money up, rolled it and tucked it into her bra.

'I was given this job.' She went into her handbag and brought out a card. It said 'Superior Edinburgh Escorts', her name underneath, a mobile number and email.

'What do you mean?'

'He was described to me over the phone,' Darcy said. 'I was told where and when I would find him.'

'And you were supposed to sleep with him?'

Darcy shrugged.

'Who gave you the job?'

'I didn't get a name.'

Jenny finished her drink. 'How were you going to get paid?'

'I got the deposit already, gave my account details over the phone. The rest was after I did the job.'

'What did the person sound like on the phone?'

'Angry,' Darcy said, finishing her own drink and taking her business card back from Jenny. 'And Irish.'

37
HANNAH

Carphone Warehouse was a scruffy blue place sandwiched between shinier Three and EE shops. Why did phone places always herd together? Across the road the castle loomed over Princes Street Gardens, tourists stopping on the pavement to take pictures as Hannah strode inside and pulled the receipt from her pocket. Mel obviously didn't have the phone on her when she was found, so where was it? Probably smashed and in a skip somewhere. The receipt said Mel, or whoever bought it, was served by Kyle.

She approached the counter and asked for him. The guy behind the counter was short and stocky, Eastern European accent, a spread of gothic tattoos up his arms and poking out from the neck of his T-shirt. He nodded at one of the other employees dealing with a middle-aged woman.

'Kyle is busy, can I help?'

'I need to speak to Kyle.'

The guy shrugged. 'Then you wait.'

Hannah hung around nearby. Kyle was about the same age as her, soul patch tuft of beard on his chin, pallid skin and bags under his eyes.

He seemed to take an age with the woman, who was all handsy with him, touching his arm and laughing at something he said. Get on with it, for God's sake, buy the phone or get lost. Eventually the woman chose something then they went to the desk. It then took another age to get a box from the back, then go over the contract, then persuade her to sign for insurance and buy a pink diamante case.

Finally, with much waving and smiling, she was gone and the Polish guy nodded Kyle towards Hannah.

'Can I help you, Madam?'

Madam. They were the same age. Hannah showed him the receipt.

'Do you remember selling this phone to my friend Melanie?'

Kyle frowned at her then the receipt. 'We sell a lot of phones in here, miss.'

Now it was 'miss'.

'Please take a look at it.'

Kyle peered at the piece of paper. 'This was almost two months ago.'

'Well?'

He laughed. 'I don't remember.'

Hannah got her phone out, flicked through the camera roll, thumbed up one of Indy and Mel dressed up for something, she couldn't even remember what now. She showed it to Kyle.

'The Scots-Chinese girl. She had a light Dundee accent.'

Kyle looked at the screen then at Hannah. '"Had"?'

'What?'

'You said "had" not "has".'

Hannah felt a weight on her shoulders.

Kyle narrowed his eyes. 'What's this about?'

Hannah looked around the shop, glossy adverts selling hi-tech shit that would be obsolete in a year or two. 'She's dead.'

'Shit,' Kyle said. 'Sorry.'

'She was strangled.'

'Jesus.' Kyle looked at the Polish guy for help, but he kept his head behind a computer screen.

'I need to find out what happened,' Hannah said.

Kyle looked at the receipt again. 'And you think this phone has something to do with it?'

'It wasn't her main phone,' Hannah said. 'She was using it for something else.'

'A burner.'

'What?'

'It's what drug dealers call it,' Kyle said, looking uncomfortable. 'Like on *Breaking Bad*. A pay-as-you-go phone you change or ditch regularly to avoid getting traced.'

'That's not what Mel was doing.'

Kyle's eyes widened. 'I didn't mean that.'

'She was my friend and she's dead.'

Kyle shuffled his feet. 'Let me see her picture again?'

Hannah held out her phone and Kyle examined it, running his fingers along his tiny beard.

'She's pretty,' he said eventually. 'I remember her.'

'Really?'

'Sure. She wasn't dressed like this.' His finger smudged the screen on Mel's tight red dress.

'Of course not,' Hannah said. 'Was she alone?'

Kyle sighed. 'It was a long time ago.'

'With a guy?'

Kyle screwed up his face. 'I don't know. Maybe.'

Hannah took her phone back and Googled. 'This guy?'

She held up a picture of Peter Longhorn from his Edinburgh Uni page, sensible smile, blue shirt.

Kyle shook his head. 'I couldn't honestly say.'

'What about CCTV?'

Kyle nodded at a camera in a corner of the shop. 'It only gets kept for two weeks then we write over it.'

'Can you check?'

'There's no point.'

Hannah let out a loud sigh. 'What about your database, the sale must be in your system.'

'Sure, but it'll just be the same information as on the receipt.'

'If she was with someone else, maybe they paid.'

Kyle looked around the shop. It was busy, people waiting to get served, to walk away with shiny new handheld dreams. 'OK.'

He went to one of the screens behind the desk and typed in the transaction number from the receipt. He typed some more info, whatever the system needed, then flattened his lips together as he turned the screen to show her. 'It was paid for by Melanie Cheng, was that your friend?'

Hannah nodded as she scanned the screen.

'What about the number, can you give me that?'

Kyle turned the screen back towards himself. 'It's against policy to give out that information.'

Hannah balled her fist around her phone. 'This is a murder investigation.'

'You're not the police.'

Hannah breathed deeply. 'No, but I was her best friend and I'm a private investigator.'

'Really?'

'Really.'

'Do you have a licence or something?'

Hannah shook her head. 'It doesn't work like that.'

'So how do you get to be a private detective?'

'Investigator.' Hannah shrugged. 'You just become one. Now can I have that number?'

Kyle looked around, unsure.

Hannah moved in and lowered her voice. 'The alternative is that I get the police to ask you, would you like that?'

'I don't know.'

Hannah looked at the Polish guy, the other young men working in the shop. 'How many burner phones do you sell here every week? What if the police had a look at your CCTV and cross-referenced it with sales for the last fortnight?'

Kyle stared at the screen for a long time then turned it to show Hannah. She plugged the number into her phone and pressed 'call'. Waited a few seconds then heard a dead tone. She redialled, the same, then a third time. Dead.

Kyle moved the screen back and looked around at the customers. 'I need to get back to work.'

Hannah tried one more time as she left the shop and emerged

into the sunshine, buses rumbling along the street, the chatter of shoppers around her. The dead tone in her ear again. At least now she had a number to give Thomas to trace calls.

She put her phone away and crossed the road, dodging a tram, thinking about who Mel was calling.

38
Dorothy

She stood with the SD cards in her fist as she stared at the view out of the kitchen window. It always amazed her how much green space there was in Edinburgh, and the Braid Hills sprawled south for miles, woodland and gorse, golf courses hidden in there somewhere, the burn down below.

She heard the toilet flush, then a while later Jacob appeared in the doorway.

'Sorry about that, when I have to go, I have to go.' He eased himself onto a kitchen chair.

Dorothy thought about the footage of him going to the toilet over and over again.

'When the body fails,' Jacob said, 'it's a real bastard.'

'You do pretty well.'

'You mean considering I'm ninety-four.'

'You look younger.'

'You're very kind,' Jacob said. 'But I feel much older. Every morning when I wake up, it's with a mixture of relief and disappointment, if I'm honest.'

Dorothy joined him at the kitchen table. 'You don't mean that.'

'I'm serious. I never wanted to end my life, even when I had to leave my parents in Germany, knowing I would probably never see them again. Even when Kristina died.'

Dorothy presumed Kristina was the wife.

'But I do now,' Jacob said. 'I don't have the balls to end it, but I wish I did. And now this.'

He waved his hand around, presumably indicating having hired a private investigator to catch a thief in his home.

Dorothy placed the SD cards on the table, wondered what info they held.

'We haven't found anything so far.'

'You will.'

'I've checked the last two days for when Susan was here. There was nothing unusual.'

'Maybe she suspects,' Jacob said. 'I left some bank notes on the worktop here yesterday during the day, but they were still there when she left.'

Dorothy shook her head. 'That's far too obvious. She probably realises you're trying to trap her.'

'Maybe she twigged that you're not a colleague,' Jacob said. 'That was quick thinking, by the way.'

'Thanks.'

'You would've been a good academic.'

'I don't know about that.'

'You're obviously very bright.'

'But not academic.'

Dorothy got up and went over to the paintings on the wall. Strong slashes of thick paint, primary colours. Ovals and ellipses scattered about the canvas. 'These are great.'

'I miss her every day,' Jacob said. 'She wasn't academic either, but so much brighter than me. She would've known what to do.'

Dorothy looked at the bookshelf. Ran a finger along the top of it. No dust.

'Has the cleaner been recently?'

'This morning.'

'Tell me about her, where did you find her?'

Jacob frowned as he turned. 'It's not Monika.'

Dorothy stared at him. 'You don't know that.'

'We've had women from the same company for years,' Jacob said, hands trembling in his lap. 'Very reliable. Kristina organised it originally, that's how long ago it was. They're Ukrainian, that's why she went to them, she wanted to help others from her homeland.'

'What's the company name?'

'Home Angels. But it's not Monika, I'm telling you.'

Dorothy walked back to the table and stood. 'We have to explore every possibility, that's all. I wouldn't be doing my job otherwise.'

'Fine.'

'Do you know Monika's surname?'

Jacob shook his head.

'I can find out,' Dorothy said. 'When exactly was she here?'

'Ten o'clock this morning.'

'Until?'

'Half past twelve.'

Dorothy scooped up the SD cards. 'But nothing else has gone missing?'

'Not that I've noticed.'

'OK, I'd better go.'

Jacob started the slow process of standing up.

'There's no need to see me out,' Dorothy said, touching his arm.

'I'm not quite dead yet,' he said, shuffling forwards on his walker.

As they went along the hall, Dorothy looked into the living room and spotted something. 'Is that an iPad?'

Jacob stopped. 'Yes.'

'The one that went missing?'

'It turned up in my bedroom.'

She gave him a look.

'I'm not senile,' Jacob said. 'It wasn't there before, I would've noticed. And I never use it upstairs, so I can't have misplaced it up there.'

He was almost on the verge of tears. Dorothy touched his arm again, it was meant to be reassuring, but she didn't get the feeling it was.

'I'll check the footage,' Dorothy said. 'And let you know.'

She left the house and walked away, thinking about families and loyalty, and about being so old that you were disappointed when you woke up every morning.

The kitchen table was covered in paperwork, boxes of files, receipts piled high, invoices spilling over balance sheets. Schrödinger sat on one of the piles licking a paw and making a soft sound in his throat. Outside, long shadows splayed over the links, dappling people heading home or to bars in town, a handful of souls knocking golf balls around the pitch and putt.

Dorothy sipped her whisky and sighed. On the one hand, she was glad the company never went digital, she barely knew how to switch a computer on. On the other hand there was this mess of files going back decades, connected by some Byzantine system only Jim understood. Maybe that was deliberate, she thought, then hated herself for thinking it.

There was a knock on the open door and Archie stood there looking worried.

'Hi,' she said.

'Hey.' He gazed at the chaos in front of her. 'What's this?'

'Join me for a drink,' Dorothy said, lifting her glass.

Archie looked uncomfortable. 'I shouldn't, my medication.'

'Just one,' Dorothy said. 'I need the company.'

Archie hesitated then sat down, as Dorothy got him a glass and poured a couple of fingers of Highland Park.

Archie sipped and sat, staring into his glass, the amber swirl of it.

'So, what are you up to?' he said eventually.

Dorothy waited until he looked up, tried to gauge something from his eyes or the way he spoke. Imagine having the superpower of knowing what someone else was thinking, what a terrifying prospect. And yet don't we all try to feel what it's like to be someone else, otherwise we turn into sociopaths?

'How's everything going,' Dorothy said. 'With the Cotard's, I mean.'

Archie shrugged. 'OK.'

'Anything you want to talk about?'

He shook his head and gripped his glass.

Dorothy put a hand on his arm. 'You would tell me if you were struggling?'

He looked up and held her gaze, like a challenge. 'Yes.'

'I often wonder what it's like.'

'How do you mean?'

'The syndrome. Do you mind talking about it?'

Archie scratched his beard. 'No.'

'Are you sure?'

'Dorothy, you saved me. You can talk about anything you like.'

'I don't want you to be uncomfortable.'

Archie waved that away. 'It's fine.'

Dorothy lifted a piece of paper from the table, an invoice for renovation work done to the embalming room back in 2009. An expansion plus an improved air-conditioning unit after the unusually warm summer.

'I think recently,' she said, 'I've had an idea what it must've been like for you.'

'How do you mean?'

Dorothy ran her thumb along her fingernails. 'I don't mean to sound flippant about your condition, but I've felt pretty dead, since Jim.'

Archie considered his whisky but didn't drink. 'It's not about feeling dead.'

'I know.'

'It's about being dead,' Archie said. 'In your mind. Before I stabilised, it wasn't like I wanted to climb into coffins and act like a corpse, I was really dead, had no connection to the living, couldn't understand how to communicate with them.'

'But none of us communicate with each other,' Dorothy said. 'Not really.'

Archie shook his head. 'I used to hang around in cemeteries because I couldn't think of anything else to do. I thought I had a connection to the dead, something I didn't have with the living.'

Dorothy stroked Schrödinger, who purred in response.

'But that brought you to us,' Dorothy said.

Archie sipped his drink and looked out of the window. 'I can't ever thank you enough, Dorothy. I can't repay you for your kindness when I needed it most.'

Dorothy swallowed more whisky, felt it burn her throat. She put a hand to the paperwork spread over the table. 'What about this?'

He looked at the table. 'What about it?'

Dorothy stared at him. 'I need to find out what happened to Simon Lawrence.'

Archie held his whisky glass like a grenade. 'OK.'

'You know something.'

He stared at his lap. 'I really don't.'

'Look me in the eye and say that, Archie.'

He did as he was told. 'I don't.'

Dorothy pressed her lips together. 'I did a DNA test.'

Archie looked confused. 'On who?'

'To see if Jim was the father of Rebecca Lawrence's daughter. Or maybe her grandfather.'

'Jesus,' Archie said. 'And?'

Dorothy shook her head.

Archie held his hands out. 'Well, then.'

Dorothy nodded at the messy table again. 'I need you to help me.'

'How?'

'I'm checking back through the business around the time Simon disappeared.'

Archie shifted in his seat. 'Why?'

'Why do you think?'

Archie sipped his whisky and touched his ear. 'I have no idea.'

Dorothy leaned forwards, elbows mussing up some of the

papers. Schrödinger flicked his ears upwards, as if something interesting might happen. Outside, young women were laughing in the park.

'Yes, you do,' Dorothy said. 'You're a smart guy, don't play dumb.'

Archie looked out of the window, as if he wanted to be with those laughing voices. There was a smell of barbecue and Dorothy pictured flipping burgers with Jim. Then she pictured him shrivelling to dust on the funeral pyre.

Archie spoke. 'You think Simon Lawrence didn't just walk away from his life.'

'Correct.'

'Maybe Jim had something to do with it.'

'More than that.' Dorothy felt like a big cat stalking her prey through the long grass, eyes never wavering.

'You think Jim might've killed Simon.'

Dorothy motioned to the paperwork in front of her. 'And?'

'And got rid of the body through the business somehow.'

She'd made him say it rather than have the words pass her own lips. Now the idea was out in the open she couldn't decide whether it sounded ridiculous or not. She was accusing her husband of murder. That's why he paid Rebecca Lawrence, out of guilt.

'It's crazy,' Archie said.

'Is it?'

Schrödinger stretched a paw and a notebook slipped to the floor with a thud, making Dorothy jump.

'Christ,' she said, leaning down to pick it up. She imagined a confession note slipping from between the pages, a neat explanation for everything that didn't make sense. But the notebook had no loose pages, just lists of supplies and costs, incomings and outgoings, the stuff of every business.

She focused on Archie, who was finishing his drink.

'If anyone knows how to get rid of a body, it's an undertaker.'

Archie was wide-eyed at that. 'You know that's not true. There are strict rules, traceability, it's not like a horror movie or something.'

Dorothy pursed her lips and picked up a page at random from the table. An invoice from nine years ago for a simple cremation at Warriston. Mari Gibson. Paid within the month, nothing untoward. The smell of the barbecue outside was stronger now and there were more voices, guys full of bluster, women gossiping and laughing, the clink of beer bottles and wine glasses, the energy and carelessness of youth. Dorothy felt the wood of her seat biting into her back, a dull ache that all the yoga in the world couldn't shift now that she was on the way to the grave herself.

She looked at Archie. 'Will you help me?'

Schrödinger leaned into her and she stroked his back, feeling his purr in her fingers. Archie watched her with the cat then spoke.

'OK,' he said. 'But it's a waste of time.'

Dorothy smiled and finished her drink. 'We'll see.'

39
JENNY

She still hadn't worked out what to do by the time she put the key in the lock. Darcy was obviously a honeytrap set by Orla, so what the hell? Hire a private investigator to follow your husband, pay someone to pick him up, providing evidence of adultery to get everything in the divorce? Poor Liam. She thought about kissing Craig yesterday. Craig had cheated on Fiona in that moment, but it was more complex than that, given Jenny's history with him. But that was a bullshit excuse, she snogged a married man, end of story. It didn't matter that he was her ex-husband. In fact it was worse.

She compared Liam to Craig. While Craig was kissing his ex-wife, Liam was painting behind his wife's back because he couldn't share his passion, and she was setting him up for a fall. Jenny wondered whether to tell Liam. Or tell Orla that she knew. Neither option was appealing. Then she thought about kissing Craig again, so stupid. And yet.

She was in the downstairs hall in darkness now. She heard voices upstairs and headed up. Archie and Dorothy were in the kitchen, a nearly empty whisky bottle between them, paperwork scattered over the table and piled on the floor. Schrödinger was moping in a window chair.

'What's this?' she said.

They both looked up. Dorothy took a second to focus.

'Simon Lawrence.'

Jenny stepped towards the table. 'The guy who walked out on his family.'

All these bad husbands and fathers, and Liam in his studio painting skulls and alien plants.

Dorothy pulled a chair out for her to sit. 'That's the thing, I'm not sure he did walk out.'

Jenny sat. 'But he disappeared.'

Dorothy nodded but didn't speak.

'So?' Jenny said.

Dorothy swallowed. She was definitely drunk.

Archie spoke. 'Your mum thinks your dad was involved.'

Jenny felt her brow crease. 'But the DNA came back negative.'

'Not involved with Rebecca,' Archie said. 'Involved in Simon's disappearance.'

He swept an arm at the papers across the table.

Jenny took a minute to put it together then turned to Dorothy. 'No way.'

Dorothy shrugged and swayed a little. She had an edge Jenny hadn't seen before, like she was on the brink of falling apart.

'Maybe,' Dorothy said.

Archie went back to examining the papers in front of him, keeping his head down to avoid getting into this.

'You know what you're implying,' Jenny said.

Dorothy shook her head.

'You just don't want to say it,' Jenny said.

'Please.'

'You think Dad was a murderer.'

Archie froze, and Dorothy stared at Jenny then lowered her head into her hands. She began to weep into her palms, tears dripping onto an accounting ledger in front of her.

'I don't know why you're crying,' Jenny said. 'It's your idea, I just said it out loud.'

Dorothy took heaving breaths, shoulders shaking.

Jenny shook her head. 'If anything, I should be crying. You're calling my dad a killer.'

Dorothy lifted her face and pulled a tissue from her sleeve, dabbed at her eyes and nose. 'This is hard for all of us.'

'You think?'

Out the corner of her eye, Jenny saw Archie slide a single sheet of paper off a pile and place it carefully on the floor, his head down the whole time.

Dorothy shoved the tissue back into her sleeve. 'I'm sorry.'

'What for?' Jenny said. 'Thinking the worst of my dad?'

Dorothy raised her chin in defiance. 'I can't help how I feel. None of us can.'

Jenny pointed at the table of paperwork. 'So what exactly is the plan here?'

Dorothy fanned her face to cool down. 'I'm looking at funerals we did around the time Simon disappeared. He has to be somewhere. If he died, why not get rid of him that way?'

'Two bodies in a coffin? That wouldn't work.'

'Maybe, if the other person was small.'

'The pallbearers would notice.'

'They'd have nothing to compare the weight to. Or maybe…'

Jenny stared at her mother. 'What?'

Dorothy's eyes were wet again. 'I don't know. Maybe he placed bits of the body in lots of coffins.'

'Come on,' Jenny said.

Archie's eyebrows were raised. 'Dorothy, that's crazy.'

'I know.'

Silence at the table, just a scratching noise from Schrödinger.

Jenny picked up a piece of paper. 'But what can you do with all this?'

Dorothy shrugged. 'Trace the funerals we did at the time.'

'Then what?'

'I don't know.'

Archie sipped his drink. 'I've already asked her this.'

'Some of them would've been cremations,' Jenny said. 'So there's no evidence.'

'The burials then,' Dorothy said.

Jenny's eyes were wide. 'What about them? Are you going to ask the council or police to exhume graves on a hunch? That's insane.'

Dorothy was close to crying again. 'I don't know.'

Jenny stood up and put her hands on her hips. 'I don't think any good can come of this.'

'We might find out the truth,' Dorothy said, sticking out her chin.

'But we could also ruin lots of people's lives,' Jenny said. 'Is it worth it?'

Dorothy was crying again, almost a choke, struggling to breathe.

Jenny went to the sink and poured a glass of water, took it to Dorothy at the table, stood with her arms folded. She noticed that the piece of paper Archie had placed on the floor was no longer there and she frowned.

'I have to know the truth,' Dorothy said, and Jenny wondered if that was ever a good idea.

40
HANNAH

Hannah smelt Indy's lamb jalfrezi even before she opened the door of the flat. Indy marinated the meat and mixed the spices herself, it was something else. Hannah hadn't eaten all day and her stomach grumbled.

When she opened the door she was met by a woman dressed in forensic scrubs, face mask, hair net, blue plastic gloves and shoe covers. She was standing in the doorway of Mel's room, two men dressed the same inside, going through the pile of Mel's stuff on the floor.

The woman in the doorway turned.

'You must be Hannah.' Her voice was muffled through the mask. 'You're responsible for this mess.'

Hannah nodded.

'Thanks,' the woman said. 'You've just made our job a whole lot harder.'

'Hey, babes,' Indy said, coming out of the kitchen with a glass of white wine.

'Hey.'

Indy kissed her lightly, handed her the wine then nodded at the people in Mel's room. 'Look, forensics are here.'

'So I see.'

They stood and watched the three forensic officers milling around, picking up pieces of paper or clothing from the edges of the giant pile in the middle of the room. Hannah had called Indy earlier to tell her she'd found a clue in Mel's room, but looking at it now, with the forensic guys in there, she couldn't believe what a state she'd left the place in.

'I'm guessing that you haven't eaten,' Indy said, rubbing her back.

Hannah nodded.

'Come through,' Indy said. 'Thomas is here.'

Indy went to the kitchen and Hannah watched her as she followed. She was barefoot in baggy yoga trousers and a blouse, hair falling from her short pony, smooth skin on her neck. Hannah sometimes forgot how beautiful her girlfriend was, took her for granted, and she'd been doing that since this business with Mel began. She didn't deserve a woman as smart and supportive as Indy, here with a kiss and a homemade curry when she needed it.

In the kitchen, Indy was stirring a pot, Thomas sitting on a stool at the breakfast bar. He stood when Hannah came in.

'How are you?' he said.

She thought about it. 'I'm OK.'

Hannah took a sip of wine. Her mum drank way more than her, a generational thing. For Jenny alcohol was rebellion, her drug to annoy the generation before, or just to get high. But Hannah's generation had found other addictions – fitness, social media, gaming, moving away from the crutches of Generation X, but crutches all the same. Maybe we all need something to keep us distracted, to keep us going in the face of all the shit.

'Want to tell me about Melanie's room?' Thomas said.

Indy raised her eyebrows. She'd obviously told Thomas as much as she knew.

'I found a receipt for her second phone.'

'And?'

'I fluttered my eyelashes at Kyle at Carphone Warehouse and he gave me the number. It's dead, obviously, but you can get a list of calls, right?'

Thomas nodded. 'That's good work, Hannah. But please let us do this stuff, OK?'

Hannah shrugged. 'I didn't know how long you were going to take to get round here. I had to do something.'

Thomas looked out the doorway. 'I understand, but you might have compromised evidence in there.'

'Sir?' This was the forensic woman at the door. 'Can I have a word?'

'Have you found something else?' Hannah said.

'No,' she said. 'No thanks to you.'

'Excuse me,' Thomas said, leaving with the woman.

Indy turned from the curry pot. 'You think Peter Longhorn will be on the list of calls?'

Hannah thought about it. The naked pictures, the unborn baby, the phone number, it was all coming together. 'Yeah.'

'What if he's not?'

'There's DNA, the baby will match him.'

Indy switched the gas off under the pots and stood for a moment. 'This is all so unbelievable.'

'I know.'

'I can't handle it,' Indy said.

Hannah turned away as she felt tears in her eyes.

'Hey.' Indy put her arms around Hannah, squeezing her, the smell of her mingling with the spices and overwhelming Hannah. Eventually Hannah realised Indy was crying too, and squeezed her tighter. They stood like that for a long time, then pulled away from each other.

'You don't have to be strong for my sake,' Hannah said.

'It's not like that. We're here for each other, right?'

'Right.'

Indy got two plates from a cupboard and began dishing up the food.

Hannah felt ashamed. Mel's disappearance and death had brought out her selfishness, making it all about her. There were so many other people affected by this, Indy, Mel's other coursemates, her poor mum and dad, Vic, all her family and friends, huge ripples of grief spreading out across the world.

Hannah's mind went to Mel's room, the phone, the pictures,

then the unborn child, a grandkid her parents would never take to the park or push on the swings.

But it was still Hannah's grief too. Hannah would never be a favourite aunt to that unborn baby, sneaking her sweets and making her laugh with stories of her mum at university.

She thought about her studies, whether she would be able to go back to learning about forces and particles, the rules that brought the universe together, the subatomic to the galactic, in the wake of all this. She had a tremor of a feeling that if she could just grasp the next thing, the next level of understanding, then all the pieces of the universe would fall into place, the equations would balance, the theories would match data perfectly and the whole cosmos would be aligned. But that wasn't realistic. There was no grand unified theory, at least not one available to human minds. We were just monkeys scrabbling in the dirt, scratching at the surface of understanding, hopelessly outflanked by the realities of the universe, crippled by the foibles and flaws of human nature. We've barely evolved from savages, still carrying millions of years of evolutionary baggage, capable of extreme cruelty, torture, rape, murder, leaving a young woman's body in the bushes at a golf course with your own unborn baby dead inside her belly as her flesh rotted away and her memories and spirit disappeared.

She stared out of the window at a magpie harassing two blackbirds in a tree. A tiny conflict in the scheme of things, but life or death to them.

'Excuse me,' Thomas said in the doorway.

Both women turned.

'What is it?' Hannah said.

Outside, the blackbirds had chased the magpie away. But it would be back looking for eggs, now that it knew there was something there.

'There's been a development,' Thomas said. 'You should check the news.'

'What?' Hannah took out her phone and opened the news app, read the breaking alert:

> ACADEMIC FOUND DEAD IN HOTEL
>
> Peter Longhorn, a physics lecturer at Edinburgh University, has been found dead near his home in the Inverleith area of the city. Police say they are not looking for anyone else in connection with the death. Longhorn had been questioned by police as part of the ongoing investigation into the murder of student Melanie Cheng. It's believed that Longhorn was discovered in a hotel room sometime this afternoon.

41
DOROTHY

Her lower back throbbed as she shuffled round the kit to an old Yo La Tengo record. The band was indie but their songs were about feel, almost soporific, and when Georgia Hubley was singing as well as drumming, there was something resonant about them. The headphones were making Dorothy's ears warm as she opened onto the ride cymbal for the chorus, shifting her weight and feeling her back groan. She hadn't been on the yoga mat since Jim's funeral, the longest she'd gone without in years, and her body was letting her know. It was stupid to have stayed away, the practice was all about connection, feeling your body and mind in balance, but she couldn't bring herself. Maybe grief was turning to depression. Maybe there was no difference between the two. Maybe she would die of heartbreak, like you heard about with elderly couples. But her heartbreak was tempered by the possibility her husband was a murderer and liar. She was hitting the drums too hard now, drowning out the melody, and she pulled back, closed her eyes, tried to sit behind the beat until the end of the song.

When the tune finished and she opened her eyes, Abi was in the doorway waiting for her lesson. Dorothy smiled and gave up the drum stool.

The lesson passed in a blur. Dorothy tried to give the girl her attention but her mind drifted. She'd put Wilco on to stretch her, and the girl was rising to the challenge, but all Dorothy could think about was the list of funerals she had downstairs, the ceremonies Jim had performed in the days after Simon Lawrence was reported missing. It was a surprisingly quiet time for the business, there was one burial three days after Simon went missing, then a gap of almost a week, then a handful of cremations in a row. Of course, maybe Jim kept the body in the fridge for weeks, got rid of it much later. But that would've been risky. If he put the body into one of the cremated coffins, that was the end of the trail. You wouldn't be able to tell anything from cremated remains, no DNA, and the amount of ashes varied hugely, depending on all sorts of factors. So she had to focus on the burial, that was all she had.

Abi had a sheen of sweat on her forehead, where a spread of adolescent spots had broken out recently. Her hair was greasy at the scalp too, and Dorothy remembered Jenny at that age, similarly out of sorts, unprepared for the world but also not giving a flying shit, so energising. Mothers were supposed to want their daughters all pulled together and sorted for facing the world but Dorothy had always loved Jenny's makeshift energy, the sense of subcultural disaffection. It reminded her of the Californian counter-cultural stuff that had been blossoming around her when she upped sticks and came to Scotland.

The song finished and Abi looked up, grinning and sweaty. Dorothy smiled encouragingly and went to put another song on the iPod.

'That was great,' she said. 'But don't overthink it, go with your instincts.'

Abi nodded seriously, taking it in. She was a great kid, would do well in the world whatever she decided to do.

Dorothy tried not to overthink things, but that grave out there loomed in her mind, casting a shadow over everything.

Archie was doing facial cosmetics on an elderly lady on the slab. Dorothy watched him apply foundation to her cheeks, forehead and neck, careful and tender, like he was putting the finishing touches to an elaborate model of a human being.

'I've made a decision,' Dorothy said, staying in the doorway.

Archie jumped and looked up.

The smell of the make-up came to Dorothy, on top of something like rotting flowers. Cool air swept around the room but she felt her cheeks flush.

'About what?' Archie said.

'I need to find out for certain.'

Archie shook his head, foundation brush in his hand. Tiny flakes of powder fell from the brush like pollen onto the back of his fingers.

'Speak to the police,' Archie said. 'This is a matter for them.'

He looked at Mrs Murdoch's face.

'You know they won't take me seriously,' Dorothy said.

'Thomas will.'

'Even he can't swing this. Exhuming a grave on a hunch? A bereaved family from a decade ago needlessly upset over something that's likely nothing?'

Archie looked up. 'That's just it, it's nothing, you've got no evidence.'

'That's why I need to get into that grave.'

Archie swallowed. 'I won't be a part of this.'

Dorothy felt the wood of the doorframe under her finger. 'You owe me.'

'That's not fair,' Archie said. 'I think you're having a breakdown.'

'I've never been clearer in my mind.'

'You need to speak to someone.'

'I'm speaking to you.'

Archie put the foundation brush down, wiped his hands. 'You're talking about desecrating someone's grave. It's illegal. You'll get caught.'

Dorothy straightened her back. 'Not if you help me.'

'I'm sorry, Dorothy, I won't do this.'

Dorothy held onto the doorframe, squeezed the wood, hoping for a splinter to pierce her skin. 'Then I'll do it myself.'

42
HANNAH

She drifted through the day of lectures and labs like she was dark matter, undetectable by humanity, just an ominous lack of substance, a hole in the calculations of the universe. She'd studied dark matter in her first-year particle physics class, how the observable universe was only five percent of the story, the other ninety-five was mysterious, unseen. But we know it's there because of the effects it has on what we can see, without it, galaxies would fly apart. Dark matter is the glue of the universe. She felt dark energy permeating the James Clerk Maxwell Building too, a sense that everyone knew what Peter Longhorn had done, and that Hannah was responsible. But all she'd done was look for the truth, try to solve the mystery of her friend, and if that started a chain reaction that led to other consequences, that wasn't her fault.

She saw Bradley Barker in the canteen, and he rose and left when he caught sight of her. She looked around for Xander but he was missing from class. Some of the other members of the Quantum Club were there, but they all looked away when she tried to make eye contact. She was repellent, driving everyone away with her actions.

She bunked off her last tutorial and walked up the road towards Greenhill Gardens. She needed to see Indy, be told she'd done the right thing.

It was half an hour's walk through Blackford and The Grange into Greenhill, passing some of the biggest houses in the city, Edinburgh old money for generations, lots of Skelf funeral customers over the years. She wondered what possessed Grandpa to start up the private investigator's. Was it to do with the missing employee? It was impossible to think of him as a murderer, but everything had changed in the last week.

She presumed Longhorn had done it out of guilt. The baby was his, Mel had told him, threatened to tell his wife, he'd panicked and strangled her, left her in the bushes. When it all came out and his wife knew, he couldn't take it.

Emilia Longhorn had backed him on the doorstep, claimed he was the victim of a stalker, but she changed her tune later. Maybe her confidence in him was blown out of the water by Mel's body turning up, or the news of the pregnancy. Hannah was getting ahead of herself, they hadn't confirmed the baby was Peter's. She tried phoning Thomas at the station but he wasn't there. She needed to know the baby was Peter's. If it wasn't, that was more dark matter and dark energy lurking in the shadows.

She reached the house and stood at the front gate staring at the address. '0 Greenhill Gardens' was so weird, like the house didn't exist, more dark matter. She wondered if there was another world somewhere in the multiverse where all the house numbers were negative, where the sun sucked energy from the purple skies, and where Mel was still alive, in her room right now studying for exams, staring out of the window and wishing she was out in the Meadows at a barbecue.

Hannah could hear drumming from the top floor of the house, a syncopated beat floating through the tree branches across Bruntsfield Links. She imagined Gran up there, hunched over, drumsticks a blur, eyes closed as she leaned in to the rhythm. Drumming was both maths and magic at the same time.

As a little kid, Hannah loved watching Dorothy play, eyes wide from the noise, amazed at the skill involved. When she'd tried it herself, it was clear some things weren't passed down through the generations. She was scared to hit the drums, even more so the cymbals, unwilling to give herself up to this bigger thing. She thought now maybe that was a mistake, maybe giving yourself over to bigger things than yourself was the way to live. Was that what Mel did, dared to get out there and connect with the universe in a more direct way? Or was she just caught up in the dragnet of everyday lust and desire, the messiness of people and their emotions? Was she trying to set herself free from society's bullshit?

Hannah felt exhausted by the grief and sadness, there seemed to be no release from it. She spotted Schrödinger eyeing up some sparrows on a bird feeder hanging from a pine branch. He was motionless in the shadows, eyes following the flutter of wings. She walked to the house close to the birds so that they flapped into the high branches away from the cat.

Indy was on her hands and knees in front of the desk, fiddling with cables, skirt stretched tight across her bum.

'That's a nice welcome,' Hannah said, touching that skirt and running her hand up Indy's back. Maybe this was the release she needed.

Indy extricated herself from the mess and stood up.

'That's sexual assault.'

'Sue me.' Hannah pulled her close and kissed her. Dorothy was still playing drums in the studio, had moved into a soft shuffle, and Hannah shifted her hips in time, Indy following suit.

Indy smiled. 'I would if you had any money.'

Hannah felt the dark matter of her atoms transforming into light, the electrons vibrating more in their orbits, the neutrons and protons hugging each other a little tighter in the nucleus.

The front door swung open and banged against the wall.

'You fucking bitch.'

Emilia Longhorn stood in the doorway, her baby in a buggy a few feet behind her, sucking on a bottle and wiggling her toes. With the sunshine behind her, Emilia looked like an avenging angel. Hannah pushed Indy aside and held out her hands to stop whatever was coming. Emilia strode forwards, lips pressed together, then launched herself at Hannah, grabbing her throat and pushing her to the ground, falling on top of her then raising a fist and punching Hannah in the eye. She grabbed Hannah's hair with her other hand and punched again, this time connecting with the cheek bone, and Hannah felt Emilia's ring slice the skin, warm blood flowing from her cheek. Hannah kicked and thrashed but Emilia didn't budge from on top of her. Hannah smelled her perfume, citrus and coconut, heard her breathing and then the baby crying outside, Dorothy's drumming still thumping upstairs, echoing through the bones of the house as Emilia lifted her fist again. She connected with Hannah's ear and Hannah heard ringing as she tried to grip Emilia's wrist and stop the blows. But Emilia ripped her hand free and was swinging her arm down when she was bulldozed by Indy in a rugby tackle, the pair of them tumbling into a display of roses and tulips, scattering blossoms and foliage over the carpet, rolling with a thud into the bottom of the banister.

Hannah put a hand to her cheek and it came away bloody. She propped herself up on her elbows and saw Indy staggering to her feet and throwing a foot into Emilia's ribs, which made Hannah wince and Emilia cower into a ball, gripping her chest and struggling to breathe.

Indy pushed hair from her face as she stood over the woman. She looked from Emilia to the baby, who had dropped her bottle on the gravel and was scrambling like a landed guppy to get it back, pudgy arms and legs flapping, plaintive cries from her mouth.

Hannah stared at the baby, helpless and now fatherless.

'Who the hell are you?' Indy said between breaths.

Emilia got to her hands and knees, then slowly stood up.

Hannah stood up too, her face pounding with pain, her body aching.

Emilia pointed at Hannah. 'You killed my husband.'

'He killed himself.'

'Because of you.'

Hannah wiped blood from her cheek. 'Because of what he did.

You threw him out of the house because of what he did. This is not on me.'

The baby was gurning now, her cry piercing. Emilia ignored her for a long moment, tears in her eyes. Eventually she turned.

'It's OK, honey, Mummy's here.'

She turned back to Hannah, her fists at her sides as she began to walk towards the door.

'You haven't heard the last of this.'

She picked up the baby's bottle and handed it to her, then pushed the kid down the driveway and into the street.

43
Jenny

She finished her coffee and decided. Got up and left the café, walked across the cobbles to the vennel and into the courtyard in the evening light. She pushed open the front door, headed to Liam's studio and knocked. She wasn't sure what she was going to say to him, but it was time to talk.

She heard a clatter, brushes on a table, and the door opened. Liam was handsome close up, green eyes and a strong jaw. He'd changed out of his work suit, which was hanging up on the curtain rail at the window, and he wore saggy jeans and a blue shirt. She could tell from the way it clung to his chest that he was toned underneath.

'Can I help you?' he said. He had a softer accent than Orla, a more open manner. There were flecks of grey through his black hair, and dark splotches of paint across his shirt. His hands were thin, long fingers, mottled with paint too.

'Hi,' Jenny said, throwing on a smile. 'I'm planning to rent one of these studios and I wondered if I could take a quick look around.'

He frowned, unsure.

'Mohammed said it was OK,' she said. 'He couldn't find the key for my one yet, but said just to pop down and someone would let me take a peek.'

She waved her hand along the corridor.

'I tried a few others, but no one else is in.'

He looked behind him at the canvas he was working on, propped on the easel.

'Sure,' he said, opening the door.

'Thanks.'

She walked past him into the middle of the room, the smell of paint and sweat coming to her.

'Good light,' she said, pointing at the window.

He narrowed his eyes and watched her closely, and she felt a flutter in her chest.

'Have we met before?' he said.

She turned, raised a hand to her temple. 'I don't think so.'

'You definitely look familiar.'

She raised her eyebrows. 'I get that a lot, must have a generic face.'

He bit on his lip, concentrating. 'I certainly wouldn't say that.'

She came round the room, glancing at the canvases stacked on the floor, the same ones she'd seen when she broke in.

'Is this place secure?'

He was at his canvas now but still watching her. 'If you'd asked a week ago I would've said yes but I got broken into the other day.'

'Did they take anything?'

He laughed and shook his head. 'I guess they weren't art fans.'

She smiled.

'I presume they were after stuff they could sell,' Liam said. 'Laptops, anything electrical. A bunch of weird paintings by a nobody wouldn't get many buyers down at the pub.'

Jenny pointed at a picture on the floor. 'I think these are great, they're not weird at all.'

The painting had the vague outline of a deer, but it seemed rooted in the forest, like it was a malformed tree, its antlers were branches with leaves and blooms sprouting from them. Other trees in the background had animal shapes, with a liquid sun pouring through the skeletal outcrops. It was beautiful and eerie.

'Thanks.'

'I mean it,' Jenny said, coming round to the work in progress. It was kind of a seascape, figures below and above the water, something like a whale carcass with ribs poking out, and a rotting ship, beams exposed at the waterline. Alien plants wrapped around them, purple and maroon seaweeds, luminous vines trailing from both structures, the balance and composition off centre and off kilter.

'Do you ever show these or sell them?'

He laughed in surprise. 'No, nothing like that.'

'You should.'

He shook his head.

'I'm not bullshitting,' Jenny said.

He leaned into a bow. 'You're very kind, but I don't think I'm ready.'

She smiled at his self-deprecation and held out a hand. 'I'm Jenny by the way.'

He shook her hand, strong and solid. 'Liam.'

She went back to looking around the room, brushed hair away from her face.

'I know where I've seen you before,' he said.

She lowered her hand and turned.

'My sister-in-law's funeral, you were working for the undertaker.'

Jenny had hoped different hair and clothes would throw him off, but he was an artist, it was his job to notice things. Or maybe he'd just noticed her. 'Yes, I work there, was that Gina O'Donnell's service?'

He nodded, thoughtful. 'What's it like in that business?'

'I've only just started, really.'

'What do you mean?'

'It's the family business,' she said. 'Skelf Funeral Directors. I'm Jenny Skelf. But I only began helping out when my father died.'

Liam took a step closer. 'I'm sorry to hear that.'

She could feel the warmth of him standing close, and wondered if he was going to touch her, a sympathetic hand on the arm.

'It's OK,' she said.

'No, it's not, your dad died, it's anything but OK.'

Silence between them for a long beat, the ghosts of all the dead swirling around Jenny's head.

'So you're an artist as well as a funeral director?' Liam said.

'I suppose so.'

'What sort of stuff do you do?'

Jenny looked at Liam's painting on the easel. 'It's hard to describe.'

Liam nodded. 'I know what you mean. It's hard to talk about this. That's why we create stuff, isn't it, so we don't have to talk.'

Jenny tried to think if she'd created anything in her life except a mess. She thought of Hannah, her creation, the one thing she and Craig got right.

'Exactly,' she said.

She walked round the room trailing a finger along the top of some stacked canvases.

'Do you think you'll take it?' Liam said.

'What?'

'The studio, you said you spoke to Mo about it. Which one is it?'

Jenny tried to remember. 'He said Derek's was free? Something about hospital.'

'Yeah, shame.'

'I think I'll take it. It's good to have your own space, a place to lose yourself.'

She touched one of the canvases then raised her eyebrows at Liam for permission. He nodded and she flicked through the stack, more animal-plant hybrids, some vaguely human forms, the colours and contours mesmerising, simultaneously familiar and otherworldly.

'Don't you want people to see these?' she said.

'Maybe one day. I'm still finding my feet.'

'They're so good.'

'That's not the point.'

Jenny turned. 'Then what is the point?'

Liam thought about the question.

'It's about finding out who you are,' he said eventually. He pointed out of the window. 'Without any distractions. Without anyone else getting in the way. Finding out what kind of person you want to be. It's about the process of doing the painting, the act of creating, not the end result of the painting itself. Life is about processes, not results.'

So this was his secret, he wanted to find out who he was by painting and spending time alone. Jenny thought about what kind of person she was, what she'd become and what she wanted to be, but her mind was blank. She was just someone whose father was dead, someone who followed people around and spied on them, who helped wives entrap their husbands so they could get a divorce, who snogged her ex-husband even though he was married with a new family, who grabbed a young man by the balls because he was cocky and she didn't like him, who hoped to hell her daughter turned out better than she did. She felt tears coming to her eyes and hurried past Liam to the door then out into a world where she didn't know who she was anymore, if she ever had.

44
DOROTHY

'Hello, Home Angels Cleaning Services.'

Dorothy stared out at Bruntsfield Links, crinkly with sunshine. The woman on the line had a heavy Eastern European accent, Dorothy's guess was middle-aged.

'Hi, I'm trying to track down one of your staff, Monika Belenko?'

'Who are you?'

'I'm the personal assistant of Jacob Glassman, you clean his house?'

'Glassman, yes.'

'I think Monika might've lost a piece of jewellery when she was at the Glassman house, I want to return it to her.'

'Bring it to our office, we'll make sure she gets it.'

'No offence, but I'd rather hand it to her directly, just to be sure. Do you have a mobile number for her?'

'We cannot give out that information.'

'I see,' Dorothy said. 'Well, Mr Glassman was very insistent that I get this back to her today. Directly to her.'

'We can't give out private employee information.'

'Well, if she's working today, perhaps you could tell me where she is? I could pop in and drop it off.'

'I'm sorry, we can't do that either.'

'That's a real shame,' Dorothy said. 'If that's the case, Mr Glassman might have to reconsider his cleaning contract with you. I believe it's a very competitive market at the moment.'

Long pause, some conversation happening with the mouthpiece covered.

'Please hold on a second,' the woman said, her voice dripping with disgust.

The house on Greenbank Crescent was a 1920s bungalow with a converted attic and a big modern extension to the side. Dorothy walked up the path and could hear a hoover running inside. She was glad to be out of the house. She'd spent several more hours watching footage from Jacob's house, nothing. She'd checked the five cameras in the same order as before, first for the times when Susan was on her daily visit, then for when the cleaner had been in. There was footage of her hoovering and dusting, mopping the floor in the kitchen and generally knocking the place into shape. Dorothy had half a mind to enlist her cleaning services herself. Then she'd looked at the footage from other times during the day, just Jacob slowly shuffling around the house, bugger all else. She wasn't sure why she was here on Greenbank Crescent, but she didn't know what else to do.

She rang the bell and the hoover went off, but no one came to the door. She rang again, heard footsteps then the door opened.

'I'm sorry, Mrs Cavanagh is not in.'

Monika had striking features, high cheekbones and a sharp nose, big green eyes. She was wearing a sky-blue Home Angels T-shirt and skin-tight white jeans. Dorothy couldn't help thinking they must be incredibly uncomfortable for cleaning, and not at all practical. Monika had a gold choker chain around her neck with a crucifix on it, her blonde hair in a bun on the top of her head, and her nails long and dark purple. You could see why even an old man like Jacob would notice her.

'I'm not here to see Mrs Cavanagh,' Dorothy said. 'I'm here to see you.'

Monika looked confused.

'Can I come in?' Dorothy said.

Monika glanced behind her, then back. 'No, this is not my house.'

She had a Ukrainian accent, but smoother than the woman on the phone. Dorothy wondered how long she'd been in Scotland, if life was turning out as she expected. She was working as a cleaner, so probably not.

'I'm a friend of Mr Glassman,' Dorothy said. 'You clean his house?'

Monika nodded. 'Nice old gentleman. Hermitage. Big house, needs a lot of cleaning.'

'I'll bet. Listen, he found this.'

Dorothy pulled out an old bracelet that she'd taken from her dresser at home. It was silver, pretty, but not worth much, she couldn't remember the last time she'd worn it.

'After you visited to clean the other day. And he wondered if it was yours?'

Monika glanced at the bracelet but didn't take it. Shook her head. 'It's not mine.'

'Are you sure?' Dorothy offered it up. 'Please take a closer look. He was adamant.'

Monika looked annoyed. 'I know what is my jewellery. This isn't mine.'

'Maybe from a previous visit.'

Monika narrowed her eyes and stared at Dorothy. 'What did you say your name was?'

'Dorothy.'

'I never heard Mr Glassman mention you.'

'Do you talk to him much when you're there?'

Monika looked up and down the street. 'Not really, I don't have much time. Schedules are very tight.'

'But you have spoken to him.'

'Of course, he's friendly. And a little lonely. He has no family nearby.'

Dorothy realised she was still holding the bracelet, so she stuffed it into her cardigan pocket. 'Do you think he's managing OK in that big house?'

Monika shrugged. 'It's not my business. You are his friend.'

'I think he's been misplacing things. Forgetting things and becoming confused.'

Monika shook her head. 'He is very sharp for his age. I do not think he is confused. Maybe you are confused.'

'So what about this bracelet?' Dorothy said.

'I don't have an answer,' Monika said, looking back into the house. 'Now please, I have to work.'

The door closed and Dorothy stood there until she heard the hoover start again. She walked away from the house, rubbing the bracelet between her fingers in her pocket and thinking about what it must be like to work in other people's houses all day. The things you must see, the lives you spy on, the secrets you keep.

45
JENNY

She sat in the body van in Learmonth Gardens, looking at the Hooks' home. It was a street of grey-brick terraced upstairs-downstairs, nothing fancy but still worth an arm and a leg this close to the city centre. She wondered how Liam and Orla afforded it, but then you never knew people's circumstances, maybe they'd inherited money or won the lottery, maybe they were drug dealers on the side. A private investigator should really look into that kind of stuff. Across the road from the house was a strip of green space, silver birch and willow trees throwing shade over the grass in the low light. A young family with a kid on a trike, an elderly couple out for their evening constitutional, life carrying on.

Jenny dialled Orla's number and listened to the ring.

'Hi,' Orla said.

Jenny imagined Orla inside the house looking smug.

'Jenny Skelf here.'

'You've got something.' There was excitement in her voice that she wasn't good at hiding. 'Should we meet up again?'

Jenny looked at the house, one of fifty in the street, and wondered what all the other occupants were doing now. Making tea, kids doing homework, teenagers on phones or the PlayStation, mums changing nappies.

'I think it's quicker to do this over the phone.'

'So you have evidence?'

'I'm afraid I won't be able to continue with this case.'

Silence for a moment. 'What do you mean?'

'I've been carrying out surveillance on your husband for almost a week now and I've found no evidence that he's cheating on you.'

'Then you haven't been doing your job properly.'

Orla was angry. Jenny wondered what Darcy told her about the honeytrap. She must've lied to get paid, because Orla was clearly expecting Jenny to have some dirt.

'I can assure you I've been doing my job properly,' Jenny said. 'Sometimes there's nothing to find out.'

'You're useless.'

'I'll bill you for my time,' Jenny said. 'And I expect to be paid promptly.'

Orla laughed. 'I'm not paying for this amateur crap. I should've known better than to get a fucking funeral director to look into him. You're not even really that, are you?'

'There's no need to be like that.'

'I know my husband is fucking some little tart behind my back, and I'm going to get someone who knows what he's doing to help me.'

Jenny watched a young mum and a little girl do cartwheels on the grass, and tried to remember Hannah at that age, so bendy and fearless.

'Your husband is a talented painter,' she said.

Orla laughed. 'Goodbye.'

The line went dead.

Jenny sucked her teeth then put her phone away and settled in for the wait.

It only took fifteen minutes.

A small white van pulled up outside and Jenny shrank into her seat as a short stocky guy with a shaved head got out and went up the path to Orla's house. Orla answered in five seconds, ushering him inside. She looked worried, and the way she touched his arm and chest gave everything away. Some people are idiots.

Jenny saw Orla and the guy come into the front room, at first having a disagreement then after a couple of minutes touching and kissing. They headed out of the room, presumably upstairs.

Jenny got out and crossed the road to the guy's van. She took a photo of the number plate, there had to be a way to trace that. She looked into the front of the van, saw a bunch of flyers for Karl Zukas, Landscape Gardener, with a number and email. She took a picture of that too. Inside the van was a mess, Maccy D wrappers and cups, empty Irn Bru bottles, KFC boxes. She saw through to the back of the van, lots of gardening tools, compost bags, turf rolls.

She went back to her own van, got in and waited. Looked up Karl Zukas online. He had a good rating on Trusted Traders, plenty of satisfied customers, mostly women. Orla was trading Liam in for this?

Another fifteen minutes and the front door opened. Jenny zoomed her phone in, took a ton of pictures then some video as Orla and Karl stood like love-struck kids in the doorway, touching each other, kissing long and hard. Eventually Karl pulled himself away and Orla went back inside, smiling like her world wasn't about to come crashing down.

46
HANNAH

She pushed herself, trying to beat her best five K, legs pounding and aching, breath ragged, face flushed. It didn't help that the Meadows were hoaching, unseasonal sunshine bringing everyone out to enjoy the last throes of summer.

She overtook two middle-aged men jogging at half her speed, and thought about Peter. He killed himself out of guilt over what he did to Mel, so fuck him. She understood Emilia being upset, but what about Mel and her family? It wasn't Hannah's fault, all she did was find the photographs, uncover the truth. If she hadn't pursued it Peter would still be alive, but only because he hadn't been caught. She refused to take the blame.

But then she thought about Emilia's baby, scrabbling for her bottle of milk on the ground. She would grow up without a dad, and nobody deserved that. She thought about her own dad and how much she wanted him to be around when she was a teenager arguing with Mum.

Her feet thumped across the grass, she was a few seconds up on her PB, she could break twenty-two minutes for the first time. She had her phone out, checking how much she had to go, three hundred metres, two hundred, she passed another man in his thirties, thickening around the middle, now one hundred metres, she sucked in air and threw her legs forwards, imagined a finishing tape, then the automated voice told her she'd reached five kilometres and she pressed pause and her legs staggered to a stop and she almost fell over, stumbling until she slammed a hand against an oak tree and bent over, chest heaving, the voice telling her she'd done it in twenty-one minutes and fifty-seven seconds as black spots sparkled in her vision and she leaned against the tree and wished Mel and Peter were still alive, Grandpa too.

She straightened up and walked down Middle Meadow Walk to the flat, cyclists zipping past, more runners, an old punk drinking from a beer can, two girls in Capri trousers and pastel jumpers laughing loudly about a boy.

She was at the lights on Melville Terrace, waiting to cross.

'Hey.'

She turned and there was her dad.

'Hey.'

'I was just coming to see you.' He held a small bouquet of white roses. 'I saw on the news about your friend.'

Hannah took the flowers and gave him a hug. She realised she was sweaty and smelly but didn't care. She began crying into his chest and felt his hand on her back. She pulled herself into the embrace, hoping to burrow into the dark forever. She was aware of people passing by, probably wondering why she was crying in this man's arms. Her breath synchronised with Craig's, their chests moving as if their hearts were connected.

Eventually she pulled away and wiped her eyes. Craig pushed strands of hair away from her cheek.

'Come on up,' Hannah said, smelling the roses. 'I'll put the kettle on.'

She led him up the stairs into the flat, Indy at the breakfast bar on her laptop.

'Hey,' she said to Hannah, taking in Craig behind. She'd always got on with him, something Hannah was grateful for.

'Dad gave me these,' Hannah said, pulling out a pint glass and arranging the flowers in it.

'I'm sorry to hear about Melanie,' Craig said.

Hannah put the kettle on, kissed Indy in passing, saw the website on her laptop.

'Any news?' she said.

Indy shook her head. 'Just what we heard last night. Anything from Thomas?'

'I've tried a few times, left messages.'

'Who's Thomas?' Craig said.

'A cop friend of Dorothy's,' Indy said.

'Dorothy is friends with a cop?'

'He's been great,' Hannah said. 'Really helped us out.'

'That's good,' Craig said. 'So this lecturer in the news.'

'He was sleeping with Mel,' Hannah said.

'And you didn't know about it?'

The kettle clicked off and Hannah got mugs from the rack, threw teabags in. 'It turns out Mel was good at keeping secrets.'

Craig took a cup of tea from Hannah. 'And this guy killed her, then himself?'

'We think so,' Hannah said. 'The police are still working on it.'

'Ms Sherlock Holmes here is quite the detective,' Indy said, touching Hannah on the arm.

Hannah shook her head. 'He mentioned something about emails but she didn't send him any, so I checked his office and found pictures of them together. She also had a second phone, we presume Peter got rid of it. But we have the number and the police are getting a list of calls. Plus there's forensics too, at the murder scene, but also Mel was pregnant. So we're waiting for DNA to confirm Peter was the father.'

'That doesn't necessarily mean he killed her,' Craig said.

'But it gives him a motive if she was going to tell his wife.'

Hannah lifted her phone from the worktop and dialled Thomas's number again. She was ready to leave another message but he answered on the third ring.

'Hi, Thomas, it's Hannah.'

'Sorry, things have been hectic around here.'

'So where are we?'

Hannah saw Craig and Indy share a look of concern. She felt in limbo, she couldn't relax until she knew what happened.

'We got DNA back half an hour ago,' Thomas said.

'And?'

'There's no match. Peter Longhorn wasn't the father of Melanie's child.'

Drouthy's was a scabby sports bar on the corner of West Preston Street and Summerhall Place. The Celtic-band logo and old-time font on their lettering had the air of a Scottish theme bar, but inside it was a standard football pub with cheap lager promos and pungent toilets. It was in the heart of the student neighbourhood and Hannah lived ten minutes away, but she'd never been in before.

She'd thought of this while she was in the shower after her run. Her dad had gone and she was chewing over the call from Thomas, that Peter wasn't the father. That meant they had to follow their other leads. She called her mum while she dried herself, and they agreed to go back to speak to Xander and Bradley, respectively. Hannah had no joy tracking down Xander, he seemed to have gone to ground. She wondered about that. Then she remembered the flatmates' names he gave her, she'd completely forgotten about the note on her phone, had never added them to the whiteboard at her gran's house. Darren Grant and Faisal McNish. They were easy to find on social media, seemed to spend half their lives watching football in the pub, and Faisal had even posted a picture of a fresh pint of Stella on Instagram an hour ago, tagged Drouthy Neebors. So here she was.

She spotted them at the bar, their eyes on the screen above the door, watching Man City against Barcelona. Hannah studied them for a moment while they were oblivious. Darren was big and broad, a rugby player's physique, shaven head and scrubby beard. He was studying agriculture, she found out online, and he looked like a farmer. Faisal was the same height but thinner, sculpted, wavy black hair and a smart shirt tucked into black jeans. He was doing law at Edinburgh Uni, a fast track to elitism if ever there was one. They were an unlikely couple, and Hannah swallowed as she approached.

'Excuse me.'

Their eyes drifted from the screen to her, and they both obviously checked out her tits under her open jacket.

'Hi, darling,' Darren said. 'Do you need in to the bar?'

Faisal put his pint down and leaned forwards. 'Let me save you the bother, love, can I buy you a drink?'

Hannah shook her head. 'I need to speak to you both about Melanie Cheng.'

Their faces went hard.

Darren's chin went out. 'Who're you?'

Faisal smiled. 'Oh, you must be the flatmate, Xander said you were playing detective.'

'Can you tell me where Xander is?'

Darren narrowed his eyes. 'Still at the cop shop, no thanks to you.'

Faisal frowned at his mate. 'We don't have to speak to her, Daz.'

'You don't have to, but it might help you.'

Faisal laughed. 'How could talking to you possibly help us?'

Over Hannah's shoulder something happened in the football match, the dozen men in the place exhaled with frustration. Darren and Faisal briefly glanced up at the screen.

'I missed that, fuck's sake,' Darren said.

'A girl is dead,' Hannah said. 'Don't you give a shit?'

'It's got nothing to do with us,' Faisal said.

'Have the police spoken to either of you?'

'Why would they speak to us?' Darren said.

'You knew Mel.'

Faisal took a sip of his pint. 'It sounds like a lot of people knew Mel.'

'What do you mean?'

Darren raised his eyebrows. 'She was a stupid slut.'

'What makes you say that?'

'She was fucking that lecturer behind Xander's back for a start,' Darren said. 'God knows who else she was shagging.'

Hannah looked from one to the other. 'Were either of you sleeping with her?'

Faisal shook his head. 'Bros before hoes. It's the mates' code. No way we'd do that.'

'But she was pretty, right?' Hannah said. 'You probably flirted with her. Tried it on a little bit. Maybe when she knocked you back you got angry. Maybe you've been jealous of Xander all along.'

Faisal laughed and nudged Darren. 'She thinks she's a cop, Daz. It's so cute. Xander was right, you are a sad twat.'

Darren scrutinised her more closely. 'He never said how hot you were, though. Sure I can't get you a glass of wine?'

Faisal shook his head. 'Don't bother, mate, she's one of them, remember?'

Darren looked her over again. 'Oh yeah. Shame.'

Their eyes drifted back to the screen behind Hannah. She looked at them for a second. There was something here, but she couldn't work out if it was bog-standard misogyny and homophobia, or something else.

'You two are a piece of work, you know that?'

Faisal glanced down and shrugged.

'I'm going to make sure the police investigate you properly.'

Darren put his pint down on the bar. 'Do what you like, bitch. Now fuck along, there's a good girl, we're trying to watch the football.'

Hannah imagined smashing the pint glass off the bar, pushing the jagged edge into Darren's face, then Faisal's. Boys her own age with the attitudes of fifty years ago. How was that possible?

She turned and left the bar as a penalty claim was denied on the screens.

'Fucking men,' she said under her breath.

47
JENNY

Jenny pulled the van into the driveway, the familiar crunch of gravel under the wheels comforting like an old blanket, and parked next to the hearse in the garage. She remembered a night when she was a teenager, some boy walking her home, God, she couldn't even remember his name, Jason something. They'd been drinking in one of the hotel bars in Bruntsfield, it was a Best Western now but back then it was independent and a good place to drink underage. Nobody gave a shit about that in the eighties. Anyway, she let Jason kiss her at the front gate, then after a time she let him put his hand up her blouse. Eventually she pulled him along the driveway, his eyes widening, and into the garage. Climbed into the back of the hearse they had then and fucked him, her on top, seeing the amazement in his eyes, feeling the cold metal of the hearse on her knees as she moved up and down on him, fingers spread out on his chest.

It had been a long time since she'd touched a man's bare chest. She thought about Orla fucking Karl, her Lithuanian toyboy, while Liam dabbed mauve onto the corner of a canvas. Human desire was a bitch. She remembered kissing Craig a couple of days ago and wondered what his chest was like under his shirt these days. She wondered about Liam's chest, thought about his shy smile. He was getting fucked over by Orla, and Jenny had the evidence. She sat thinking about that.

She went inside still chewing it over. The ground floor was silent, Indy and Archie away home. Light dappled through the stained glass on the staircase as she went up, woodpigeons cooing in the trees outside. She'd resented all this quiet as a teenager but now she craved it. People change, their bodies change, their minds change, their selves change. Hannah once told her that all the atoms in your body are replaced by new ones every seven years. If every plank of a ship is gradually replaced, is it still the same ship? What had Liam said to her about his paintings, it wasn't about the end product, it was about the process of making the work. We are a series of actions, we are our cumulative experience and that's it.

Dorothy was sitting in the kitchen, Schrödinger in her lap, a piece of paper on the table in front of her. She looked like she'd been crying.

'Mum?'

Dorothy shook her head, stroked the cat, who stretched his neck.

Jenny sat and placed a hand on her mum's knee.

'What is it?'

Dorothy looked out of the window. The skies were blood red bleaching burnt orange at the edges. 'I need your help.'

Jenny squeezed Dorothy's knee.

Dorothy took a deep breath and turned. 'I need you to help me dig up a grave.'

Jenny took her hand away. She didn't speak for a long time.

'What do you mean?' she said eventually.

Dorothy pointed to the piece of paper. 'I think your dad got rid of Simon Lawrence's body in someone else's coffin.' She tapped the paper lightly, as if she was scared it might attack her. 'This one.'

'How do you know?'

Dorothy put her fingertips to her forehead. 'I know how his mind works. There were no cremations for a week after Simon went missing. He wouldn't want the body in the fridge that long, so I think he buried him.'

'Mum, you realise what you're asking.'

Dorothy's eyes were wet. 'I do.'

'I think you're—'

Dorothy snapped around and Schrödinger slid off her lap, slinking across the room. 'You think I'm mad?'

'I didn't say that.'

'You didn't have to.' Dorothy tapped the paper again. 'Say you'll help me.'

Jenny put her hand on top of Dorothy's. 'Give this to Thomas.'

'*He'll* think I'm mad.'

Jenny made a face.

Dorothy gripped her hand tight. 'I have to know. I have to find out what he did. He was lying to me the whole time. Everything I believed in was built on sand.'

Jenny thought about Craig's affair with Fiona. She thought about Orla fucking Karl behind Liam's back. She thought about Peter Longhorn and Melanie Cheng. The lies, the deceit, the betrayals.

'It's illegal,' Jenny said.

'I know.'

'It's immoral.'

'I know that too.'

'It's hard work,' Jenny said. 'Digging is hard work.'

'I know.'

'You're seventy years old.'

'Thanks for reminding me.' Dorothy leaned forwards so that their faces were inches apart. She held Jenny's hand, gripping tight. 'I'm a strong woman. You're strong too.'

She wasn't talking about physical strength.

Her grip was tighter, Jenny feeling it in her knuckles, across her wrist.

Dorothy was whispering now, they were so close. 'I need my daughter to be strong. I need to do this.'

Jenny stared at her mother's face and swallowed.

She didn't have a choice.

She found her way through King's Buildings more easily this time, even though it was getting dark. She strode into the James Clerk Maxwell Building and up the stairs, still a surprising number of people around. Maybe being a student or academic was like any other profession now, working longer and longer hours for less money, fuelled by the fear of dropping behind.

She stopped at room 4.16 and stared at that Quantum Club poster. No one had really properly explained to her what they did in that club, and she wondered if Hannah had overlooked something there, if there was anything more sinister to it.

She knocked. A long pause. She didn't know he was here, but it was all she had to go on. She was about to knock again when she heard a noise inside, maybe the squeak of a chair.

She pushed the door open and there was Bradley on his own in the office. She half expected him to have a woman in here, or his trousers round his ankles and his cock out wanking over porn on his laptop. But he was just sitting looking annoyed at the sight of her in the doorway.

'Go away,' he said, sounding tired.

'Why didn't you answer the door?' Jenny said.

'Because I didn't want to speak to you.'

'How did you know it was me?'

'I didn't,' Bradley said. 'I don't want to speak to anyone.'

Jenny looked around the office. Same cramped set-up as before, nothing seemed out of place or different. It smelled of nervous sweat.

'Please leave,' Bradley said.

'Did the police interview you?'

'Fuck off, will you?'

'That's a yes.' Jenny took a step into the room and Bradley stood up. It was dark outside the window, making the office seem more intimate, claustrophobic. Jenny felt the energy shift when he stood up, looming over her. He seemed to feel it too.

'You don't seem very upset about Mel turning up dead.'

He shook his head. 'You don't know me. You don't know what I'm feeling.'

'Says the dick-pic guy.'

'That was a mistake.'

'Only because it got you into trouble.'

He took a step forwards. 'No, you got me into trouble.'

'You did it to yourself.'

He swallowed hard. 'I have nothing to feel guilty about.'

'Is that what you told the police?'

'I told them that you assaulted me on the roof,' Bradley said, moving towards her. They were close now, she could see the tiredness in his eyes.

'I bet they laughed you out of the station,' Jenny said.

'They took it seriously.'

'This is the age of Me Too, you don't get to be a victim.'

'Assault is still assault.'

She could see his laptop screen, at least it looked like actual work, equations and diagrams, a graph demonstrating some fundamental truth about the universe.

He saw her looking. 'What, you were expecting porn?'

Jenny raised her eyebrows. 'That sounds like a guilty conscience.'

'I don't feel guilty,' Bradley said.

'You must be worried about the DNA match.'

'What DNA match?'

'Between you and Mel's baby.' She was out on a limb here, but you never know.

He paused at that. He was right in her face now, and he reached out a hand and placed it on the open door next to her. He smiled.

'You're a sad little cow, aren't you? I looked you up online, mid-forties, divorced. Is this how you fill the emptiness? Wandering around making false accusations about innocent people? I feel sorry for you.'

Jenny felt her face flush and looked down at her hands.

'Oh, that hit home, didn't it?' Bradley said. 'The truth hurts.'

He grabbed her upper arms and squeezed, stood there looking in her eyes.

'Get off me,' she said, pulling away.

'Not so fucking brave now, are you? How about if I did to you what you did to me? What if I grabbed your cunt right now?'

Jenny stared at him, tried to find some truth in his eyes, but it was just hate and disgust, she'd seen those a million times before.

She was ready with her knee, about to lift it into his crotch when he thrust her out of the door so hard that she smacked her head against the opposite wall. She breathed hard, legs shaking.

'Don't come back here if you know what's good for you,' Bradley said, and closed the door.

48
DOROTHY

The front gates were locked but she expected that. The adjoining house, built into the high cemetery wall, was dark, everyone asleep at this time of night. She drove the van down Milton Road, turned right at the end into Brunstane Mill Road and parked in one of the spots at the bottom. The path beyond led to fields in one direction, Newhailes House stately home in another, Brunstane Burn to the right. That was the way in.

She turned to Jenny twitching in the passenger seat.

'Ready?'

Jenny shook her head. 'No.'

'Come on.'

She got out and went to the back of the van, took out the holdall containing shovels, picks and torches. She heard Jenny's door open and close then locked the van and walked over the burn into the darkness of the park. She led Jenny along the burnside path, past the private golf holes at the back of millionaires' houses, then too soon they were at the back of Portobello Cemetery. The burn was narrow and shallow here, a fallen tree making an easy bridging point. They crossed then scrambled through undergrowth to an old chain-link fence full of holes, several posts leaning askew. It was easy to squeeze through.

She took out the torches and handed one to Jenny.

'Go that way,' she said, pointing up the hill. 'I'll go left. Remember it's Barbara Worth we're looking for.'

Jenny looked petrified and Dorothy didn't blame her. Part of Dorothy couldn't believe they were here, but she had a sense of fate. From the moment she found out about the payments to Rebecca, she had been heading here.

She shouldered the holdall, felt the weight against her muscles, the strap biting her skin. She patted Jenny's shoulder then shooed her away, began checking the graves as she walked. The headstones here in the bottom part of the cemetery were less than ten years old, some very fresh, so she didn't waste much time, just cursory glances as she passed. She walked up one row then down another. She did ten rows then moved up to the next regiment of graves, the death dates getting closer to Barbara Worth's. As the graves got older there were fewer flowers propped against the stones. How quickly we forget. The cliché was that we live on as long as we're remembered by those we leave behind. But that wasn't long.

Dorothy tutted under her breath at every headstone that wasn't Barbara Worth. She sensed movement above her head and saw bats flitting from tree to tree, frantic wings against the glow of the sky over towards the road. She heard an owl calling and another returning the call, and she thought about her and Jim, until death parted them.

Another row of dead ends, then another as she circled back to where she'd left Jenny. She could see Jenny's torch in the distance, angled down, careful not to attract attention. Not that anyone could see, there were small copses of trees breaking the sightline, more trees along the burn behind them, high walls at the front, as well as to the left where the railway line ran, and to the right where the posh houses were. No one wanted to see a graveyard when they were on their decking sipping Prosecco.

She was beginning to lose her nerve. The bag ached on her back, the adrenaline being replaced by doubt and shame. Because what they had planned was shameful. But then she remembered how Jim lied and paid out thousands of pounds over the years, how Rebecca presumed it would last forever. How Simon disappeared, a mystery she had to solve for the sake of her sanity.

Her phone rang in her pocket and she jumped. The sound of it sliced through the darkness. She answered.

'I've found her,' Jenny said.

Dorothy flashed her torch three times like they agreed, then she saw Jenny's torch do the same. She walked in that direction, pulling the strap on her shoulder as she went.

She found Jenny standing with her back hunched, a hangdog expression on her face.

'There.'

And there she was, Barbara Worth, 1940–2010. Something satisfying about the neatness of the dates, three score years and ten wasn't so much these days but it was enough for Barbara. Beloved wife, mother and grandmother, the outline of a winged figure carved into the black granite. No flowers or tributes, just a clutch of dandelions sprouting from the grass.

'We don't have to do this,' Jenny said. 'There's still time to turn back.'

Dorothy stared at the gravestone for a while then crouched and touched it, running her finger along the engraving. There was a shadow of moss along the bottom edge of the dates and Dorothy scraped it away. Then she touched the grass beneath her, felt the dampness and the earth underneath, the beating heart of the planet, the thrum of the city echoed in tremors that sank to the centre of the Earth, way past the few feet Barbara occupied.

'If you want to go, that's fine,' Dorothy said.

Jenny stared at her.

Dorothy dropped the holdall and undid the zip. 'But I need to do this.'

She pulled out a shovel, ran a finger along its edge, and looked at Jenny. The way Jenny's torch was pointing, her face was mostly in shadow. Dorothy saw her eyelashes illuminated like some fantastical night creature. Eventually Jenny held out a hand, her mouth tight.

Dorothy handed her a shovel then placed the blade of her own shovel against the earth. She put her heel against the shoulder of the shovel and pushed until she felt the earth break underneath her.

'Sorry, Barbara,' she said.

She could smell her own sweat mingled with the stench of mulch and loam, the earth damp and clinging to the blades of their shovels. They'd been at it for two hours, setting the turf to one side then digging out the soil on the other. Dorothy's back was aching, her shoulders hunched, but she kept on, stopping for an occasional swig from a water bottle.

She paused and looked at Jenny. Digging in a solid rhythm, dirt smudged across her cheek and caked on her hands, like a prisoner digging to escape.

Dorothy looked at the hole. She was surprised how far down they'd got already, the earth easy to shift, worms shrinking from the air when exposed, that owl still hooting in the trees somewhere. At one point a fox came padding along the path, spotted them and calmly headed away. The night was still dark, the sky black, only their torches propped against the headstone to see by.

They were properly in a hole now, a few feet below ground level, and Dorothy began digging again, the earth flying behind her shoulder as she heaved each shovelful out of the earth. The secret was rhythm, and she understood how those working songs came about for slaves in the cotton fields or building railroads. Jenny was digging like a woman possessed, maybe working out aggression from something else, her anger and grief at Jim, or the adultery case, or everything with Melanie.

They shifted more shovelfuls, Dorothy's shoulders bending to the work. She pictured the Earth spinning through space at thousands of miles an hour and tried to think how irrelevant all this was, but the truth was it mattered to her more than anything. And it would matter to Barbara Worth's family, but she couldn't help that.

Jenny's shovel thudded into the ground beneath them and Dorothy felt the reverberations through her feet. It felt different from solid ground, it was wood.

Jenny looked round, panting. Dorothy breathed heavily as she leaned on her shovel, then she reached out of the grave and grabbed one of the torches, played it over the blade of Jenny's shovel as she scraped at the earth, spooning it out to expose the grubby oak casket underneath.

They redoubled their efforts even though Dorothy didn't want this to end. As long as they kept digging, she would never have to find out. If they dug all the way to New Zealand she could stay blissfully ignorant about what they were doing, what Jim had done.

Much of the casket was exposed now and the thunk and scrape of their efforts shifted more earth every second. Soon they had the entire lid of the coffin exposed and Dorothy recognised it as the Lindisfarne model, solid oak, not veneer, upwards of a thousand pounds, the most expensive casket they sold. So Barbara's family had money to spend. And money to sue if it came to that.

Jenny stopped digging. The six brass turnkeys along the sides of the coffin lid were exposed, a dull gleam where the torchlight hit them. Dorothy placed her shovel out of the grave and Jenny followed suit. They stood there on the coffin, Dorothy thinking.

Jenny shook her head. 'We don't have to.'

'We've been through this.'

'Are you sure?'

Dorothy nodded. She got to her knees, felt the dampness of the remaining dirt against her trousers, and tried to unscrew the first key in the top left corner. It was tight and she scraped earth from the thread, squeezed the screw between thumb and forefinger and pressed. Finally it started to budge anticlockwise, stiff to begin with then faster as the dirt was pushed aside and the thread caught better.

She turned and saw Jenny doing the same at the bottom end, first one screw, which came easily, then another, which she had to lean into, sticking her elbows out, to get it moving.

Dorothy went back to her own end, started on the second one, scraping away the dirt, feeling the rawness of her skin, the breeze around them, the rustle of leaves on the trees above, that bloody owl and its mate still calling back and forth. Why couldn't they just get it together?

She had the second key out and into her pocket, then moved to one of the middle ones as Jenny crawled from the other direction to do the final one. They were turning the keys at the same time, squeaks as the threads unravelled, the shanks of the keys rising as they turned. Then they were out.

Jenny rose and helped Dorothy to her feet. She shunted herself out of the grave backwards, sitting on her bum at the side of the hole, then helped Dorothy do the same. Dorothy got the pickaxe from the holdall and leaned into the grave, jammed the point of the axe between the lid and the body of the coffin, and waited a moment.

She shared a look with Jenny but couldn't work out what she was thinking. She thought of Jim's shard of bone in her pocket, she carried it everywhere now. She thought of letting go of the pickaxe, leaning back, producing the bone and stabbing herself in the heart with it. Or at least cutting at her wrists. But that was even more crazy than digging up Barbara Worth.

She pursed her lips and swallowed, then levered the pickaxe tip between the casket's lid and body. They separated easily with a pop, the seal broken after a decade of peace. She got her shovel and reached into the hole, stuck the blade under the coffin lid and lifted it up.

Jenny pointed her torch into the grave.

There was Barbara, or what was left of her, a sagging pile of bones, decayed flesh and disintegrated material forming a thin mulch on the floor of the coffin, her skull intact, wisps of flesh and skin still hanging off, worms and slaters hiding from the light, crawling between collar bone and shoulder blade.

'Christ,' Jenny said.

Dorothy stared for a long time then slipped into the coffin like she was sliding into a swimming pool. She landed with a squelch and thought she might be sick.

'Mum.'

Dorothy looked up. She wondered how she must appear to Jenny, wild-eyed, covered in mud, standing amongst human remains in an open grave.

'I have to check,' she said. She put a hand against the wet earth on the side of the hole and crouched down, lifted Barbara's skull with her fingertips. A large earthworm slid out and burrowed away. Dorothy felt some of the coffin base give under her foot, solid earth below.

There was nothing underneath Barbara's skull except more of her decomposed scalp. Dorothy saw a glint of an earring in the mud. She shifted the shoulders and ribcage, lifting them and peering underneath. More of the same, fragments of cloth and skin yet to be returned to the planet. She scanned the rest of the coffin, lifted Barbara's hips, obviously a woman's hips. Nothing there.

She looked round the rest of the grave, the stink of decomposition in her nose, sweat cooling on her brow, her fingers shaking, her nails clogged with dirt and God knows what else. Finally she stopped examining the casket's contents and looked up at Jenny pointing her torch on this horror scene.

'It's only Barbara in here,' Dorothy said, hands on hips. 'I was wrong.'

49

JENNY

'You look like death warmed up.'

Jenny turned to see Hannah in the kitchen doorway. She came in, switched the kettle on and sat opposite Jenny at the table.

It was already afternoon, Jenny sleeping late after last night. It felt like a fever dream, as if it hadn't really happened, or happened to someone else in a parallel universe. But the feel of the dirt was still under her nails, the smell of wet earth was still in her nostrils. To Jenny's amazement Dorothy was downstairs working, arranging a funeral with the husband of an elderly lady who passed away in the night. How could she be functioning, physically and emotionally? Jenny just wanted to curl up and make the world go away.

'How did it go last night?' Hannah said.

Jenny waited for Hannah to tell her that she somehow knew her mother and grandmother spent the night desecrating a grave. It had taken them less time to fill the hole back in but it was still hard work, especially clouded by Dorothy's disappointment about the lack of a second body. The whole escapade was pointless.

She realised she hadn't answered.

'How do you mean?'

The kettle clicked off, the rushing boil of water dying away.

'Speaking to Bradley?'

Jenny switched lanes in her mind, thought for a moment. 'I didn't get anything. The police have spoken to him, I presume they have his DNA.'

Hannah began making tea. 'Just because Peter Longhorn wasn't the father of Mel's kid, doesn't mean he didn't kill her.'

'But it makes it less likely.'

'I don't know,' Hannah said, bringing the mugs over. 'Maybe he killed her because he found out she was pregnant by someone else.'

'But he knew she had a boyfriend.'

Hannah shrugged. 'Who knows what she told him, or what he figured out?'

Jenny looked at the whiteboard. 'So what now?'

'I'm heading round to speak to Xander.'

'Didn't you find him yesterday?'

Hannah shook her head. 'No, he was still at the police station. But I tracked down his flatmates.'

'And?'

'They might not be guilty, but they knew her, and they're misogynist arseholes. I flagged them up with Thomas.'

Jenny sipped her tea. 'Are you sure this is all a good idea? Shouldn't we leave it to the police?'

Hannah shook her head. 'I don't trust the police to do this. I need to keep investigating.'

Jenny looked at the board again. Hannah had added Faisal McNish and Darren Grant to it. 'All these guys circling around Mel. I'll never understand men.'

'Me neither.'

Jenny gave a rueful smile. 'As my own failed marriage demonstrates.'

She wondered where Schrödinger was, maybe out trying to mate or hunting birds. Something macho, anyway.

'What Dad did to you was shit,' Hannah said. 'I'm not stupid, I don't worship him.'

Jenny looked out of the window at the new buildings of Quartermile glinting in the sun.

'Women have strange relationships with their fathers,' she said. She reached out and held Hannah's hand. 'Your gran is convinced my dad was lying to her for years.'

'But there's no proof apart from the money, right?'

Jenny remembered Dorothy in a spotlight, standing in a grave, sifting through bones to get to the truth. But there was no truth, at least not the kind she was looking for. 'No, there isn't.'

'Well, then.'

Jenny sipped her tea. 'We think our dads are perfect but we know what men are like in the real world. And dads are just men, after all.' She looked at Hannah. 'You made the right choice with Indy.'

Hannah frowned. 'It's not any different. Men and women, straight and gay, we're just trying to get along, not hurt anyone, but it doesn't always work like that.'

Jenny smiled. 'How did I have a daughter so wise?'

Hannah got up and looked at the whiteboards. They were updated, new lines drawn, names scored out, funerals conducted, suspects added.

'What about your adultery case?' Hannah said.

Part of Jenny couldn't believe the world was still turning after last night. She'd presumed they would get caught. How can you just walk into a cemetery and dig someone up and no one even notice? The way they'd left the grave would be noticeable if anyone paid close attention. They'd cut the turf and laid it to the side first, then when they'd filled the hole back in they'd stamped it back down over the earth, but the cuts in the sod were easy to see. Maybe it was only a matter of time until someone saw it and twigged, the groundskeeper or a relative. Then there would be an appeal for information in the local paper, a disgusted husband or brother standing next to the grave. Maybe they would dig it up again to make sure she was still in there. Maybe there was CCTV they hadn't spotted. Maybe that bloody owl would blab to the world about what it saw.

She realised she hadn't answered Hannah again.

'He's innocent,' she said.

'Really?'

'I think so.'

'Some men are OK, then.'

Jenny shrugged, thinking of Liam's eyes, those paintings. 'Maybe.'

'So is the case closed?'

'She was setting up a sting on him. She hired an escort to seduce him while I was on his tail.'

Hannah's eyes were wide. 'Wow. But he didn't bite?'

'Wasn't interested.' Jenny scratched her neck. 'There's more. His wife is the one sleeping around. I saw her with a landscape gardener.'

'Have you told him?' Hannah said.

'Not yet.'

'Are you going to?'

'I don't know. Technically, I'm off the case and it's none of my business.'

Hannah looked at her. 'But?'

'I should tell him.'

'What's stopping you?'

Jenny got up, stared at the boards, all the death and deceit, all the secrets and lies. 'It's not always easy to do the right thing.'

She thought about her mum holding Barbara's skull in her hand, about some faceless man strangling Mel to death, about Orla sharing an orgasm with her gardener. She thought about Archie and his condition, thinking that he was dead. Then she remembered something from the other night, something she'd forgotten until now. The piece of paper. When she was comforting Mum, Archie had slipped a piece of paperwork onto the floor right here in the kitchen. Then when she looked again it was gone. She hadn't realised at the time, but after last night it suddenly came to her. It was another burial from ten years ago.

She pushed her chair back and headed towards the door.

'Mum?' Hannah said behind her as she took the stairs, down to reception, where Indy was manning the desk.

'Is Archie in?'

Indy shook her head. 'He's at the Western General on a pick-up.'

Jenny went to the embalming room. Empty. She walked through to the workshop where Archie made up the coffins, no one around. She went to his desk, tools and wood scraps, swathes of material for coffin linings. She looked at the mess, the shelves of paperwork. She saw Archie's jacket hanging up and went through the pockets, just cigarettes, a lighter, breath mints. She pulled out the first drawer of the desk, rummaged through the junk in there, no paperwork, then the next drawer down. She looked again at the shelves, folders of invoices and receipts, years of stuff to go through. It could be anywhere.

She turned and looked around the workshop. Stood thinking. There were three coffins on workbenches in different stages of completion. The nearest was very rough, just four sides, no bottom attached yet. The second was a complete structure but had no lining. The third was lined on the inside with silky white fabric. She stared into it for a few seconds then ran her hand around the material, from the head down to the feet. Felt normal. Then she ran her hands around the sides, from the bottom back to the top. It felt different along the headboard. Not rough wood underneath, something smoother. Paper.

She pulled at the material, ripping staples out of the wood, tearing the sheer fabric until she had the underneath exposed. She recognised the yellowing lined paper as she lifted it out and unfolded it.

Ailsa Montgomery, buried in Piershill Cemetery.

The date on the piece of paper was the day after Barbara Worth's funeral.

50
HANNAH

Xander's flat was on Clerk Street above an old man's pub called The Grapes which everyone called The Sour Grapes due to the faces of the regulars smoking outside. The street was a main route south, maroon buses queuing up at the stops, the pavements cluttered with a mix of students, locals and tourists who'd lost their way.

The guys from The Grapes eyeballed Hannah as she pressed the buzzer for Shaw, one of four surnames on their panel.

A voice came on the intercom. 'Yeah.'

'It's Hannah.'

The door clicked and she went up the dark stairwell, posties' elastic bands piled at the bottom of the spiral stairs, two clarty bikes chained to the banister.

She knocked on the door and waited. She was about to knock again when Xander opened the door looking blurry. He'd sounded hungover on the phone and he confirmed that with bleary eyes and the smell of stale booze.

'Can I come in?'

'No.'

Hannah looked past him and he tightened the space between his body and the door.

'Got another girlfriend already?'

'What kind of person do you think I am?'

'I don't know, that's why I'm here.'

Xander looked at her with loathing. 'You don't have a monopoly on grief. Or anger.'

'I never said I did.'

'Well, you're fucking acting like it.'

'I just want to find out what happened.'

'Join the queue.'

Hannah put her hands out in appeasement. 'Look, can I come in so we can talk?'

'Say what you have to say here.'

'You're acting very uncooperatively for someone who wants to know what happened.'

That made him straighten up. 'Fuck off, Hannah. The police interviewed me at the station and took a DNA sample. I had to get a solicitor. Then I find out Mel was sleeping with Longhorn. Then I find out she was pregnant, it wasn't Longhorn's and it wasn't mine either.'

'It wasn't?'

'So you don't know everything.'

'The baby wasn't yours?'

Xander slumped and breathed out like a deflating balloon. 'Which means she was sleeping with someone else.'

'A third guy.'

'A third guy,' Xander said, like a zombie. 'A third guy who probably killed her. And she was my girlfriend. So stop acting like an avenging angel out for the truth, like you're something special, when we all want to know, we all want to get the cunt who did this.'

Hannah rested a hand on the doorframe and thought about a third guy. Bradley Barker, Darren Grant, Faisal McNish, someone else walking about out there with a guilty conscience, or maybe not feeling guilty at all, maybe thrilled or proud or turned on by the memory of what he did.

'And you had no idea?'

'None.'

A flicker of something on his face made Hannah pause. 'What?'

He shook his head. 'It never occurred to me there were other guys, but...'

'But what?'

He looked awkward. 'She had an appetite.'

Hannah squinted at him. 'How do you mean?'

'Sex. She was, you know, full on. Like, she wanted to do some crazy shit, but I wouldn't.'

Hannah felt another part of her image of Mel crumble. Was it this easy to keep so many sides of yourself secret?

She felt herself deflate just like Xander. This was sucking the life out of her. Maybe she didn't have the stomach to be an investigator, if that was even what she was. She had exams coming up, coursework, she wanted to sit in the sunshine right now with Indy flicking through a no-brain magazine full of opinions on people's dresses or diets. But that was a lie too. She would get bored doing nothing, and frustrated that someone was out there who hadn't paid for what he'd done. Mel and her family deserved answers. The police would do all they could, but they didn't care like she cared, it wasn't personal for them. Plus they had to obey the law, follow due process. But she could do what she wanted, if only she knew what that was.

'I know you mean well,' Xander said. 'But I'm not the enemy, we're on the same side.'

Hannah wished she could know that was true.

'Here,' he said, ducking behind the door. He appeared with a bin bag of stuff, nothing heavy from the way he held it out to her. 'Take this, it's Mel's clothes that she left here.'

'Didn't the police want this?'

Xander shrugged. 'They never asked. Anyway, I trust you to find out what happened more than I trust them.'

She took the bag and opened it. A couple of T-shirts, some nightwear, a sweatshirt and an old jacket. The smell of Mel's perfume came off the clothes and made Hannah feel sick.

'Thanks,' she said, slinging it over her shoulder.

Xander swallowed hard. Maybe she was wrong about him, maybe he wasn't hungover, maybe he was just sad. Or both.

'Find the bastard who did this,' he said.

'I will,' Hannah said, but she wasn't convinced by her own words.

She went downstairs and along Clerk Street and was turning into Hope Park Terrace when her phone rang. Thomas.

'Hannah.'

'Have you got something?'

'The phone you gave me,' he said, 'it's a dead end. She only called one number but it's another burner, not registered. Whoever it was, they were being careful. We tried the number, of course, but it's dead. And we tried a physical trace, nothing. I'm sorry.'

Hannah watched the traffic clogging up towards the Meadows, people crossing on the green man, getting home to loved ones, their lives without mystery, and she longed to be one of them.

She got up and walked around the kitchen, arching her back and rubbing at her shoulders. She'd been looking at the footage from the Glassman house for two and a half hours with nothing to show for it but a crick in her neck and a pain across her forehead. But she needed the distraction. She hadn't got anywhere with Mel, with the dizzying array of arseholes who seemed to have been circling her when she died, and there were only so many times you could confront someone on their doorstep and hope to get anything out of it except a restraining order.

So she'd thrown herself into this. Gran had a funeral on today and she'd asked for help to keep on top of the data coming in from the spy cameras. Hannah told her how to Dropbox them over to her so she could scan them at home.

But so far, nothing. Gran had explained about the cleaner as well as the carer, but that hadn't been any use either. And the rest was just mundane stuff, Jacob trying to make a cup of tea on his own with shaking hands, him watching *University Challenge* and talking to the television set. The cameras didn't have audio, so she didn't know whether he was getting any of the answers right.

She went back to the laptop and sighed, sat down again. Opened a new file, from late yesterday evening, the camera that she'd placed in the wardrobe of Jacob's bedroom. He was obviously aware of the camera there, walked over to check it was still in position, stared blankly into the screen, then left the room with pyjamas in hand, presumably to get changed in the bathroom. It must be strange, Hannah thought, having your every move watched. Well, not every move, thankfully she didn't have to see his bare butt.

The footage jumped to him re-entering the room and climbing slowly into bed. He found reading glasses and flicked through an old paperback for a few minutes before placing the open book on the covers, removing his glasses and turning the light off. The camera switched to low-light mode with the bedside lamp off, but there was nothing to see, just an old man asleep in his bed. Hannah imagined him getting up and sleepwalking, or a jump-scare from a horror movie, the face of a terrible demon screaming into the camera lens, or the pale shadow of a ghost standing at the foot of the bed pointing at Jacob.

But instead the footage just clicked forwards on the time stamp to a few hours later, Jacob rising to visit the bathroom, then re-turning and settling in again. Then another jump, another visit to the toilet, another return, then it was morning and Jacob was waking up.

God, this was boring.

She went to check the other cameras for the same period through the night. She presumed Dorothy hadn't looked at any of them yet, there was no note of it in the file where they logged what they'd watched.

She opened a file for the kitchen-cam, the one that started at midnight.

And almost fell off her chair.

A young woman walked calmly into the kitchen, went to the fridge and started making a sandwich. She pulled a bottle of red wine from a rack and unscrewed it, getting a glass from the cupboard. She knew her way around.

Hannah gazed at the screen as if it was the best movie she'd ever seen.

The woman was wearing joggers and a loose T-shirt, but she had her back to the camera while she spread butter on bread, added cheese and ham, put it all together. She had blonde hair, long with a fringe.

Hannah checked the file on Susan Raymond that she'd put together for Dorothy. It wasn't her, totally different body shape and hair colour. Then she went online, searched for Monika Belenko and Home Angels, came up with a Facebook profile of a glamorous young woman. The hair colour was right, but the wrong style. Maybe she'd had the fringe cut recently.

The woman cleared her sandwich stuff back into the fridge and left the room.

Hannah clicked on another file, opened it, and there was the woman in the living room, the television on a comedy channel. She was playing with an iPad, sitting on the sofa, eating the sandwich and sipping her wine. The glow of the iPad lit her face a little better, and she didn't look much like the Facebook profile, but Hannah wasn't sure. And anyway, if it was the cleaner, what the hell was she doing in the house in the middle of the night?

Hannah opened more files, not closing down the previous ones, so that umpteen windows cluttered her laptop screen. There was nothing on the dining-room one. The kitchen one showed the woman coming back in to fill up her wine glass, take a sip while standing at the window, then leave again. She was picked up by the living-room camera, this time on her phone, scrolling through with her thumb.

Hannah checked the final camera, the upstairs hall, and she froze.

The first bit of footage showed a hatch in the ceiling gently opening from above, then a ladder from the attic unfolding down to the floorboards. When the ladder was fully extended, the young woman came down it, checking that the coast was clear. She had bare feet on the ladder rungs, and Hannah could see more clearly now that her clothes were nightwear.

'Holy shit,' Hannah said. 'She's living in the attic.'

51
DOROTHY

She was glad Arthur Ford was being cremated, she couldn't stand the sight of an open grave today. She stood outside Mortonhall Crematorium watching the mourners trickle inside, a few stragglers smoking last-minute cigarettes before paying their final respects.

The crem building was a modernist concrete construction like giant garden slabs piled up at random angles, but it did the job of hiding the industrial chimney of the incinerator. The place had been spruced up in the recent renovation, after it almost burned down three years back. That accident had at least drawn attention away from the baby ashes scandal before that. That had knocked the city and Dorothy was still fielding questions about it from customers, even though it was the council and nothing to do with Skelf's. She pictured herself standing in the grave last night, and wondered about the scandal of that.

There were three funeral cars pulled in behind the hearse. Six frail old men in threadbare suits lifted the coffin out of the hearse as Dorothy watched, her brain wired from lack of sleep, haunted by visions of a skull staring at her from the mulch of a grave.

She led the way, the six men with the weight of the world on their shoulders behind, then Archie bringing up the rear. She walked into the building, felt her shoulders relax when she heard the hubbub die and the rumble of a hundred people rise to their feet. There was safety in familiarity now, something to grasp hold of.

Once the coffin was on the plinth, she stood back and let the minister do his thing, try to bring some meaning to Arthur Ford's death. Dorothy lingered at the door and Archie joined her. She tensed up, couldn't help herself. A tremor ran through her body and she felt so tired suddenly that she thought she might throw up.

A string of relatives got up and said nice things about Arthur, ways that he had been kind in the world, examples of his sense of humour, his charity, the Rotary Club, bowls, three children and four grandchildren. Dorothy wondered who would get up at her funeral, what they could say to cast her in a good light. Maybe she would bypass the whole thing like Jim did, get Jenny and Hannah to throw her in a skip on the outskirts of town. Save everyone the bother of lying and saying she was a good person, a person who didn't destroy the last resting places of the innocent.

Eventually Arthur was lowered into the plinth via the motorised mechanism, down into the fiery pits of hell. Or the incinerator. The pine coffin would be sparking into life, splintering and burning, his body cooking inside, water vapour turning to steam, skin shrivelling to old leather then crisping and bursting into flames, fat from his body dissolving, a million chemical reactions that would transform him into something else.

The congregation filed out and dispersed, Arthur's wife stoic but shellshocked by the whole thing, three daughters by her side crying into handkerchiefs.

Then they were into the funeral cars and away to a modest reception at the bowling club, to raise a glass of something to his memory.

Dorothy got in the passenger seat of the hearse beside Archie and heaved a sigh.

'You OK?' Archie said.

Dorothy took a long time to answer. 'Not really.'

Archie didn't start the engine, just sat watching the last few mourners walk to their cars or out of the gate to catch a bus.

'There was something on the news this morning,' Archie said.

Dorothy stared at her hands. She could feel the dirt still under her nails despite scrubbing and using a nail file.

'Apparently someone disturbed a grave in Portobello Cemetery.'

Dorothy felt tears in her eyes as she looked out of the window away from Archie's gaze.

'The groundskeeper alerted police,' Archie said. 'But they think it was just a prank. A sick joke. They think the grave wasn't dug up, just the surface layer messed with.'

'Right,' Dorothy said, her throat dry.

'Dorothy.'

The tone of his voice made her turn. He was almost crying and that made her tears come. She wiped at her cheeks with her hands.

'Don't speak,' she said, swallowing hard.

They sat for a long time, no sound except their breathing, the windows steaming up.

Eventually Dorothy reached into her pocket and pulled out the piece of paper. She unfolded it carefully and offered it to him. He stared at it but didn't take it.

'What's that?' he said.

'Jenny found this,' she said. 'It's another burial from the same time.'

'Where did she find it?'

Dorothy hesitated, pressed her lips together. 'Sealed under the lining of a coffin in the workshop.'

'How the hell did it get there?'

'You really don't know?'

Archie shook his head.

'Come on, Archie.'

'Honestly, Dorothy.'

He took the piece of paper, which trembled in his hand as he squinted at it.

Dorothy took the paper back and stared at it. Thought about Ailsa Montgomery. 'I'm going to dig her up tonight.'

'Good luck.'

'You're coming too.'

'No I'm not.'

'You owe me, Archie, you said so yourself. You owe me your life.'

'That's not fair.'

'Life's not fair.'

'I won't do it.'

'Then consider yourself out of a job,' Dorothy said. 'As of now.'

Archie looked across and held her gaze. 'This is a bad idea.'

She stared at him then folded the piece of paper and put it away in her pocket.

Her phone rang. Hannah.

'Gran, there's something on the camera footage,' Hannah said. 'The Glassman case. You're not going to believe it.'

52
JENNY

The King's Wark was quiet, which made this harder. The sun had set outside, the dim light in here making it more intimate. Liam was in his usual spot at the bar, two-thirds through his lager, crossword in front of him. Jenny thought about what she had to say.

She'd sat in the café across from the studio vennel for two hours until Liam left, then waited another twenty minutes. When she finally got up she hoped he wouldn't be here, that he'd skip his drink and head home to his loving wife. Ha. Her heart sank when she pulled open the door and saw him on his stool. The fates had decided, she would go through with it.

She walked to the bar and stood next to him. He didn't notice her, intent on his paper. Jenny waited to be served, it was a barman she hadn't seen before, a guy in his late twenties, hipster beard waxed at the corners, gelled quiff, arms sleeved with tattoos of birds and boats.

'Double gin and tonic, thanks,' she said.

Liam looked up at her voice. He smiled and her heart sank.

'It's the artistic funeral director.'

'Hi.'

She put out her hand and regretted it, it was too formal, a stupid gesture, but he smiled and shook it.

'Can I get you a drink?' she said, nodding at his pint glass.

'I'm fine.'

'Sure?'

He thought about it for a second, smiled. 'OK, pint of Amstel.'

She got the drinks and passed his over. 'Cheers.'

They clinked and drank, Jenny taking a big gulp, feeling the edge of it.

'So did you take the studio?' Liam said.

'What?'

'I presume as you're here, that you've taken the studio round the corner.'

'No, I didn't rent it in the end.'

'Shame,' Liam said, and he seemed to mean it. 'We could've been artistic buddies.'

Jenny put on a thin smile. She pictured a different universe where she worked on paintings or sculptures, the graft of creating, then sat here afterwards putting the world to rights with Liam, the glow of the fire on winter nights.

'Why didn't you, out of interest?' Liam said.

She drank more gin, swallowed it down like juice.

'I'm not really an artist,' she said.

Liam shook his head and sucked his teeth, almost tutted. 'I know what you mean, but that's not the attitude. It's not like you apply to the council to get an artist's licence. Everyone's creative in some way, it's about giving yourself permission, finding a way to express yourself.'

'That's not what I mean.' Jenny pulled at her ear and swallowed.

Liam waved this away. 'I think you should take the studio. Everyone needs a place where they can get some headspace. That's what the studio is for me, a place where I can be myself away from the noise of the world. You don't know what you're capable of until you really give yourself the chance.'

You don't know what you're capable of. Jenny thought about digging up the grave last night. She drank more gin and tonic, her glass almost empty. She raised her hand in case Liam was going to say anything else, she couldn't stand to hear him speak.

'I have to tell you something.'

He took a drink and put his pint glass down. Staff glided behind the bar like ghosts, conversations behind Jenny murmured on like incantations of the dead. She imagined everyone stopping talking to stare at her, a spotlight shining on her as she spoke.

'I lied,' she said, scratching her cheek. 'When I came to the studio, I wasn't looking to hire a place.'

'Then what were you doing?'

Jenny looked away then back at him. 'I needed to speak to you. I was working.'

'The funeral thing?'

'No. As well as the funeral business, we run a private investigator's. I was investigating you.'

'Me?' He thought it was a wind-up.

She nodded and drank the last of her gin.

'Why?' he said.

She breathed in and out, shifted her weight. 'Your wife hired me. She thought you were having an affair.'

Liam laughed. 'This is a joke, someone put you up to this.'

'She hired me at her sister's funeral to look into you. I've been following you for the last week.'

'I don't believe you.'

'I sat outside your house, followed you to work, then to the studio. I've been in here twice before when you were in.'

'Orla wouldn't do this.'

'That's not all.'

His hand was tight on his pint glass, veins showing across his knuckles. 'What do you mean?'

'The other night,' Jenny said. 'The woman in the skirt chatting you up.'

Liam took a moment to twig, then remembered. 'What about her?'

'She was an escort. Orla hired her to sleep with you.'

'Fuck off, you've lost the plot.'

'I spoke to the woman after you left,' Jenny said, wishing she hadn't finished her drink so quickly. 'She confirmed it. Orla was trying to set you up as an adulterer, to take everything in a divorce.'

'You've made a mistake.'

Jenny shook her head. 'There's one other thing.'

'I don't want to hear it.'

Jenny was worried Liam's grip would smash the pint glass, beer and blood everywhere. 'I saw Orla with someone.'

Liam didn't speak.

'A guy called Karl Zukas.'

Recognition in his face. 'He does some gardening work for us.'

'Orla is sleeping with him.'

'Bullshit,' Liam said. 'You're some mad stalker. Is this because your dad died, a weird grief thing?'

Jenny went into her bag and brought out an envelope. She'd laughed when Orla mentioned brown envelopes, but she hadn't been able to think of any other way to do this. So here she was sliding an envelope across the bar towards him.

Liam stared at the envelope. 'This is a sick joke.'

Jenny looked at him, her face flushed. 'I wish it was.'

He stood up, releasing his grip on the glass.

'Goodbye,' he said.

Jenny held out the envelope. 'I'm so sorry, Liam. But I had to tell you.'

He went to walk away and she pressed the envelope to his chest. He paused, hands at his side. He held her gaze for a long time, then eventually grabbed the envelope and strode out of the pub clutching it in his fist like a death sentence.

53
DOROTHY

'Are you sure about this?' Thomas said.

Dorothy looked at him. They were sitting in his car outside 11 Hermitage Drive. Dorothy turned and looked at the house, up at the roof. Quite a bit of space up there, by the look of it. An old lady walking a terrier in a coat gave Thomas a stare as she passed. A black man in a rich area, really? Dorothy turned back to him and nodded.

'I've seen the footage.'

'I mean, are you sure you want to come in with me?'

'Of course, Jacob doesn't know you.'

They got out and went up the path, rang the bell and waited. It was a long time before Jacob answered.

'We need to talk,' Dorothy said.

'Who's your friend?'

'Thomas Olsson, he's a police officer.'

'So you found something?'

'Can we come in?'

Dorothy looked up the stairs as they went to the kitchen. Wondered if she was up there now. Wondered if she would make a run for it. But why would she if she didn't know they were on to her?

Jacob turned at the kitchen table. 'So?'

Thomas smiled at him. 'I think you should sit down.'

Jacob frowned but sat.

'When was the last time you were in your attic?' Thomas said.

Jacob laughed, pointed at his walking frame. 'Look at me. When do you think?'

Dorothy took a seat at the table too. 'Has anyone been up there recently?'

'No,' Jacob said, confused. 'What is this?'

Dorothy gave Thomas a look.

'We think someone is living up there,' Thomas said.

'What?'

Dorothy nodded. 'We have footage. She comes down at night when you're asleep.'

'Susan?'

Dorothy shook her head. 'It's not Susan Raymond. We think it might be Monika.'

Jacob coughed, swallowed hard. 'I don't understand. How can someone be living up there?'

Thomas glanced at the ceiling. 'Can we take a look?'

'You think she's up there now?'

Dorothy shrugged.

Jacob made a vague hand gesture towards the ceiling, giving permission.

'Wait here,' Thomas said to Dorothy.

She shook her head. 'No, I need to see.'

Thomas knew better than to argue.

'We'll be back in a moment,' Dorothy said to Jacob, who just sat there shaking his head.

She followed Thomas up the stairs and they stood under the hatch in the ceiling. On his tiptoes, Thomas could just reach the hatch, lowered it quietly, the ladder unfolding automatically.

They stood and listened. No sound.

'Don't bother telling me to stay here,' Dorothy said quietly.

'OK, but I'll go first.'

Thomas placed careful feet on the ladder and up he went, Dorothy behind. Thomas paused before peering over the top, then glanced back and shrugged, continued up the ladder and into the attic. Dorothy got her head through the hatch and looked around. She half expected someone to come running at her with a baseball bat, or to grab her hair and shove her down the ladder.

She kept up the ladder, taking in the room. It was a large space, the slope of the eaves not too steep. It was floored, cheap chipboard, with piles of cardboard boxes here and there, a set of golf clubs and some old dumbbells in a corner. There were two small skylights that had sheets pinned over them, spreading diffuse light into the space. And over against the far wall was a mattress with a pile of bedding on it, including a sleeping bag, a duvet and a blanket. Next to the mattress was an open sports bag full of women's clothes, a bag of toiletries, a pair of trainers, a bottle of water and a torch. There was also a small basin, which smelled of urine as Dorothy got closer. Thomas was ahead of her, soft steps towards the bed too, and as they got closer Dorothy saw the bed covers move, then she heard a snuffle and saw the top of a woman's head sticking out from the sleeping bag.

She exchanged a look with Thomas, who crouched down next to the woman then gently shook her.

'Hey,' he said. 'Wake up.'

The woman jumped and shrank away from his touch, scuttling against the wall and pulling the sleeping bag against her chest.

'I'm a police officer,' Thomas said.

The woman looked from Thomas to Dorothy then back again, trying to shake the sleep away.

'Who are you?' Dorothy said, because the woman definitely wasn't Monika Belenko.

The woman shook her head, looked past them at the hatch.

'I wouldn't recommend it,' Thomas said.

'Why don't we go downstairs and have a chat?' Dorothy said.

'No, thanks,' the woman said. Scottish accent.

Thomas stood up. 'It's that or come to the police station.'

The woman seemed to deflate, shrugged.

'I'll put the kettle on,' Dorothy said.

The woman thought for a long time then stood up.

Thomas led the way down the ladder, then the woman, then Dorothy last. The woman let herself be taken downstairs and along the hall, into the kitchen. Jacob was still sitting where they'd left him. He frowned when he saw the woman, then his eyes widened.

'Amy?' he said.

'Hi, Jacob.'

'You know each other?' Thomas said.

'She delivered my post,' Jacob said. 'She was my postie until a few months ago. What is this?'

Amy lowered her chin to her chest. She seemed vulnerable in her T-shirt and pyjama bottoms when the rest of them were fully dressed. Dorothy pulled a chair out for her at the table and put the kettle on, began making tea. Amy rubbed at her forehead then eventually sat down across the table from Jacob. Thomas stood near the doorway, in case she made a break for it.

'I'm sorry,' she said eventually, her head still down.

Dorothy put tea in front of her and Jacob, stepped back.

'You've been living in my home?' Jacob said. 'I don't understand.'

Amy finally looked up, held her hands out as if to say she didn't understand it either. She scratched at the table, rubbed her hair, looked around for help.

'Come on,' Thomas said, not unkindly.

Amy shook her head. 'I got made redundant by the Post Office. Cutbacks, the usual shite. Pretty soon I couldn't pay the rent. I had flatmates, but they weren't friends. I had nothing, just a bag of clothes. No family. It's amazing how quickly you can just slip through the cracks.'

She touched her mug but didn't drink. She looked around again, gave a sad smile. 'This place looks different in daylight.'

'How did you end up here?' Dorothy said.

Amy turned to her and frowned. 'Who are you?'

'I'm a private investigator. Jacob hired me when he thought stuff was going missing.'

Amy turned to Jacob. 'I'm so sorry.'

Jacob narrowed his eyes. 'You didn't answer her question, how did you get here?'

Amy shrugged. 'Any of you ever slept on the street? It's fucking awful, you can't imagine how bad. I only did it for a few days and I wanted to kill myself. Then I got thinking. All those big posh houses I delivered post to. Some of them were probably empty. So I started retracing my routes, checking out the houses. But most have good security, full of families. Then I remembered you, Jacob.'

She swallowed and pulled on her earlobe.

'I knew you lived here alone, you told me. We always chatted at the door if I had a parcel that was too big for the letterbox. And you weren't very mobile, probably didn't use half of the house. Plus you were, you know, nice. Harmless. So I just thought, why not?'

'But how did you get in?'

'I knew you didn't lock the front door during the day. And I remembered you moaning that you kept falling asleep in front of the television. I just came by a few times, sneaked a look in the window. Waited till you were asleep, walked right in and up the stairs.'

Thomas folded his arms. 'When was this?'

Amy ran her tongue around the inside of her cheek, thinking. 'Three months ago.'

Jacob's eyes were wide. 'You've been living in my attic for three months?'

She shrugged. 'Sorry.'

'I have a question,' Dorothy said, watching her closely. 'How did you think this was going to end?'

Amy shook her head. 'I didn't think that far ahead. I was just staying off the street.' She finally took a sip of her tea and looked around at the three of them.

'So, how does it end?' she said.

54
HANNAH

Hannah stared at the mess of Mel's room. Mel was never coming home, why bother making things neat? The drawers were still piled on the floor, their contents strewn all over the place. Forensics had taken away a few items in plastic bags, but they had refused to tell her what the items were, or why they were taking them.

She righted the bedframe and flopped the mattress on top, then slumped down with a sigh, lay down on Xander's bag of Mel's clothes that she'd dumped in here earlier, before all that nuts stuff with Jacob Glassman. She stared at the ceiling and wondered what Mel was thinking last time she was in this bed. Was she fucking Xander, lost in an orgasm, or thinking about Peter Longhorn? Or this third guy. Maybe she was worried that the third guy was dangerous. She was pregnant but hadn't told anyone, so maybe that was preying on her mind. Maybe she wanted to tell the father, and she wondered how that would go. Did she want to keep it, get rid of it, give it up for adoption? You never got answers once someone was dead.

The bullshit of television dramas where everything gets wrapped up after six episodes was such a lie. We need that resolution, sure, because we don't get it in real life. Real life is a mess, non sequiturs, inconsequential moments, no building tension to a satisfying climax. Real life didn't need hooks before the advert breaks or cliffhangers at the end of an hour. Real life just left you bereft and lonely, grieving for people who would never come back, wishing you'd lived differently in some unspecified way. Real life was a bastard. And then you die.

She lifted a pillow off the floor. There was a long black hair on it, one of Mel's, and she rubbed it between her fingertips, watching it spin. She'd read somewhere that hundreds of years ago they believed that the face of a murderer would be imprinted on the eyes of his victim. Then there was muscle memory, the way your body could do certain things when your mind couldn't, like play a musical instrument or drive a car. And she remembered a silly show on television where someone got a heart transplant and started dressing differently, liking different food and music, their new tastes exactly matching those of the donor. Maybe this hair was the key, maybe if she absorbed the information locked in its proteins she would know who killed Mel. Maybe on a quantum level the quarks and leptons in her own atoms would mingle with Mel's, creating an energy field that connected them. She could become Mel and live her life over and figure out what happened to her.

She placed the hair back on the pillow and lay there listening to her breath. Eventually she sat up and took in the room again. What would happen to Mel's stuff? Who tidies up after the dead? What's the point of keeping physics notes for a degree that no one is ever going to get? What about all the technical stuff, bank account, university enrolment, rent, voter register, national insurance number. There were a million incidental details that defined a life and they all had to be terminated after you die. How could anyone face that?

She thought about phoning Vic, see how he was doing, how his mum and dad were coping, but she couldn't face that conversation. She was a coward. Maybe this private investigator stuff was a way to deflect herself from thinking about how she actually felt about her friend dying. She knew all about coping mechanisms from Indy working at Skelf's, and from her gran and grandpa. And that was another piece of avoidance, Jim had died ten days ago and she'd scarcely given it a thought, filling her mind with second phones, mystery lovers, DNA matches and dead babies.

And maybe the biggest piece of avoidance now was Peter. It was her fault no matter how many times she told herself it wasn't. He might have been fucking Mel but he wasn't the father, and Hannah had exposed him to his wife. OK, the guilt was his, but Hannah drove him to a situation where he couldn't see a way out, and that was just awful.

So there was guilt, grief and loss, what a pile of shit.

She wondered how Dorothy coped with this stuff every day. It was other people's grief, but how the hell do you not take it on without becoming a heartless bitch?

She opened the bin bag and emptied the clothes onto the bed. She lifted a T-shirt, a vintage skinny-fit with Hong Kong Phooey on it, a cartoon character from the 1980s that looked like a terrible piece of cultural appropriation. Hannah had been with Mel when she bought it in Armstrong's. Mel loved it because of the cultural thing and her parents were annoyed by it. So maybe Mel always had a mischievous side. It was easy to think of her as the good girl, but none of us are defined so easily, we all play different roles within different groups of people. That's what helps us connect.

Hannah lifted the T-shirt and inhaled a mix of Mel's perfume, maybe some sweat, that second-hand fustiness underneath. She lifted each piece of clothing in turn and smelled them, feeling queasy. Finally she got to the jacket, a sporty waterproof material, again retro like something worn by a B-girl breakdancer in Harlem at the birth of hip-hop. Hannah checked the pockets, empty, then as she threw it back on the bed she noticed a zipped pocket on the inside. She tugged at the zip, a little stiff, held the material around the zip for purchase, and opened it. She slid two fingers in and felt a piece of paper. She pulled it out, a receipt for two drinks, a dirty martini and a bottle of Birra Moretti. It was from the bar of Malmaison, a boutique hotel at Leith waterfront.

She turned the receipt over in her hands. The date was two weeks ago. Mel surely knew she was pregnant then but maybe one dirty martini didn't make any difference.

She picked up her phone and called.

Eventually Xander picked up. 'What?'

Hannah stood up. 'Did you ever go to Malmaison with Mel?'

'What?'

'It's a simple question, did you ever drink with her there?'

'At their prices? I don't think so.'

'You're sure.'

'Do you have something?'

'I have to go.'

She hung up and called again.

'Hello, Hannah.' Thomas's voice, always calm.

'Mel was drinking in Malmaison with someone two weeks ago and it wasn't Xander.'

'How do you know?'

'I have a receipt, found it in her jacket that was at Xander's flat.'

'It could've been Peter Longhorn.'

'But it might not have been,' Hannah said, pacing the room.

'If you bring the receipt in, I'll send an officer there to ask.'

Hannah thought about that. The police hadn't even asked for Mel's stuff from Xander's place. She could deal with this quicker, she was a private investigator after all.

'Hannah?' Thomas said. 'Are you still there?'

'Yes,' she said, putting the receipt into her pocket. 'I'll bring it round to the station.'

She hung up, threw on Mel's jacket and headed out the door to Leith.

55
Jenny

She looked round The Pear Tree beer garden and tried not to feel sick. It was partly down to the gin, partly guilt about Liam. He seemed like one of the good guys and she'd destroyed his marriage. Then there was her dad's death, the loss but also the revelations. Standing in a grave that she and her mum had dug out together, the shame of that. And Mel, with more men than sense and pregnant too, all of it making a mess of Jenny's head and heart.

And there was Craig too, sitting across from her with the smile she knew so well. Yet he'd betrayed her too. And now he'd betrayed his wife. Jenny felt guilty about that, and guilty for calling him when she left The King's Wark, crying on the phone, feeling embarrassed and stupid but she didn't care, and when Craig offered to meet her, part of her was mortified but another part wanted to feel that old familiarity and said yes.

'You're too hard on yourself,' Craig said, resting his hand on hers. God, she still missed that touch.

It was dark in the beer garden, fairy lights along the wall making everything fuzzy round the edges, or maybe that was the gin. A group of freezing Italians sat at the next table, scarves and winter jackets despite the evening warmth. Their own table was wet from the sweat of their glasses, a flyer there for a student club night on Cowgate. She remembered clubbing in Sneaky's, then that dreadful place on King Stables Road, then Studio 24 down from The Venue, and she wondered if any of these places were still there, if kids still drank snakebite and took speed, if they stayed up all night smoking weed to come down and yammering about nothing and everything, instead of helping their mums dig graves and ruining marriages.

'Maybe I need someone to be hard on me,' she said.

She hadn't intended the double entendre but Craig made a face and they both laughed. It was pathetically gratifying to have someone still consider you a sexual being, and she hated that she felt that way. Hated what she was thinking about Craig and his stupid wife who'd stolen him from her. Hated that she realised there was no going back, but fuck it, she was drunk and upset and he was here with his hand on hers.

'It sounds like you did this guy a favour,' Craig said, his fingers stroking the back of her hand. That skin on her hand had been elastic and tight when they first met, when they were young and naïve and full of energy. And now it was slack along with the rest of her body, driven south by age and gravity, as if she was melting into the floor unnoticed by the world. But not unnoticed by Craig.

'I don't know,' she said, sipping her drink, feeling the burn.

'Come on,' Craig said. 'It's one thing to have an affair—'

Her raised eyebrows made him put his hands out in defence. 'I know, I know.' He bowed his head in mock deference. 'I can never make up for what I did, I get that.'

She chewed her lip, a mix of thinking and signalling.

'But this woman isn't just sleeping around, she set him up for a fall. That's another level of devious bastardry.'

'And you would know about devious bastardry.'

'I'm just saying.'

They both took a drink, Jenny looking around, Craig watching her.

'Did you fancy him?' Craig said eventually.

'This isn't the playground.'

'Just asking.'

She smiled. 'He is cute.'

Craig raised his eyebrows.

'And he clearly works out,' Jenny said.

Craig made a show of his guns and she laughed despite herself.

'I've always been secure about my masculinity,' he said.

He was right, that was one of the things she liked about him, he wasn't threatened by the idea of other men.

Silence for a moment, not uncomfortable.

'How's everything else?' Craig said. 'Is Hannah OK?'

Jenny shook her head. 'She's taken this thing with Mel really hard.'

'Understandable.'

'She thinks the police aren't doing enough so she's driving herself insane chasing shadows.'

The Italians at the next table finally had enough of the chilly air and trooped inside, leaving Jenny and Craig alone in the beer garden. It was near closing time but Jenny didn't want this to end. She sipped the last of her drink and scudded the glass on the table. Maybe she was drunker than she realised.

'There's just so much death around,' she said, waving her hands.

Craig spluttered into his pint. 'You live in a funeral director's.'

'Good point.' Jenny closed one eye and pointed like Columbo.

Craig finished his lager and looked at her glass. 'One for the road?'

'I'd better head home.'

'I'll walk you.'

She smiled and stood. She remembered kissing him against the wall last time. She was in control then and she was in control now. She could nip this in the bud anytime she liked. She could, but she wasn't going to.

56
DOROTHY

Piershill Cemetery was easy to break into. She walked with Archie down Fishwives' Causeway, a dark lane that ran off Moira Terrace towards Portobello. The lane ran round the back of people's houses and split in two, the narrower part heading over the railway, the gloomy metal bridge covered in graffiti, then running between Craigentinny rail depot and the graveyard. The back of the cemetery was just a low wall, easy to clamber over. In fact it was much harder to get into the railway sidings, spiky railings, CCTV cameras, trespassing signs. Nobody cared if you trespassed on the dead.

Dorothy felt her legs and arms ache as she slid onto the manicured grass. Archie dropped the holdall he'd been carrying and followed her. Dorothy took out her phone and checked, no calls. She'd been trying to get hold of Jenny for hours, since before the business with Jacob Glassman's postwoman. But Jenny wasn't answering. Maybe she'd had enough of digging up dead people. Understandable. Dorothy was still reeling from the woman in the attic, was struggling to get her head around it. So easy to fall through the cracks, that's what Amy said. And so easy to just occupy someone else's space. She thought about the loft in the Skelf house, how she would feel if she discovered someone up there. Thomas had taken Amy down to the station to make a statement and charge her, though he wasn't exactly sure what to charge her with. He called later in the evening to say that she'd be spending the night in the cells until she could see a duty solicitor in the morning, but he'd found a place in a Women's Aid shelter for her after that. It was only temporary, but she could speak to social services, try to sort out something more permanent.

Dorothy thought about living nocturnally, sneaking about like a rodent, reducing your life to mere existence. But did any of us really do anything so different to that? Were any of us really much more connected?

She took a torch from her pocket and switched it on, they needed it here away from the streetlights. There were houses overlooking the cemetery to their left but they were far away, a long stretch of grass between. There was something about untouched land in a graveyard, waiting to be filled up by the deceased, which tugged at Dorothy.

'OK?' she said to Archie as he straightened up, holding his back.

'Not really,' Archie said.

He lifted the holdall and they began walking along the rows of gravestones. There were some large chestnut trees further up the hill giving them cover from the main road where night buses still ran.

They didn't split up like Dorothy and Jenny had last night. Dorothy needed someone by her side, now that she knew what was coming.

The graves were laid out chronologically and they found Ailsa Montgomery after just a few minutes. She was a beloved sister, mother and grandmother, three generations out there still missing her after a decade, getting on with the white noise of life but now and then feeling a blip of grief, a bump of loss that threw them off balance. Dorothy wondered if she would ever get to the stage with Jim where she mostly didn't think about him. She didn't know if she would live long enough to take his death for granted and maybe that was just as well.

'Don't go through with this,' Archie said.

Dorothy thought about his condition, the death fixation, the medication, the therapy. None of this could do him any good.

'Let's go home,' he said.

She thought about Archie hiding that piece of paper in the coffin. 'You could just tell me.'

He looked around at the other graves then back to Ailsa. 'There's nothing to tell.'

Dorothy swallowed and nodded. 'Then we dig.'

She took shovels out of the holdall and handed one over. She propped her torch against the gravestone and paused with the blade of the spade on the ground. The grass was better tended here than last night, no moss or dandelions, evenly cut. It would be more obvious that this grave had been disturbed.

Archie looked at her and waited. She nodded to him and he reluctantly placed his shovel blade against the grass. She pushed down on her own shovel, which sank into the soil. Archie watched her for a long moment, then joined in.

It was easier this time, psychologically. It's true that people can get used to anything if it becomes normalised. Maybe Dorothy would be digging up corpses for the rest of her life.

Once the turf was placed aside she pushed up her sleeves and set about scooping shovelfuls of dirt into a pile by the grave. Her mind ran blank after a while, the repetitive lifting and dumping, over and over, worms glistening as they wriggled in the torchlight, stones like alien eggs half buried in the earth pile.

After two hours they were close to the depth they needed to be. Another forty minutes and she expected the clunk any moment, so when it came it felt preordained, as if she was always meant to be here doing this monstrous thing.

She exchanged a look with Archie and redoubled her efforts, spurred on by the knowledge she was close. Archie kept digging with reluctant movements. She was scooping and clearing, soil lifting into the air behind her as their breath billowed from their mouths like lost souls.

Finally the coffin was mostly clear of dirt, just a smear left. This was a cheaper coffin, light pine, but it had held together well. Dorothy began unlocking the bolts at the corners and Archie eventually did likewise, then when they were all done Archie helped Dorothy out of the hole then climbed out himself. She wedged the shovel blade between the lid and coffin and they creaked apart like something from a horror movie.

She turned to Archie. 'This is it.'

Archie lowered his head.

Dorothy breathed in the smell of damp dirt and sweat, blinked heavily as she lifted the lid and balanced it against the wall of the hole.

Crumbs of dirt fell into the open coffin as Dorothy lifted her torch from the headstone and pointed it.

Two bodies.

Her heart hammered against her ribs and spots flashed across her vision. She breathed, tried to be mindful, closed her eyes and opened them again.

There were some remains of clothes, strips of cloth, an emaciated leather belt, then at the top end of the coffin were two skulls, one higher than the other. Below that were two tattered ribcages like shipwrecks emerging at low tide. From the size of the remains it looked like a man and a woman. One was Ailsa.

Dorothy turned to Archie who was staring into the coffin.

She looked back and saw a slater disappear into the earth beneath a shoe. Two ladies' shoes down there, and the other two feet just bare bones behind. She looked at the woman's hands, bones folded across sunken ribs. The man had been wedged in along one side of the coffin, Ailsa pushed up against the other side. She was small, there was room for two of them. People might've noticed at the funeral if they knew how much a body weighs, or a coffin, or any of it. Certainly Jim would've known. And Archie.

She turned to him. 'Simon Lawrence.'

He shook his head.

'You knew all along,' she said.

He just kept shaking his head, his eyes glowing wet as he wrapped his arms around himself.

Dorothy touched her face, felt the grains of dirt, wiped them away with a smear. 'Tell me.'

'I can't.'

'Damn you, Archie, if you don't tell me what happened, I'll throw you in this grave and fill it in.'

Archie rubbed his forehead and scrunched his face up, tears falling onto the earth at his feet. He swallowed hard over and over. Eventually he looked up and gave the slightest nod. He sat carefully at the edge of the grave and Dorothy did the same. Their legs dangled into the hole like two kids sitting on a school wall at break time.

'It was Jim's idea.'

Dorothy felt her throat close up, tried to push out a juddering breath, placed a hand against her chest like she was having a heart attack.

Archie began rocking over the grave and Dorothy wondered if he might throw himself in.

'We had to get rid of him,' Archie said. 'The longer we kept him in the fridges, the more chance we would be found out. And there were no cremations. So Jim decided to do it this way.'

'Archie, what happened?' Dorothy said, trying to keep her voice level. 'How did Simon die?'

Archie seemed in a trance.

Dorothy wanted to slap him. 'Did Jim kill him?'

Archie was crying again, tears tracing through the dirt smudges on his cheeks and dripping into the coffin.

'No,' he said finally. 'Jim didn't kill him.'

'Then what?'

Archie wiped at his eyes. 'It was an accident.'

He swallowed, tried to compose himself. 'I left work one day but forgot my jacket with my keys in the pocket. I came back, went in through the garage so as not to disturb anyone upstairs. I walked into the embalming room and Simon was there. He was with someone. One of the deceased, Zoe Wilson, she was young, a suicide. He was on top of her with his trousers at his ankles. Moving in and out. Talking under his breath to her.'

Dorothy felt the darkness close in as she placed a hand on the grass.

Archie shook his head. 'I hauled him off. He fought me. He wasn't even sorry, didn't give a shit, just wanted me to shut up. We struggled, then I managed to push him off me and his head hit the treatment table. He went straight down, blood coming out, and just lay there. I watched him die. Didn't try to save him. I wanted to be dead too, more then than ever. He was the lucky one, he got to die, he got to be nothing, invisible.'

Dorothy looked into the grave.

Archie sighed. 'Eventually I went upstairs to get help. Jim was there in the kitchen, you were out somewhere, thank God. I made him come downstairs and I tried to explain. He looked at Simon and the woman for a long time, then we began tidying up. We put Zoe back in the fridge, then put Simon in there too, with no marker on his door, until we could think what to do.'

Dorothy pictured Jim and Archie lifting Simon's body onto the table, putting him in a body bag, sliding him into the fridge, cleaning up the blood. She thought about the young woman, not even safe from predatory men in death. She thought about Rebecca sitting at home all these years waiting for her loving husband to return, to be a father to their daughter, never knowing what he really was. And she thought about Jim's decision to cover everything up. There would've been a murder charge, court case, necrophilia, for Christ's sake. The Skelfs would've been ruined, Archie's life ruined, Rebecca's life ruined, Zoe Wilson's family devastated.

'I'm so sorry,' Archie said. 'You can't imagine.'

Dorothy felt a chill run through her body, the energy in the air all around them, permeating everything, bringing them here, giving them a decision to make. Eventually she stood up, using her shovel to help her. Archie watched.

She pointed to Simon and Ailsa in the grave.

'Help me fill this back in,' she said.

57

HANNAH

She strode along the cobbles of The Shore past seafood restaurants and pubs, all closed at this time of night. The Water of Leith was slick black on her left, boats bobbing a little, the slap of low waves bumping against their hulls.

Malmaison was at the bottom of the street, a sturdy old sailors' mission with a clock tower, fancy plants and standing heaters next to the deserted outdoor tables. She strode past reception and up to the bar, hotel bars were open into the early hours. A couple of businessmen in tailored suits were drinking brandies in a corner, ties loosened, a good deal struck today. A weary young guy behind the bar gave them an evil stare, which he switched to Hannah when he saw her.

'We're closed,' he said. 'Except for guests.'

He had her pegged as someone who couldn't afford to stay here. The bar was all black with random red pipes jutting out like an industrial warehouse, and above the barman was a large neon sign that read: 'Don't Worry Help Is On The Way'.

Hannah shook her head. 'I don't want a drink, I was hoping you could help me.'

He perked up a little. He was about her age, tall and thin, a tousle of black hair and a few days of stubble, kind eyes now that he was paying attention. His nametag said 'Rakim'.

'What kind of help?'

'Were you working here two weeks ago?'

'I'm always working here.'

She got the receipt out of her pocket, checked the date. 'On Wednesday the seventh?'

She thought he might check the rota but he just nodded. 'I do six nights a week, fits in with my studies.'

Hannah got a picture of Mel on her phone and showed him. 'Did you see her in here?'

He took her phone and peered at it, angled the screen to get rid of the glare from the neon message above them.

'She might've been in this jacket,' Hannah said, spinning round to show it to him.

He looked at her then back at the screen. Frowned for a long time. She's a pretty girl, Hannah thought, come on. Presuming he's straight, of course.

'Maybe.'

'Really?'

'I think so.'

'She was with someone,' Hannah said. 'Probably a guy. She bought a dirty martini and a beer.'

'OK.'

'Do you remember the guy?'

'I don't know.'

'He might've been a lot older?'

Rakim laughed. 'Older guys with cute young women? We get that a lot.'

Hannah pointed at her phone. 'Please, try to remember.'

'What's this about?'

'She was murdered.'

That made him pay attention. 'Wait, is she the girl on the news?'

'She was my friend.'

'Shouldn't the police be doing this?'

'I'm trying to help them.' She flicked up a picture of Peter from the web on her phone. 'Was it this guy?'

Rakim took the phone, stared. 'No.'

'If you know it wasn't him then you remember something.' She flicked back to her camera roll, got up a photo of Xander and Mel. 'Was it him?'

'He was older. In a suit.'

'What did he look like?'

The two guys in the corner pushed themselves to their feet, unsteady, and headed to bed. Rakim watched them go.

'You know how many middle-aged white guys in suits we get in here?'

'So he was middle-aged?'

Rakim nodded. 'Forties, I'd guess. Dark hair. He wasn't ugly or fat. Like, it wasn't crazy they might be together, not necessarily a call-girl situation.'

'Is that all you remember?'

Rakim fiddled with a bar towel. 'Sorry.'

Hannah looked around the empty bar. 'What about CCTV?'

'They wipe it from the hard drive every seven days.'

Hannah rubbed at her temple then placed her hands on the bar, felt the stickiness of a million drinks under her fingers.

'There has to be something,' she said. 'What else do you remember?'

He shook his head and looked above them, that neon sign throbbing in the darkness, mocking them.

'I'd like to help you,' Rakim said. 'But I just don't know.'

Hannah got the receipt back out of her pocket and looked at it.

'So she bought these drinks, did she buy others? Did they have a meal? One drink is not much, did the guy buy drinks the rest of the night?' She pointed at the till on the bar. 'Can you check through the purchases that night?'

Rakim shook his head. 'That stuff's not stored.'

Hannah looked around again then realised something. 'But this is a hotel so maybe they put food and drink on a room tab?'

Rakim ran his tongue around his teeth, leaned forwards. 'If they had a room, yeah.'

Hannah looked towards reception. 'Can we check?'

'I could get fired for that.'

Hannah gave him big eyes. 'I won't tell anyone.'

He stared at her for a time then tapped the till screen. 'I can access it from here, the system's integrated.'

He punched info on the touch screen, waited, pressed the screen some more, frowning, then again until finally he smiled and turned the screen to face her. He looked over her shoulder, checking no one was around.

Hannah scanned the names that the rooms were booked under. There were about thirty and she didn't see any she recognised. She scanned again, looking for Cheng, Longhorn, Xander's surname Shaw, anything that might pop out.

'Can we print this off?'

Rakim looked around again. 'Should be able to, but it'll come out in the office, I'll need to go get it.'

'Please.'

He turned the screen back, pressed it some more. 'I can't believe I'm doing this.'

'You've been a massive help.'

'Don't go anywhere,' Rakim said, walking through the back.

Hannah swivelled the screen and looked at the list again. In the other columns alongside booking name were the type of room, breakfast options and payment details. She clicked all the information open and began again through the list, running her finger down the screen to keep her right. She only looked at double rooms, compared payment details with booking name. She was down past the first dozen entries, then the next handful, when her finger stopped and she suddenly felt like she was drowning.

There was a double room booked under McLaren but the credit-card payment was a different name, McNamara. First initial C.

It was just a coincidence, it had to be. There was no way.

Rakim came through from the back. Hannah's hand shook as she took her finger from the screen. He offered her the printout but she went into her phone again, pulled up a picture of herself with her dad, one that was taken a year ago when they were out for a meal, a selfie where they were both grinning like idiots. She showed the phone to Rakim.

'Is this the guy who was with Mel?'

He didn't hesitate.

'Yeah, that's him. So you know him?'

58
Jenny

'Nightcap?' She felt like a kid again and enjoyed it, this familiar feeling between them. She was wired from booze and pictured herself under him, feeling him inside her, the skin of their bellies touching, that connection they always had, reading each other's thoughts and being each other's best friend.

Craig looked up at the house, windows dark. 'Are you sure? I don't know if Dorothy would like me to come inside.'

Jenny thought about her mum, pictured her standing in the grave last night.

'Mum will be fast asleep,' she said.

Craig looked at his watch, exaggerated movements, drunk and comical. 'In that case I would love a nightcap.'

She led him inside, both of them goofing it, sharing a look that they knew this was dumb, but what is life if not a bunch of dumb mistakes that feel good at the time. Plus they were loaded, so fuck it.

The big house was quiet and dark, giving Jenny a tremor in her heart. She thought about the bodies lying in the fridges through the back, the dead guy in his coffin in one of the viewing rooms. She thought about her dad, he was part of this house, part of her life since the day she was born, and now he was a pile of dust that Dorothy didn't know what to do with.

She took Craig upstairs to the kitchen, pulled whisky from a cupboard, found two tumblers and poured. He wandered to the whiteboards and perused them. She took her jacket off, placed it on the back of a chair and brought the drinks over, the smell reminding her of her dad after a long day's work.

Craig nodded at the whiteboards. 'So you ladies are really taking this investigator thing seriously?'

Jenny shrugged, thought of Liam. 'It's kind of fallen into our laps. Hannah is obviously distraught about Mel, looking for answers, and Mum has something she needs to find out.'

Craig squinted at the scribbles on the board. 'To do with Jim?'

'Maybe, we're still not sure.'

Craig took a sip of whisky and Jenny copied him, felt the burn, felt alive.

'What about your adultery sting?'

'I told him what his wife did,' Jenny said, cringing at the memory. 'He didn't take it well.'

'Marriages, eh?'

Schrödinger padded into the room and slunk around the table, his back raised, fur up. He approached Craig with a soft hiss then slipped out of the door.

'I don't think he likes me,' Craig said.

'Rival male in the house.'

'Is that what I am?'

'He's the alpha male around here,' Jenny said. 'Since...'

She didn't want to talk anymore, didn't want to mention her dad or mum or daughter or any of it. Just wanted to be here in the bubble of the moment. What was it Liam said, we are our processes not our results? This was a process, her life was a process, you can't judge a life by results. Divorced, jobless, homeless, fatherless, these were the results not the process.

She leaned in and kissed Craig, felt his surprise melt into reciprocation. His whisky glass moved to the side as he pressed into her, his other hand on her waist, a movement against her hip that she responded to.

She pulled away for a moment, keeping eye contact, and took his whisky glass from him, put it on the table with her own, then touched his cheek. Always smooth shaven, he'd never gone for the hipster beard, nothing really different about him in the years she'd known him except they weren't together anymore, but they were together in this moment and that's all that mattered, processes not results, and kissing him again was a process she wanted to get on with.

'Jenny,' he said, doubt in his voice.

She ran her hand down his chest. Kissed him again, pushing her tongue into his mouth, gently at first, feeling him move his hand from her hip to her breast, her nipple already responding.

He pulled away. 'This is wrong.'

'We've all made mistakes.'

'Doesn't mean we have to keep making them.'

'That's life,' she said. 'Making mistakes and dealing with it afterwards.'

His eyes looked glassy, wet. 'What if our mistakes are too big?'

'There's nothing so terrible that we can't fix it.'

'I'm not so sure.'

She stroked his brow. 'You're here with me, that's all that matters.'

The phone began ringing downstairs. Jenny looked at the clock on the wall, it was after three. They were supposed to answer it twenty-four hours a day, but some things were more important. It was probably a wrong number, but even if it was a bereavement it could be dealt with in the morning. They would still be dead, after all.

Nine rings then it went quiet.

She placed a soft kiss on his cheek, tried to get the mood back, but he looked out of the window.

'What's the matter?' Jenny said.

He rubbed at his forehead, straightened his back. 'Something happened.'

'What do you mean? Between you and Fiona?'

'No.'

'Is Sophia OK?'

His daughter's name made him flinch. 'She's fine.'

'Then what?'

He shook his head and chewed his lip.

Jenny saw her phone light up through the thin material of her jacket pocket on the back of the chair. She looked at the clock again, thought about the downstairs phone ringing.

She stared at Craig for a long beat then pulled away reluctantly.

'I better check that,' she said. 'It could be important.'

She went to her jacket and took the phone out. Realised she'd had the ringer switched off since she was with Liam earlier. She had seven missed calls, two from Dorothy earlier, five more recently from Hannah, and now a text. She glanced at Craig, who was still looking away, then opened the text. Her vision was blurry from whisky and gin, and it took a moment to focus:

Dad knew Mel. They were together. I'm freaking out. Call me.

She stared at the text, her thumb hovering over the screen as if she might swipe it away. She swallowed hard and tried to think. She was scared to look up but she did it anyway. Craig had turned and was watching her, tears in his eyes.

'What is it?' he said.

But he knew. He knew she knew. So much between them, the connections of the past, the thread that has always linked them. She gave it away in her face as she looked at him.

'Is everything OK?' he said, taking a step towards her.

She couldn't help it, flinched at his movement and stepped backwards towards the kitchen drawer where the knives were.

'Oh,' he said. 'I see.'

He was still walking as he talked, hands out in front of him.

She stepped back, phone still in her hand, Hannah's message glowing at her, breaking her heart, breaking her connection with Craig, although that would never really be broken, not even by this. That was the worst thing, she would still be tied to him after this was over.

'It's not what it seems like,' Craig said, as if he'd been caught flirting with a waitress. 'You don't know what happened.'

She made a grab for the drawer but Craig was on her, fist into her stomach making her double over breathless, trying to suck in air, as he took the phone from her and grabbed her by the hair, yanking downwards, making her lose balance and stagger so that she fell into the corner of the kitchen table, which jabbed at her temple, pain rushing through her like a drug. She blinked and tried to stand up, heard the drawer open, the rattle of cutlery, then she was pulled into the seat and felt the knife against her throat, the point pushing into the skin, taut as she angled her head away.

He stared at her with a look of infinite sorrow, his eyes wet with tears as if this was all deeply upsetting for him. He glanced at the phone screen and shook his head.

'I never wanted this,' he said softly. 'I never meant for any of it to happen, you have to understand.'

'Craig,' Jenny said, feeling the pulse in her neck against the knife blade, her blood begging to be let out.

He pulled a seat over and sat next to her, leaning in, the knife never leaving her throat. 'Whatever you're going to say, don't.'

As if this was a marital tiff, an argument about taking the bins out or drinking too much at a party.

He shook his head and looked at the whiteboard, the picture of Mel up there surrounded by men.

'You know me,' he said. 'You know I'm weak.'

Jenny swallowed. 'This isn't weak, it's evil.'

'I'm not evil.'

'You killed someone. She was pregnant.'

Tears were on his cheeks, dripping onto the kitchen table.

'It's like she put a spell on me,' he said. 'I couldn't stop thinking about her. I was sick with her, diseased. She was so full of life.'

Jenny thought about slapping the knife away from her neck. 'You're just another pathetic old man fucking young girls. It's the oldest story in the world.'

Craig didn't seem to be listening. 'She was there when I popped round to see Hannah one time. Hannah wasn't in but we got chatting. She actually saw me as a man, you know? Not a dad or a husband or a sad old loser. I felt invisible before I met her, do you know what that's like?'

'Every middle-aged woman on the planet knows what that's like.'

Craig shook his head. 'I'm not a bad man.'

Jenny couldn't believe his bullshit. 'You killed her.' She leaned forwards, not caring about the knife, feeling it stretch her skin. 'Your daughter's best friend. She was carrying your baby.'

'It was just supposed to be fun,' Craig said under his breath. 'Nothing serious. But she got clingy. Wanted to tell Hannah about us, but I talked her out of it. Wanted me to leave Fiona.'

His hand was shaking, the knife with it. The tip gently pierced Jenny's skin and she felt a prick of pain, blood dripping down her neck.

Craig hadn't noticed. 'Then with the baby, she went crazy when I suggested getting rid of it, said she was going to tell everyone what kind of man I was. She had her phone out, was calling Fiona to tell her. I couldn't let her ruin everything.'

'I can't believe you're making excuses.'

He gave her a resigned look like he had no control over his actions. 'If I had more courage, I would kill myself. I've thought about it. A bottle of whisky and some pills in the bath. But I'm not brave enough, I'm not strong enough.'

A noise in the doorway made them both turn. It was Schrödinger coming in without a glance in their direction, heading for the chair by the window. While Craig's head was turned Jenny raised her hand and swept the knife from her neck, the knife clattering on the floorboards and making the cat jump. Jenny rose from her chair as Craig turned to her, and threw her fist as hard as she could into the side of his head, connecting with the temple, feeling her knuckle crack with the impact. His neck snapped back and he almost toppled from his seat as Jenny's chair scraped the floor. She was up and sliding past him towards the door, Schrödinger looking at them now, then she was beyond him as Craig swore and held his face. A couple more steps and she was at the doorway, then she felt him grab her hair and yank her off her feet, some of her hair ripping out at the root. She landed on her hip with a thud and was dragged backwards, rucking up the rug underneath her, splinters from the floorboards pricking her hip where her skin was exposed.

She swung her hands above her head, scratching at Craig's fist in her hair, heard him breathing heavily then the cat hissing. She looked over to see Schrödinger with his back arched, tail high. Then she felt a kick to her lower back, kidneys screaming, then another and another, so she lowered her hands and tried to protect herself. Craig pulled her head down and it thumped against the floor sending sparks across her vision, pain stripping her body. She felt her hair released and tried to push herself up, got as far as one elbow when Craig came round and swung his foot into her face, a red burning in her ear and a crack in her cheek as she fell onto the floor again. She could see dust bunnies and toast crumbs under the table, then she heard the knife being picked up from where it had landed by the window.

Schrödinger made a spitting noise and Jenny turned to see Craig's foot connect with the cat's midriff and lift him into the air, claws out, hammering against the glass of the window and bouncing onto the floor.

Craig stepped towards her with the knife held out, looking at it as if he had no idea what to do with it, like it was an alien artefact.

'Wait,' Jenny said, holding her hand up. Her body and face ached, pain soared through her, and she had a brief thought that this would destroy Hannah most of all.

'No,' Craig said, hunkering down and staring into her eyes.

He looked at her with something like love then slid the knife into her stomach and held it there.

59

DOROTHY

Dorothy's phone started ringing as Archie turned the van into Duddingston Low Road. The two of them had been silent since they filled in the grave.

She looked at her phone: Hannah. She looked at the clock on the dashboard, quarter past three. The purple tracers of dawn laced the sky behind them as they drove west.

She answered.

'It's Dad,' Hannah said. She was out of breath, her voice shaky. Dorothy felt the connection to her granddaughter through the phone pressed to her ear, a thread linking them.

'What?'

'He was sleeping with Mel.'

Dorothy removed the phone from her ear and stared at the screen, the timer counting the seconds they'd been connected, Hannah's name on the screen. She stared at Archie, who glanced across then back at the road.

'Are you sure?' she said.

'I can't handle this,' Hannah said.

'Have you spoken to your mum?'

Hannah sniffed down the line, a rumble and rattle in the background. 'I've left a million messages, she's not answering.'

The van swung round Arthur's Seat, past the Commie Pool, heading into Newington. Zero traffic this time of night, all the lights going their way. It felt like they were drifting through deep space.

'Where are you?'

'In a taxi to yours.'

'We're heading there now.'

'Where have you been?' Hannah said.

Dorothy looked at Archie then out at Grange Road as they drove along it.

'Doesn't matter,' she said. 'Have you told the police?'

'I woke Thomas up. He's sending two officers to Dad's house...'

She broke off, crying.

'Hannah, listen,' Dorothy said.

'I keep telling myself there's a mistake. This can't be it.'

'How do you know about them?'

'A receipt. The hotel barman saw them together. They had a room booked. Gran, I feel sick.'

Dorothy breathed as Archie frowned at her. The car went across Whitehouse Loan, another green light like they were blessed.

'You need to stay calm,' Dorothy said.

'I can't breathe.'

'Where are you now?'

A pause as the thrum of the taxi leaked down the line. 'Just coming to the Meadows, not far.'

'OK, we're almost home,' Dorothy said. 'We can sit down and talk about it.'

'Gran, I'm so scared. If he...'

Archie drove the last part of Greenhill Gardens then pulled into the drive and switched the engine off.

'It's going to be all right,' Dorothy said.

She knew it wasn't going to be all right.

She looked up at the house and saw the kitchen light left on.

Hannah hung up and Dorothy opened the van door. The movement made her shoulder burn with pain, she was aching from her earlier exertions, needed time to recover. Time to digest what Archie told her and think about what to do. And now here was this awful new thing landing in their laps.

The holdall with the shovels and torches was still in the back of the van. Archie opened his door and Dorothy touched his arm.

'Leave that stuff until tomorrow,' she said.

Archie hadn't said a word, not as they filled in the grave, not as they trekked to the van, over the wall at the back of the graveyard, not as they drove over here.

'Go home,' Dorothy said. 'We both need rest.'

'I'm sorry,' Archie said, head down as he closed his door.

'I know.'

A long silence. 'Should I come into work tomorrow?'

Dorothy was still touching his arm, felt the warmth of his skin. 'Of course, where else would you go?'

Archie shrugged, a tiny movement. 'I thought you might want me to go to the police. Or at least, you might not want me here.'

Dorothy took her hand away. 'We can talk tomorrow.'

He hesitated. 'Is everything all right with Hannah? She sounded upset.'

Dorothy shook her head.

'Do you want me to hang around?'

'It's fine.'

'You don't deserve any of this, Dorothy. You're a good woman. You take on others' troubles, that can get to you.'

'I'm OK. Or I will be once I have a decent night's sleep.'

'Take care,' Archie said.

Dorothy eased out of the van feeling every muscle cry out. She closed the door and watched as Archie started the van, turned and left. There was no sign of Hannah's taxi yet. Two weeks ago Dorothy would've said Craig wasn't capable of this. But since then she'd discovered Archie had killed a man who was raping a dead woman, her husband had helped him get rid of the body and covered it up, and predatory men were everywhere.

She knew she had to tell Jenny about Craig and that knowledge pushed down on her with intense force as she went in the front door and began trudging up the stairs, calves burning, hand squeezing the banister, dirt on her fingers, her mind full of dead bodies, heart full of sorrow.

She was halfway up the stairs when she heard footsteps, and remembered the light in the kitchen. She'd presumed Jenny left it on when she went to bed, but perhaps she'd woken in the night. Dorothy listened again but all was quiet.

She reached the top of the stairs and stopped in the kitchen doorway.

Jenny lay in the middle of the floor, blood pooling from her stomach and running along the grooves between floorboards, soaking into the rug and darkening the material. She had her eyes closed and a knife handle sticking out of her gut, the knife Dorothy used to slice pineapple.

Craig stood over her, breathing heavily, hands covered in blood, more red stains on his jeans and shirt. He wiped at his nose then turned to Dorothy. His eyes were wet, cheeks flushed like he'd been for a run. He held Dorothy's gaze for a moment then looked at Jenny, then he ran towards Dorothy and grabbed her arms and tried to push past her. She stumbled into him, lifted her knee to his crotch and his head jolted downwards before coming back up. He heaved her over to the side and rammed her against the wall, smacking her skull on the whiteboard. She felt dizzy as he let go of her arms and put his hands around her throat, began to squeeze.

She struggled to breathe and squirmed to escape his grip but he was too strong. She tried the knee thing again but he was wise to it, standing to the side, and she connected with the outside of his thigh. She scratched at the wall behind her, praying for anything she could use to distract him, throw at him, pull off the wall to save herself. Nothing. His fingers squeezed her neck and her lungs burned. She scrabbled at his hands on her throat, felt herself growing faint, then remembered something. She felt into her cardigan pocket and placed her hand on the bone that she'd carried since Jim's cremation. She pulled it out and made a fist, the point poking out from her tight knuckle. She pushed her fist with all her energy into the underside of Craig's chin, feeling Jim's bone go through the fleshy part of his mouth and tongue. He roared and let go of her throat.

She pulled the bone out and jammed it in again, same place. He gripped her arm and yanked it away, but she held on to the bone then forced it into his chest below the ribs, felt it run through flesh then muscle.

He tried to suck in air as he swung his fist into her face, knocking her to the ground. She still had hold of the bone in her hand, Craig's blood soaking her fist, splashing from his chin and running from his chest. He looked at that wound, placed his hand over it, stumbled as if he might pass out, then righted himself. He pulled his vision into focus and stared down at Dorothy.

'Dad?'

Dorothy heaved in a breath as she turned and saw Hannah standing at the door. She raised a hand, the one with the bone, and pointed it at Craig. She tried to focus but her vision was blurred, tears and pain. Craig was staring at Hannah and holding his chin and chest.

Craig and Hannah stood motionless as if this moment was trapped in time forever, father and daughter, injured women lying around them both in a tragic tableau.

Then Craig sparked to life. He ran at Hannah and knocked her out of the way as he stumbled through the door. Dorothy heard him clumping down the stairs, crashing into the banister with a crack.

Hannah righted herself and looked at the door, then back into the room.

'Let him go,' Dorothy said between breaths, her hand shaking at her raw neck.

Hannah looked at the doorway again.

'I can't,' she said.

60
Hannah

She followed him down the stairs, heard him clattering out of the front door then the crunch of his footsteps on gravel, uneven as he staggered forwards. She reached the front door as he disappeared into the street, heading right towards Bruntsfield Links. It was dark on the grass away from the lit pathways, maybe he thought he could disappear.

She ran after him, birds already chirping in the trees above. She turned the corner, went to the edge of the park and paused. The sky was glowing in the east above Arthur's Seat. Straight ahead the castle was spotlit against the bruised sky. Sodium light spilled from the park's paths, darkness over the grassy undulations in between.

Hannah looked for movement. He was injured and found out, the police would get him, he couldn't escape. But that wasn't enough for her.

Shadows twitched to her right over by James Gillespie's. It was him, stumbling over the mounds, an animal desperate to escape. She ran towards him, jogging at first then picking up speed. He must've sensed something, heard her footfall, because he sped up, zigzagging to the left and down the hill, veering towards the road then away again.

She was gaining on him. Her feet solid beneath her, her gaze steady, like a lioness on the plains with a gazelle in her sights. He was clutching his ribs and chin. Hannah tried to remember what his injuries were, but it all happened so fast. There was a lot of blood, and she wondered whether she should go back and help Mum and Gran. But Gran was conscious, she could call an ambulance.

He picked up speed and staggered into the glare of a streetlight, then went across Whitehouse Loan, glancing round and seeing her. He ran into the larger part of Bruntsfield Links where the pitch and putt was. It was almost like he was running towards Hannah's home. But he was just running away from everything he'd done, every lie he'd told, every action that hurt the ones he loved, if he ever loved anyone.

She ran faster, crossed the road, there was more light now, pre-dawn over Salisbury Crags and the glare of the city as they got closer to the clutter of the Old Town. He couldn't escape and he must know that. He ran away from the golf holes and tried to go up the slope away from the main road but the incline made him lose his footing and fall.

Hannah was fifty yards away, would be on him in a few moments, as he lurched to his feet and took a few steps forwards. She remembered once seeing Schrödinger stalk a sparrow in the garden, when he broke cover and pelted for the bird it just sat there flapping one wing, the other broken, and the cat hesitated, unsure what to do with such an easy kill. Then he ripped its throat out.

'Dad,' she said between breaths.

He looked round, kept going forwards but his steps were pitiful, his hand at his chin black with blood dripping onto the grass.

She was twenty yards away.

He turned and looked at her, his body swaying like a skyscraper in an earthquake, and he stopped trying to run or even walk, just stood clutching his rib and his chin, staring at her.

'Don't,' he said.

Hannah stopped a few yards away.

'I'm sorry,' he said. His voice was ragged between wheezing breaths.

Hannah shook her head, could feel her hands trembling and tears in her eyes.

Craig crouched over. He took his hands from his wounds and placed them on his knees. Blood ran down his neck like an oil spill. The front of his shirt was soaked, more blood oozing from below his ribs.

'You don't get to be sorry,' Hannah said.

'I don't know what to say.'

Hannah scratched at her wrist, tears down her cheeks. 'You're my dad.'

He shook his head. 'I'm just a man.'

'She was my friend.'

'It wasn't about you.'

Hannah felt bile rise in her throat.

'You're my dad,' she screamed.

Craig looked at her. He seemed unable to focus, his balance wavering. His back bent in slow motion then his legs gave way and he slumped to his knees like he was praying.

'The worst thing is,' Hannah said, 'this isn't over.'

'It's over,' Craig said after a long pause.

'No. Mel is dead. Her parents will always be without a daughter.'

'I didn't mean any of it.'

Hannah walked towards him.

'And I will always have a murderer for a dad,' she said.

She was aware of flashing lights behind her on Melville Drive.

He was on his knees, panting, head down.

She got onto her knees next to him and took hold of his hair. Lifted his head up to look at his face. His skin was waxy and grey, eyes just black holes.

'I wish you were dead,' she said.

He focused on her for a moment. He smiled and tried to raise a hand but it flopped at his side.

'Me too,' he said.

61
JENNY

Jenny looked around the chapel. All of Melanie's friends and family were here, Cantonese music burbling in the background, a large buffet of homemade food on a long table, Mel's body in an open coffin at the front, pictures of her and flower arrangements scattered around. Most of her family were in bright silky clothes, a lot of red, which Dorothy had explained was lucky. Jenny smiled at two small kids feeding each other dumplings from napkins in the corner.

She touched her bandages. It only hurt when she breathed. Seven days since the stabbing and surgery and it felt like a year. Partly from the pain, every movement making her stitched-up stomach muscles rage. But the time also dragged because she was chewing everything over, the ripples in the universe that would reverberate through their lives forever.

She still needed help to get dressed this morning, four days after her release from hospital. Surgery went well, no major organs touched by Craig's knife so it was really just a patch-up. They implanted a wire mesh to help her muscles knit together then observed her for two days to make sure she avoided infection or complications.

Jenny managed to get her blouse on herself but Dorothy needed to pull on her tights and shoes for her. To have your mum dress you like she did forty years ago was a humbling experience. Dorothy said Jenny didn't have to be here, but she wanted to do it for the Chengs. She had her doubts when Victor asked the Skelfs to do the funeral. After all, they were connected to Mel's murderer. But the Skelfs also found out the truth about Mel and got Craig arrested. Jenny wanted to be here for Mel, for her parents and brother, for every young woman controlled and lied to by an older man. Even if she could hardly move and was worried her bandages were visible through the thin blouse.

Craig was still in hospital, his injuries more serious than Jenny's. Dorothy really did a job on him. Surgery on his mouth had been long and complex, leaving him unable to speak. The chest wound punctured his lung and they were still draining it and fighting infection in his chest cavity. A police officer was stationed in the room and Craig was on suicide watch having tried to jump out of the window when he first came round. Jenny thought about that.

Despite not being able to talk, he had confessed, grimly typing out a statement in front of Thomas. It was much the same as he'd told Jenny. He and Mel were walking along the path by the golf course and arguing. She tried to phone Fiona and tell her about their affair, about the baby. He panicked, strangled her in a fit of rage, then dragged her body deep into the bushes and ran.

Jenny thought about Craig's suicide attempt. He was a murderer and a liar, and he had betrayed women over and over again. But he was also a father to Hannah and Sophia. And of course Mel's baby, DNA tests confirmed it.

It was such a colossal mess. Jenny wondered if Fiona had been to see him in hospital. Jenny had toyed with the idea when she was released from her ward, to see him face to face, get answers, confront him. But there were no answers.

She'd had trouble sleeping since she got home, nightmares of stabbing and strangulation, violence and retribution. She dreamed of killing Craig and felt sick when she woke up sweating, stomach wound screaming in the dark.

'Are you OK?'

It was Victor, eyes wet as he swallowed.

'How are your parents holding up?' Jenny said.

'They're not really, none of us are.'

'It's hard.'

Vic looked round the room at his relatives. 'But we're glad we know the truth. We're glad there's justice.'

Was this justice? A young woman was dead, what could compensate for that? Jenny wondered if she wanted Craig to kill himself, but she couldn't even work that out.

'Have you seen Hannah?' Victor said.

Jenny scanned the room but couldn't see her. 'I'll go and find her.'

She suddenly needed distance from this and she was already stepping away, her stomach burning. She touched Vic on the shoulder and left him looking lost.

Indy was sitting at reception looking equally lost. Jenny sometimes forgot how hard all this must be for her too.

'Is Hannah about?'

Indy pursed her lips and looked upstairs. 'She needed a moment.'

The front door opened and Jenny turned. Liam stood in the doorway looking sheepish, but he smiled when he saw her.

'Hi,' he said.

'Hi.'

'I saw you on the news.'

'I'm famous now.'

Liam looked into the chapel, saw everyone milling about. 'This is a bad time.'

'No,' Jenny said. 'We can talk through here.'

She led him to an empty viewing room and realised it was the same room she spoke to Orla in. When was that? Less than three weeks ago. Ripples and reverberations, echoes and feedback.

'How are you?' he said.

'OK.'

She wondered how long people would keep asking how she was. At some point they would stop and she'd miss it. Because maybe then would be the time she really needed to talk about how she was.

She ran her fingers across the bandages under her blouse.

'Just don't make me laugh,' she said. 'I'll burst a stitch.'

'Jesus.' Liam was paler than she remembered, dark circles under his eyes. But then she wasn't exactly radiant herself.

'I owe you an apology,' he said.

'You don't owe me anything.'

'Actually, I owe you a lot more than an apology.' He held her gaze for a moment then turned to look at the curtains. 'You were right about everything.'

'Wow, can I get that in writing? It could come in handy for my next argument with someone.'

He smiled and she remembered what he looked like talking about his paintings in the studio. We are our processes, not our results.

'You opened my eyes,' Liam said. 'I can't thank you enough.'

Jenny shrugged.

'I've moved out and filed for divorce,' he said. 'I asked her about the gardener, she denied it but it was obvious. She's actually a really bad liar when confronted.'

'I suspect most of us are.' Jenny thought about lies. 'I'll give you the rest of the photos I took, if that'll help with the divorce.'

He looked at her as if it had never occurred to him. 'That would be a help, yes. I'll pay you for your time.'

Jenny waved her fingers, a small gesture. 'No need.'

'You're trying to keep a business going, aren't you?'

'I suppose.'

'Then I'll pay you.'

Jenny stared at the plinth where the coffin would go for a viewing. Thought about the thousands of deceased who had passed through here on the way to the ground or the furnace. All those stories, all that life, snuffed out.

'Anyway,' Liam said, 'it sounds like you have plenty of your own stuff to deal with.'

'Yeah.'

'Was he really your ex-husband?' He looked ashamed to have read about it.

Jenny felt a lump in her throat, tried to swallow. The pain in her stomach tugged at her.

'I'm sorry,' Liam said.

'Don't be.' Jenny couldn't think of anything else to say.

Liam took a deep breath and it made Jenny's muscles ache to hear it.

'What was it like?' he said eventually. 'When you were following me?'

Jenny hadn't been expecting that question, had to think about it for a few moments. 'I don't know.' She ran a finger along the plinth, hoping for a splinter to snag her skin. 'I suppose it felt creepy, like I was doing something wrong. But it was also kind of thrilling, watching you and finding out about your life.'

'I'm pretty boring.'

'I wouldn't say that. Anyway, boring is underrated, I wouldn't mind some boring in my life right now.'

That got a small laugh out of him.

'This might sound crazy,' he said. 'But after all this calms down, maybe we could meet up for coffee or a drink sometime.'

He glanced up then away. She watched him acting nervous and thought about Craig standing over her, the kitchen knife in her guts. She thought about him with his hands around Mel's throat, Dorothy's throat. She thought about standing in someone's open grave with her mum, dirt under her nails and a weight in her heart. She thought about the funeral happening right now, the pain of losing a daughter, and she thought about life and how it was stupidly short and you had to try and live it even if it killed you in the process.

'I'd like that,' she said.

He shuffled on the spot, smiled, held her gaze. 'OK, great.'

He looked around like an actor waiting for his prompt.

'I'd better go,' he said. 'But I'll be in touch.'

'Sure.'

He was suddenly energetic, out of the door and down the hall, then gone.

Jenny rested her weight on the plinth, just the latest dead soul to sit on this piece of wood in this room, and she tried to think of a possible future.

62
HANNAH

Hannah looked out of the window at Bruntsfield Links. Clouds scudded across the sky throwing patches of light and shade on the grass, shifting like a shoal of fish. She thought about collective consciousness, how fish and birds move in groups in a way that suggests they have knowledge of each other's minds. Insects too. Maybe humans are the same, maybe we move in patterns that acknowledge each other's intentions, have awareness of others' thoughts. Recent experiments across disciplines pointed to a more connected universe, quantum biology, psychology, biochemistry. No man, or woman, is an island, and all that.

She felt Schrödinger rub against her leg. She knelt and stroked him, tickled his chin, and he gave off a subsonic rumble of a purr that she felt against her hand. Signals and communication everywhere.

She straightened up and went to the whiteboards. Mel's name was at the top of the funeral board now, removed from the investigation board. She thought about the names connected to Mel – Xander, Bradley, Peter. They had been connected, of course, just not the way Hannah imagined. She thought about the name that wasn't on the board. Her dad lying in hospital, his body repairing itself, drawing energy from a drip and his food, mending his torn skin and flesh, blood swilling round his body, his neurons firing. She pictured him kneeling on the grass a week ago, blood pouring out of him, looking like a lost boy praying for forgiveness, or maybe just for life to end. Then she thought about Peter Longhorn, his body buried or cremated by some other funeral director.

'Hey, you.'

Indy came through the door. A shared look, like a sad smile but a hundred times stronger, the burden of loving someone in a world of pain.

'Hey.'

Indy held her arms out and Hannah went to her, let herself be held like a baby as tears came to her eyes.

Neither of them spoke for a long time, just breathing and tears. Then eventually Hannah pulled away and wiped at her eyes and cheeks with her sleeve, sniffed.

'Vic was asking for you,' Indy said. She tucked a strand of hair behind Hannah's ear and left her hand on her cheek for a moment.

Hannah went to the kitchen table. The rug still had bloodstains on it, it took a specialist cleaner to get it out and he didn't have an appointment slot until next week. The blood was both her mum's and dad's, their DNA mingling like they did when Hannah was created, or when they kissed each other or fucked. She was the combination of their lives, just like the stain on the carpet.

'I can't be down there,' she said.

Indy watched her but didn't move. 'They wouldn't have come to Skelf's if they had a problem with it.'

Hannah touched a finger to the table. 'Maybe they don't have a problem, but I do.'

'You have to go easy on yourself,' Indy said, pain in her voice.

'Do I?' Hannah said. 'My dad killed our friend. And his own baby.'

'Exactly. Your dad, not you.'

Hannah looked out of the window, more clouds desperate to get somewhere. 'I can't help how I feel.'

'It'll take a while,' Indy said. 'But it will get better.'

'It doesn't feel like that.'

'I know.'

Indy was talking about losing her parents and Hannah felt ashamed all over again. Being selfish when others had gone through so much, the Chengs downstairs, Indy with her parents, wives without husbands, children without fathers, parents without daughters.

She breathed, in and out, as the murmur of people drifted up from downstairs, a door opening and closing, conversation filling the air.

'What about Peter?' she said eventually.

'It wasn't your fault,' Indy said. She hesitated, reached out a hand but let it drop.

Hannah gave her a look. 'We both know that's not true.'

Indy folded her arms. 'Peter made his own decisions.'

Hannah picked at an invisible mark on the table. 'I backed him into a corner.'

'He was having an affair with a student who died,' Indy said, voice rising. 'It would've come out.'

'What about his daughter?' Hannah was crying again. A tear landed on the table next to her finger and she wiped it away. 'That kid is going to grow up without a dad.'

Silence for a long time. Words didn't matter, just vibrations in the air, molecules moving to transmit meaning from a brain to a mouth to the air to an ear to another brain.

'Come downstairs,' Indy said at last. 'For Mel.'

Hannah looked up and saw sadness and worry in Indy's eyes, radiating from her like heat from an open furnace.

She wiped her cheeks and nodded, walked past Indy with a touch of her forearm, then went downstairs, legs unsteady.

At the bottom she almost walked into Xander coming out of the chapel.

'Oh, hey,' he said, shuffling his feet.

'Hi.'

'I was hoping I'd see you,' Xander said. He was wearing a white shirt tucked into jeans. 'I wanted to say sorry. You were just trying to help and I was a dick.'

Hannah looked past him into the packed room, saw the end of the coffin where Mel's feet would be resting on the soft lining.

'I was a dick too,' Hannah said. 'We both just miss her.'

Xander nodded. He was the grieving boyfriend, it was easy to forget that. Everyone is the main character in their own story, has their own life to lead, full of sorrow and joy, boredom and excitement, life and death.

'OK,' he said, and headed to the toilet.

Hannah went into the chapel, pulling at her skirt to straighten it. She stood watching Yu and Bolin hunched over in the front row. Her throat tightened, her stomach was a stone. Vic saw her and came over, took her in his arms and held on, powerful grip, strong cologne, his body against hers.

'Thank you,' he said. 'For everything.'

She pulled away and shook her head, looked around the room again. There was no escaping this, she was part of it, linked to everyone here, everyone on the planet, drowning in sorrow, sinking in sadness, looking for a reason to keep going.

63
DOROTHY

She rang the doorbell and waited. Looked up Craigentinny Avenue to where there were now roadworks. Guys in hi-vis and hardhats watching a digger tear up the tarmac, dust and noise in the air, rumbles under her feet. A few cars were stopped at the temporary lights. A disruption to ordinary life, just a little thing to throw you off balance, that's all it took.

Rebecca opened her door and straightened up. Her hair was a mess and she wore a loose T-shirt and joggers.

'Can I come in?' Dorothy said. She had to raise her voice over the sound of the digger up the road. Some dust caught in her throat and she swallowed.

Rebecca folded her arms across her chest. 'No.'

'Please, it's important.'

Rebecca looked her up and down and considered it. Eventually she unfolded her arms and turned inside.

'Two minutes.'

She walked into the living room and Dorothy followed. There was a laptop open on a sofa, a recruitment agency website, and Rebecca closed it as she sat down. Dorothy went to the other sofa and sat, hands in her lap.

'Is Natalie at school?' she said.

'What do you want?'

Dorothy had thought about this moment every day since she discovered Simon's body. Since they dug him up then put him back. She thought about what Archie said, if he could be trusted, and about the repercussions, the waves spreading from their discovery. Jim, Archie, Simon and his family, the family of Ailsa

Montgomery. The family of Simon's victim. If Dorothy told the truth all of them would be affected and it would be painful. Rebecca was still missing a husband, or at least his body. And what if Archie wasn't telling the truth? He'd lied to her since Jim died, and Jim lied to her for a lot longer, so who could she trust?

She'd looked inside herself, tried to find the strength to make a decision. She'd gone back to yoga despite her injuries. She tried to meditate but the chaos was too much to block out. She played the drums for long sessions, trying to lose herself in the rhythms, but no use. She would always end up back in Piershill Cemetery, standing with mud on her hands, the smell of earth in her nostrils, staring at two skulls in the ground.

'I never heard from your lawyer,' she said.

Rebecca sighed and looked at her lap. 'I can't afford a lawyer.'

Dorothy nodded. 'Some information has come to light.'

'What kind of information?'

Dorothy looked at all the pictures of Natalie on the mantelpiece, a happy daughter without a dad. Maybe she would want to track down her father when she was older. What if she knew the truth? What about Archie's accusations about Simon? No evidence now and there never would be, but the accusation would be out there.

'I found some paperwork,' Dorothy said. 'Going through Jim's things.'

'And?'

Dorothy gulped, felt her stomach knot up. 'It seems I was mistaken. About your husband and the life assurance.'

Rebecca sat up, put her fingers against the arm of the sofa. 'Really?'

Dorothy nodded. 'It wasn't a conventional insurance policy but there was an agreement between Simon and Jim. You were right.'

'OK.' Rebecca was clearly wary of saying anything in case this vanished the way her husband did.

Dorothy spread her hands out. 'So I'm willing to reinstate the payments to your account.'

Rebecca swallowed, her body tight. 'That's very kind.'

'Our paperwork is quite specific though,' Dorothy said. She looked again at the framed pictures of Natalie on the mantel, a homemade Mother's Day card with a sparkly unicorn on the front. 'The payments are only to be made until your daughter turns eighteen.'

Rebecca pressed her lips together.

Dorothy wondered what kind of man Simon was, what kind of father he would've been to Natalie. She thought about what Archie said he did.

'Would that be acceptable?' she said.

Rebecca took a breath. 'Yes.'

Dorothy pressed her hands together and stood up. 'Well, that's all I came for.'

She walked to the door and turned. Rebecca stood there, arms trembling, blood risen to her cheeks.

'Thank you,' she said.

'I wish you and Natalie all the best,' Dorothy said, and she meant it.

The pump gurgled and thrummed as it pushed embalming fluid into the body. Archie tapped the gauge, checking the flow into the carotid artery at the collarbone, the blood sliding out the other side and draining away through the hole at the bottom of the table.

Dorothy glanced at the names of the dead on the refrigerator, either waiting for treatment or to be dressed and viewed, then moved on into the next life. The business of death never stopped. People are always going to die and we're always going to grieve and it's always going to hurt. All you can do is keep going, because what else is there?

Archie noticed her as she came to stand by the body. He didn't speak, just raised his eyebrows. She hadn't spoken to him much since that night, didn't want to cloud her thoughts. He'd kept his head down, put coffins together, done embalmings, helped at services, driven the hearse, done his job as well as he always did.

'I went to see Rebecca,' she said.

Archie stroked his beard, gave the embalming tube a shake. The colour was coming back into the man on the table, skin turning from old leather to a more healthy pink, the dehydration wrinkles filling out, artificial life returning to him. It was a trick, all of this. Dorothy preferred what they did with Jim's body, it was more honest.

'I didn't tell her,' she said.

'OK.'

'I didn't think it would do any good. As long as what you told me was true.'

'It was.' Archie's blue-gloved fingers tapped the deceased's hand to massage the veins, bringing the dead back to life. 'I swear.'

She wished she was sure, but the truth is no one is ever sure about anything, not really.

'OK,' she said, turning to leave. 'I'll let you get on with your work.'

She stood outside 11 Hermitage Drive and waited. She looked at nearby Blackford Hill, thought about all the neighbourhoods of the city you could see from up there, the tendrils of life spread out like a single organism, each reliant on being part of the greater whole for its continued existence. And the graveyards, cemeteries, mortuaries and crematoriums that linked the city too, the network of the dead, just as important as the living.

Amy opened the door.

'Thanks for coming,' she said, and waved Dorothy in.

Dorothy hadn't believed it when Thomas told her a few days ago that Jacob was dropping charges against Amy. But the more she thought about it, the more it made a weird kind of sense. Then Jacob called her yesterday, and his reasoning confirmed what she'd guessed. He was lonely, needed help around the house. She was homeless, needed an address to get her Job Seeker's Allowance and on the housing list. She was welcome to stay with him for now.

He certainly seemed happy enough with the arrangement, sitting at the kitchen table with a cheese sandwich in front of him. There was another sandwich across from him, and two full wine glasses on the table.

'Sorry, you're eating,' Dorothy said.

'Nonsense,' Jacob said. 'Sit.'

'Can I get you anything?' Amy said, coming past her into the kitchen.

Dorothy shook her head and looked at them both.

'So this is really happening?'

Jacob shrugged, pulled a tiny piece of bread and cheese from his sandwich. 'Looks like it.'

Amy took a bite of her sandwich, then a large glug of wine.

'This doesn't seem weird to either of you?'

Jacob made a face. 'Less weird than a lot of other families.'

Dorothy supposed that was true.

'What about trust?' she said to Jacob. 'She stole from you.'

Amy had the good grace to wince at her words.

'Only out of necessity,' Jacob said.

'And I'll pay him back,' Amy said, mouth full of food. 'Once I get on my feet.'

Dorothy nodded to herself, watched them eat.

'And how does your daughter-in-law feel about this?'

Jacob grinned. 'She hates it. Which is an added bonus.'

Amy got up and lifted a tote bag from behind the table.

'Here are your cameras,' she said, handing it over.

'And here's your cheque,' Jacob said, sliding it across the table. 'Thank you so much, for everything.'

Amy nodded. 'Yes. Thank you.'

Dorothy picked up the cheque and hoisted the bag on her shoulder, then lifted her eyes to the ceiling for a moment and turned to go.

'I'll see myself out,' she said.

Middle Meadow Walk was busy with students, mums, office workers, people getting on with life. A young woman and her parents walked past, her in bright, baggy clothes and large-rimmed glasses, the parents in Berghaus fleeces and comfy shoes. Dorothy thought about her daughter and granddaughter, all they carried with them in the world.

She spotted Thomas, steady, confident walk. He was in a fitted grey suit, no tie. She rose from her seat and accepted his kiss on the cheek as he sat. He'd taken her hand when they kissed, and still held it.

'How are you?' he said, more than just small talk.

'I'm OK.'

He meant the business with Craig, not Simon, and she had to shift gears in her mind to accommodate. She still had marks on her neck from Craig's fingers, bruises on her body from being thrown about. At her age, these things took a long time to fade. You carry ghosts of injuries all the time when you're old. She raised a hand to her neck as the waiter took their order.

Thomas smiled. 'Here.' He took something from his jacket pocket and placed it on the table. It was Jim's bone in an evidence bag.

She raised her eyebrows.

'It's clear you were acting in self-defence,' Thomas said. 'And he's confessed, so there won't be a trial.'

She could see dark stains on it, Craig's blood.

'You were very brave,' Thomas said.

'Jenny and Hannah have been braver.'

'How are they holding up?'

Wind riffled the leaves on the trees above them as their coffees and pastries arrived.

'As well as can be expected,' Dorothy said. 'It was Mel's funeral today.'

'You Skelf women are strong.'

Dorothy cocked her head to the side. 'You think?'

'Come on, you're the strongest women I've ever met.'

Dorothy sipped her coffee, watched the stream of people up and down the street. Magpies in the trees were cackling, pigeons picking at crumbs in the gutter.

Thomas shifted in his seat. 'What about Simon Lawrence?'

Dorothy tried to think how much he knew. The missing person, the negative DNA test. He would've heard about the disturbed grave, but she hadn't told him anything about her search, and there was nothing to link the two.

'I'm letting that lie.'

Thomas gave a slow nod of the head. 'Probably for the best.'

Dorothy pictured the skulls in the dirt.

Thomas drank from his latte. 'For what it's worth, you know what I thought of Jim. He was a good man.'

She touched his hand on the table, looked him in the eye.

'I'm glad to have you, and not just because you get DNA tests done super quick.' She touched the evidence bag still on the table. 'Or because you can sneak evidence out of a police station.'

He laughed. 'So that's how it is.'

She put on a mock shocked face and felt him squeeze her hand. A look passed between them.

She took Jim's bone and placed it in her bag and sat there, happy in silence, just in the moment, with a friend on a sunny day, the world still spinning through the universe.

64
JENNY

Jenny took a handful of her dad from the ashes casket and weighed it in her hand. She felt the grit against her fingertips, the only father she would ever have.

She watched Hannah take a handful from the casket, which Dorothy was holding out. Hannah pushed her upper lip against her teeth, a look of determination that Jenny recognised from her as a toddler, from twenty years of knowing her daughter.

Dorothy was last to dip her hand into the small wooden casket. She did it with care. She had a stillness about her even now, her hand full of her husband's remains.

Jenny looked around Bruntsfield Links. Just an ordinary day for commuters along Bruntsfield Place, for students heading to university and art college, for kids mucking about on their lunch break from Gillespie's. The elderly couple ambling along Whitehouse Loan, the dog walkers throwing tennis balls for two collies by The Golf Tavern. Heavy clumps of white cloud cruised above them, away over Arthur's Seat to the sea. A bin lorry crunched its way along Greenhill Gardens behind them, the creak and crank of the mechanism lifting rubbish into the jaws at the back.

Jenny looked at her mum. 'Do you want to say anything?'

Dorothy stared at the ashes in her hand. 'I don't know.'

Maybe there wasn't anything to say that didn't sound trite and contrived, anything that made a difference to grief and longing, any way to express the absence of people you love.

'Go easy, Jim,' Dorothy said, opening her fingers and letting the dust fall.

Jenny looked at her hand then behind at the big house. They

were fifty yards away, so they would be looking at her dad every time they stared out of the kitchen window. Jenny thought about what had happened up there and Hannah's chase across this piece of grass. Maybe that would always be mixed up in their minds with this, but there was no avoiding it. Everything is connected anyway.

She let her dad slip through her fingers then brushed at the remaining ashes, which were taken by a breeze into the air. She smudged a bit between forefinger and thumb then popped her thumb in her mouth and sucked it clean, tasting the bitterness.

Dorothy had told her and Hannah everything about Simon, how Archie found him in the embalming room, how her dad helped get rid of the body, how Archie eventually told Dorothy what she hoped was the truth. Hannah had listened, but still seemed in shock about her dad.

Hannah dropped her share of her grandfather onto the grass, scattering it like seeds with a shake of her hand. It's funny how we do that, as if we're sowing something for the future, spreading the souls of the dead far and wide.

Jenny watched as Dorothy tipped the casket and began emptying the rest of Jim onto the grass, making sure he was evenly scattered so there were no visible mounds of ash. Way below the grassy surface were the hundreds of plague victims buried centuries ago, when Bruntsfield was outside the city walls, considered safe. Jenny imagined her dad's ashes sinking through the layers of dirt, soil and loam, mingling with the ancient dead, then further still, the remains of dinosaurs or other ancient beasts, early life drowning in mud or dying from cold, all the ways it was possible to die. It was hard to stay alive sometimes.

Dorothy had finished, the casket upside down in her hands, the wind flapping at the bottom of her dress, people walking past on the paths, some curious, some oblivious. She turned to Hannah and Jenny.

It's hard to stay alive, but sometimes it's the only choice we have.

Schrödinger sat in the window seat and lifted his head to watch the three women come through the door. He licked at a paw and settled back down. He'd been tentative for a few days after his injuries, but he brought Jenny a mangled sparrow while she lay in bed yesterday morning, so he was back to normal.

'I'll put the kettle on,' Dorothy said, and started making tea.

Jenny touched Hannah's arm as she looked out of the window at where they'd just been. Hannah lowered her head then turned to the whiteboards. Jenny thought about fathers and daughters.

There were three funerals on the slate. Archie had gone to prep Olivia Barlow for viewing, Indy was at reception taking calls, everything was back to normal.

Dorothy poured tea and the women sat in silence. Jenny ignored the bloodstained rug on the floor. She touched the bandage around her waist, pressed until she felt discomfort then pressed some more.

'Are you OK?' Hannah said, seeing her hand on her stomach.

'Fine.'

'I don't know how to handle this,' Hannah said.

Dorothy took her hand. 'We have each other, don't underestimate that.'

Hannah shook her head and Jenny wanted to hug her, squeeze until she made the big bad world disappear.

She heard the front door open downstairs then someone talking with Indy at the desk. She sipped her tea as the sun appeared between clouds and bathed Schrödinger in warmth. The steam rose from her mug and evaporated, becoming one with the universe.

Footsteps upstairs, then Indy appeared in the doorway.

'There's a woman downstairs looking for a private investigator,' Indy said. 'Says she's being harassed by her neighbour.'

'Why doesn't she go to the police?' Dorothy said.

'Her neighbour is a cop.'

Hannah raised her head and looked at Indy.

'Well?' Indy said. 'What will I tell her?'

Jenny shared a look with the other women. She spoke to Indy. 'Tell her we'll be down in a minute.'

ACKNOWLEDGEMENTS

Massive thanks to Karen Sullivan and everyone else at Orenda Books for their continued love and dedication. Thanks to Phil Patterson and all at Marjacq for their hard work and support. I'm also indebted to Creative Scotland for their belief in this book and their financial support during its writing. This novel was partly inspired by my time as writer in residence at William Purves Funeral Directors, and I want to thank all the staff there for their kindness and help. Needless to say, all characters and events in this book are fictional, and any mistakes with respect to details of the funeral business are entirely my own. And the biggest thanks once more go to Tricia, Aidan and Amber, for everything.